Claire Varley's debut novel *The Bit in Between* was released in 2015. Her fiction and non-fiction work has been published widely, and she has coordinated community development projects in Australia and overseas, including remote Solomon Islands and with refugee and asylum seeker communities in Melbourne's outer north.

This book was written and takes place on the lands of the Kulin nation, and the author pays her respects to Elders and community past and present.

Also by Claire Varley

The Bit in Between

The Book of Ordinary People

Claire Varley

MACMILLAN
Pan Macmillan Australia

First published 2018 in Macmillan by Pan Macmillan Australia Pty Ltd
1 Market Street, Sydney, New South Wales, Australia, 2000

Cataloguing-in-Publication entry is available
from the National Library of Australia
http://catalogue.nla.gov.au

Typeset in 11/16 pt Sabon by Post Pre-press Group, Brisbane
Printed by McPherson's Printing Group

Images on Part openers from Shutterstock.com

The author and the publisher have made every effort to contact copyright holders for material used in this book. Any person or organisation that may have been overlooked should contact the publisher.

MIX
Paper from
responsible sources
FSC
www.fsc.org   FSC® C001695

For John, my heart, and Mojdeh, my liver.

In memory of Yiayia who loved unconditionally and completely.

Prologue

Slowly, thoroughly, the traffic came to a stop. Cars halted mid-creep, bumpers kissing, grinding the Tullamarine on-ramp towards standstill. It spread neatly and efficiently along Bell Street, branching off in rivulets: Sydney Road, Nicholson, St Georges, High Street, blooming to the north and south in a seemingly choreographed dance of inconvenience and ire. Tram brakes groaned, peppered motionless between stops, as cars amassed along the urban vertebrae. The word went out, relayed from station to station: traffic was banked up across the tracks and all trains were to remain still until signalled otherwise. People listened to their car radios, volume up high, or streamed updates through their mobile phones. The choppers reported the same ominous message: gridlock, gridlock, as far as the eye can see, and from where their eye in the sky hovered, it was far far far indeed. On the ground, reactions varied. Some reached for mobiles, sending pre-emptive apologies for imminent tardiness. Some silenced engines, reclining their seats for the wait, weary already before the work day had begun. Others were livid, pounding their steering wheels at the very injustice of it, because it was 2016 and the future was now and how on earth could this possibly still keep happening in the modern infrastructure economy and by Christ you better believe someone would be losing votes for this. In the most northerly north, the drivers sat with practised patience amid the building blocks of their half-built estates, one road in, one road out, smug that finally others felt their pain. And in the inner north, passengers spilled from trams, their legs primed for the walking they'd always promised themselves they'd attempt, lungs opening curiously to the mid-autumnal air.

Here they are, these unremarkable strangers, caught in a moment of stasis before the everyday continues:

Evangelia Kouros sits in her car stuck in Reservoir's High Street, her children bickering from the back seat about trivial nonsense and her head pounding with the promise of a headache. She watches a woman attempt to escape the traffic, zigzagging her little hatchback in a hundred-point turn that bumps and grazes a pole, the curb, a nearby bumper, and Evangelia mutters under her breath.

In the Clifton Hill pool, DB Arnolds swims his regular morning laps, his head in the clouds and his heart in his mouth, oblivious to both the traffic jam around him and to the *ting ting ting* of the increasingly frustrated texts from his increasingly frustrated wife who, with a first period year nine History class and their child still in his car seat, will twice be late this blustering leafy morning.

On the South Morang line, Aida Abedi tears a tissue into a thousand pieces somewhere between Thomastown and Lalor, anxious she will miss her appointment with her case worker and have to wait another procession of weeks for the next. Each piece forgets itself as it piles onto her lap, for she is waiting, always waiting . . .

In his boxy Thornbury apartment, the Failed Hack pulls the blanket over his head to drown out the angry horns bleating from the street outside, and turns to the wall, wide-eyed and weary from yet another night unslept.

And in a fluorescent-lit CBD office, bright-eyed and coffee-ed, Nell Swansea has missed the entire thing because she has been here since seven-thirty, tapping away at her keyboard as another day begins its crawl towards the end.

Time passes, emergency response vehicles weave towards the freeway, and the north has no choice but to wait.

Part 1

1

Aida

I've always hated waiting, ever since I was a small girl. Tugging at my mother's coat as we queued to buy barbari bread, yowling restlessly from the pavement as we trudged through Tehran's endless foot traffic, stealing past the stovetop to smell if the rice was done cooking. Even in the womb I couldn't bear to wait, kicking impatiently at the fleshy walls around me while my father and older brothers prayed for the Iraqi bombs to stop falling from the sky. My mother told me many years later that my movement inside her reminded her to be strong – that after nearly eight years of war she could hold out a little longer. My brothers, both of them stubborn grown men now, told me that during the air raids my mother would cradle her full belly and shake her head sternly at their anxious cries, refusing to acknowledge the danger. 'Why would they bomb our family?' she would ask them, her face firm with disbelief. 'We have never done anything wrong.' As if cowering in the bunker were all a game, as if being sardined in the darkness with her least favourite sister-in-law and the neighbour she was certain pilfered clothes from our line were all an amusing pastime. As if people she knew – school friends and colleagues of my father – hadn't died already, lifeless and cheated beneath the rubble of war. She would refuse to be scared because this, she was certain, was what they wanted: Saddam, Khomeini, Khamenei – all of them, she was sure, were hoping to render us powerless through fear. When it came to people, she trusted few and feared none.

There were many things she could have feared at the time of my birth: that she would go into labour just as a bombardment began and would be forced to deliver me on the floor of a crowded bunker with my aunt Simin shouting useless commands and my uncle Asadollah hiding his eyes for shame in the corner. That the announcement of my birth would be eclipsed by the wretched news from the frontline that some close relative had been lost – riddled with bullets or frozen by chemical weapons – causing them to mourn a new martyr instead of celebrating my birth. That we'd be flattened, all of us, and she'd be interred for the eternal here-after alongside her light-fingered neighbour and least favourite sister-in-law. Perhaps she had faith too in the missiles Deputy Commander-in-Chief Rafsanjani sent shuddering back across the border, as if the two opposing warheads would meet mid-flight and obliterate each other. Either way, I was born in the dying months of the war and to my mother at least my birth represented a new beginning for our country.

She is sentimental like this, my mother, but hides it well, like the way you don't notice weight so much on tall people. In hind-sight her sentimentality is obvious, but in person it lurks behind an exterior of dry levity and unimpressed eyebrow lifts. Don't tell her I said that or there'll be trouble, even though we've oceans between us now. She rarely disciplined us when we were small, using the mere suggestion of physical punishment as punishment in itself. Her displeasure would be made known by the purposeful easing off of her house slipper followed by the steady drumbeat of the faded plastic sole slapping against her palm. My brothers Alireza and Amin used to refer to it as 'Maman's angry heartbeat', and the sound would send us scuttling across the living area and into the hidden crevices of our wardrobes. Eventually, when the cautionary metronome died down, we would sparrow-call each other from our respective hiding places, whistling and chirping an invented cryptography until we dared to emerge. Our mother, now seemingly engrossed in the kitchen in some repetitive preparatory task, would ignore our tentative steps, waiting until the moment we were but metres from her before she would whip around, pelting us with flour or the wilted peel of vegetables. Shrieking with laughter, we would dance about in the fine powdery shower or scoop up the vegetable clippings as if preparing for a nutritious snowball fight. My father, disturbed from his reading, would peer out from his study, his index finger keeping place on the page somewhere between Alexander's burning of Persepolis and the Parthian rebellion. Taking in this scene of mayhem, his brow would furrow into a mighty Persian scowl as he tilted his head to one side then the other. Then, taking note of the ingredients coating our shoulders and noses, he would look my mother dead in the eye and predict what was for dinner.

These things – these are the things I remember. The smell of it all, of the soft white flour frosting Alireza's hair, or the tang of sweat dancing across Amin's heavy brow. That steady drumbeat played out on my mother's fleshy palm, its creases and folds dried and calloused from a childhood spent farming and a marriage of household chores. The bristles of my father's moustache as it brushed my ear, tickling and irritating and whispering good night. These are the things I remember though both time and geography have distanced me from them. When every day becomes too everyday and nothing seems to change. If you want me to tell you my story, it begins and ends with memories like this. Perhaps this is not what you want but this is what is here, swirling through my head as I lie sleepless in the relentless dragging night, jamming my ears from the cries remembered of the hopeless and the resigned. My father used to tell me that if you write too much about the past you become stuck there, that this is where you remain. He would know, with his history books and lecture notes gathering temporal dust on the sagging bookshelf. But perhaps sometimes this is for the best – better than this present, anyhow. These are the things I remember as I wait.

Aida blinked once, twice, and she was back in the world of the almost living. She tucked her notebook away and looked around the waiting room. A man was arguing with the young woman behind the reception desk. Stooped and exhausted-looking, he swung his hands in frustrated circles that haloed the young woman's passive face as if in despondent religious ceremony. This happened a lot – every time she was here, in fact – except that each time the language and cause of the frustration changed. She had once seen a woman break down in weary tears, her thin body collapsing across the benchtop and scattering leaflets all about the place like a colourful, informative rain shower. Another time, a teenage boy refused to leave, chaining himself to the chair with a complicated twist of limbs before eventually wandering off, bored with being ignored. Aida glanced at the clock on the wall. Fifty-five minutes past her appointment time and twenty since she'd rushed in red-cheeked and frantic from the train station. Sarah seldom kept to schedule. Her clients were never made to leave until they were ready – and rarely were they ready – which meant Aida had spent countless hours perched uncomfortably on the faded maroon waiting room chairs, her eyes scanning the various posters and public health messages on the walls. *Have you been tested?* one of them asked Aida from the wall near the clock, two concerned-looking youth staring out at the world. *Yes,* she wanted to reply each time, *though not in the way you think.*

Sometimes, as she sat in the waiting room, flashes of the past would claw out of the places she'd hidden them. Long ago, fresh out of high school, she had entered and won an essay-writing competition for the nation's university students. How proud

10

she'd been, life stretching before her so promisingly. Sometimes here, pressed between the tired, sweaty, anxious bodies, she wanted to scream it out into the dense silence. *I won the national essay-writing competition! I don't belong here!* But she knew the whole room was most probably full of people like her, forgetting daily the awards and victories of their lives past.

She stretched her neck, the right side straining reluctantly the way it had for months now, then checked her mobile. There was a handful of new messages from her mother, who had taken to the messaging app with unbridled fervour after Aida had assured her that unlike international phone cards, it was free. *What is the weather like? Have you touched a koala? Do they have saffron? Have you heard anything yet?* She used it to keep Aida updated on the progress of Aida's friends: who was pregnant, who was divorcing, who had been harassed by *gasht-e ershad*, the guidance police. Aida scrolled through her mother's gossip, the distance and intimacy of it both unsettling and comforting her. There were few other people who messaged her now. Shirin, occasionally, and once or twice something from Afshar, though these were like hen's teeth since he had been swallowed up by his new wife and the stresses of fatherhood. Aida massaged her neck with her other hand, the insistent knot having reformed itself at some point during the night. She had hoped to start the new year free of the constant pull and strain, but the Gregorian, lunar and solar celebrations had all been and gone while the ache remained. She kneaded it harder, wincing, her free thumb working her mobile. Another message appeared as she did: *Your father woke me with his coughing again – is it morning there too?* She placed her mobile carefully in her lap, as if her mother might notice from the other side of the world that her only daughter was ignoring her. She would respond to them later, when the world felt less urgent. She counted back the hours in her head. It was 4.00, no 5.00 am in Tehran. Her mother would soon rise to start

11

her chores as the city rumbled awake around her. Her father would lift himself gingerly to his elbows before commencing the clockwork procession of phlegmatic coughs that brought his bronchitic lungs to life each morning and sent her mother into fits of worry. *Phlegm all over his good pyjamas*, she'd messaged once. *You have to scrub it out by hand.* These types of messages were more frequent now, the minutiae of the flu her father could not seem to shake. *Two different doctors and still no better*, her mother would write, and it worried Aida to reply. She pushed the phone deep into her pocket, out of sight for now.

It had been a month since their last appointment, when the only news Sarah had had was that she'd found a new housemate for Aida. Her previous housemate, unsettled by the endlessness of waiting, had moved to a regional area where her brother worked picking apples and where she thought the prospects of her protection visa application might be improved. Her brother earned slightly less than the benefits payment had been but it was worth it, her housemate had said, for the purpose it gave his days. Aida had struggled with the rent, existing on flavourless packet noodles, until Sarah had found the new housemate. Or housemates. 'A housemate and a half,' Sarah had joked when Elham had walked into the room with Niki clinging to the hem of her shirt. This was their first introduction – Niki's face coiled into a tired scowl as she clawed at her mother for attention. Her dark hair springing from two uneven pigtails, she had looked at Aida with a contempt and displeasure far beyond her years.

'She's tired,' Elham apologised quietly in Persian, attempting to prise away Niki's hands as they stretched the material of her shirt and exposed the flesh on her belly.

Niki's response had been to let out a high-pitched shriek, slapping at her mother as she buried her face into her trouser leg. Aida watched Elham cringe, her body moving wearily with the demands of her daughter.

'I think you're going to be great housemates,' Sarah said encouragingly, her voice rising to compete with Niki's increasingly deranged howl.

A week or so later Elham and Niki had moved in, the grand sum of their worldly possessions held within the zippers of two large chequered storage bags. A tired red and blue stripe, they were the symbol of transience the world over. Aida lent her some bedding then helped her float the sheet across the narrow mattress.

'It's only a single,' Aida apologised, but Elham shrugged.

'We'll fit.'

Niki, ensconced in the far corner gripping a well-worn teddy bear, eyed them suspiciously then hurled herself dramatically onto the faded carpet.

'No room,' she cried, mixing an English 'no' with a Persian 'room'.

Aida watched her, uncertain, a lifetime of avoiding small children rendering her ill-equipped for this situation. Elham simply sighed, grasping a naked pillow and a pale blue cover. In response to this, Niki's howl increased threefold, her little legs beating at the floor with indignation. They sounded out a steady beat, a miniscule army preparing for battle. Aida hesitated, then reached for the second pillow. As the tantrum progressed, Aida racked her brain for something to say.

'How old is she?' Aida asked finally, watching as Elham carefully smoothed out the sheets.

'Three,' Elham replied, holding out her hand for the pillow.

'Not three, FOUR,' Niki shrieked, her head popping up momentarily like a scandalised mongoose before burying itself in the carpet again.

'Three,' Elham repeated, pronouncing the word carefully in both English and Persian. 'Nearly four. Three and confused.'

And Aida had nodded her head, unsure of what else to say.

13

She'd left then, in search of painkillers as the tantrum continued, leaving Elham to unpack their two little worlds into the bedroom built for one. In the weeks since, they'd spent little time together. Like many others Aida knew, Elham's bridging visa had expired and Immigration didn't seem to be issuing new ones to the thousands like Elham waiting to hear the decision on their protection claims. This meant that unlike Aida, even if Elham were able to find work, it wouldn't be legal to take it. A further divide between the already divided. Still, between taking Niki to kindergarten a couple of days a week, her own weekly English classes at the community centre, and seeking out the food truck to buy discounted produce, Elham was rarely home. When she was, Aida was out searching for work, long days spent walking the streets of Melbourne's outer north handing out résumés to bored hospitality workers half her age who promised to hand them on to their managers. They passed each other in the hallway, exiting the bathroom or out by the temperamental second-hand washing machine with an armload of clothing. Elham ate early, she and Niki huddled around the small table as Elham patiently cut up Niki's food and ignored her protests. Often when Aida entered the kitchen hours later she would find the collateral from their meal – upended bowls and rice trampled into the linoleum – and like a domestic detective would link it to the protestations and clamour heard earlier. As far as she could see, Niki did not approve of anyone and took issue with everything. She was an activist, stubborn and forceful, at war with the trials of life at three (nearly four). Aida had taken to avoiding her, gently nudging her bedroom door shut as the patter of angry little feet approached, and carefully stepping over discarded toys so as not to invoke her wrath.

The waiting room thundered with anticipation and boredom. It was always full now, since the sea of letters had started instructing them they had a month to submit their applications for temporary protection. They'd come in trickles then waves, some people gripping their letters, others still waiting to receive them. Sixty-odd pages, one hundred and one questions, twenty-eight days of panic, then do it all again in three to five years' time. Not to mention the interviews and the Freedom of Information applications for copies of interviews they'd given years ago when they'd first arrived, and the terror of getting it wrong because their right to appeal had been severely diminished simply because they'd got on a boat.

Another ten minutes passed before Sarah finally appeared in the doorway, ushering out an elderly couple clutching folders full of paperwork. The woman, her face set with deep lines, held the files to her chest, the end of her headscarf draped protectively over them as the man guided her towards the door. Sarah motioned cheerfully to Aida. As she settled herself inside the consulting room, Aida placed her phone on the desk. There were several more messages from her mother, who by this time would be setting out the plates for breakfast, spooning soft cheese onto her father's plate and placing the sugar bowl alongside their teacups, all the while maintaining a steady stream of wandering updates to her only daughter across the sea. *No appetite anymore, Aida-joon . . .* Sarah placed Aida's dense file on the desk, balancing a pen along its top edge.

'Sorry for the hold-up. We're just so busy right now. It's been worse since they cut funding again. I'm back to four days. It's crazy. Anyway, how are you? Did you get stuck in that traffic out there? I hear it's chaos.'

Sarah leant her elbows against the desk, casually resting her chin on her knuckles. She looked tired, her eyes rimmed with dark crescents, and for a moment Aida forgot herself and thought to offer her some tea. Instead, she raised her eyebrows expectantly.

'Nothing,' Sarah responded. 'You?'

'Nothing,' Aida replied, drawing her lips tight.

'It'll come in the mail,' Sarah assured her, and Aida nodded obligingly, for this was their act.

'Has anyone else heard?'

'Not that we know of. I hear people have, but no one we work with, yet.' Sarah emphasised the 'yet' as if this could reassure any of the feelings swirling through Aida's gut.

'What about you?' Sarah asked, though they both knew Aida knew no one any more.

Sarah changed the topic.

'How is Elham? And Niki?'

Aida shrugged. She didn't mention the cuts she'd seen carefully lining Elham's arms like notches on a tree trunk. They'd looked old, healed now, so she didn't bring them up. Nor did she mention Niki's night terrors, her tantrums, or her endless fascination with casting Aida's toiletries into the toilet bowl. She did not say: Elham is embarrassed to speak in front of me and subservient to her child. Or: Niki's tantrums are like a shrieking unstoppable fireworks display. Or: sometimes I think to leave the front door open just a little so Niki might run away for just a few hours until a well-meaning neighbour brings her back.

'They're all right.'

Sarah nodded encouragingly. Her fingers drummed the top of the heavy file.

'Have you talked with her much? About her application? Because I'm a little worried . . .' Sarah caught herself.

Aida folded her hands in her lap. You didn't ask people's stories. Sarah should know this by now.

'We don't talk about things like that.'

Sarah straightened her shoulders.

'Never mind. Forget I said anything. I have something for you,' she announced, reaching for a bag by the desk.

Aida eyed it warily. 'Donations?'

'Yep.'

'What have we got, then?' Aida asked, making a show of opening the bag.

She peered into it, fishing around dramatically before seizing something from the bottom.

'A worn shoe! Adidas, I think. Yes. And does it have a partner?'

She rifled through the bag some more.

'No, no partner!' she announced. 'There's always a single worn shoe with no partner. Who would donate such a thing?'

Sarah grinned. 'So there's nothing you want there?'

Aida shook her head, handing back the bag. This had become a running joke between them – the well-intentioned yet utterly useless items that found their way into donation bins. Holey sheets, jeans with busted zippers, toys so deformed by love that they looked as if they might come alive at night to roam and maim. She sometimes suspected Sarah purposefully collated the worst of the lot in order to present them at Aida's next visit like a carnival of the misguided and bizarre. It made her laugh, amid the constant no-news drudgery. Aida smiled then rose from the desk.

'I'll let you know if I hear anything,' Sarah said, her forced optimism a mask against the uncertainty of their meetings.

'Of course,' Aida replied as she took her phone from the desk. 'Me too.'

And she left as she'd left so many times before, waiting, as always.

It was a fair walk home from the train station but Aida enjoyed it, particularly on these warm afternoons when the leftover summer sun clung to the mid-autumn days as if winter were implausible. When mild northerlies collected the leaves from where they'd fallen and sent them tumbling all about the place. It was a kind heat – comforting and cleansing – so unlike the heat of the island that smothered its detainees, stifling and unrelenting, seeping them from themselves day by day. The narrow streets of the outer north seemed speckled with a hodgepodge placement of brick houses, exhausted factories and empty, fenced-off subdivided blocks waist-high with weeds. The clutter of homes pressed alongside each other like stock on a shelf, so unlike the lonely houses of the east adrift in their spacious yards. She'd journeyed out there once, via train then bus, and had been surprised by what she had seen. The ease of the houses sprawling lazily across those giant blocks, all neat lawns, solid fences and pronounced ambitions. She imagined them – the old Iranians – Baha'is and monarchists who came after the '79 Revolution, and each night dreamed of an Iran that no longer existed. Sitting inside these houses, their lives reassembled in this foreign country that now felt like home. She wondered if she should knock on the doors, unannounced and unexpected, peddling her face from house to house in search of her country people. She'd offer a cheerful 'Salam' and wait for the eager hands to drag her inside, insisting she drink tea and take pistachios and fruit. Plying her with Persian-language books and newspapers and tales of lives unshackled by the drudgery and terror of temporary visas. She'd entertain them, cracking jokes and juggling witticisms the way she'd done as a child whenever bedtime drew near, building face by face her new collection of friends, confidantes and allies. In reality, Aida knew it was far more likely that most of those doors would never open, not for her anyway. Not for the new wave of Iranians who got on boats and left behind the country many of the settled diaspora thought they deserved.

Here, though, here in the north the buildings and factories coughed and spluttered together like patients crammed into an emergency room. She crossed the street then wandered past the small collection of shops that loosely defined the suburb's centre. The streets were busy. People bustled, laden with shopping bags, dragging their children along the pavement. A cluster of paunch-bellied men sat around one of the tables outside the coffee shop, stroking their moustaches in contemplation before slamming their backgammon pieces down and slapping their thighs in victory. At the end of the shops stood a large McDonald's, incongruous amid the clutter of small businesses. Aida inhaled as she passed, the oily pungent smell catching in the back of her throat and pricking her eyes. All her life she had longed for McDonald's, the images, the ads, the fantasy of it hoisted high above all else in her childhood dreams like a beacon of hope and culinary virtue. She remembered the first time she'd eaten it, not long after her release in Australia, her hands clawing at the wrapping like a waylaid hiker recently rescued from the desert. Fumbling and salivating with a two-decade-long expectation. It was a slap in the face. She'd looked forlornly at the service counter, the be-hatted teenagers too busy with new orders to aid her. Perhaps there'd been a mistake? A key ingredient left out or a rogue batch of off patties? A uniformed young man passed by, his arms wrangling a bloated rubbish bag like a stubborn debutante. She'd reached out, her arm urgently pressing his.

'There's something wrong with my burger,' she said, holding it out for inspection.

'What's wrong with it?' he asked, distracted.

Aida considered the exhibit in her hand. 'Everything,' she replied softly.

The young man had observed her briefly, his fingers tugging impatiently at the stretched polyethylene of the rubbish bag. He held it open for her, the gaping mouth expectant, and she'd thrown the burger in.

At first, after all those months behind wire, she'd savoured every moment, every opportunity to do and smell and touch things. The sharp pain of hot water splashing on her naked nape, the exhilaration of eating at times of her choosing. Of strangers, each meeting brief and fleeting, whose stories she would never know when before on the island she'd known every horrible story because at night the sky sung with them. But eventually the tedium had set in. And then the limitlessness and newness of it all had faded beneath the oppressive coat of waiting. Endless waiting. She felt it now, the coat tightening sharply around her chest, binding her body as her breaths staccato-ed and stabbed. She felt it now, in the fire travelling her cheeks, the murmuring yelps swirling in her belly, clawing for release. White-knuckled, Aida clenched her eyes shut, forcing her breaths to lengthen. *Three things*, she thought, blocking out the clamouring and the panic. *Three things different and three things the same.* This was something her father had taught her, a private trick for fighting off the terror of the unknown: the night before exams or wandering the halls at the start of each school year. Three things different and three things the same.

Three things different:

The driver's side of the car

Footballs aren't round

Sugar doesn't come in cubes

Three things the same:

The sun that rises first on me then on my family

Politicians mostly lie

My stinky breath in the morning

She smiled at this last one. She'd been awoken that morning by Niki erupting out of nowhere, imperiously demanding she help find Cyrus. She'd just as swiftly backtracked, one pudgy accusing finger pointing at Aida's mouth in shock.

'Stinky breath,' Niki had whispered, eyes like affronted dinner plates, before she'd repeated it again with gusto.

At this point Cyrus had slunk out from under Aida's bed, arching his skinny back and flicking his tail in irritation at this vulgar wake-up call. He padded towards the door, Niki following him. Aida had watched, equally mortified and bothered by the fact she had successfully been heckled by someone who had clearly wet herself during the recent night's sleep. Niki had sashayed out, her backside still haloed with telltale damp, repeating 'stinky breath' in a mocking voice until she was out of earshot.

Turning onto her street, Aida checked her breath again. The familiar houses greeted her from behind their roller-shuttered windows. Her small brick house stood squat in its concrete yard, a carport to one side with an uneven steel roof sloping so far down it made it unusable. The letterbox, detached from its post, rested precariously on the uneven brick fence. Aida paused before it, sucking in her breath, then lifted the lid tentatively. Its emptiness stunned her, the way it repeatedly stunned her five days out of every seven, although relief mingled with this reservation. She lifted the gate so it wouldn't scrape across the ground as she opened it, then approached the house. As she stepped through the entry the cats bolted past, their little black bodies lithe and determined. Niki was home, then, Aida thought to herself. The cats had been a constant since Aida had first moved in, mewing and begging outside the back door each night. It was only after Elham arrived that they'd been allowed inside, enticed by the leftovers she set down for them. They'd named them then. Elham had insisted Aida do the honours, so she'd decided on Shahrzad for the smaller one because she kept them up all night and Cyrus for the larger one because he swiftly claimed a majority of the house as his own. This suited Niki well enough, though she struggled to tell the difference between them and simply referred to them both as Cyrus. Sometimes Aida wondered if Niki even realised there were two cats, her arrival usually sending both skittering off in separate directions as she lunged after one with a joyful lack of awareness.

Inside, the house was cold despite the warmth of the day. She could hear Elham pottering about the kitchen, the smell of cooking rice and spices wafting through the dark hallway and tickling her empty stomach. Elham's soft voice wandered the corridor, singing in dialect. Niki was nearby too, destroying something by the sound of it. Aida slipped off her shoes then wandered towards the kitchen. Her phone buzzed as she did so, a new message from her mother. *Have you heard anything yet? Baba sends his regards. He's taken to bed with his cough again – this cold weather we're having is doing no one any good.* She hesitated, texting a simple *nothing*, then pocketed her phone as she entered the kitchen. Elham looked up from the pot she was fussing over, her brows knotted in concern.

'*Salam.* Any luck?'

Aida shook her head.

'I don't know how you get about so easily,' Elham sighed. 'I've barely left the suburb. This city is so big.'

'Tehran's bigger,' Aida reminded her.

'And I didn't see too much of that either,' Elham replied.

She turned back to the stovetop. Aida could smell onions and coriander. Her stomach grumbled expectantly. She knew nothing of cooking.

'You want some when this is done?' Elham asked, giving the bubbling green stew an experimental stir.

'I've eaten,' Aida lied.

'There's plenty for everyone,' Elham insisted, but Aida shook her head.

'You sure?'

'I'm sure.'

Elham frowned, her *taarof* failed. But Aida couldn't bring herself to eat Elham's food, knowing how little money she and Niki received each fortnight. For Aida, she could make the money stretch, limiting herself and rationing when additional expenses made things tight. But Niki was too young to possess such self-control, her appetite tremendous and demanding as for the first time in her short life she had access to foods unimaginable on the island. The house was often a wasteland of the discarded indulgences Elham showered upon Niki. Half-shrunk lollipops sunk head first into the couch cushions, spat-out jubes cemented across the Cyruses' coats. Aida had once found a trail of crushed chips leading to the bathroom, where Niki sat splayed across the empty bath like a Bacchanalian emperor amid a sea of gutted plastic packets after finding her mother's secret hiding spot. Denying her resulted in an avalanche of tantrums, one spilling into the next, terrifying both Aida and Elham that someone nearby might call Child Protection or a tactical response team. Besides, how could Elham deny a child who had been born into a world of denial? Where bland, over-boiled foods and unidentifiable meats were the standard daily fare, and fruit as rare as diamonds?

Aida filled a glass of water from the tap then sat at the small table watching Elham. Sometimes it was like watching two different people – one at ease in this little cold house but the other a shadow beyond its walls. Not long after they had moved in Aida had accompanied Elham to a doctor's appointment. She hadn't wanted to, but Elham had seemed so nervous that she hadn't had the heart to say no. They'd sat in the waiting room watching the muted television as it flashed images of Syrians scattered across the Greek coastline, while Niki tore apart the toy box and shrieked at the other children. The doctor, an elderly man whose kind eyes reminded Aida of her father, had invited Elham to talk. Elham had leant towards Aida.

'That accent, all nose and phlegm!' she exclaimed. 'What is he saying? I can't understand him.'

Aida translated, watching the change in Elham's posture. Eyes downcast and fingers trembling, Elham explained in whispered Persian how her body felt always on the edge of collapse.

Like her breathing was gone, like her mind would explode from the racing. How sometimes at night her body shook so much it woke Niki. How the darkness bled into her mind and hauled up images of the boat, the rocks, and the wall of water engulfing them all. Then she had waited expectantly, hands clasped in her lap, and Aida realised she had to translate this too. She did so, her jaw tight and her mind rigid against itself. When she finished, the doctor tilted his head to one side.

'Can you ask her to tell me more about this?' he'd said, pen poised over notepad. 'More about what she's been through?'

At this Aida froze. Elham looked at her expectantly and Aida considered lying. She was saved by a bang from the corner as the medical waste bin fell on its side, Niki standing victorious and purposeful above it.

'Niki!' Elham snapped, and Niki's face had twisted into an outraged scowl as she burst into tears, leaving the overwhelmed doctor to rifle through his drawers for a lollipop as he warily eyed the used syringes, wipes and rust-hewed dressings.

Now, several weeks after this visit, Elham diligently took the antidepressants she'd been prescribed, waiting each day for their effects.

After she'd finished eating she set aside some scraps for the cats then went to settle Niki in bed. Aida sat on the couch, absorbed in the headlines of the nightly news. There was a piece from back home, something about a visit from the Australian Foreign Minister and the ensuing inevitable talks of involuntary returns. Her mother would message about this, she was sure, her longing to see her only daughter muted by the fear of what might happen in the event of her forced homecoming. There would be safeguards, the Minister assured people, but no one believed this. The report cut to footage of a protest in Melbourne's city centre, thousands of people waving signs for humanity. *Bring them here! Not in our name!*

Aida looked up as Elham entered the room. It was a rare occasion that the two women found themselves alone together. Aida drew in her legs, making room on the couch, and Elham sat down beside her. Aida reached for the remote. She knew that Elham refused to watch the news, that the sadness of others was too much to process alongside her own, so she flicked through the channels until she found a US sitcom with loud canned laughter. These shows demanded nothing of either woman and the American accents didn't strain on their ears as the Australian ones did.

'This?' Aida asked, and Elham shrugged agreeably.

On screen a young woman was dancing about with an uncooked turkey on her head.

'Turn key,' Elham said in English.

'Turkey,' Aida corrected her.

'Turkey,' Elham repeated.

'Use it in a sentence,' Aida suggested.

'We cannot eat the turkey because oven is break and the landlord will not fix,' Elham announced in awkward English.

'Close enough,' Aida said.

They watched in silence, curled up side by side on the couch with the cats nestled between them. Aida glanced at Elham, her young face intent on the television screen. She was so tiny it seemed impossible Niki had come from her, yet once that small body had carried this screaming, demanding child across the sea and into this world. She reminded Aida of another woman from the island, a Feyli, effectively stateless and lost, who had filled her belly with cleaning products to avoid an empty future. But she didn't want to remember that woman from the island. She didn't want to remember any of them. What she really wanted was to ask Elham if the pills were working, if the nightmares and the shaking and the panic had stopped. If it made some things easier and made others forgotten. Instead, she cleared her throat and adjusted her legs.

'Niki is asleep?' she asked, and Elham gave a half-nod.

'*Enshallah*,' she replied, mimicking a pious mother with a comic tilt of her head.

Aida laughed and turned to say more, but Niki's cry interrupted them.

'Of course.' Elham smiled with feigned exasperation as she pulled herself from the couch.

She'd tried to show her photos. A few days before, scrolling through her phone to parade her family before Aida. Aida had humoured her, but had none of her own to share. She'd deleted the ones her mother had sent via the phone app, the ones of her father, gaunt and pale. What use were photos if you couldn't bring yourself to look at them?

'Where are your people, Aida?' Elham had asked softly. 'Everyone I know is up in Brisbane but what about you?'

She'd ignored this and Elham hadn't asked again.

Aida turned back to the television, flicking through the channels until she found the twenty-four-hour news station. There again was the Australian Foreign Minister shaking hands with her Iranian counterpart. They stood together, caught in the flash of the world's press as a sea of journalists fanned their microphones before them. Aida scanned the faces, moving forward to crouch close to the television screen. This had been where she'd seen herself, back when she'd first decided to study journalism. Pushing her way to the front, elbows lethal and determined, questions ready to hurl above the others as she landed her headlining story. Instead, here *she* was the angle, another nameless story to be reported and forgotten. Her cheek rested against the screen for a moment, the down of her skin prickling with static, before she switched it off. There was a faint click, a flash of hazy colour remaining as if clinging to the memory for the briefest of milliseconds, then the room fell into darkness.

2

DB

Dear Jonesy . . .

Ben 'DB' Arnolds swam his laps one by one. Though, to be honest, it was less one by one and more one-by-one-by-stop-to-adjust-goggles-by-one-by-squint-at-the-lane-timer-for-a-moment-by-one-by-quick-sip-of-water-by-no-no-you-go-first-I-insist-by-one-by-gosh-these-goggles-are-being-a-bother-today-by-one-by-is-that-the-time-maybe-just-a-few-more-with-the-kickboard-by-one.

He used to be good at this – good in the sense that the physical exertion hadn't always made him feel like vomiting – and he still had some of the better-coloured ribbons from his high school swimming carnival days. He'd even done a triathlon once, the swimming bit anyway, because it was one of those work team-building ones where everyone did a different part, and they'd not done too shabbily either. But now it was a constant morning battle to haul himself up and down the lane for long enough to tick off the exercise portion of his daily routine. He'd slow to a crawl sometimes, his mind elsewhere, until he'd catch a glimpse through the water of the elderly folk huffing their way up the walking lane in their reef shoes and realise they were beating him. Then he'd picture the lane traffic piling up behind him and speed up in panic, racing to the end where his goggles would no doubt need adjusting. This, more accurately, was how DB swam his laps. But regardless of how he swam them, he swam them just the same.

As he swam, DB made lists. Things that needed doing that day, things that needed paying that day, things to tell Jonesy when he replied to his email later in the day. Jonesy was in Doha at the moment for a conference and had attached a picture of himself at the Corniche with the futuristic skyline in the background. DB had been to the Corniche once and found it glitzy and overblown, so he'd tell Jonesy this, and also embed a picture of the place he'd found that did their toasties with two types of gruyere, a subtle throwback to their uni days when a cheaper variation of this had been their standard post-night out fare. Something in his shoulder was twinging with each stroke but DB ignored it, just as he ignored the murky amoeba-like clouds that floated about the water of the local swimming pool. There were better pools, but it was on his way to work so it would have to do.

Jonesy had certainly lifted his game of late. It had been easier when he'd been stuck in his Trafalgar office for hours on end. But since he'd got the promotion and commenced what seemed to be a never-ending world tour of business dealings and experience-havings, his emails had stepped it up a notch or two. DB enjoyed it, their chummy back-and-forth. And he knew Jonesy would be blown out of the proverbial water when DB got his promotion. Not that it was set in stone. Or even chalked lightly on stone. Or verbalised in the vicinity of the stone. But he could just tell from the particular look Old Man Williams gave him when they bumped into each other in the elevator – a certain knowing glint in the eye – that the future had a corner office in it and was indeed promising. Not that it wasn't well deserved. And it would certainly help with the mortgage. He'd worked it out the other day in a moment of distraction and at this point, with them both working fulltime and providing they didn't have any more children, he and Sylvie would have it all paid off by the time they were one hundred and thirty, or dead, whichever came first. But this was, unfortunately, the kind of sacrifice one had to make if one wanted to live in Northcote these days. And technically, if you checked the local planning maps – which DB had – they were actually on the very cusp of Westgarth, if you were a bit creative with fence lines – which DB was – and this made their piece of the world very impressive real estate when it all came down to it. And this meant they'd be able to get somewhere nice on the peninsula when they retired at one hundred and thirty, and if they didn't make it that far Rudy would find himself with a very nice inheritance to blow as he pleased.

DB paused at the end of the lane, pretending to drain some water from his goggles, grappling for breath. A woman in a neon cap completed her lap and he nodded for her to go before him. He waited a few more gasps, then threw himself into another lap.

Rudy. He was an earnest little thing, four years old and curious, though not curious enough to have mastered the potty or approached the toilet, which he observed with wild-eyed suspicion as if it were a compact trapdoor to hell and seating himself atop it would eventuate in immediate brimstone-y freefall. This was becoming a bit of a big deal as apparently the staff at his kindergarten did not get paid enough to change nappies and Rudy was becoming a sore – and smelly – point. Sylvie fretted over this, their weekends largely spent enticing and cajoling him while he shrieked like a nanny goat whenever the toilet was in sight. But DB saw the valour in it. He was a cautious and perceptive child, much like his old man, and he knew the end of a good run when he saw it. It was admirable, really, though Sylvie didn't seem to think so. Instead, she saw their child's occasional shortcomings as a direct reflection of their abilities as parents, which was something DB would never have imagined of a woman who in her pre-mothering days had more than once turned up to work in yesterday's clothing, having pulled an all-nighter at one of the various clubs and pubs they used to frequent back when they were fun.

Rudy was currently going through A Stage. It had started with the dead bird. It must have flown down the chimney at some point while they were away on the Noosa holiday, and from what they could gather had made itself at home, shat all about the place, then died rather ceremoniously in the middle of Rudy's little bed. They had buried it in the garden accompanied by its duvet shroud, and since then Rudy had been fascinated with what happened to other living creatures when they died. His insistent questioning meant DB now knew that elephants grieved their dead, that shark and whale carcasses were scavenged by bottom dwellers, and that sometimes the Antarctic winter preserved frozen penguin corpses for decades. While not exactly things to tell Jonesy – *That merger sounds like a winner! Did you know cats like to crawl into small spaces to die?* – it demonstrated to DB the kind of sagacity one needed to get ahead in life. His son would be great on trivia teams. He would impress the ladies. Or the gents. Didn't matter. DB was progressive like that. The Discovery Channel fuelled this obsession, and Rudy spent a great deal of his time sitting before it like a dear sweet addict, eyes wide and body deceptively limp as he could within seconds hurl himself shrieking across the polished floorboards if someone were to interrupt his viewing. While Sylvie insisted they would be just as happy with non-subscription television, DB felt their monthly payments were entirely reasonable if it meant maintaining Rudy's habit. He had intellect, his son. And intellect required cultivating.

Sylvie was of the opinion that if they spent less money they would require less money. This was, DB suspected – quietly, and never in her presence – because she had grown up poor, so what was the worst that could happen to her? He, on the other hand, hadn't, and it certainly wasn't something he was keen to have a go at. This difference had become starker post-Rudy's birth, as the decisions they made seemed to suddenly matter so much more. Besides, he loved his job and loved what it allowed them to do. He loved the ways his ears popped in the elevator on the way up to his desk and how his suits fit perfectly because the tailor knew his body by rote. Sylvie poked fun at his sartorial choices, particularly his love of a well-cut business shirt, but what was he to do? He was a tall man with wide-set shoulders. Tailored shirts were a necessity. Most of Sylvie's childhood clothing had been sewn by her mother, so she'd practically cried with laughter at the matching Ralph Lauren polos he'd recently brought home for himself and Rudy, pretending to vomit onto the year nine History essays she was marking at the kitchen table.

'He can't wear that to kindy. Do you want him to get beaten up by all the kids in tracksuits?'

Then she had turned back to scrawling red ink across a poorly formed dissection of the causes of World War I, emitting the occasional chuckle and snort as she recalled the matching polos.

The kindy. This was a delicate subject in their household. Despite living in an area with ample quality kindergartens, the fact they both worked fulltime meant they depended greatly on Sylvie's parents to help out with Rudy. While DB had investigated options like Montessori and Steiner learning models, Sylvie was a champion of council-run centres, preferably in areas with respectable vaccination rates. After much heated discussion, they had fudged their address and enrolled him in a kinder north of Bell Street, closer to Sylvie's parents' outer suburbs home. This in itself had in fact been a compromise as Sylvie had wanted them to go the whole hog and sell up and relocate closer to her parents. So the geographic victory of their place of residence was somewhat dampened for DB, as it had, to him, come at the cost of his child's early years education, but battles were battles, and wars were wars, and the true war was still to come because Rudy was a decade away from high school and DB was damned if he would be a child of the public school system. DB's parents, both lawyers and utterly progressive in a closed-minded kind of way, were openly disapproving of their choice of kindergarten when there were perfectly good ones this side of the divide. It wasn't the location, they had told DB and Sylvie, but Rudy's future they were worried about. Why couldn't he just go to the lovely Montessori kinder DB had gone to? Because, Sylvie had informed them coolly, he would be going to the perfectly fine council-run one she had attended. And then everyone had been very quiet for the rest of the meal and Sylvie had refused to go to any more Sunday night dinners. She tolerated his parents, which wasn't fair as he quite liked hers.

Sylvie spoke to her family daily, whether it was in person when dropping off or collecting Rudy, or over the phone a half-dozen times throughout the course of the day. They were always in each other's lives, always so aware of where they all were and what they were all doing at any given moment. They would ring each other to ask about a third party's whereabouts, often prior to calling the person in question. *Sylvie, it's your mother. Will your brother be home at nine-thirty if I ring him this morning?* DB had originally found this unsettling, until eventually he realised he had been pulled into this Carmen Sandiego vortex a year or so into their relationship, and found himself an integral part of this intense Zambetti communications tree. Most likely Tony would be at the gym at nine-thirty because he'd missed his session on Sunday due to his hangover. Yes, it was strange he wasn't answering, but he might be stuck in traffic because there was always traffic these days. No, no one needed to call the police yet. Yes, Tony was such a good boy to his mama.

Tony was, DB had discovered long ago, actually a bit of a drop-kick, but no one could ever argue this with Guiseppa Zambetti, who had formed her opinion the moment she'd first heard his newborn wail and never wavered since. Besides, he had been named for her long-dead brother who had passed away in his late teens in a motorcycle accident, and it still made Guiseppa weep just to think of him. Sylvie, who had been named after her paternal grandmother who nobody particularly liked, had long ago given up attempting to equal Tony's familial status, though understandably, and for reasons DB suspected had something to do with money, her standing had risen significantly once DB came into the picture.

Sylvie's grandparents had grown up in villages where people died often and dramatically. Smallpox, whooping cough and, once, though DB sometimes questioned this, a wolf had apparently snatched a toddler straight out of its pram while its mother was engrossed in buying tomatoes at the *mercato*. Subsequently, and despite the distinct lack of wolves in Australia, they had raised their children with a constant awareness of the potential for imminent death. This was a parenting technique Sylvie's mother had carried over to her own children. Her fundamental understanding of the telephone was that it allowed one to check for certain that loved ones were presently still alive, and provided concrete evidence that if left unanswered they were at the very least severely maimed or kidnapped. She had started insisting during her evening phone calls that Rudy be put on the line, in something DB was increasingly certain was some kind of telephonic proof of life. As if she didn't trust their assurances that he was alive and well and staring golem-like at the television as a pack of lions tore apart a gazelle. When DB mentioned this to Sylvie, she gently teased that he was jealous because his parents could go a whole week between Sunday dinners without clarification that he was still living, forcing him onto the defensive. 'We speak regularly. Daily, even.' His family engaged in a long-running and suitably competitive race to solve the nine-letter word in the newspaper's puzzle section, conducted via a group messaging app. *DECIDUOUS. ORATORIAL. CHIHUAHUA, you inept fool.* This was how they kept in contact. Besides, they valued quality over quantity, which in DB's mind tended to be preferable. You paid for quality, as his father often liked to say, to avoid the burden of quantity.

There were many other things Sylvie's family did that his did not. Guiseppa was always popping by with food, delicious casseroles and lasagnes that kept them from living off takeaways after they got home late after work. Her parents vocalised their joy, often at DB's accomplishments: success in the courtroom, affixing a new number to the letterbox, completing all his meal. Sometimes they spoke to him in Italian and he would dazzle them with a clumsily executed '*Molto bene!*' and they would applaud him as if he'd just delivered a poignant and stirring oration, while Sylvie, who understood the language but rarely spoke it, would roll her eyes at the praise.

'It's like they think you're a simpleton,' Sylvie would marvel.

'It's like they think I'm a god!' he would crow.

Money was another area where their families differed, specifically in the giving of it. Having worked their way eventually onto the bottom rungs of the lower middle class, Sylvie's parents had contributed to the purchase of the house, writing a cheque to cover the last few thousand to secure DB and Sylvie's deposit in a loan it was understood they would never pay back. His had gifted them a potted lemon tree that had died not long after they'd put it in the ground. While Guiseppa and Nino did not expect the loan to be repaid, they maintained an unwavering determined insistence that one grandchild – while much revered – was not nearly enough to meet their quota. Despite her absolute adoration for her son, Guiseppa had long ago come to peace with the fact that if Tony had indeed fathered children, the likelihood was that she – and probably he – might never meet them. DB knew she lived with a secret hope that one day they would appear unannounced at the door, teenaged and longing for a nonna, like the storylines in her favourite Italian soap operas. But until this time came, she and Nino took solace in applying a constant malingering pressure on Sylvie, as if she was the heir to a royal lineage under strain to ensure its very existence. The heir and the spare, that's what they wanted, because you never knew – and Christ forbid it – when a wolf might snatch Rudy from their clutches. And it wasn't that he and Sylvie didn't want more children, but they really should have done it a year or so ago before they'd upgraded the family car and landscaped the yard. All was not lost, though, because they'd be in a sound financial position when the promotion came through. With careful planning we can have it all, he liked to tell Sylvie, and he'd watched a great many TED Talks on this very subject. Financial security was a frame of mind, after all. Sylvie had rolled her eyes at this, but she was not by nature a planner. So it was up to DB to do the planning for both of them, and he'd managed it down to a fine, somewhat precarious line. And as long as nothing interfered with that line, everything would be just fine.

There was a tap at his toes and DB realised he had dropped his pace again. He pulled himself forward, returning to the email for Jonesy he'd been composing in his head. His mentee Nell had spent half the previous Friday with cappuccino froth caked across her top lip, which had been somewhat amusing, so maybe he'd include a line about that. Of all the grads Williams & Williams employed, he seemed to have been lumped with the crusading one, and she seemed to spend a considerable amount of time questioning the very foundations upon which the legal system was built, which for a lawyer was not an ideal position to take. It wasn't that they were bad questions – insufferable yes, unintelligent no – but that they forced DB to think of answers to things he had never really thought about before. And she somehow found ways to make the legal system – which was seemingly a straightforward and transparent beast – into a windy labyrinthine being waiting about to trip up people like himself. A minotaur! That was it. She'd somehow made a minotaur of the law. This was how he would put it to Jonesy, who would no doubt be prompted to remember the handful of Classics classes they'd taken together in first year. But minotaur or no, the promotion would clear him of this because none of the department heads had to have mentees, and he made a mental note to put this in the email too. Then an update on Rudy – *fascinated by nature* . . . And Sylvie . . . well, they were sleeping separately now, nothing weird, just that he'd been snoring a bit more at night, muttering and whatnot from the stress, and, occasionally, apparently, shrieking from his financial night terrors, and it made sense because they both needed a good night's sleep and god knew they had enough rooms . . . *Sylvie is doing well*. And as for him, the best part of the week had been not having bowel cancer. He'd been worried – worried about how long it took to take a shit these days – but the doctor had told him this was just how things were now, so that too was a victory of sorts. *Do you think about fibre as much as I do these days, Jonesy? Life, eh!*

DB dragged himself from the pool, towelled off and headed towards the change room. He would grab a coffee, jump on the tram, shoot off the email to Jonesy on the way into work, and get on with the business of starting his day.

3

Evangelia

My mother Xanthoula Georgiou (nee Anastasiades) was born in the port city of Lemosos, Cyprus, in 1941 to a Rhodian mother and a Greek-Cypriot father. Her father was a fabric merchant who owned a textiles store in central Lemosos. Like many women at the time, her mother did not work but stayed home to raise my mother and her two brothers Athanasios and Niko. As the eldest, my mother went to school so that she would be able to watch over her two young brothers and make sure they behaved. My grandfather's store did very well until the war with the British when it was destroyed by fire. They stayed on for another year, trying to rebuild their lives, but things became very difficult with the fighting so they were sponsored by my mother's uncle to come to Australia. My mother was sixteen at the time. They stayed with her uncle in Northcote, before they eventually bought a house of their own. My grandfather worked in the Pelaco factory because of his knowledge of textiles, and once more my grandmother stayed home to continue raising the family.

A few years after arriving, my mother was introduced to my father and they were married in the Holy Church of the Annunciation of Our Lady in East Melbourne. After a time, they moved to their own house in Northcote. My father worked for many years in the brickworks while my mother volunteered at the church and looked after the home. It was some time before they were able to have children, but my mother prayed every week and eventually my sister Lydia was born in 1968. I was born in 1971. My mother continued her duties raising our family and when we had children of our own, she helped Lydia and me to care for them. She continued to live in the same house in Northcote even after my father passed away of a heart attack at the very young age of sixty. Unfortunately my family were not so lucky and my mother died young too, at seventy-five.

Evangelia read back over what she had written. Shit. It was utter shit. It sounded like a eulogy which was exactly what she didn't want it to sound like, and what was worse, it sounded like the most lifeless eulogy on earth. She saved the file, naming it *MumsStoryVersion1_ShitVersion*, then pushed her chair back from the desk. The wheels squeaked as they rolled and she spun it gently in a full rotation. Her head hurt – had been hurting since the bloody traffic jam dropping the kids off at school that morning – which was another headache on top of the existing headache still hanging about from the school holidays. She needed sugar. Maybe there was some of the baklava left that Peter or the kids hadn't eaten yet. Unlikely, though. It had been the first sweet she'd allowed in the house since the funeral and they'd gone at it like feral animals, elbowing each other out of the way and getting the sticky syrup all over their uniforms. Even Peter, who was meant to be partaking in Lent, had tried half-heartedly to convince her it was allowed.

'*Nistisima* my arse,' she'd scoffed, rolling her eyes. 'Your sister may as well throw in the cow for all the butter she uses.'

But he had ignored her, shovelling the wedges into his mouth as though he'd crossed the great desert himself, buttery syrup dripping down his chin and into his dark whiskers which he'd kept long, even after the forty days were through. It was one of the many moments in her life that Evangelia was glad not to have company.

That had been one of the pluses since the funeral. That beautiful period when people weren't supposed to visit, and they were expected not to socialise, and she'd been able to sit around at home in her tracksuit pants without fielding a thousand calls from Lydia or the other school mums about why she wasn't at whatever fundraiser the school was currently holding. That school. It was like the Sydney Opera House. Once they finished one expensive renovation they started on another. The new music centre, the Olympic-sized swimming pool, the state-of-the-art theatre. And it wasn't like she could refuse to help out on the basis that her children declined to participate in anything extracurricular. If it were a user pays system, Lydia would be bankrolling the whole thing with her overachieving children. If there was a stage, Lydia's kids would be on it. They'd even made a performance out of the funeral, keeping quiet the secret that they'd brought along cuttings from her mother's garden so that Yiayia could 'take some of her garden with her to heaven'. And there were her own children, forgetting to bring the expensive roses she'd organised from the florist and having to make do with an ugly bouquet of daffodils that Peter had managed to find in the back of the little cemetery shop. This had set the tone for the rest of the *mnimósina*, with Nick and Xanthe squabbling in the car on the way to the nine days service, which graduated to actual physical fighting at the forty days while the priest was reciting the prayers. It had started like all their fights, over something trivial, which never seemed trivial when you were eight and ten years old and everything that happened to you seemed entirely important and unfair. Nick had turned to his sister, whispering in a too-loud-for-church voice, 'Why is it forty days?' and Xanthe had rolled her eyes at her little brother and replied, 'Because of Jesus. Don't you even listen to anyone, you idiot?' and for some reason it had made sense to Nick to elbow her in response, which Xanthe had taken as an invitation to hurl her *koliva* at him, and then they'd both started clawing at each other because, embarrassingly, her children were scratchers.

The only blessing – which wasn't really a blessing but an embarrassment – was that there hadn't been many people there, but then there hadn't been many people at the funeral either. Not like her father's, because he had lived his life outside the home – the Greek Club, the brickworks, the market – while their mother's world had revolved largely around the kitchen. And, to make matters worse, each time they seemed to get the Italian, a man who had converted to Orthodoxy after many years as a Catholic priest, and it unsettled Evangelia to have this man pronouncing her mother's eternal blessings with his harsh y's and ridiculous rolling r's.

The embarrassment of the tiny attendance at the funeral had nothing on the embarrassment of a few weeks earlier, though. They'd gone to church for her mother's three-month *mnimósino*, she and Lydia, and realised too late that neither of them had remembered to hand over the slip of paper with their mother's name and the money to the Italian, so they'd sat through the whole service for a bunch of strangers.

'We look like those crazy old ladies who sit in on other people's funerals,' she'd later hissed at Lydia, though, if she was honest with herself, deep down she was partly pleased that Lydia had slipped up. Before, it was their mother who held this knowledge, the name days and twelve months and other important dates. She'd managed it all with military precision, all the cemetery visits and overseas phone calls and lighting of candles on her little shelf of icons and memorial cards. Lydia was the oldest so it was meant to be her job now. She knew Lydia didn't see it like this, though. Lydia was – and it nauseated Evangelia to use the phrase – a self-described 'cultural'

Greek, a phrase she brought out often in defence of her pref-
erence to pick and choose what suited her from their Hellenic
heritage. From what Evangelia could see, it basically meant
that anything Lydia wanted to do was 'cultural' and anything
she didn't was 'a relic of a conservative and patriarchal tradition'. Lydia wanted to attend church for the *mnimósino* and
afterwards invite people into her home to drink port and tell
her how strong she was. Lydia didn't want to wear black or
refuse social events during the forty days of mourning because
it was an imposition on her personal life. This had not been
the case fifteen years ago when they'd buried their father, but
according to Lydia, that was different. There had been more
people watching, for one thing, and a proper Greek priest. So
this time Evangelia alone had clothed herself in black, shuttered
herself inside and ensured that no well-intentioned person made
the mistake of bringing sweets to the house or calling them
away. During those weeks she'd thought about her mother a lot,
how her soul was meant to be wandering the earth, revisiting
all the places she'd lived, but she'd only really lived in three
places so it wouldn't have been much of a trip. She'd probably
skipped off to Heaven early, so the joke was on Evangelia
sitting alone by herself dressed in black and not eating pastries.
To Lydia, this was all an unnecessary act, a pointless show from
a bygone time of village gossip and nonsensical superstitions. It
was not, according to Lydia, how things were done anymore.
Lydia liked to tell people how things should be done, and the
person she liked to tell most was Evangelia. *Only drink filtered
water, Eva. Don't let your children watch television on school
nights, Eva. Your husband's cholesterol is a symbol of the love
you have for him and the state of your marriage, Eva.*

Lydia and her husband, Darren, who was not an actual
Greek but was, according to Lydia, culturally so, had raised
two handsome blonde children who engaged in various cultural

41

activities such as Greek dancing and bouzouki playing and language lessons, and were far better at these than their dual-Greek-parented cousins. Sometimes Evangelia would complain about this to her husband but, being the youngest child and only son, and therefore possessed of a hearty and secure sense of self, Peter brushed this off as he did much of Lydia's behaviour.

'We own a *gyros* shop and you're constantly busting my balls – what's more cultural than that?'

Then she would press him to list her older sister's faults, and he would rummage around in his memory, offering vaguely satisfying barbs.

'Her *tiropita* has hairs in it sometimes. This is a fault.'

Much of the problem lay in the fact that Nick and Xanthe were incredibly lazy, and this was exacerbated by the ready proximity they maintained to assorted technological items. Both had laptops, iPhones, iPads, iPods – which were apparently different – and the Xbox they'd pleaded for but rarely used because it meant sitting together in the living room as opposed to alone in their bedrooms. Sometimes, and far more recently of late because their *yiayia*'s passing had meant spending substantially longer periods in Lydia's vicinity, Evangelia would bundle all the technology into a box and refuse to let them use it until they'd demonstrated some act of Greekness to her. They would whimper and plea, before eventually offering a sad little *sirtaki* as if they were at the end of a long and exhausting aerobics class, and Peter, who was meant to be the disciplinarian, would look at her like she was a monster.

Evangelia stopped spinning her office chair and glanced at her watch. She should probably put something onto the table soon or else Peter's appetite would get the better of him and he'd end up eating a meal before their actual meal, and god knew where in the stratosphere his cholesterol was these days. One of the problems with owning a food service, he told her often, was that he spent the day in a constant state of hunger due to the meat juices circulating through the air. He maintained himself at work – there were customers there, after all – but, once home, became ravenous and tore apart the pantry, particularly on nights like tonight when he let one of the staff close up so he could join the family for dinner. He'd put on weight recently but instead of connecting this to his eating habits, he'd become convinced he was suffering some kind of debilitating ailment. He'd google things as he ate, and sift through the many possible illnesses that could be behind this baffling yet steady weight gain. So far he'd considered hyperthyroidism, oedema and a range of unlikely cancers. Evangelia did her best, bringing him salads and healthy meals when she dropped by the store to pick up the takings or work on the books or the thousands of other things she did to keep the place afloat. She'd often find them on the next visit, untouched and mouldering. This was another thing that Lydia commented on, as if the fact Evangelia didn't have a job title equated to her not having a job. As if running a small business – and a house – was not a job. Lydia had a job because she was cultural. She was a university lecturer and taught subjects on social identity and cultural anthropology. Darren had been one of her students and was noticeably younger than her. If you thought about it too much – which Evangelia sometimes did by accident – it was a little nauseating. Peter referred to her as Kyría Robinson, which Evangelia still found hilarious.

She really should be starting on dinner. Evangelia scuttled her chair back to the desk and shut down the computer. Her mother's story would have to wait a little longer. She left the office and walked down the corridor to the open living area. As she'd suspected, Peter was sitting on a stool at the counter eating his way through a tub of dip. She pressed her lips together, emitting a soft click of disapproval, but he didn't hear her over his ruminations.

'Ten minutes of Greek practice or I'll take your technology,' she ordered Nick and Xanthe, who were draped across the couches on their iPads with the TV on in the background.

They put them down begrudgingly and started calling across to each other in bored, put-upon voices.

'*Yassou*, Niko.'

'*Yassou*, Xanthe.'

Evangelia opened the fridge and pulled out some leftover pilaf. She placed it on the bench and returned for the salad ingredients. Her meals were simple these days; it hurt to cook her mother's recipes. To see the scratchy letters marking up alterations and improvements on the page. *Prosthéste ládi.* Always more oil. Twice the eggs. Leave out the dill if you are making it for Lydia.

'PCOS,' Peter said, not looking up from his phone. 'It says that one of the symptoms –'

'Keep scrolling,' Evangelia interrupted.

'Oh.'

She started cutting the cucumbers and tomato. As she did, she listened to the children's stilted Greek. This is what she heard:

'Where are you from?'

'I am Nick.'

'What is your job?'

'Australia I am.'

'I'm carpets.'

'Good night.'

'Good night.'

Evangelia sighed. How many years of Greek School had they been paying for now?

'*Oi, Niko. Pós se léne?*'

What are you called? That shouldn't be too hard. Nick stared at her blankly.

'*Nai.*'

'Yes? That's your answer? Yes?'

Nick glanced over at Xanthe, who gave her brother an encouraging nod.

'*Nai.*'

Evangelia sighed again. 'Petro, *ta paidiá sou eínai hazá.*'

Xanthe narrowed her eyes. '*Hazá* means stupid.'

Evangelia snorted. 'That word you know.'

She finished preparing the meal and they sat down to dinner. She watched them as they bickered while eating, alternating between teasing and amusing each other. They'd waited years for these children, eventually needing IVF to get things going with Xanthe before Nick came along naturally. Her mother had prayed for them, lighting candle after candle in churches across the northern suburbs, even asking an acquaintance who was visiting Rhodes to visit the Panagia Tsambika on Evangelia's behalf. Lydia, of course, had had no trouble at all, falling pregnant at exactly the moment she had planned to and saving their mother who knew how much in candles, though it probably had something to do with Darren's decade-younger sperm.

They finished eating and everyone went their separate ways. Evangelia sat on the couch next to Peter, who immediately drifted off. As she flicked through the TV channels, she also scrolled through her emails on her mobile. There was mostly junk but she sifted through it anyway, the way her mother used to study each of the supermarket catalogues when they came in the mail. There was an email from one of the local TAFEs where she'd done a bookkeeping short course years ago. As she scrolled down the list of new courses she noticed one titled *HerStory: A Women's Guide to Biography.* Evangelia read through the description. By the time Peter had woken himself with the vigour of his snores, Evangelia was enrolled.

4

Rik

North Facing Window: Gladys O'Reilly
April 2016
By Rik Lee

Gladys O'Reilly has seen a lot of changes in the last nine decades. 'I'm a northerner through and through. Fifty years in Northcote and it'll be fifty in Coburg soon enough.' She remembers the fuss and excitement when Northland opened in 1966, the first self-contained indoor mall in Victoria. 'It was very European. We'd go down to gush over the fabrics in Buckley & Nunn and make a day of it.' So enamoured was she of the new shopping hub, Gladys ended up securing work in the makeup section of Myer, where she stayed until her retirement in the mid-eighties. 'Once the children were all grown – and with Barry's blessing, of course – I put on my best dress and presented myself at the counter and gosh near argued my way into a job! It was the eye shadow that did it. Galactic blue. Done subtly.'

Gladys fondly recalls the area's shift in demographic. 'Once the Greeks and Italians arrived, you couldn't move without bumping into a fancy tailor! They did all of Barry's suits and I found a woman who would create the most lovely dresses for a pittance. It was all the children you see, lots of mouths to feed. Big families, like us Irish Catholics. Lovely people.'

After years crammed into a single-fronted terrace, Gladys and Barry built their new home on a large plot in Coburg, big enough for the whole family. 'By that point most of the children were married and close to starting families of their own – except for Maureen, but that's another story, bless her for trying – so there was plenty of space for when the grandchildren visited. It was quite the design – triple fronted, brick veneer, lovely castellated fence. We argued about if it would date but it's safe to say it's stood the test of time.'

Gladys still gets about with the help of her walker and is a well-known presence along Sydney Road. Her favourite thing about living in the north is how easy it is to pop down to the shops now that there are so many Coles about the place.

Rik Lee, failed hack and man-about-nowhere, carefully closed the pages of the small suburban newspaper, placed it to one side of his little plywood kitchen table-cum-desk, then gently folded himself face down as if performing a particularly graceful yoga move. He waited a moment then gently struck his forehead against the surface, firmly enough to elicit a satisfying thud, and turned his face to the wall. Outside car horns blared angrily and he pressed his ear into the table to block them out. His cheek squished into what he suspected was an errant splotch of oats from the porridge he had been eating, and he imagined it spreading out, contagion-like, into his pores.

Of all the pieces, this one had been by far the hardest, and not just because she'd asked him repeatedly where he was from until he gave up and told her his paternal grandparents were born in Hong Kong, which had seemed to satisfy her. The old woman's house had smelt like urine, the carpets stained in mortifying patches, and the hallway lined with cheery smiling photos of the family members who had allowed this. It was appalling, the state things got to when people were no longer able to care for themselves. When he'd tactfully broached the subject Gladys had shrugged her shoulders complacently while she dunked a milk arrowroot biscuit into her teacup. She told him that someone from the council popped by twice a week to help her wash and she occasionally had a nice chat with the young people who stopped by to enquire about her electricity provider. Then she'd rattled open a kitchen drawer to show him where she kept her painkillers, explaining that when the district nurse came to visit she'd ask Gladys to rate her pain from one to ten and would dole out quantities of tablets accordingly. Gladys had a nice collection as she always exaggerated the pain and was saving them for a rainy day when she was too much of a burden for people. He'd become quietly outraged then, imagining for a fleeting moment that this article would become a call to action for better services and companionship for the area's elderly, but he'd just as quickly pushed this thought away. No, this was a nice simple story about a nice simple old woman who lived in a nice simple house in the north. As his editor had informed him on his first day writing the column a month or so back, rallying cries were not what people wanted when they sat down to *North Facing Window* of a Monday afternoon with their cuppa. What they wanted from the column, she reminded him often, was a glimpse into the front windows of their fellow northerners, people not so different from themselves.

'That piece you did on the couple with the vertical garden – people liked that. We got oodles of letters. That's the kind of thing people want to read about. Keep those coming and you'll make me a happy woman.'

She had even supplied him with a simple dot-point formula to follow: *Who are they? What do they do? Something fun and interesting other northerners might want to know! What is their favourite thing about living in the north?!!* He wasn't even entirely sure that anyone living this side of the river actually called themselves northerners but his editor, caught up in a George RR Martin fervour, seemed determined they would. And, as if by telepathy, he found that as soon as he phrased a question thus: 'What makes you a proud northerner?', people quickly adopted this, parroting it back as if they had been saying it for years.

Rik stared at the paper folded on the table. Once, though who could remember these things now, he'd almost been a finalist for a Walkley (which he knew wasn't the same as actually *being* a finalist), and he knew that was meant to count for something (though honestly deep down he knew it didn't).

When it came to mildly shocking exposés into corrupted local identities, the paper had Lotti. Lotti wrote pretty much everything that wasn't the *North Facing Window* column or the pre-packaged items for syndication across all the state's suburban mastheads. She was approximately half Rik's age and spent much of her time chasing down leads about dodgy dealings among the local councillors and championing the community's abiding need for more CCTV. This was the exact position Rik had held when he'd started out at this very newspaper nearly two decades before, fresh out of university and ready to change the world. Now, older and wiser, he knew this was a young person's game, and required the naïve belief that the world could ever be changed with words. Leave him to his reminiscent geriatrics and his innovative modern-living home-gardening techniques, thank you very much. Besides, he was lucky enough to get this gig, what with the state of print media and everything that had happened. Thankfully only Lotti seemed to know, her investigative nous leading her to the simple google click that told the tale of the mess he'd made of his career as Rik watched on in horror from his desk nearby. Only, she'd never said anything to anyone, which meant she was either so embarrassed on his behalf that she felt it better not to mention any part of the catastrophe, perhaps in fear that he might once more lose the plot, or else she'd stored it away for safekeeping and future stand-overing, which was more likely as this was exactly what Rik would have done at her age. *Come at me*, Rik thought, staring around the cramped little apartment where he had preferred to work since the google incident. *Take what you can find.* There was nothing much of any worth in the apartment, save for the monstrous sideboard he'd inherited from his grandmother and felt too guilty to give to charity with the rest of it. It sat there, a relic to a once glorious past, housing IKEA cutlery instead of antiquities, and catching his toe as he wandered the small apartment at night.

He glanced at it now, and from nowhere a voice cried into the silence. *Stop, please, I only want to help!* No! Rik squeezed his eyes shut, his hands flying to his temples. The headaches were getting worse – migraines more likely, for they throbbed and blinded with equal abandon. He took some of the foreign painkillers from the indecipherable packet in his pocket, then splashed his face with cold water at the sink. He sat back at the table, head in his hands, and eventually the pressure subsided. He thought about the next few hours, took a cavernous breath, then levered himself up from the sticky table, reaching for his jacket. There was no rest for the wicked and right now the wicked was running late for an interview about a man and his bluestone cobblestones crusade.

5

Nell

Reference: 3284/16BA
Williams & Williams
Queen Street, Melbourne 3000

11 April 2016
Jolly Jumping Jungle Gym Pty Ltd
Plenty Road, Bundoora, 3038
Dear Mr Nigel Miller,

Re: Jolly Jumping Jungle Gym Corporation

We refer to your initial appointment of 5 April 2016 and confirm your instructions to act in the above matter.

Confirmation of Instructions

You have asked us to advise you on the contractual validity of the Terms and Conditions of Entry Form in protecting Jolly Jumping Jungle Gym Corporation (JJJGC) from any action by all parties. We have been informed that possible negligence on behalf of JJJGC employees in maintaining adequate and responsive provision of cleaning services may have contributed to an incident that occurred on the slip'n'dip tunnel slide during the occasion of a joint birthday/confirmation party in March 2016.

Summary of Advice

JJJGC may owe a duty of care to minors even with the terms and conditions of entry, if foreseeable risk can be established outside the scope of exclusion clause.

In this case, duty of care may cover provision of adequate training to employees in maintaining hygienic regulation.

The Contract

The Terms and Conditions of Entry Form appears to have present the main features of a validly formed contract, including agreement expressively reached between JJJGC and clients to provide a safe environment and equipment for all events held at the premise including hygienic regulation

Nell paused mid-sentence and looked up from her computer, frowning. On the opposite site of the partner desk, DB's eyes were glued to his own screen, his fingers jabbing at the keyboard with furious purpose like a titan pummelling a tiny organ.

'Do we have to say "hygienic regulation"?'

DB's brow was already furrowed as he cast his eyes towards her.

'Do we have to use that term?' Nell repeated, clicking her thumbnail impatiently against the nub of her index finger. 'Because it doesn't really convey a child urinating at the top of a slide and another child slipping on it.'

DB brought a hand to his forehead and pressed it firmly, as if to contain his brain.

'Yes, that's the term we use. It's still the term we use. No matter how many times you ask, it will remain the term we use. And before you go on, remember what I said last time – it is a semantics thing, yes, but it is the law, and we are nothing but confined to the rule of law, and there is no room in the law for empty platitudes or emotional appeals, and I feel that the number of occasions you ask me questions like this suggests that we could perhaps save ourselves an abundance of time by simply not asking these kinds of questions of our superiors because the law remains ever so clear on them, to the point of tedium, despite how we generally feel about it all.'

Nell bit down on her lip, then gave him a short nod. DB returned to his work and Nell resumed staring at her computer screen. *Hygienic regulation* . . . It sounded so . . . well, it didn't say what she wanted it to say. Really, it needed to be clearer . . . Straightforward. Plain English. Because the law may indeed be black and white but the terms they bandied about never seemed to be, and DB was a pedant for legalese. And if everyone just said exactly what they meant then the world would be a much easier place for everyone to navigate, and people wouldn't get themselves into these kinds of situations to begin with. It was frustrating – always so fist-clenchingly, jaw-splittingly frustrating – and seemingly more so as each day went by. She remembered what it had been like all those months ago when she had first started. Hovered over the sink, bracing herself against the walls of the toilet stall, willing herself not to throw up. Holding her hand under the cold tap for a moment before pressing it against the back of her neck, careful not to touch the top of her new business blazer or the bottom of her carefully pinned blonde bun. Glancing in the small mirror above the sink, as she breathed in and out, excited, terrified, and with an energy she could now only faintly recall, like a long-gone lover whose features have faded and fuzzed.

Here she was, finally, part of the coveted Williams & Williams graduate solicitor program. How thrilling it had all seemed back then. Sitting bolt upright as the interview panel – headed by Mr Arthur Williams AO himself! – had smiled warmly as they worked through her CV, ticking off each item.

'Sandstone University,' Mr Williams had murmured. 'Very good.'

She had waited tensely, her eyes dancing from the white walls to the white office furniture to the white orchids arranged stylishly in the centre of the table. It was like a meeting in heaven with Marie biscuits. She'd reached for a biscuit out of nervousness, then panicked at the thought of eating it in front of the panel. It had spent the rest of the interview peeping up from where she'd stowed it on her lap out of sight. Meanwhile, they'd nodded approvingly at her credentials which carefully hid her twelve months of post-university job-seeking – an internship up in the Northern Territory and volunteer stints with several community legal centres, including one working with women escaping their abusive partners.

'We're very much about corporate social responsibility,' Mr Williams had commented, and Mr Blake, another panel member, had told her about their commitment to a yearly Christmas dry goods drive as well as their inter-firm football and netball teams.

Williams & Williams specialised, among other things, in commercial law, they reminded her. Was this something she was interested in?

'Absolutely,' she'd lied, and they'd nodded approvingly.

'Very good, Helena,' said Mr Williams, placing the emphasis in the wrong part, but Nell hadn't corrected him. To Mr Williams she was Helena. The only other place she was Helena was on her birth certificate and in the occasional frustrated sigh from her mother. Mr Williams sat back, satisfied, his generous belly straining against his expensive cotton shirt.

And then, with a handshake, Nell was no longer part of the great teeming masses of inexperienced, overqualified graduates desperately seeking employment. Her first days had passed in a blur of introductions, inductions, office equipment demonstrations and stretches of time spent huddled over the various forms required to receive pay, accrue superannuation, and contribute at an appropriate rate to the great taxation system from which everything seemed to emanate, circumnavigate and evade. At one point Nell sat back, documentation spread before her like a paper trail leading towards adulthood, and felt a rush of excitement and dread. *So this is what it feels like in the real world.*

It was in these first few days of the graduate program that they had each been introduced to their mentor, an experienced solicitor tasked with guiding them through the minefield-maze of the legal profession. She had been assigned to support an associate named Ben, a man who seemed to consist entirely of well-cut suits and strictly enforced deadlines for everyone but himself. He delivered his correspondence through short, succinct statements volleyed at her across their partner desk, and pithy emails with no conjunctions. They met for the first time over lunch, his paisley silk tie draping gracefully into his reheated stroganoff as he outlined eagerly the many opportunities that awaited them. The rumour was that not long before Nell had started, he had blown apart a particularly tricky patent case with a chance discovery of new evidence, and had failed to reach such grand heights since. At the time it had earned him the fleeting coveted attention of Mr Williams, who had commended him for his dynamism and bestowed upon him the appellation Dynamic Ben. It was a momentary favouritism that, just like the nickname, Ben – now DB – had been courting ever since. Indeed, the only people who still referred to him as DB were Nell – by dint of his constant insistence – and DB himself.

Nell's work mainly revolved around drafting instruction confirmation letters and contracts for DB, or sifting through the firm's prehistoric paper files and online database for past precedents. File after file of convoluted, complicated waffle. Oh, but they'd sounded so interesting, those area titles, all those months ago – Mergers and Acquisitions! Competition and Consumer! Except that DB and Nell seemed to spend a majority of their time engaged in dispute resolution over minor contract disagreements, or else Compliance, which apart from Insolvency and Recoveries, everyone agreed was the worst.

Despite his proclaimed dynamism, DB rarely seemed to attract interesting cases. In lieu of this, he had developed a growing obsession with formatting, causing Nell to spend hours reworking documents to ensure they met his specific, changing demands while he feverishly watched a point just beyond her shoulder. Initially she had thought he was studiously overseeing her progress for opportunities to correct or coach her, but she soon realised he was in fact monitoring the elevator lobby for chance glimpses of Mr Williams. In the event of a successful sighting, he was prone to developing a sudden insatiable urge for coffee and would hurry towards the lobby in the hope of catching some one-on-one time with their boss. Usually he would return defeated, and slump behind his computer stabbing dejectedly at his keyboard while helping himself to the stash of mini Turkish Delights secreted in his middle drawer.

When not in pursuit of Mr Williams, DB fielded the occasional phone call from what Nell had originally assumed was a wife or girlfriend, but eventually realised was in fact his mother. They talked – bickered would be more precise – about what Nell worked out was a semi-regular Sunday dinner, and a recurrent point of contention was something called Woofer who had seemingly taken over DB's childhood bedroom. And there were words too – using three syllables – barked triumphantly into the phone for no discernible reason. All in all, she could fit in the palm of her hand the things she was learning from DB.

Despite her grad year having officially ended and Nell now technically being a proper Williams & Williams junior staff member, she and DB continued to share a workspace. Williams & Williams prided themselves on adopting what they termed an 'integrated approach' across all their legal services, and one aspect of this was a mentor/mentee relationship that, it seemed to Nell, was expected to last in perpetuity. Williams & Williams had modern partner desks – more IKEA than ye olde worlde England – shared between mentor and mentee. The theory was that this would create a joint space in which learning would be transmitted freely and easily, a two-way exchange intended to bring experience and innovation together in an our-powers-combined legal virtuosity. Instead, it acted like some kind of sporting net over which they took turns lobbing reluctant requests and clarifications at each other, unless they had reached a point of contention, in which case DB tended to revert to his terse emails.

Far from the excitement Nell had imagined in those halcyon first days, for the most part it was a steady trudge of memos submitted with sluggish reliability, template contracts with only a few clauses added or deleted and the contact details changed, files reviewed to make sure they'd been costed correctly, and periodic mentor/mentee 'catch-ups' in the staff kitchen, during which she provided occasional interjections to DB's regular monologues that demonstrated the general disjuncture between the lawyer in his head and the one that loafed about his desk each day. They disagreed frequently, arguing about the merit of the cases they worked.

'They can't all be foreigners, Nell,' he'd reminded her one afternoon, and she'd had to google what this meant.

A foreigner, it appeared, had something to do with elaborate shelf companies and off-the-books Panama-style cover-ups, and she had disliked DB just a little more after this. She watched him now, stabbing away at his keyboard. Nell turned back to her own. She deleted the bit that read 'hygienic regulation' and in its place wrote 'urinating on the play equipment', then sent the file zinging through the greater world wide web towards DB's inbox. He could deal with it himself.

*

Often Nell drifted into daydreams on the tram heading home each night, drawn-out imaginings in which she stumbled upon some magnificent piece of Socratic reasoning that shifted the very foundations of the legal establishment, sending it spiralling towards unprecedented civic and moral equity. She'd overshot her stop the first time she'd made the journey from the city centre to Seymour's inner north home. *Her* home, she corrected herself, though it still sounded strange. That first time she'd wandered the streets for a while, the GPS on her mobile flailing to find itself, until she eventually recognised a park draped in a large *Refugees are welcome here* banner and found her way back to the little terrace house. Her explanation to Seymour was that she was plotting routes for future jogs, but she knew he saw through this. 'When did you last jog?' he'd asked, and she'd pretended not to hear.

Today, Nell watched the streets stumble into dusk, the light falling in dappled intervals along the seemingly never-ending passage of Sydney Road. It was still warm for April, and though she knew that this more than likely heralded the inching ever closer of the catastrophic climactic tipping point, it was quite pleasant nonetheless. Seymour would probably have something to say about this. Seymour had something to say about everything. He was very particular about things like environmental justice and what should and shouldn't go in the recycling, though without Patrick to inform him, his arguments had become overwhelmingly more symbolic than factual. The night before he had been halfway through a lecture on why she shouldn't put her meat scraps in the worm farm when he'd stopped mid-sentence, confusion plastering his face and said, 'Just because, okay? I'm your older brother and please just do as I say because your questions are insufferable.'

It was only now that Patrick was gone that Nell realised that much of what she had previously thought of as her brother's wide-ranging intellectualism was simply the repackaging of Patrick's thoughts coupled with Seymour's own innate sense of self-righteousness. Without Patrick, Seymour was like a rudderless boat on the sea of opinions, forging ahead blindly with neither logic nor reasoning to guide him. A man on a stump with not much to say. In the weeks since she'd moved in, settling her belongings into what had previously been Patrick's study, she had already been on the receiving end of loosely structured orations on the harmful impacts of too much screen time and why her first order of business should be to petition her workplace for standing desks. Both, though passionate and articulate, generally revolved around the theme that she should do these things because he told her to, and his near decade's seniority over her seemed less apparent as the days wore on. And because she loved her brother, who was so clearly falling apart at the seams, she tried not to argue these points. Instead, as she lay awake each night in a room that still smelt of Patrick, she pondered the myriad ways her brother reeled and unravelled before her. Sometimes, as she heard the soft murmurs on the other side of their shared wall that were either tears or YouTube, she wanted to rap lightly against the plaster and call to him through the anonymity of the partition: *It's okay, this wasn't my plan either. I thought by now I'd have saved if not the whole world then at least a portion of it. That my superior legal skills would have brought justice and equity to all, when instead I spend much of my time deep in discussion with my mentor about whether narrow margins are appropriate for external communications and briefing him on the minutiae of legal precedents for contractual disagreements that would put Mr Westminster himself to sleep. And who would have thought I'd be voted out of yet another share house? Inexplicably, another, and forced into your spare room?*

These days, when he was not at the gallery, Seymour oscillated between exuberant, near manic activity and hours spent in the Seymour-shaped groove on the couch. The other week she had returned home to find him hovering over the kitchen counter, striped apron and mountains of white powder piled before him like a gluten-hungry Tony Montana. He was making bread, he had informed her, his eyes electric behind the fine dusting of flour across his nose and brow, Adele playing over the sound system. They had both smelt it then, the charcoal-scented tang, and Seymour's face had fallen as he dove for the oven. Thick acrid smoke filled the room. The siblings stood mute, their eyes on the ruined loaves as Adele sang out her heartbreak in the background, duetted by the screech of the smoke alarm. Eventually, Seymour had shrugged acceptingly then turned back to his flour mounds.

This evening she found him sprawled across the couch in what she had taken to thinking of as his 'house clothes': a combination of faded grey tracksuit pants and a Woodstock-style cotton shirt. With his shaggy blond hair and three-day growth he looked like an anglicised later years Jesus caught in a mid-life slump. He looked up briefly, his blue eyes meeting her own before oscillating back to the television. She glanced at the screen. He had somehow managed to find a station almost solely devoted to *Friends* reruns. He and Patrick used to watch *Friends* together, he'd told her one night, and she'd gently suggested he consider washing the ice-cream stains from his crotch.

By day, his transformation was remarkable, washed and

dressed in the vintage suits he wore to the gallery, where he charmed and chattered with his usual breezy touch. The gallery had been the love child of he and Patrick, a lifelong ambition harboured from behind the desk of other galleries until Patrick one day suggested he take the plunge and go out on his own, which had, just quietly, involved plunging somewhat substantially into their mother's share of the Family Money. He had wanted to call it *Gallery Oh!*, after the sound he hoped punters would make on surveying its art, however Patrick had pointed out that this sounded more like a strip club – somewhere white-collar workers and retired high court judges went to relax in discrete, glittery style. Instead, they had settled on *PS*, a seemingly romantic entanglement of their initials, until the graffiti started declaring it *Gallery Piss*. At that, he had simply removed the sign and since then it was known affectionately as *Seymour's*.

Leaving him to his viewing, Nell peered into the fridge, poking at a few plastic containers.

'Is this porridge or risotto?'

Seymour offered an ambivalent shrug. Patrick had been the cook, she'd since discovered, and not much had rubbed off during the course of their decade-long relationship.

'*Little Shop of Horrors* is opening soon,' she called out, shoving a container into the microwave.

She'd seen an advertisement for the stage show on the tram. The movie had been a staple of their childhood, so much so that Seymour had used it as inspiration for his sobriquet long ago when he'd turned against his birth name. She looked expectantly at her brother.

'Patrick loves *Little Shop of Horrors*,' he said softly.

She sighed inwardly. Patrick, it seemed, loved pretty much everything that involved getting up off the couch and showering. The Patrick-sized hole in the house was obvious, not just from the faint outlines on the walls and carpets where long-standing furniture no longer stood, but in the tilt and swing of Seymour's moods.

Patrick had been sent overseas to cover the war and who knew when he would return. Their mother had asked which war and Seymour, adrift without Patrick to feed him information of current affairs, had simply replied, 'All of them.' To Nell, it looked like a break-up, but a break-up it apparently was not, and he'd chastised her once for even suggesting this. It was simply that it was easier on them both to limit contact, what with the unpredictability of foreign internet and all, and it made sense to put Patrick's belongings in storage so that Seymour could offer the spare room to Nell, who everyone knew did not thrive in share houses. And the fact Patrick had spent most of his career reporting on the arts had no bearing on his ability to report the real stories from the sidelines of war. If one needed to label it – which Seymour felt they really did not – it was simply a break, with no 'up' involved, though to Nell there clearly appeared to be one hell of a 'down' taking place. So off to war Patrick went, lugging behind him all of his clothing, a heavy oak desk and assorted other antique furnishings. Indeed, the only thing of Patrick's remaining was a collection of dark hairs in the sinkhole that remained coiled in the spokes like a little memorial to a waylaid saint. Grabbing the mystery meal from the microwave, Nell squeezed into the gap between Seymour's socked feet and the couch arm.

'Porridge,' she reported, her mouth full and disappointed.

'Porridge is an ideal breakfast,' Seymour murmured, eyes glued to the screen. 'It's low GI or a super food or something like that. Cleans you out, I think. I don't remember. Something to do with your duodenum. Bon appétit.'

Credits started rolling and he began to flick through the stations, slow and methodical, before resting on the national broadcaster.

'Isn't Mum meant to be on tonight?' Nell asked.

'They bumped her at the last minute. Prudence was available instead. Mum rang earlier. She's livid.'

Their mother had, in the eighties, authored what was now considered a foundational work of feminist critique of the traditional Australian canon. *Bush of the Bush: Putting Women in their Place* had been phenomenally successful in a way that none of her subsequent books had managed. As part of the failing publicity for her most recent book, *Out of Focus: Women in the Public Archive*, a friend had wrangled her a spot on a national current affairs show, though this too, it seemed, had fallen through. This would not have been received well: for someone who critiqued for a profession, their mother was perhaps one of the least capable of receiving criticism. The opening music began and the siblings watched on, treasonous in their mother's absence. Prudence, their mother's academic rival and real-world arch nemesis, was, as always, impeccable. At one point Seymour's face lit up.

'Prudence is once more dressed in the heady red shades of inner east suburban solidarity,' he observed wryly.

'Pardon?' Nell was confused.

'Patrick would have laughed,' Seymour muttered to himself, and they went back to watching in silence.

Ten minutes later Nell lay coiled around her laptop, the doona cocooning her into the bed as she stared glumly at the screen. In fairness to the world in general it was never a good idea to google oneself, yet self-google she had. *Did you mean* Ned *Swansea?* the browser asked earnestly. She scrolled through a couple of pages, finding only foreign doppelgangers, and then eventually links to Seymour. There he was, perfect teeth and soulful eyes, wearing a stupid trilby on a ridiculous angle that she had since seen him twice bin then rescue after proclaiming it a poltergeist of Patrick's incessant desire to transform him.

'Nobody actually wears trilbies,' he'd muttered into the open lid of the bin before letting it snap shut. 'Only embarrassing wannabes and elderly men with names like Lorenzo or Alf.'

Moments later he'd nudged the bin back open with an embarrassed foot and swiped the trilby out.

'I'll take it to the op shop later,' he snapped, though Nell suspected it had joined the secret pile of Patrick-scented mementos he'd started hoarding in the back of his wardrobe. Nell closed her laptop and lay back in the darkness waiting for sleep to arrive.

*

The next morning passed slowly as Nell spent it reworking the Miller letter DB had sent back to her with comments. *Hygienic regulation*, she noted, was back. She took an early lunch, placing an order at a café down the street, then waited by the window. The foot traffic at this end of Collins Street was a teeming sea of neutral tones set against the languid sky. Suits of black, grey and brown weaved and zigzagged, as office workers wasted their breaks with tedious errands and personal tasks as their lunches sat on their desks awaiting their return. Heads were cast downwards against the rain and already brisk gaits quickened, leaping and dodging over and around the fast-forming puddles. Inside the café, fine-suited professionals scrolled through their phones, shooting off urgent emails and knocking over hasty phone calls. She waited for her order, listening to the conversations taking place around her.

'We went to Geelong,' a young woman was telling another. 'But the nice part. My parents have a place down there that's super close to the beach. But the nice beach.'

Taking her sandwich from the waiter and shoving it into her bag, Nell edged her way out of the café. The rain was heavier now, beating at the pavement as if washing the city of its past.

She opened her umbrella gingerly, then stepped into the deluge. She made it halfway down the block before reluctantly ducking under an awning for relief. She could feel the water seeping into her stockinged feet and she grimaced. Dry feet were a fundamental part of maintaining a balanced mood and Nell could feel the grumpiness creeping up on her. Her feet and underwear – so long as these two things were dry she could do anything, which was why she avoided rain and boats. As she grumbled about her feet, she noticed a similar displeasure on the faces of other thwarted lunchtime shoppers and errand runners. One young woman in particular was looking especially annoyed with her grime-splattered boots. Nell's brain suddenly clicked.

'Rani?'

Of all their university friends, Rani was the only one to land the kind of job they'd all talked of finding, working for an outer suburbs community legal centre. While the rest of them had their office perks like travel opportunities, healthy bank accounts and agency-sponsored after-work drinks, Rani alone claimed to have a balanced conscience that she liked to mock-flaunt at their frequently less frequent catch-ups. Infrequent, Nell realised; they'd not seen each other since before Nell landed the position with Williams & Williams.

'What are you doing in the CBD?' Nell asked, leaning into the hug.

'Ruining my boots, for one thing,' Rani grimaced. 'And meetings. Funding issues. Again. I swear it's like we spend half our time trying to convince the government not to cut funding instead of actually helping clients. But at least it means a day somewhere with proper coffee. Speaking of, should we? Want to get out of this rain and humour an old bird from the 'burbs?'

They settled into a snug laneway café that smelt of roasting beans and things without gluten. As their coffees arrived, Rani finished her story about the refugee client she'd recently helped get out of an unwarranted public transport fine then looked at Nell intently. All Nell had to contribute was: 'Sometimes DB refuses to read my work unless it is the right font. Arial. Size twelve. This is the right font. Sans serif or death, that's his current motto.' But she didn't share this because, compared to Rani's story of helping extricate the vulnerable from an outrageously unfair system weighted against them, her own story made her sound like a glorified assistant for a moderately insane typesetter. Rani, it turned out, was leading a team of graduates at her community legal centre, and also volunteered one day a week assisting people seeking asylum at the local refugee legal centre.

'It's so busy right now.' She shook her head. 'Silence for years and then suddenly thirty thousand people issued with letters telling them they have a month to lodge an application for a temporary protection visa. You can imagine what that's been like. And then you've got the Minister going and making ridiculous comments about queue jumpers and illegals on the television, so all our clients are suddenly getting harassed on the street more than usual.'

Her workplace, too, was overwhelmed, thanks to a renewed national interest in domestic abuse.

'We've got more family violence than we know what to do with. That's the thing they don't seem to get. Fine, put however many millions into an awareness campaign, but as soon as those ads hit the telly, who do you think is suddenly seeing more clients than we've got capacity for? It's brutal. I mean, we just can't make it to every hearing because there simply aren't enough of us, and we know clients aren't showing up because they're scared to be there on their own. That's what's criminal. The money from the Royal Commission can't come soon enough.'

Rani folded a sugar sachet in half and shoved it into her empty glass.

'You're not looking to do some pro bono stuff, are you?' she asked, her face twisted in mock servitude. 'Corporate social responsibility and all that jazz? We'd kill for some more lawyers. Little bit of warm and fuzzy to go alongside those decent salaries you get? Anyway, just a thought. I better keep going. Can't afford to be late for a funding meeting in these times of rampant budget trimming. Keep fighting the good fight, Swansea.'

Rani raised a comic fist in the air then she ducked through the door and out into the rain.

Back in the office, DB watched as Nell shrugged off her blazer, tapping his finger on his watch, head moving disparagingly from side to side like a grim laughing clown from a carnival alley.

'I know, I know,' Nell muttered, unpausing the program that tracked her billable hours.

She spent the afternoon tinkering with a costs disclosure that DB had asked her to rework, her mind on Rani's half-joked offer. She saw the version of herself that veered leeward from the one that had accepted the Williams & Williams position, the one who had written essays at university with titles like *The Lawyer as Conduit for Equity* and *A Short Discourse on Justice and Access*. That innate sense of justice had been the reason she'd studied law in the first place. And embarrassing as it was, yes, true, she'd also been inspired by the slick, articulate lawyers that traipsed the made-up courtrooms of the silver screen, battling for the disenfranchised and downtrodden, eloquent and impassioned and having hot TV sex with one another in their chambers. Because they did *good*, those spunky television lawyers, fighting for what was right and fair and just. She sat at her side of the partner desk for hours, ignoring the ache in her back and the strain behind her eyes, her fingers mechanically wandering the keyboard as her mind remained elsewhere. When DB rose from his side, his workday complete, Nell straightened her back.

'Can I speak to you for a moment before you go?'

DB looked pained. 'Can't it wait until tomorrow?'

He hurried off towards the elevator without waiting for her response. After a while, the elevator returned, this time depositing Mr Williams on their floor. He strode towards one of the head of department corner offices. *Near miss, DB*, Nell smiled to herself. Mr Williams noticed her and offered a friendly wave. Nell returned it, blushing, then stood to collect her blazer. She paused. It was now or never, wasn't it?

'Mr Williams?' she called out. 'Can I please speak to you for a second?'

Part 2

6

Aida

In the century leading up to my birth, Iran had seen two revolutions and two coups d'état. This was modern Iran, the back-and-forth power struggle as the monarchy, the mullahs and the mercantile circled each other for supremacy. The reality is the stuff of Hollywood movies – exiles, betrayals, the CIA lurking in the shadows – though Hollywood has yet to tell this tale without the pizazz and licence that make fiction of fact. Yet for most of my childhood my head swam with tales of old Persia, fuelled by the stories from my father and grandfather of the time before the Arab invasion brought Islam to our nation. This was when the Persian Empire spread from the Indus River in the east to modern-day Ethiopia under the rule of Kourosh – Cyrus the Great – when our stories were equal parts history and mythology.

My grandfather would tell me tales of the mighty Achaemenid descendants of Cyrus – Darius, Xerxes, Artaxerxes – building brick by brick their glorious new capital in Persepolis. He took me there once during a family holiday down south, my brothers running off in search of undiscovered treasures as the two of us wandered hand in hand through the ancient city buried for centuries under dust and sand and forgetting. I posed for a photograph before a statue of the homa bird, a griffin-like creature thought to live its life in flight, never resting permanently in any one place.

In this picture my arms are spread wide as if I myself am flying, my mouth pouting in a narrow, funnelled attempt at a hooked beak. I remember how my grandfather laughed at this, his thin body rocking back and forth in the way my father's does now. Those thin bodies that were once as tall and handsome as cypress trees, before time left them wilted.

I was far more fascinated by Naqsh-e Rustam, the ancient necropolis carved deep into heavy rock high up in a nearby cliff face, for I knew the name Rostam from the stories told to me by my father. Here the great Zoroastrian kings were laid to rest, their bodies placed in the rocky burial chambers touching neither earth nor fire. Did I want to ride a camel? my grandfather asked, indicating to where my brothers mock-raced each other along the road despite the scowls of the weathered camel handlers. But I was more interested in scrutinising the gaps in the rockwork and the fine bas-relief accompanying them, imagining myself prone inside as the vultures picked my bleached bones clean.

'Does it hurt?' I asked him.

'Does what hurt?' he replied. 'The camels?'

'History,' I said, and he had no answer to this.

My happiest memories are of visiting my grandparents in their small village near Kashan, where they retired after my grandfather made his money in Tehran. The joyful anticipation that radiated between my brothers and I as we tussled in the back seat of the car, bidding farewell to crowded, cramped Tehran. The carefree whistle in my father's exhalation as he returned to the home of his ancestors. My mother's stoic brow, steeling herself for my grandmother's questions and critiques. Sometimes Damavand, the tallest mountain in the Alborz range that hugs the north of the city, would manage to peep through the pollution long enough for us to wave goodbye, and then we would be on our way, stopping only in Qom to dodge the mullahs and buy sweet sticky sohan for my grandmother. My grandparents' village lay in the desert – not the golden soil of Yazd or soft dunes of Maranjab – but hard, rocky desert of stone and shrubs that was dry yet fertile given the right conditions. The houses in their tiny village were squat and block-like, stacked side by side like a child's plaything. There had been a school once, and a factory for making hinges, both now closed as the village shrank. A doctor visited the clinic once a week to tend to the ageing occupants, who were all related to us in one way or another (and sometimes both), for this was a place where cousins sometimes married cousins to build up their real estate. Despite its appearance, the village soils still thrived, and with the help of hired youth from a larger village nearby produced pomegranates, walnuts, figs, almonds, apricots, plums, blackberries, tomatoes, eggplants, cucumbers and turnips. Roses, too, with rosewater forming the backbone of their income.

We'd pile out of the car, the sharpness of the air hitting our lungs so different from Tehran's bitter chemical fug. My grandparents' house had two main rooms, both lined from wall to wall with carpets of all colours and styles: Mashhadi, Kashani, a bold nomadic weave depicting the tree of life. Here we would sit down to eat and later to sleep, half in one room, half in the other, all haunted by the apnoeic snoring of my uncle Asadollah, who never seemed to be roused by the frustrated manhandling of the would-be sleepers around him. Huddled together around the korsi, its coal fire fighting off the cold desert night, my father and grandfather would take turns telling us stories from the Shahnameh. Of wise Sam, abandoned Zal, and of course the mighty Rostam, each trying to outdo the other with poetic phrasing and flourishing details, as Uncle Asadollah prayed hastily in the corner because he'd forgotten to do it earlier. His belly tucked into his striped pyjamas, he wheezed and panted each time he lowered himself to the ground in a secondary soundtrack to our evening. And often this is how I would fall asleep, my head resting on my mother's shoulder as familiar voices sung me into sleep.

It was early still but late enough to pull herself out of bed after another restless night. Aida closed her notebook, sliding it beneath her pillow. After she dressed, she crept out of the house. As usual the letterbox was empty, save for some flyers and junk mail. Sometimes, even though she knew the postman didn't call until the afternoon, Aida checked it in the morning just in case. Just in case she'd missed it the day before, just in case it had landed in a neighbour's letterbox first. Just in case she was losing her mind. She chided herself, looking around to see if there were any neighbours about, but thankfully the street was clear of anyone who might puzzle at her incessant routine. *This is what I have become*, she thought to herself. A degree from one of the best universities in Iran and her day revolved around checking the letterbox and giving out résumés that went straight into rubbish bins.

She pulled the sleeves of her jumper down over her knuckles. The weather was changing now, autumn settling in with a mild chill that had plunged their little house into premature winter. It had been raining, too, a light drizzle that was steadily building in purpose. She looked up as the front door slammed. Elham stood wrestling an umbrella open as Niki steered a course straight for the nearest puddle, her face set in maniacal determination.

'Niki!' Elham called warningly, just as Niki landed, showering herself with stale, dirty water. She looked utterly impressed with herself. Elham greeted Aida, tilting her head towards the letterbox.

'Nothing?'

'Nothing.'

'No news is good news,' Elham offered, her nose wrinkled. 'What will you do today?'

'Keep looking for jobs,' Aida replied, her eyes on the heavy clouds. 'Rain, hail or shine!'

Elham made a clicking noise with her tongue. 'You'll drive yourself crazy, all this looking. And you want to work where?

In some shop or café when you are a journalist who studied English?'

Aida shrugged. It didn't work like that. Here she had no contacts, no understanding of the system. No permanent visa, which was the most important part. Elham clicked her tongue again.

'Give your mind the morning off. Come drop Niki at kinder.'

Aida began to decline the offer but stopped. Elham was right. It was getting to her, day after day of silence and rejection fuelling the uselessness that permeated her entire being. It had been enough before, when none of them had work rights, but now to have the right but not the opportunity – this was far worse.

'Okay.'

Elham raised her eyebrows, surprised. 'Really?'

'*Areh,*' Aida smiled.

Beside them, Niki was eyeing the puddle again, considering a rematch. She raised a boot-clad foot in the air.

'Let's go now, then,' Elham said, smiling back. 'Niki! *Nakon!*'

Niki watched her mother, a single foot still hovering over the water. Elham raised a stern eyebrow and Niki lowered it, guiltily, until it rested at the edge of the puddle.

'*Berim,*' Elham announced.

And off they went indeed, Aida and Elham huddled beneath the umbrella and Niki stomping through the rain. They walked the few blocks to Niki's kinder, joining the hodgepodge procession of patterned umbrellas and prams advancing in caravan towards the building. At the entrance, Aida watched Elham key in a code to release the gate. Niki paused then turned to Aida.

'Come,' she commanded in aloof English, marching into the building.

Surprised by the attention, Aida followed her. Torn between her usual state of wilfully ignoring Aida and her innate desire to showcase her kinder, Niki toured Aida through the building, pointing out various areas, barking their names with casual indifference.

'Kitchen – toilet – painting – playground – naughty corner,' she rattled off, her hands gesturing casually as if she were welcoming a film crew through her newly renovated home.

They paused before a large glassed area that looked out onto the play equipment outside. Its surface was peppered with the smudge and smears of a hundred little hands. Oblivious, Niki pressed her nose against the glass.

'Rabbit,' she announced, pointing to an A-frame hutch in one corner. 'Detention.'

Aida glanced at the wire mesh that kept the rabbits inside, but Niki had already resumed her tour. They viewed the reading area and the art cupboard before Niki suddenly bored of her new occupation and raced off in the direction of the other children without a backward glance. A tall girl with dark braids was throwing a ball to another little girl, and Niki leapt between them, delighted. The three of them dove for the ball, giggling and tumbling, then chased each other across the room. Elham watched them, her face momentarily pained.

'They can't put her back in detention. Look at her here.'

Niki successfully wrestled the ball from the others, hysterical with power and joy. As Aida and Elham made their way towards the exit a brightly dressed woman caught up with them. She was soft and round, her open face anxious to please.

'I'm Heather,' she introduced herself. 'One of the centre managers.'

Elham nodded hesitantly at Heather then looked to Aida with uncertainty. She reminded Aida of her own kinder teacher, Parisa-joon, and she wondered for a moment if they were all pumped out of a floral-scented perennially nervous mould in a factory somewhere. Heather rested one hand on the other, both atop the curve of her stomach.

'I just wanted to have a quick chat about Niki,' she said, a jolly fake smile on her face. 'Is that . . . do you . . . is that okay?'

She looked at them both nervously and Aida's mind filled with images of all the terrible things Niki might be responsible for: never-ending tantrums, her fascination with casting things into the toilet, the rabbit – please don't let it be anything to do with the rabbit, or the toilet, or both.

'What is it?' Elham asked in Persian and Aida shrugged.

She nodded for Heather to continue.

'Let me start by saying that Niki is a lovely little girl. Just lovely.'

Aida translated for Elham, who looked sceptical.

'My Niki? Are you sure she's got the right child?'

Aida smiled at Heather.

'She says thank you for saying such kind things.'

'And she's made lots of little friends here,' Heather continued. 'Oodles of them.'

Aida translated and Elham frowned.

'She has the wrong kid. Here, show her the picture in my phone.'

Aida ignored the phone. 'Elham says making friends is one of Niki's strong points. That and demonstrating patience.'

'What is she getting at? Who is this woman? Find out what she wants,' Elham commanded under her breath.

'Just like her mother,' Aida continued. 'The whole family thrives on their warm and trusting nature.'

Elham elbowed her.

'I know you're not translating what I say.'

Heather watched, confused, then reset her uneasy smile.

'There are a couple of things I'm a little concerned about.'

'See! I knew it,' Elham said in rapid Persian. 'It's the tantrums, isn't it? She never listens, either. Or the pinching. She knows she's not meant to pinch but you think she'll listen to me?'

'Her speech isn't as advanced as we would expect at her age but more than that . . . it's . . . the drawings, mostly,' Heather continued, her gaze shifting away from them in discomfort. 'They're, well, we can't put any of them up on the walls, if you get my drift. Some are . . . troubling and, well, we've had a complaint. Nothing formal yet, but one of the parents . . . Niki can be . . . rough. I'm sure she doesn't mean it. But we need to ensure all the children feel safe. And it makes me wonder about how things are for Niki. I understand your situation, and really we want to support you. Those times you've been late to pick her up and she's joined the long day care kids, we've not charged you for that. But the pictures and the rough play and, well . . .' She trailed off, her discomfort filling the gaps for Aida.

Aida translated for Elham, who fell silent. It was a long silence, punctuated only by the incongruous giggle and shriek of children playing nearby. Elham's voice was small, her eyes set on the ground before her.

'You think I don't know this?' she asked. 'I see this. I know it isn't normal for her. But how is she supposed to understand normal when all she has known is detention? When all she has seen . . . You think I don't feel shame about this? You think I don't feel like I am failing her? Mothers are meant to protect their children but how can I do this for her? I tell her to be gentle but what can you expect? What do I tell her? No, Niki, draw rainbows and pussycats instead. Nice things. Just forget everything else. How do I do this? There is nothing I can do.'

Tears filled her eyes and she turned away from them, ashamed. Heather clasped her hands in front of her, waiting uncomfortably for Aida to translate. Elham turned back to Aida suddenly, her eyes full of fear.

'What if they take Niki away from me?' she whispered. 'You hear all those stories of Child Protection . . . Don't tell her I said all that, Aida-joon. Please.'

Aida cleared her throat.

'Elham is a good mother,' she told Heather. 'It is not easy for people like us. She is doing her best.'

'I . . . I didn't say she wasn't,' Heather said. 'It's just, well, we can organise something. Some help perhaps?'

'Can you get her a visa?' Aida asked sharply. 'Promise her she won't go back into detention?'

Heather's face fell. 'Now, look, I . . . my concern is . . . I *care*. I've signed the petitions online. My husband too. But I have no control over those things.'

The woman was red-cheeked, wringing her hands nervously.

'I'm sorry,' Aida apologised. 'That was very improper of me. I'll talk to Elham about getting someone to help with Niki.'

As if conjured by some spell of coincidence, Niki appeared beside them, casting her arms around Elham's legs.

'Of course,' said Heather, offering them both what Aida now knew was a smile of hope and pain. It was the one given by anyone employed to help them. 'When you're ready, of course.'

As they left, Aida thought of all the children she'd seen, caged and anxious and not knowing any better. No room for their imaginations because of the abundance of reality. Then she tried to think of them no more.

*

When Elham returned home with Niki that afternoon Aida had a surprise for them.

'It's a bed, Niki. A late birthday present. A little mattress just for you. So you don't have to sleep crammed together on that single bed anymore.'

Niki gave the mattress a cursory glance, her eyes drifting over the purple daisies and stars of the sheets.

'No,' she replied shortly, coiling herself around Elham.

'Niki-joon, look at the lovely gift *khaleh* has given you!' Elham gushed, but Niki refused to.

'No,' she said again, her voice muffled by Elham's thigh.

Elham gave Aida an apologetic look.

Aida waved it off. 'It's nothing.'

She watched Niki huff out of the room. She had missed Niki's birthday the week before and only now had the money to buy her a gift. Aida didn't mention that because of the mattress she would be eating noodles until her next payment came through. Nor the difficulty she'd had lugging it home from the high street, balanced beneath her umbrella, after spotting it in a store while dropping off résumés. Nor the particularly strange breed of catcalls this had produced.

'We've never slept apart,' Elham confided, her voice low.

Aida was mortified that she had not considered this.

'Of course,' she assured Elham. 'It's there whenever you need it. I'm sure the cats will love it, anyway.'

Later, Aida wandered into the kitchen to find Elham scraping the remains of Niki's meal into the Cyruses bowl. Elham glanced at her a moment, shaking her head at the wasted food, then her face suddenly lit up.

'Oh, something happened to Niki today! Niki-joon!' she called. 'Come here! Come show *khaleh*.'

Niki wandered back in, heavy-footed.

'Show her. Show *khaleh*,' Elham insisted, and Niki reluctantly opened her mouth.

'She fell off the play equipment,' Elham explained. 'Knocked a tooth right out. But she's such a brave girl, aren't you?'

Niki nodded stoically, her tongue working the new gap in her mouth. 'Tooth fairy,' she informed them.

Elham and Aida exchanged confused looks.

'She was saying this before,' Elham said. 'What are you saying, *azizam*?'

'Tooth fairy,' Niki insisted, her voice rising with frustration.

'Fairly?' Aida guessed. 'What's not fair?'

'I don't understand you, *azizam*. Maybe it's the missing tooth or maybe she knocked her head when she fell. Niki, what are you saying?' Elham asked again, prompting the child to flash red.

'TOOTH FAIRY!'

The two women looked at each other, lost. Somewhere in the back of Aida's mind a distant memory shuffled its feet.

'Wait, this is sounding familiar.'

She pulled out her phone and typed *tooth fairy* into the search engine. She opened the Wikipedia entry and scrolled down. When she was finished, she began at the start and read through again. Elham watched her intently.

'What? What does it say?'

Aida looked down at the screen, bewildered.

'Tooth fairy . . . A *pari*. When children lose their teeth the tooth fairy comes in the night to take them away.'

Elham's face squirrelled in confusion.

'What? The children?'

'No, the teeth.'

'It takes the teeth? Oh, like the little mouse! My mother used to tell me that. The little mouse comes at night to take your teeth away.'

'Yes, but the tooth fairy leaves money in return.'

'For the teeth? Who gets the money? The parents or the child?'

'The child.'

Elham considered this.

'The little mouse makes more sense. Mice are always hoarding things. But why would a *pari* want to buy teeth? A *jinn* maybe. A jinn would exchange your teeth for money, except it would be an ancient *dirham* that turned out to be cursed, and would ruin the fortunes of you and your descendants for generations.'

Aida could see her mind ticking over.

'But we're in Australia now, so *pari* it is. Okay, Niki-joon. Time for bed. Let's leave your tooth out for the tooth *pari*.'

Niki threw back her head to protest but Elham raised a finger.

'You want your payment, don't you? You better get into the new bed *khaleh* gave you or the tooth *pari* might accidentally give your payment to Maman and take away my teeth.'

Niki eyed the two women suspiciously, processing her options. Finally, she nodded cautiously.

'But Maman help me sleep,' she countered.

'Okay, *azizam*,' Elham agreed. 'You go put on your pyjamas and I'll be there soon.'

Niki sauntered off, casting a prudent glance over her shoulder, the little tooth clasped firmly in her fist. In the kitchen, Elham opened her purse.

'How much do you think this jinn leaves? I have no coins.'

Aida checked her own purse.

'Me neither. I have a ten-dollar note. Is that too much? It seems like too much. Surely a child's tooth isn't worth much?'

Elham shrugged her shoulders sceptically.

'Who knows in this country? You pay five dollars for bread so ten doesn't seem unreasonable for a human tooth.'

'Maman!' Niki called out from the bedroom.

'You go settle her,' Aida said. 'I'll find somewhere to get some change.'

'You sure?' Elham asked, her face uncertain. 'It's raining.'

'Of course. Imagine what would happen if she woke up to nothing. Go.'

The rain was heavier now, bucketing down in great powerful slabs. Aida huddled under the umbrella, her shoes soaked through. Water coursed through the gutter beside her, leaves and garbage barrelling urgently down the street. The little corner store was still open, a bucket waiting expectantly by the door for umbrellas. Aida's was the sole lodger. It was a small store, poky and labyrinthine, the shelves housing an eclectic assortment of products, many of which were coated with a preserving layer of dust. There were loaves of white bread on the counter, a selection of videos for hire, and a handwritten sign advertising the option of dry-cleaning services should patrons be that way inclined. It reminded Aida of the little stores at home, the one near her parents' place where she'd go sometimes to pick up jam and herbs and *pofak* cheese puffs if there was change to spare. An elderly woman, wizened and bored-looking, stood behind the counter, a feather duster keeping busy over the easier-to-reach stock. Such was her height that only two of the four shelves were dust-free. Aida approached the counter, pulling the ten-dollar note from her pocket.

'Excuse me,' she said. 'You wouldn't happen to know the correct amount of money the tooth fairy leaves, would you?'

The woman stared at her for a moment, her face expressionless, before she called out something in another language through the open doorway behind her. Aida thought it might be Vietnamese, and for a moment wondered if this woman too had come by boat. Soon a young man came skulking out. The woman said something to him and his face contorted in confusion.

'What were you looking for?' he asked Aida, stepping up to the counter.

Aida smoothed the note in her hand.

'I was wondering how much money the tooth fairy leaves. For a tooth. A small tooth, maybe this big.' She squeezed her thumb and forefinger close. 'Three, no, just turned four years old. Knocked out in the playground, if that makes a difference,' she added helpfully, unsure whether the tooth fairy modulated payments like insurers did.

The young man thought for a moment.

'It depends. I mean, in this economy, you wouldn't want to go for anything lower than a dollar, I reckon. It's not like the old days when twenty cents would buy you a decent bag of lollies. And any higher is just excessive, because what's a four-year-old going to do with all that coin? A dollar, I reckon. Just to be safe.'

Aida held out the note.

'Thank you. Could I trouble you for change?'

The woman looked annoyed and stepped forward to say something, but the young man brushed her away.

'It's fine, *Ba Noi*. Look at the rain.'

He fished some coins out of the register.

'Here, take this too.'

He handed Aida a small chocolate bar from the counter.

'Just think of it as the tooth fairy making an investment for the future.'

His unexpected kindness unsettled her, and she turned her face away.

Aida arrived home to a smell both familiar and faraway, her mind lost for a moment as she scrambled to place it.

'You've been burning *esfand*!' she exclaimed, the oaky smell reminding her of her mother, who would routinely wait until guests had left before flushing the house with the burning seeds in case they'd inadvertently brought bad spirits inside. It brought seventy-two angels, her mother insisted, who purged the house of evils.

Elham looked embarrassed.

'It's all this talk of jinns . . . I know it's just a children's story but better to be safe than sorry. We need all the luck we can get.'

Aida smiled, and placed a coin and the chocolate bar in Elham's palm.

'Here.'

Elham pocketed them.

'I'll take it in later, in case she wakes up before morning. You hungry? I'm reheating some *tahchin* from yesterday.'

Aida held up a hand.

'It's okay. I have leftovers.'

'You mean that monstrosity that stank out the kitchen? The smell of it – like Mashhadi perfume but cheaper. I gave it to the cats.'

Aida glanced into the kitchen. Cyrus and Shahrzad had distanced themselves from the leftovers, eyeing them with disdain and mistrust.

'You see? Even the animals won't touch it. You cook like we're still in the camps. Please, just eat some real food with me.'

Aida hesitated. Cyrus was prodding at the leftovers with his paw, forcing it from his dinner plate. A chunk tipped over the edge onto the linoleum and he stepped back, satisfied.

'Fine. Thank you.'

They sat at the table, Elham's delicious food before them.

'I'm exhausted. Look at the time,' Aida sighed.

'Just like home, right?' Elham said. 'None of this dinner while it's still daylight business they have here.'

'I have an idea,' Aida said, leaving the room and returning moments later with a sheet.

She spread it on the floor, a makeshift *sofreh*, then took her plate from the table. She sat down, legs crossed, and began to eat.

'Just like home,' she smiled.

Elham let out a whoop of laughter, her eyes bright, then joined her.

'You know what would make this more like home?' she said. 'My mother complaining about the traffic on the way to the bazaar. '*Ai*, nothing but red lights the whole way! And the man beside me in the taxi looking into my bag like a pervert!'

'The price of saffron!' Aida cried, clutching at her cheeks in pantomime of her own mother. 'And you wouldn't guess how long I had to wait in line for this *sangak*! You'd think it was the bread of the Shah himself!'

Elham snorted with laughter.

'And this rain! It's like a horse's tail! I remember just before I left going to buy meat and it was twice the price it was the week before. Twice the price!'

Elham's face changed and she stared into her rice.

'It's funny the way you don't think about how it might be the last time you ever do something, but then it is. The last time I buy meat from the butcher in the bazaar. The last time I squeeze into the crowded bus. The last time I hug my mother and kiss her cheeks. You don't realise how big these small things are.'

Aida stopped eating. Elham seemed suddenly shrunken by her grief. She knew what was coming next. Her heart started to race as she settled her spoon on her plate.

'You know . . .' Elham started, but Aida cut her off.

'You know what I do when I start to think like that?' she said, and Elham looked at her expectantly.

'I think of three things different and three things the same. My father taught me this. It makes things less scary. Reminds you of the things you have. Why don't you try?'

Elham looked dubious. 'Your father is a psychologist?'

'An academic, but he figures it's the same. Just try it,' Aida insisted. 'Three things that are different.'

'Fine,' Elham said, picking a grain of rice from her lap. 'One – people eat dinner very early here. Two – the tooth jinn, obviously. Three – people say confusing things here like, "How are you going?" What does this mean? How am I going? By train, of course, but I'll probably be late because they're never on time.'

'Good.' Aida smiled. 'Now three things the same.'

Elham sat back, stretching her feet before her and rubbing her thighs.

'This is hard.'

She thought some more.

'One – I'm still scared to walk the streets at night. Two – most television is silly. Three – saffron is just as expensive.'

'Do you feel better?' Aida asked, and Elham lifted her shoulders.

'Distracted, I guess. It stops you thinking what you were thinking. Your father is a clever man.' Elham pulled herself to her feet, her arms wrapped around her body. 'Does it help you hold off those thoughts forever?'

'I suppose so,' Aida replied softly, but her voice was drowned out by the rain.

*

Later that night, as she lay in bed listening to the rain pound down upon the roof, Aida checked her phone. There was a message from her mother. *Back to the doctors. More tests. Have you heard anything? Sending you love.* Her stomach tightened at this, her chest, her muscles, everything retracting with cautious resistance. Everything was okay. Of course it was. It had to be. Because she was here and not there, and if something happened she couldn't be there, so it had to be okay. Her heart started beating out a new rhythm, one of panic and dread, and she squeezed her eyes shut to disrupt it. *Three things*, she thought, but nothing came. She raised herself from bed, pulled a cardigan over her pyjamas, then padded softly out of her room. The air was cool and sharp as she stepped onto the porch, mist rising from the thundering rain and settling across her exposed skin.

Three things different:

The colour of money

The tooth jinn, obviously

The spaces between people

Three things the same:

The smell of rain

The colour of night

The stories. The ones that people tell, that follow you for always.

She stared out, the world constricted under the pressure and closeness of the rain clouds. And she imagined them, all those stories, breaking out from the well inside her and pouring liberated into the night.

7

Nell

High-Profile Law Firm to Trial Free Justice For All
Media Release
For immediate release
9 May 2016

High-profile law firm Williams & Williams will trial a pro bono legal venture allowing community legal centres access to the firm's experienced legal team. A pilot case will be the first of what is expected to be a successful and productive partnership between one of the country's top-tier law firms and the state's network of community legal centres. Managing Partner Arthur Williams AO said the firm was delighted to be able to make its lawyers available in a time when community legal centres are overwhelmed and often unable to respond to demand.

'By its very nature, the strength of the legal system lies in the ability of every member of society to access it equally and without discrimination or disadvantage, whether that be based on income, geography or other barriers,' Mr Williams said.

In its trial period the program will focus on supporting community legal centres to manage the increased caseload of family violence victims with a view to broadening its scope in the future should this prove successful. Associate Benjamin Arnolds said that with more than one woman a week dying at the hands of her current or former partner, family violence was a scourge on the nation.

'The shocking fact is that in Australia women are most likely to experience physical and sexual violence in their home at the hands of a male current or ex-partner. Williams & Williams has a role to play in helping victims to live free from violence,' Mr Arnolds said. 'Everyone deserves their day in court and Williams & Williams are here to make sure that fantasy becomes a reality.'

The program will be opt-in for interested Williams & Williams lawyers whose participation in the program will be in addition to regular caseloads. The initiative will commence with a pilot case to test the feasibility and sustainability of the program.

ENDS

All media enquiries are directed to the Communications team at Williams & Williams.

Nell scrolled back to the top of the media release and read through it again. They'd kept most of what she'd drafted, including the bit about equal access to the law, and she was happy they'd attributed this part to Mr Williams instead of DB. DB had got some good lines too, despite the earful she'd copped after he found out she'd gone straight to Mr Williams, but Nell didn't care. She was excited. This was exciting. This was real lawyering. She put her mobile on the table and looked around the busy restaurant. Seymour was making his way back from the bathroom where he had gone to wash the sleep from his eyes, having stumbled out of bed moments before they'd had to leave, as he did every year. It was, after all, a day of traditions.

Every Mothers' Day they met at the same Southbank restaurant at the same brunch-friendly hour for invariably the same meal every year. This altered occasionally depending on whatever food intolerance was currently in vogue for Seymour, but for the most part it was a day long steeped in tradition. They wrangled over the complimentary bread, complained about the funky river smell and each took turns bemoaning the fact they'd not brought sunglasses, every single year. Wait staff came and went, but the Swanseas remained, with the subtle irony that none of the family were particularly enamoured of the restaurant. But no one could quite remember when – or why – the tradition had started, and thus did not have the confidence to break with it.

In keeping with tradition, today their mother was fashionably late, sending her tardy apology through a series of hastily typed text messages that the siblings combined to decipher. The messages were equal parts jovial and shouty due to their mother's comfort in interrobangs. Unimpressed with lacklustre book sales, she had taken to agreeing to every media request that came her way in a frenzied effort to improve figures, and it seemed that a last-minute interview had held her up today. *Out of Focus* was not the game changer she had hoped it would be, and their mother – who had based her whole research career on looking for women where history had ignored them – now found herself being left out of writers' festival line-ups or, increasingly, replaced by higher-profile academics, often, invariably, Prudence.

'Mimosa?' Seymour suggested, and they sat in comfortable familial silence as they awaited their mother's eventual arrival. Olivia Newton-John was singing her hopeless devotions through the sound system.

'Mother would not approve of this song,' Seymour said with mock severity.

'Mother would not approve of that entire movie,' Nell agreed. '*The Rise and Victory of the Male Gaze as Told Through Sandy's Black Leather Doo-Wop Onesie: A Thesis in Twenty Parts with Appendices.*'

The gentle mockery of their mother was another family tradition that caused them equal parts merriment and self-reproach.

Hers was an endearing, earnest feminism that exhausted others with its fervour and left them all feeling lacking. This made her easy to taunt, though deep down both siblings would, if demanded, admit to being proud of her, even though she sometimes ruined perfectly good architecture and historical monuments by insisting they represented phalli. Seymour rooted around in his satchel, a deviant grin on his face.

'Look!'

He stuck his hand into the small gift bag he'd retrieved and pulled out a credit card-sized rectangle of paper. Nell peered at it. It was purple and green with their mother's name and the simple credential *Feminist* underneath.

'Card-carrying feminist,' Seymour announced proudly. 'Did it in Publisher. It's laminated and everything. I made us all one.'

He handed them over. Nell took hers. She had forgotten yet again to get their mother a gift, another Swansea tradition.

'Yours says *Baby Feminist* because you are just starting out. Mine says *Male Feminist* for reasons that should be apparent.'

Their mother arrived around the same time their meals did and, as predicted, she crowed for a full minute on receiving Seymour's gift.

'Oh, you wonderful children!' she beamed, stretching to accommodate them both in a hug. 'Apologies for being late. I was on my way then I had this phone call from a radio show wanting to grab a quick interview. Couldn't say no, could I, what with it being Mother's Day and all that commercial rot? They're niche. Internet radio. Is that a podcast?'

She reached for her wineglass.

'Anyway, how are you all? How's Patrick?'

Seymour ignored the question, instead launching into a description of the new exhibition he was curating.

'There's this artist called Vince – Vince Pemblebrook, like a Dickens character, which is probably why he just goes by Vince like Madonna or a Brazilian soccer player – and anyway, he does this thing where he takes Australian history and folklore and reimagines it in a modern multicultural context. Poems and paintings and stories and things. *Wog on a Tuckerbox*? You may have seen that piece. It won a bunch of awards but caused all this controversy because what doesn't these days? Anyway, so his thing is "reimagining the dominant discourse and narratives of Forgetful Australia", which is what he calls the past because it seems to forget that there was anyone but straight white men wandering about the place. And we've finally got him doing a show, only he got very into the idea of all the gallery staff contributing their own pieces too because of some kind of artistic socialism or creative redistribution thing he is going through. So it's meant to be reclaiming our own stories through reimagining the stories of others.'

Nell nodded, waiting patiently until it was her turn to speak.

'You'll be recontextualising gender, I imagine?' their mother asked, causing Seymour to guffaw at the very suggestion that he might not.

'Obviously! Currently the working title is *Australians All Let Us ReVoice*. Either that or *The Mystery of History: Australia as it Wasn't*. What do you think?'

Their mother tilted her head to one side, fingers steepled.

'Casually oppressive. I love it.'

Nell looked from one to the other. This had long been a habit of theirs, falling into a secret humanities code whose expansive and flourishing language Nell's law degree had not equipped her for.

'Casually oppressive?' Nell scoffed. 'What's that even supposed to mean?'

Seymour sighed. 'You'd know it if you experienced it, Nell.'

He and their mother exchanged a bemused look, causing Nell's cheeks to flash an irritated mauve. Sometimes the two of them spiralled down a path that suggested possession of a higher knowledge Nell would never obtain from the pithy confines of legalese.

'Anyway,' Seymour continued. 'This is really important. It has the potential to be my legacy show. My seminal controversy. My *The Field* at the NGV, if you will. One of our staff members has an uncle who owns a souvlaki store somewhere in the outer suburbs and we may get him to cater – you know, the whole *Wog on the Tuckerbox* thing – but I'm not sure if that's edgy or naff . . . or racist?'

He fell into the silent perpetual quandary of the small-L liberal.

'Well, I've some news too,' Nell announced, raising her mimosa ceremoniously as if preparing to toast the future happiness and wellbeing of a recently married couple.

Her mother and Seymour looked over expectantly, only to be interrupted by the buzz of a mobile skittering into the water carafe. Their mother glanced at the screen.

'It's one of the regional stations. They must have heard the other interview. Sorry, kids.'

She gave them a powerless shrug, her elation clear, then answered the call. As she chatted, Nell and Seymour continued to eat in exaggerated silence, great pantomimic delicacy required so as not to scrape cutlery on porcelain.

'Why, speaking of that, you'll never guess what my children gave me just today,' their mother laughed into the phone. 'My son Seymour – he runs a gallery with his life partner Patrick – just this morning he gave me a little card with *Feminist* on it, so now I'm officially a card-carrying fe – yes, feminist! . . . I know! . . . Isn't it just!?'

Nell exchanged a bemused look with her brother. In any public discussion Nell's law degree and Seymour's sexuality were not far from hand. They both knew this display of liberalism brought their mother great and unabating joy. Indeed, among her circle of progressive left-wing academics, their mother felt Seymour's homosexuality practically a personal achievement and she was campaigning hard for marriage equality. Prudence, for instance, would kill to have a feminist, artist or queer activist in the family, but had to instead contend with an accountant and a Latin tutor, neither of whom were particularly engaged in politics of either the personal or political. 'I mean, Latin!' their mother was wont to crow at poor Prudence's expense after a few glasses of pinot. 'Keep waiting on that time machine so you can actually use it!' And she would laugh, heartily, like the villain in an action movie just before they are thwarted by the hero. Presently, she had adopted a serious tone, her voice creeping tentatively through the mobile.

'Of course, it hasn't always been easy. It's been a hard slog . . . That's right, a single mother for most of that time . . . Oh yes, tremendously difficult, but it's the passion that drives the work.'

Seymour locked eyes with Nell.

'You just manage,' he mouthed, brow stern.

'You just *manage*,' their mother continued. 'As women so often have throughout history. Which brings me back to the book, because there's been this idea of women as representing the archetypal mother – of building the nation – though of course, its sovereignty was never ceded – but this idea of building the nation through birthing its citizens, while not really being in and of themselves a part of it . . . Well obviously, but women have done a damn lot more than open our legs for the nation . . . I know this is live . . .'

Eventually the interview finished. As she ended the call, their mother seized her wineglass, looking around expectantly.

'I told them about the card, kids! They loved it. Great material.'

Her face fell suddenly.

'Bugger. I forgot to mention the biography class.'

Seymour looked confused.

'What biography class?'

'The one I'm teaching,' their mother replied. 'A women's biography class. Everyone is doing them these days. Writing courses, I mean, not women's biography. But that's why I'm doing the class. It starts this Friday.'

The siblings exchanged a look. Their mother was one of those academics who got by teaching a minimum of subjects due to her otherwise prolific output and lack of natural disposition to instruction.

'And you're the one running it?'

'Obviously I'm the one running it, Nelly. It's not a skill I need any further work in, is it? Anyway, enough about me. What were we talking about?'

'I said I had news,' Nell reminded her, and told them about the pro bono scheme. 'It was my idea. Well, kind of. And I'm working on the first case. DB and I. Our initial focus will be on family violence. Isn't that great, Mum? Representing family violence victims.'

Their mother gazed into her wineglass, collecting the contents in a careful centrifuge. Seymour, too, was silent.

'What?' Nell asked.

Their mother didn't say anything, reversing the direction of her wine.

'What?' Nell demanded.

'Nothing,' their mother replied. 'Nothing, that sounds wonderful, Nelly. It's nothing . . . Just . . . "represent".'

She looked like she'd tasted something bitter and clove-like. '*Represent*. Such a vile word. So . . . loaded.'

'What are you talking about?' Nell said. 'That's what lawyers do. We represent people.'

'Well, it's semantics, isn't it, really?' their mother continued, eyes focused on her pinot gris. 'People should represent themselves, really, but that's neither here nor there, I guess.'

Nell exhaled patiently. She was embarrassed she hadn't thought of this.

'Forget I said anything,' their mother said, hands raised as if caught up in a bank robbery. 'Far be it from me to rain on your parade, only . . .'

It was an infuriating pause with no intention of remaining final.

'Only what? You're mid-downpour anyway, so only what?'

The wineglass stopped suddenly, liquid surging over the rim.

'Well, for a start, don't call them victims. These women – and overwhelmingly they will be women – are more than just victims. They're survivors, for one thing, and people for another. And the law, it has this habit of reducing them to nothing more than a testimony, or some poor vulnerable creature in need of saving with no consideration of their complexity and humanity. I mean, what has the legal system done for them in the past? What does it do for them now? Demand evidence that is impossible to produce? Ask them to prove themselves? Make them tick a little checklist for how a victim should look and behave and act? "It's just a domestic." "A bit of a misunderstanding." "Two to tango," and all that nonsense.'

'That was the past, Mum. Things are different now. You should be happy about this. This is a chance to really do some good.'

Their mother gave her a look as if she – their mother – was wearied by a personal sagacity garnered from far too much living, and that her daughter would one day understand all this, but not yet.

'The past is a hard thing to leave behind, my darling. It doesn't like to be forgotten. And "good" isn't the easiest thing to do, either.'

Seymour caught Nell's glare and rapped his knuckle on the table, pulling attention.

'Moving on,' he announced, glass aloft. 'Happy Mother's Day!'

Nell sucked her teeth, avoiding their eyes.

'Happy Mother's Day,' she muttered, brushing her glass against the others with the enthusiasm of an inmate.

'Anyway, enough of that,' their mother said, flicking the topic away with one hand. 'Before I forget, I brought you both some bookmarks. For the book. I had them made up. Publicity and the like, see?'

She pulled a wad of vibrant bookmarks from her bag, halved them, and held a bundle out to Nell and Seymour. Nell glanced at the bookmark on top, its letters crisp and bold.

'I'm still not completely wedded to that font, but anyway. Go put them places,' their mother instructed, hands thrown forward like she was instigating a drag race.

'What kind of places?' Seymour asked.

'All kinds of places. The gallery, your office, Nell, wherever you buy lunch. Just, just leave them everywhere you can think of. You know, places where women go.'

'So you mean everywhere?' Seymour clarified. 'Because it's 2016?'

'Except men's toilets,' Nell added, putting aside her hurt feelings to join the gentle familial jest.

'Well, no,' Seymour agreed. 'Not even men brave those. So we leave them everywhere but men's toilets, right, Mum?'

Their mother nodded cautiously, not entirely sure whether she was once more the butt of their joke.

'Anywhere you think. Here's some for Patrick too.'

This shut Seymour up and he pretended to be suddenly taken by the detail of the bookmark. Nell looked down at the pile in her own hands, their mother's face beaming from the corner.

Where are all the womyn? the bookmark asked. She shoved them into her bag, and promptly forgot about them.

*

They met with the client early on Monday morning. Rani had emailed through information, though it only arrived moments before their meeting because the server had been acting up at Rani's office again. Nell printed it off and hurried after DB.

Hi Nell,

Thanks for picking this up for us. Very excited about the new program! Lots of publicity already! This should be a simple enough case to start with. We said we'd do it but it's a cross-application and we're down a staff member and someone else is on personal leave so we just can't make it to court on the day, and you know how quick the turn-around is on IVOs. Legal Aid can't help out because the client doesn't pass the means test. Her only other option is to self-represent but she's likely not to turn up, given that scenario, and you know how busy the duty lawyers are at court, plus she'd get a different one each time she shows up, etc etc. Ex is a lawyer himself, very charismatic, lots of connections, you know the story. We've lodged her paperwork already, basically just need you to show up on the day/hold her hand/explain what's happening, etc. Details attached. Really appreciate you doing this. Give me a buzz if anything comes up!

Talk soon,
Rani

Nell watched as DB turned the page and scanned the attachment. As his eyes roamed the paper, she stole a glance at the client. The woman sat straight-backed in the consulting room chair, her hands clasped together on her lap as if posed for a school photo. Blow-waved bob, subtle makeup, neat simple clothes that would have come with an impressive price tag. Her knuckles, Nell noticed, were mottled white, in stark contrast to the manicured nails. The woman cleared her throat as DB read through the document, a crisp high-pitched sound that reminded Nell of someone about to commence a lengthy monologue, only nothing followed. Apart from a polite hello when she'd first arrived, the client was yet to say anything. DB, on the other hand, was murmuring to himself as he worked through the document, a gentle indecipherable susurration reminiscent of a children's television character. Every so often he nodded his head, ticking things off as he found them, his voice rising in an audible swoop. DB paused at the end of the document then laid it before him on the table. He had, Nell noted, adopted a strange swagger, as if modelling himself on the kind of shoot-from-the-hip devil-may-care lawyers one encountered in the unrealistic courtrooms of the silver screen. He triangulated his fingers, touching them to his lips, then proceeded.

'Okay, Madeline, let's walk through what we've got here,' DB said.

The client, Madeline, unlocked her hands, drinking from the water glass in front of her before hooking them back together. She nodded once, eyes on DB.

'The police attended an incident at your family home a fortnight ago and found the kitchen in a state of disarray. Broken plates, glassware shattered, things like that. Your husband had some obvious physical injuries, cuts and the like, and you yourself were, to quote their words, in a bit of a state. The police have reported you were difficult to calm, possibly intoxicated, and they've taken you to the station to settle down as your two young children were about and they were a bit worried about them seeing you like that. Husband's gone off in an ambulance to get some stitches, mother-in-law's come round to watch the kids, and you spent the night asleep on a bench at the station. By the time you've woken up your bruises have come through and the police can't work out who started it so no charges are pressed. Says here you weren't very cooperative, telling them it was all a bit of a misunderstanding and refusing to say much more. Meanwhile, your husband has popped down to court to get himself an interim intervention order and you've come home to find new locks on the doors and been served with an order telling you not to approach or contact your husband or the children. How does that sound so far?'

'He also changed the banking passwords,' Madeline said, unblinking.

'Rani tells us that you want to contest the order against you and you've also filed a cross-application to get an IVO against him?'

He referred to the document. '

'Yep, okay. You've not submitted anything to the Family Court for parenting or property matters, I take it?'

Madeline shook her head.

'And you've said there's been a history of violence? Nothing reported, though?'

Madeline nodded once. Nell watched her, her poise at odds with the topic being discussed.

'And you've given us some more information here, including more details about the altercation last month.'

DB checked the documents in front of him again. They'd had very little time to prepare for this meeting, what with the hoops that needed to be cleared to get the program happening in the first place, then finding a time in both their already packed schedules when they could meet with the client. The first mention was the following Monday and they were running almost entirely off the information Rani had gathered in her one and only appointment with the client. It was rushed and uncomfortable, the paperwork hastily completed, and not in keeping with Williams & Williams' normal work approach, but as Rani had assured them, all fairly straightforward. Holding her hand, as Rani said, and waiting for the judge to switch the orders.

'Is there anything in particular you want to know about next week?' DB asked, motioning to Nell to refill his water glass.

She ignored him, focusing on Madeline instead. Madeline re-laced her fingers, swapping the dominant hand, then pressed her lips together.

'Will I be able to see the kids after Monday?'

She reminded Nell of the women who used to congregate at the gates of her high school at three-fifteen, perched high in the seats of their hand-washed four-wheel drives. Slipping easily out of the diesel-beasts to chat airily among themselves as their progeny spilled from the school buildings, funnelling into two channels headed towards either their beaming parents or to loiter with delinquent idleness around the bus pick-up area. She saw it in this woman – the ease with which a certain lifestyle allowed one to carry oneself – and knew from the way he reclined confidently in his chair that DB saw it too. DB gave Madeline a generous smile.

'If all goes to plan we should have you walking away with the intervention order in your name ready to go home to your kids. I can see we're asking for your husband to be excluded from the family home, and there's always the opportunity to ask the magistrate to include the kids on the order if you think he's a threat to them.'

Madeline nodded once more, then cleared her throat. 'And I don't have to say anything? He won't be able to ask me questions?'

'Not at this stage. We'll do all the speaking on your behalf.'

She sat back from the table. 'Then I have no more questions.'

Nell showed her out then returned to DB. His face was pulled into an excited little smirk, his fingers drumming against the printouts.

'Walk in the park,' he said with a grin. 'Simple mix-up. Interim order issued to the wrong person – it happens. We'll be back to the office by lunch. Home run for our first test case. Old Man Williams will be pretty chuffed. Might even buy us lunch if we're lucky. Dumplings at the good place. Or that Korean joint if we've got the time. Love me some kimchi!'

He sat back, pondering the many possible options for their future culinary reward. Nell bit the inside of her lip, not entirely comfortable. A gut feeling. The one lawyers were meant to listen to.

'She didn't say much, though. Do we even have enough information? It doesn't feel . . .'

DB's focus was elsewhere, his gut preoccupied with fantasy meals accompanied by a liberal side order of praise.

'Here in the paperwork. Gave your pal Rani some good details about the incident. He started the fight, she was defending herself, got all het up because they'd had a glass or two over dinner, etc etc. Kids were shaken up because they've never seen Mum like that. Refers to a couple of other incidents in the past as well. Not a lot of detail but not unusual given the timeframe.'

Nell didn't respond. Open and shut. There you go. They'd have things sorted by lunch. Only it felt wrong . . . Madeline's calmness felt wrong. DB turned to leave, then paused.

'My parents used to do this stuff,' he mused. 'Criminal, family law and whatnot. I'm fifth generation lawyer. My great-great-great-granddaddy was Ned Kelly's lawyer, or something like that.'

He set off with a merry whistle, bothering everyone in the open-plan office. For the rest of the day, all Nell could think of was the woman's silence. She read and re-read the paltry handful of pages Rani had sent through, memorising them back to front. There was the intervention order application but most of that was personal details and administrative stuff, just a couple of boxes to detail the actual incident and anything that had happened before. DB would be doing all the speaking, of course, but she wanted to be prepared just in case. She owed it to the woman to be prepared. Her mother's words drifted into her head but she pushed them to one side. Open and shut. Kimchi.

Later she found herself curled into the corner seat of a tram that smelt like fast food and urine. She hugged herself against the cold, thinking over Madeline's calmness. It unsettled her still. Distracted, she once more overshot her stop. By how far she couldn't tell, night-time gathering swiftly around her. Nell stumbled out at the next stop, crossing the street in search of the nearest return point. She waited a while, stamping her feet in the chill, before she decided to walk instead. She marched briskly, her breath tumbling out in waves. She didn't know this part of the north, farther from the city than she usually roamed. She passed a store, a vibrant red-green-white flag plastered across the window alongside its Australian equivalent. *Persian Grocers*, the sign announced cautiously, as if worried its conspicuousness might attract a brick. She thought about Madeline as she walked, her stoicism set against those knuckles wrought white with tension. The rest of her body controlled as if all her worry was banished into the small spaces between each taut finger. Nell's mind drifted back to her university days, when she'd supported other lawyers doing similar work. Mostly secretarial duties, but occasionally they'd let her sit in as they gathered material for affidavits. It was startling, all the different ways that anger could play out; in utter silence, in rambled disbelief. In abuse hurled at anyone who would listen. But Madeline was different. Had seemed so controlled. Soon

104

Nell came across a small crowd spilling out across the pavement of a little suburban mall. A young man stood busking in the streetlight, the familiar chords of Adele tumbling from his piano accordion. Seymour's song, one of the ones he listened to on repeat when he was mopey and nostalgic and thought no one could hear. When the young man finished, he held out his hat, upturned for change.

'Help me continue to make a living doing what I love,' he said, gesturing to the crowd.

Nell watched him, his crooked smile full of hope. She pulled out her wallet, rooting around for something gold. There was only shrapnel, five and ten cent pieces that were more an insult than encouragement. She slunk away, embarrassed, then stood in the shadows a moment listening to him play.

8

DB

Jonesy!

Loved the pic of the Eiffel Tower. Definitely looked like you were holding it up. Solid work on the acquisition too, bro. You'll have a happy bank account waiting for you when you get home.

To news here, Williams & Williams are taking a foray into the world of pro bono legal work and yours truly has been selected to run the first case. Not exactly the ideal situation but I suspect it's Old Man Williams testing the ol' mettle with an eye to future promotions. So silver lining and whatnot, despite the fact we've only got a couple of prep days before court. Bit of a bugger alongside the rest of the workload but them's the breaks, isn't it? Reminds me of that time you had five hours to make a six-hour flight in order to convince the Saudis that they couldn't walk away from that deal or you wouldn't get that sweet bonus come Christmas. Praise be to Allah for private jets, right? In a similar fashion, I believe this is my Saudi deal, if you will. My hurdle to overcome in order to fully realise my full potential here at Williams & Williams and what have you.

Shouldn't be too difficult – intervention order, pretty clear-cut. Get a good result and there's no way they won't be giving me some more higher-calibre stuff and sending me up a floor. Nell the Lionheart has thrown herself into things so that's a blessing at least. Emerges every so often to ask questions then back to her notes like some kind of burrowing woodland creature. Could be worse, couldn't it?

Also, guess who got a nice big pic in the paper? Link attached. Makes me look a bit like that actor from

'Are you texting at the table?'

DB dropped the phone onto his lap and looked up innocently at the gathered Zambetti family.

'It would never cross my mind to do such a thing.'

Sylvie went back to quietly seething, grinding her fork into an innocent slither of tomato. For the life of him DB couldn't work out why. Her parents had been impressed, particularly because they'd seen him in the paper. Guiseppa had cut out the article and carefully stuck it on the fridge where it was surrounded by photographs of Rudy spanning birth to the present, and Tony from back when he had hair. They'd announced a celebratory dinner, tacked onto the usual mid-week dinner they had with Sylvie's parents, with the promise of cake after the meal.

'Look at this man!' Nino had cooed, brandishing the clipping for all to see. 'The next Prime Minister right there.'

DB smiled graciously, checking to see if his son was watching. Rudy seemed occupied with scraping the flesh off a potato.

'And the suit,' Nino continued. 'What a husband, am I right, Sylvie?'

Sylvie made an unreadable face.

'You're both just impressed by anyone who wears a suit to work.'

This was true. Nino had recently bought a second-hand vacuum cleaner from a dodgy door-to-door salesman all because the man had been wearing a suit. And to this day Guiseppa still gushed about how sweet Rudy had looked in his little baptism outfit, all sensibilities vaporised at the incongruence of an infant in a three-piece suit.

'Do they pay you more?' Nino asked, his untouched meal cooling before him.

DB winced. 'Not exactly. No. But there could be a promotion at the end of it.'

Sylvie's huff was almost imperceptible. Guiseppa, on the other hand, laid down her cutlery, her mind seemingly blown by the generosity of her son-in-law.

'You're doing it for charity? What a gentleman. But it's good you get that promotion too. Then you'll be comfortable when the baby comes along and Sylvie stops working.'

'I'm not going to stop working. I like working,' Sylvie muttered. 'And I'm not pregnant. And it wouldn't be such a strain if we didn't live in the second coming of the Hearst Castle.'

Nino paid her no attention, his eyes gleaming with possibilities.

'Maybe they'll make you head of what do you call it? Social corporate responsibility. Mr Benjamin Arnolds – Head of the Social Corporate Responsibility Department.'

DB smiled politely. Head of the Cuddles Department? No thank you. Beside him, Sylvie let out a racehorse-like snort.

'Good luck with that.'

Her father looked at her, abashed.

'Do you know what he did last week?' She looked around the table for a response. 'At the kindy?'

Ah. So this was why she was angry.

'Rudy comes home with a complaint – one complaint – that another kid is mean to him, and Mr Compassion over here calls the kindy and gives the teacher an earful. I've had the staff apologising to me all week about it.'

DB put down his fork. 'It wasn't one complaint, it was two, delivered over the course of the one evening. One count of pinching and another count of crayon snatching. And I will not stand by while my child is bullied at his own kinder. During story time, no less.'

Guiseppa's hands flew to her throat. 'Someone is bullying my Rodolfo?'

Rudy was short for Rudy, but despite this, Guiseppa insisted on Italianising it.

'Not bullying,' Sylvie insisted. 'They're kids. And the other child is an asylum seeker. Imagine what she's been through. You want to talk about unfair treatment of children, that's where you start.'

'Rudy has the right to be safe,' DB said, causing Guiseppa to grip the table edge in terror.

'He's not safe?'

'He's fine, Mum. Stop it, Ben. Rudy, baby, do you like playing with Niki?'

Rudy offered a light shrug.

'Sometimes she won't share.'

Guiseppa looked anguished now.

'She has to share. They need to make the children share. Why won't the teachers make the children share?'

'Children have to share,' Nino agreed, shaking his head at the state of the world.

Sylvie's teeth grinding was practically audible so DB gallantly changed the topic.

'Did you tell Nonna and Nonno that you're going to have a birthday party?' he pressed Rudy.

'I'm going to have a birthday party,' Rudy informed them, eyes remaining on his plate.

'Eat up, Rodolfo baby,' Guiseppa encouraged him. 'Just like your clever daddy.'

'A big party with all the kids from kindy,' DB announced, looking to Sylvie for support. 'We're working on the invites right now. Shortlisting the fonts as we speak.'

'Not all the kids,' Rudy interrupted. 'Not naughty Niki. She won't share.'

'Well, obviously. All the kids except naughty Niki,' DB agreed.

'Sure, don't invite the one kid who really needs it,' Sylvie muttered.

'Why don't you have the party here?' Nino asked, gesturing around the room proudly. 'Lots more room in our backyard.'

'What an idea!' Guiseppa cried. 'Rudy can wear his little suit!'

DB glanced briefly about the Zambettis' formal dining room. There was just so much cut glassware . . .

'Rudy's pretty keen on having it at our place, aren't you Rudy?'

Rudy shrugged.

'Because of the petting zoo we planned to hire, right, buddy?'

Rudy's ears perked up. 'Right! The petting zoo. Before all the animals die.'

'But it's so far for all those parents to travel,' Guiseppa said. 'They all live around here. Near the kinder.'

'It'd be a bit far for the petting zoo, all the way out here,' DB replied. 'And the balloon guy. And the DJ.'

He glanced once more at Sylvie, who was presently draining her wineglass. He waited for her reaction – one of approval and support – but it seemed there was quite a bit of alcohol to imbibe.

'What if they dob?' Nino asked, pouring himself some more wine.

'If who dob?' DB queried.

'The children. Or their parents. You said on your form you live here. What if they tell the council you don't? No more kindy for Mr Rudy here.'

Guiseppa was nodding in agreement. DB placed his cutlery down on the plate.

'No one is going to do that. People don't do that.'

'You never know.' Nino shrugged. 'The things you see on

the telly. Maybe it's safer if you just come out this way. You know, find a nice place nearby. All his friends are here . . .'

DB eyed Sylvie, trying to work out if this was all a grand set-up. She was presently occupied with cutting her food into tiny portions, which she pushed angrily around the plate, causing them to careen into each other like soggy billiards.

'You leave him alone. He's doing fine,' Guiseppa said, playing peacemaker, her hands raised before her as though she were testifying. 'Sure, it would be easier for everyone, and then maybe they could give Rudy a sister, but that's their decision. If they move here they move here. And in the meantime we'll have another little party for Rudy at our place, just in case any of his little friends can't make it all the way to yours.'

She checked their plates to see if anyone needed more food.

'Anyway, another topic. Sylvie, have you spoken with your brother today?'

*

They drove home in the dying light, soft rain falling as Rudy sat glued to his iPad. DB checked to make sure his earphones were in.

'You know, it's not a terrible idea.'

Sylvie turned to him slowly.

'What isn't?'

'The whole double party thing. It could be fun. Rudy gets a morning with the olds then the afternoon with the petting zoo. Who could ask for a better fifth birthday?'

Sylvie turned back to the road ahead, bringing her feet up to the dashboard. Her face was drawn, shadows collecting about her eyes in the dim light. From this angle she looked like her mother, something DB saw often these days, but had swiftly learnt never to mention. The practical short haircut in place of the waist length tresses, the neutral mix-and-match tones where once op shop vintage had reigned supreme – all reminiscent of Guiseppa's stoic approach to middle age. Sylvie yawned, her face transforming slightly, and for a moment DB caught a glimpse of the past.

'You think I have time to organise two parties?' Sylvie sighed, rubbing her eyes.

'Who said anything about you organising it? I've got this, Sylv. You won't have to do a thing.'

'Why can't we just have it at Mum and Dad's? No one is going to come all the way to our place.'

DB tightened his grip on the wheel.

'Why do we keep coming back to this?'

'To what?'

'It's all sticks past Bell Street. We may as well move to the middle of nowhere.'

'It's not. It's perfectly fine. It's where I grew up. And if we wait long enough it'll be the next big thing and we'd be the savvy investors who got in early.'

'Yes, but only after a decade of boredom. They call them fringe areas for a reason,' he sniffed. 'Look at this place,' he continued, gesturing to the suburbs around them. 'It's like a maze. A heartless maze. There's no infrastructure, no public transport. Nothing. Nothing but a big shiny maze with a minotaur lurking at its centre.'

DB sat back in his seat, impressed with himself. He was really getting some mileage out of this minotaur metaphor. He'd have to let Jonesy know. Beside him, Sylvie's brow was furrowed.

'What are you even talking about?'

'The minotaur,' DB repeated, sailing through an amber light. 'The outer suburbs are a big labyrinth-bound minotaur for young families like us, waiting to entice us in then gobble us up.'

Sylvia pursed her lips, reaching for the radio.

112

'Raw milk and unvaccinated preschoolers. Let's talk about which suburbs have the real savages.'

She turned the volume up and they were drowned out by Missy Higgins. DB reached over and turned it down a fraction.

'Please, Sylvie. Not the outer suburbs. Trevor in Accounting is from there and he's always so tired.'

Sylvie didn't say anything but cleared her throat, signalling a change in topic.

'Are you able to knock off early tomorrow? Mum and Dad have a dinner thing with friends and I'm meant to stay late to supervise practice exams.'

DB scrunched up his face.

'I may have promised I'd put in some extra hours because this pro bono thing will be eating into my normal workload and I really want to get a jump on that.'

'How late?'

Late enough that they'd buy pizza for the whole office. He shrugged helplessly.

'That's fine. Our child can just stay home by himself. I mean he's, what, almost five now.'

In the back, Rudy let out a gentle cackle, his face lit up by the iPad, and they continued their drive to the centre of the north.

*

The weekend came and DB spent much of Saturday morning squirrelled away in his home office catching up on work. The pro bono mention was on Monday and you could never be sure how long you'd be stuck waiting to be called, so he didn't want to risk losing a whole day away from the office. Every so often noises came from the house proper – bumps and clangs and bouts of hysterical tinny laughter – but he did his best to block it out. He emerged at midday, his stomach grumbling, and made a beeline for the refrigerator. He remembered there being

113

a particularly creamy brie in there at one point and he hoped it was still salvageable. Sylvie was set up at the kitchen table, her feet resting on a chair opposite. She insisted she had a system but to DB it looked like someone had hastily ransacked a classroom then abandoned their haul for want of something worthwhile. This had been endearing at first, her eccentric approach to order, and DB had foolishly assumed it would change with age as the weight of responsibility made these things matter. It hadn't, and where once he had delighted in the fact she kept her documentation in an assortment of shoe boxes, at thirty-seven this seemed closer to a travesty.

'Year eight History?' he asked, taking a bite out of a cold chicken drumstick and turning to the pantry. He half-hoped he might find a surprise supply of Turkish Delight but he knew Sylvie never bought them because she thought they tasted like rubber.

'Year ten English,' she countered, not looking up. 'Practice exams. *Richard III.*'

'They found his remains under a car park,' DB mused, peeping behind some canned goods. 'Ironically buried under a big R.'

'Don't tell Rudy or we'll never hear the end of it,' Sylvie replied. 'You'll take him with you?'

'Under a reserved parking space, if memory serves. It was the back that gave him away. You could say they had a hunch . . . Take who?'

'Richard the Third. He'll be accompanying you to golf?'

'Pardon?'

'Rudy. Your child. You'll be taking him to golf with you? I've been watching him all morning and I've got loads more to do.'

DB glanced over at Rudy who was happily ensconced in front of the Discovery Channel. Something – a seal of some description – seemed to be in the process of maiming something else. DB squinted at the screen. He couldn't quite make it out. The seal surfaced, whipping the object into the air where it cartwheeled in a bloodied arc before the seal snatched it back up again.

'Oh, it's a penguin,' DB cried out.

'Huh?'

'On the telly. You couldn't tell because the seal had torn it apart somewhat . . .'

Sylvie's eyes jerked towards the television.

'For god's sake. This is why you're taking him to golf with you.'

She leapt up and marched to the coffee table, grabbing the remote and switching off the television.

'Who's up for a round of golf with Grandfather?' DB announced cheerily as Rudy collapsed into a shrieking thrashing rage.

*

The car park was alive with activity as DB's father swung the Merc aggressively towards a parking space. About them, grown men in chequered trousers and brightly hued tops dove for cover, their expensive cart bags collapsing onto the rockery.

'Are you sure you want to park in this space? It's members only.'

'I am a bloody member,' his father barked, circling the wheel sharply.

'Since when?' DB asked, flinching as his father shaved past the beamer parked to their left.

'Since today. I come here every second Saturday without fail and if that doesn't make me a member I don't know what does,' his father huffed, shifting the car into reverse and preparing for another attack.

'I'm sure it has something to do with an invitation, an exchange of money and some paperwork, but what would I know,' DB replied, his body tensing as the car lurched forward again.

He knew better than to offer to park the car on his father's behalf. Real men parked their own cars, which he supposed was a marked improvement on the previous decades when real men had drivers who wore little demeaning caps and were paid the minimum wage.

'How are we on your side?' his father demanded, skewering the car forward in little hops.

'We're about to hit –' DB began, as the car grunted into the BMW.

The BMW trembled a moment, then burst into a procession of lights and sirens. His father threw his hands in the air as if giving up on some utterly lost cause.

'You were meant to keep watch.'

A crowd was gathering, dusting themselves off from their recent escape.

'Stay here,' DB muttered, unclipping his seatbelt.

The car was sandwiched against the BMW so DB had to slither into the back seats and out the opposite passenger door. Rudy watched from his car seat, his eyes delighted as he surveyed the damaged car out the window. DB walked round to the BMW. There was a sizeable dent, exactly the shape of his father's bumper, which had slotted into it like a piece of miscoloured joinery.

'Bloody oath!'

DB turned. Standing there, hat on a jaunty angle and pants hitched high above his belly, was Mr Williams.

'You just don't expect this in members parking,' Mr Williams continued as DB felt the blood rush from his cheeks.

'Mr Williams, sir. It's DB. From work.'

Mr Williams looked momentarily confused. 'Who?'

'D– Ben Arnolds. From the Banting-Nicholson patent case. I'm working the pro bono case . . .'

'Ah, yes. Young Ben Arnolds. What's this DB business?'

'Just a family nickname. It's nothing.'

There was the sound of a car door opening.

'Benjamin, what's going on?' his father called.

Mr Williams looked towards the Mercedes.

'My father,' DB said hurriedly. 'He's . . . he's getting on.'

DB looked over his shoulder. His apparently fragile father was hoisting his golf clubs from the boot. Rudy had crawled out of his car seat and now wrapped himself around DB's legs.

'I'm so sorry about the car,' DB began, but Mr Williams held up a hand.

'Nothing insurance can't take care of. Is this your little fellow?' He hitched his trousers at the thigh, then bent forward onto one knee. 'What's your name, son?'

'Rudy Rodolfo Zambetti Arnolds Elephant Seal,' Rudy replied.

'That's not his name,' DB interjected.

'And are you here to play golf with your daddy and granddaddy?'

'I guess,' Rudy said reluctantly. 'The penguin was dead so Mummy got angry. But it's natural.'

He gave a little sigh to suggest that these things tended to happen in life. Mr Williams held out his hand and Rudy stared at it for a moment then Mr Williams took his hand back.

'Clever little chap. Full of moxie. Now you pass on my details to your father and have his people call my people about this little bingle. And don't let it get to you, young Ben Arnolds. I've big things in mind for this pro bono business should it all go to plan.'

And he raised his eyebrows in a way that suggested to DB that some of those things most certainly involved an office with a view of the Yarra.

Later, once they'd moved the Mercedes to allow Mr Williams to remove his own vehicle from the scene of carnage, DB followed his father out onto the golf course. Rudy travelled seated atop his grandfather's golf cart until his grandfather decided that was enough of that. They played a few holes in relative silence, Rudy trotting diligently beside them, picking up sticks and leaves to place in his little backpack. Occasionally, DB's father would give an order and DB would relay it on to Rudy.

'Fetch the ball, son.'

'Fetch the ball, buddy.'

Then, as DB was preparing to tee off, his father let out a low whistle.

'Yes?'

'Oh, nothing, nothing. Just thinking that there's something almost spiritual, isn't there, about three men and a round of golf.'

DB stepped back from the tee. 'What do you mean?'

'Three generations of Arnolds men. Five generations of lawyers. Sometimes life is so fortuitous one wants to pinch oneself.'

DB peered at his father. Perhaps he was having a turn?

'Niki pinches me,' Rudy announced from where he sat on the green, colliding two golf balls into each other. 'Not always, though.'

'Well, you better be pinching that young Nick back,' DB's father advised. 'You show him who the alpha is.'

'Okay, firstly, Niki is a little girl, and Rudy, don't you pinch her. Don't pinch anyone. And secondly, he's in kindergarten, Dad. There are no alphas.'

His father brushed this off.

'There's always an alpha, Benjamin. Now best you hit that ball before the sun goes down.'

DB lined up the ball and took a swing. It veered off to the side, landed with a *thwack* in a sand bunker.

'There's always an alpha,' his father repeated, then set off with a whistle.

It was a merry whistle, looping and modulating as DB set himself up in the sand preparing to chip at the ball. He busied himself a while, trying to work out the angle, then looked up again.

'Where's Rudy?'

His father raised his eyebrows to the opposite end of the bunker.

'He appears to be making sandcastles. That's where you need to aim, by the way, if you want to redeem yourself.'

'You mean aim at my child?'

'Of course not. Aim over him. Forty, forty-five degrees, I'd say.'

DB repositioned himself, practising the shot in his head. As he prepared to swing, his father gave a throaty cough.

'I just want you to know you're doing well. The house, the job, the promotion. Rudy, even with this whole toilet training fiasco. You're on the right track, Benjamin.'

DB felt the praise pierce his chest and dagger towards his heart. He smiled to himself and swung with a sudden burst of confidence, then watched the ball sail gracefully and smoothly straight into his son's back.

Later, DB stood outside his house with a subdued Rudy, waving as his father drove off down the street.

'Don't worry,' his father called as he pulled away from the curb. 'I did the same thing to you, only it was your head.'

Rudy's hand hovered protectively over the little round bruise on his shoulder as he nuzzled into his father's neck. His backpack had absorbed much of the impact, but it was tender still. They stood like this for a while, DB taking in the front of the house.

The wide sweeping verandah. The restored heritage eaves with the delicate rail and ornate brackets. The double garage that was so envied in these parts. He'd worked hard for this so that his family could have what he had had, so that he could leave something tangible behind for them.

'One day all this will be yours, buddy,' he whispered to Rudy, who gave the house the briefest glance.

'I want Mummy to see my hurt.'

DB pressed his lips into his child's hair. He smelt of sweat and sand and the chocolate they'd used to bribe away his tears.

'And my nappy,' Rudy added. 'I want Mummy to change it.'

DB held the kiss a little longer, savouring the jumble of scents, then pulled away.

'Fair call. Let's go in and see Mummy.'

9

Evangelia

Evangelia hadn't been nervous until the moment she shifted the car into park in the TAFE parking lot. Then, as the engine cooled, a barrage of previously unconsidered worries came bursting to the surface: what if they had to read each other's work? What if everyone else was better? What if the general consensus was that she was wasting her time trying to tell this unremarkable story? And, above all, *what if Lydia somehow found out?* It wasn't that Lydia would disagree, but more that she might laugh, and this was far worse. It was a habit she'd picked up from their father, a deep dismissive laugh at things that seemed pointless or petty. The laugh that had echoed about the rafters as their mother wrung her hands in worry at Lydia's refusal to stay inside for the forty days before the *sarantismos* following the birth of her babies, when she'd taken them out into the world, vulnerable to the ever-lurking *mati*. When she'd clamoured to stop Lydia pouring down the sink the blessed water saved from their christenings. When Evangelia had announced her intention to marry Peter. It was a laugh that said so clearly – *what you are doing is foolish.* It had been there in the previous weeks, thundering down the line when Evangelia had expressed her reservations about celebrating Easter while still in mourning. *For god's sake, Eva, it's not like we're even going to church. We'll have a barbecue and load the kids with chocolate and no one will burn for their sins.*

The worry worsened when Evangelia found her way to the classroom and sat at the table farthest from the front. They were set up in a U-shape and she hated this because she couldn't hide. She pulled the brand-new pencil case from her bag and the leather-bound journal too, and felt instantly embarrassed at her choice. Everyone else was pulling out laptops or setting up their iPads with little detachable keyboards. In comparison, her journal, which had looked so writerly in the shop, now seemed closer to a dream journal or something equally juvenile. Evangelia slipped the journal off the table, discreetly ripped a chunk of pages from its binding then shoved the rest of it back in her bag. She took a biro from the pencil case and hid this away too. She might look like she'd shoplifted her stationary but at least she didn't look like a loser. She understood now Nick and Xanthe's obsession with having the right pencils and book contact and shoes and all the other bits and pieces they hefted to school each day. They – like she – were terrified of being judged by their peers. In this instance, her peers seemed to consist of a couple of older women in cardigans and an intense-looking young man, but still. Judgement was judgement, no matter who it came from.

An older man dressed in knee-high socks and sandals drifted in, and then a woman with a neat grey bob with a striking dark fringe entered, taking the focal position up front. She pulled some papers from her satchel, slipped the glasses that had been resting in the bob down onto her nose, scanned the papers, then repositioned the glasses in her hair. She stood back, placing her hands on the black tunic hiding her hips, then surveyed the room.

'Is this everyone?'

Evangelia glanced about the room. How were they to know? The woman counted the participants, checked her list again (glasses down, glasses up) then counted once more. Five each time.

'Righto.'

The woman looked disappointed.

'Let's get started then. My name is Carole Swansea and I'll be your tutor for the course. I'd like to acknowledge the traditional owners of the land on which we meet, the people of the Kulin nation, and pay my respects to any elders past, present or emerging. A bit about me. My books include *Bush of the Bush* and my recent release, *Out of Focus*, and in my other life I lecture in feminist literature and critique, with a particular focus on biography and historical non-fiction that helps rewrite the dominant gendered narrative. This is my first time teaching a technical writing course but I'm sure we'll all muddle along together just brilliantly.'

Muddle along? Evangelia pursed her lips. She hadn't paid all that money to muddle along. Also, she'd never heard of this woman so clearly her books mustn't be that flash. This was a terrible mistake. She could already hear Lydia laughing at her, holding her hands to her chest as if to stop her heart from tumbling out. Carole was now perched on the end of her table like the teacher in one of those movies where they send a hip young grad to a tough inner-city school ruled by feisty urban kids brimming with hidden talent, except she was not, and neither were they.

'So why don't we go around the room and you can all tell me a bit about yourself. Who you are, why you're here?'

They were Gwen and Sita, both from Zonta and presently retired, who were working on a biography of the first woman elected to their local council, and they were incredibly pleased to meet Carole because they loved her work and found it utterly inspiring even though it was a pity she kept getting cut from the telly and perhaps one day she might like to speak at one of their morning teas? They were Damien who had recently finished high school and was taking some time to work out what he wanted from life, but he thought it might be being a biographer because he had read a really good Dylan biography and his mum had got him this class as a present but he didn't have anything much he was working on at the moment because he mostly wrote free verse poetry like Dylan and he could share that if they wanted? And they were Terry, who had amassed a considerable bottom drawer of World War II biography since his early retirement but hadn't had much luck getting it published, so perhaps this was something Carole could help him with? Carole had steepled her fingers at this, then asked him if any of the people he wrote about were women, what with this being a women's biography class and all? Terry had nodded his head at this as if he were only hearing eighty per cent of it, then applied considerable thought as he stroked his goatee.

'There'll definitely be one,' he said brightly, problem seemingly resolved.

Finally it was Evangelia's turn to introduce herself, and she did so with both her fight and flight responses jostling for supremacy.

'My name is Evangelia and I'm here to test the waters, I guess. I'm working on my mum's story but I'm not sure if I'll keep writing it or not. So we'll see, you know. Anyway, that's me.'

'Righto,' Carole said, eventually, and she looked about the room with something very close to disappointment.

She reached for her piece of paper again (glasses down, glasses up) and consulted it. She seemed at a loss for a moment before she steepled her hands together once more and brought them to her lips.

'Let's start with the beginning.'

The beginning, it seemed, was very literally the beginning of time as Carole began a potted history of the purposeful exclusion of women from the narrative arc of antiquity. Evangelia scribbled notes on her paper scraps, trying to catch the jumble of new phrases Carole expounded.

Binary norms – Cartesian dualism – gendered division of labour – public/private spheres – personal as political – the exclusion of the academe – control of the narrative – Oedipal paradigms (Was that what she'd said? Disgusting . . .)

Nearby, Gwen and Sita were nodding vigorously, typing each thought bubble into their iPads in the same determined index-finger jabbing motions that Peter adopted when typing. Eventually Carole paused for breath and rested back on the edge of the desk.

'So I guess that's why we're here. Questions?'

Terry raised a finger to attract her attention.

'So you're saying there's not much history written about women because no one thought to write it?'

Carole gave a more-or-less gesture.

'Remarkable!' Terry slapped the tabletop. 'Well, I'm definitely the man to fix that. So you're telling me that if I go out and find a woman who hasn't had her dues and write it all up into a nice little story my chances of getting published are higher?'

Carole's nostrils flared but she maintained her composure.

'That may very well be the case.'

Terry slapped the table once more and Evangelia decided she would avoid sitting near Terry in future.

'This course is already paying for itself,' he crowed, scribbling into his notebook.

The next thing they did was an exercise where Carole asked them to define what 'biography' was.

'Let's start by saying what it isn't,' she suggested.

Gwen immediately stuck up her hand. 'Biography is not fiction.'

Sita jumped in with, 'Biography is not irrefutable.'

Terry slapped the table.

'Biography is not memory.'

Carole nodded, surprised. Terry was on a roll.

'Biography is not lies. Biography is not apolitical. Biography is not propaganda.'

'Biography is not confined by space and time,' Damien offered. 'Biography is not a swimming pool.'

'Okay, we're getting a little esoteric,' Carole held up her hands. 'Let's bring it back to reality a bit. Evangelia?'

'Biography is not autobiography?'

Evangelia surprised herself with this answer, the stuttered result of intense panicking. But the more she thought about it, the more she saw it made sense.

'Tell me more,' Carole prompted.

'Like, even though I might be the one telling the story and I might even be a part of it, it isn't about me.'

'Fabulous point and one that many biographers forget,' Carole said. 'So often the work says more about the biographer than it does about the subject.'

She reached for her sheet of paper. Evangelia thought about this for a moment then raised her hand again.

'Only, sometimes it *is* about you. It's about how you interpret things. Like, even if you're writing something that isn't based on your own memories, you still have to decide how you want to write it. So maybe it's the opposite?'

'That's a really interesting point,' Carole said. 'And something I want each of you to think about before next week. Where do you stop and truth begins – and does this place even exist?'

Carole checked her watch. 'So for the rest of the course we're going to divide up our time like this: for the first half of the class we will be looking over examples of women's biography and discussing the themes, successes and failures, and then the other half we'll be workshopping your own material.

It can be something you've already written or something you work on across the course. No more than a thousand words at this point. You've got my email address so please send something through to me by the start of each week so I can circulate it to the group before we next meet. Questions?'

Terry's hand shot up.

'Not related to getting published?'

Terry's hand shot down.

'Great. I'll see you all next week then.'

Evangelia took her time packing up. She wanted to ask Carole about what she'd said – if you ever could remove yourself from what you were writing, and if this wasn't possible, what did that mean for how stories were told? But Carole slid her papers into her satchel and was out of the door before Evangelia got a chance.

*

Peter had needed to stay late at the shop that night, so Lydia's son Andreas had caught the bus with Nick and Xanthe up Spring Street to drop them there before he headed home. It wasn't an arrangement Evangelia was entirely happy with – Lydia never forgot a favour owing – but she felt more comfortable knowing they had someone with them as they passed the local high schools and mosque. They were sitting at one of the lacquered tables doing their homework when Evangelia arrived, a huge half-eaten plate of chips between them.

'Please tell me there was salad on that plate and that you ate it all,' she sighed.

'We could tell you that if you want,' Xanthe said.

Evangelia pushed through the plastic curtain into the little office at the back. Peter was hunched over the desk, moving papers about and flicking coins first into his palm and then into sealable bags. He looked exhausted.

'That class of yours better be worth it,' he grunted, then started recounting a pile.

He was always snappy after a long day at work, something he had previously blamed on his blood sugar and more recently on his mystery affliction.

'Nice to see you too,' Evangelia replied shortly.

He was the only one allowed to be tired and this irritated her. As if it wasn't work getting the children to school and double-checking the orders to the suppliers and reviewing the invoices and taking the aprons to be laundered and all the other things she did so that they didn't have to pay someone else to do it. She thought of her mother and the decades she'd put into managing the never-ending parade of domestic need, and Evangelia was instantly annoyed. If she'd not had to do all those things, then maybe Evangelia would have something to write about. Maybe she'd have been the first female councillor or have done something heroic in war. But instead she'd been stuck at home mending their clothing and making the food stretch between pay cheques and hiding from the Waltons man whenever he came knocking for payments.

Evangelia watched her husband, oblivious and distracted. They'd forgotten Mothers' Day – Peter and the kids – and Lydia had been busy speaking at a rally for the boat people or whatever it was, so the day had passed unnoticed. Lydia had invited them all to the rally to see her speak, but Evangelia had declined. The last time, Lydia had gone off on a rant about how their father had arrived in the country with nothing and had worked hard for everything he had, and people had clapped and cheered and told Lydia how articulate she was. So while Lydia had spent the afternoon standing in the tray of a ute with a megaphone in her hand, Evangelia had sat crying in the bath, trapping a bath bomb underwater and watching it dissolve in her fist.

'Have the kids eaten?' she asked.

'They had chips.'

'Chips?'

'Yes, chips. You know what chips are. They had chips because they were hungry. There wasn't anything else.'

'Nothing else? This is a food store. You couldn't make them some salad? Even a bloody *gyros* or something? Just chips? Like we're one of those families on *Today Tonight* with the malnourished children?'

Peter thumped the handful of coins he was counting back on the table. Evangelia thought of Terry and her irritation ratcheted up a few notches.

'Yes, just chips. I need to get this stuff finished before the weekend. What do you want me to do? Send them out on the street by themselves to find something? It's dark out there.'

'I know it's dark out there,' Evangelia snapped. 'You know when it wasn't dark? Before. Before it wasn't dark. Before there was lots of light and they could have gone to the hot chicken store and got some chicken and salad. Heaven forbid those children should actually eat salad every once in a while.'

The hot chicken store was Peter's closest rival and she knew this would rile him.

'You think I would let my children eat chicken from that *malaka*? You know how much steroids are in his meat? You think I want them looking like some kind of East German swimmer? Don't even mention that name to me. Hot chicken store! My god!'

He let out an outraged cry and threw his arms in the air, receipts fluttering from the desk in a graceful arc. Sometimes – often – when they were fighting, Evangelia had the ability to drift away from her body and look down on the profound inanity of the things they were saying. They fought about stupid things – this did not escape her at all. The problem was, they had been arguing for so long that it seemed natural, and they were both so enthusiastic about it. She drifted back into herself.

'Anyway, fine. I'm gonna take the kids home. You need anything?' *Like chicken?* she thought, but she didn't say this because they were done fighting for the time being. Peter drew his arms open in a sign of conciliation and for a moment he looked like a hefty Christ seated before the money lenders.

'Nah, I'm fine thanks, babe. This work, eh? It'll be the end of me. I reckon we're gonna have to take on a new staff member. They're killing us at the lunch rush.'

She bit her tongue. She had been saying this for months now, every time Peter complained about how busy things were. But he always had some reason why this wasn't feasible, often connected to money and usually connected to his not wanting to part with it. But she couldn't complain, because it was his inability to part with his earnings that had put them in the position to send the kids to the fancy private school and keep them in a way of life vaguely proportional to Lydia's. And it could be worse – Peter's sister had insisted on sending her son to a public school and he now worked in an art gallery, so god knew they were doing the right thing by their children. Besides, his relatives in Greece had been struggling for years now, what with the pension cuts and high unemployment, and despite this still managed to give to the steady stream of refugees washing up on their shores. They sent them money, Peter and Evangelia, every month for the last few years, and she knew that some of this went straight into helping those poor people, so she couldn't complain about the state of their finances or Peter's reluctance to part with it.

'That sounds like a great idea, Petro.'

'Thanks, babe.'

'We'll see you later tonight, okay? Don't stay too late.'

*

Once the children were in bed Evangelia sat down to write. She was tired but her brain was awake, stirred by the evening's class.

But when she brought her hands to the keyboard she watched them hover uncertainly above it. She thought of her mother, the familiar stabbing in her chest like someone had thrust a knife into it. Her mother had never wanted much, not that Evangelia was aware of anyway. She'd never wanted a big life and all her wants seemed to be reserved for her family. For them to be healthy, successful, educated. For herself, the wants seemed so minimal. The shops and church were within walking distance from her home, as was Evangelia's house. And Lydia was a short bus trip away. Nothing else seemed necessary. Evangelia had always just assumed – what? Her happiness? That she hadn't expected more of her life? Of course she probably had – everyone did. But she'd never made any representation of this to the living, not to anyone Evangelia knew. Her mother was an open book with remarkably few pages. There had been no surprises when selling the house. No grand discoveries hidden in the bottom of drawers. Not a single item in the entire place that wasn't familiar and homely and unbearable to pack into new boxes destined for op shop shelves. She knew other people who had dug a little deeper and found things: a father who had been part of the guerrilla resistance during independence and planted bombs in British buildings; a grandmother who had hidden Allied soldiers in the woodshed while the Germans bombed the Dodecanese; an uncle who had jumped ship on Mussolini and fled across the Alps to a new life. But the only things in her mother's closet were the same battered black coat she had been wearing for decades and the same orthopaedic sandals she'd buckled up rain, hail and shine. These were now stored in Evangelia's own wardrobe like faded ghosts, waiting to fill her eyes with shocked tears each time she went searching for a blouse or jacket because it really was true that her mother was gone and these were the last things she had that smelt of her. It had been like this in church too, each time they'd gone. Not so much the funeral when everyone's perfume drowned everyone else's out, but at the viewing, the nine days, the three months – each time she would breathe in the smell of the church's elderly, their soapy stale milk scent as they whispered the cross to themselves, and this would hurt too. But what was remarkable in that?

Evangelia thought back to a school project Xanthe had completed the previous year, when she'd grilled Evangelia for answers about their family history. She had asked why Xanthe didn't ask Yiayia herself, but Xanthe had been too impatient to struggle through the stilted English, made less intelligible in those days as old age fought for a resurgence of the mother tongue. So Evangelia had answered the questions. *What did Yiayia do during the war?* She waited for it to end. *What did Yiayia do when she moved to Australia?* She raised her family. *What did Yiayia do for fun?* Trips out east to pick the cherries, holidays at Lakes Entrance, church fundraisers when she would rise before the sun to bake and set up, then finally kick off her shoes and dance around the courtyard with her friends as the sun went down. *No, no, no – that's not interesting enough to write down!* It was a life too unexceptional even for a nine-year-old.

Nearby, her phone flashed. It was a text from Lydia, followed in quick succession by others. She – Evangelia – had forgotten a school fundraising meeting. Had been meant to bring refreshments. Had left them all thirsty. Had been put on the roster to collect donations for the upcoming silent auction. Had been volunteered by Lydia because she was the only mum without a proper job. Evangelia pushed the phone away. She stared at the blank page before her now, angry that it remained so.

10

Rik

North Facing Window: Italo De Luca
May 2016
By Rik Lee

The bluestone laneways of Coburg and Brunswick run like veins through the middle northern corridor. Quarried from Merri Creek, often by prisoners from nearby Pentridge Prison put to hard labour, they have been part of the area's aesthetic for more than a century and a half. But not for long, if one man has anything to do with it.

Since falling and breaking his arm a couple of years ago, Italo De Luca has been on a one-man mission to bring an end to the cobbled laneways surrounding his Brunswick home. 'They're no good,' Italo says, kicking at a paver. 'Look how uneven! My wife, she can't even come here because she has the walker and the wheels won't go.' Italo is a well-known face at council meetings, regularly presenting his petitions which can hold upwards of thirty signatures. 'I live here a long time. Sixty years. That's my house there. You see my driveway? Concrete. You see the pavement out front? Concrete. How hard is it to put some in the laneway too?'

Italo's first job after arriving in Australia from southern Italy was at the Queen Victoria Market unpacking fruit and veg in the early morning hours. 'Was no good. Too cold in the winter. Later I

save my money and bought the taxi and things change. What a job!
I saw the whole city. From the airport all the way out to the east.
Toorak, you know! Those streets – wide enough for three taxis.
Not like here. But it's my home, I love it.'

Italo's favourite thing about living in the north is how easy it is
to get to the airport, providing there is no traffic.

Rik hit send, the email hurtling off into the world. A fair
day's writing, all things considered, though he'd collected the
interview a few weeks earlier. He went to the fridge and cut
himself a thick slice of cheese then ate it silently sitting at his
kitchen table-cum-desk. After spending some time doing this,
he grabbed his notebook and an umbrella and stepped out into
the grey world. Rain fell in bursts, dull clouds heaped across
the sky with little interest in travelling anywhere. He watched
them as he waited at the tram stop, but the only things he could
imagine were other clouds. A big cloud, a slightly bigger cloud,
a cloud that looked like all the rest of the clouds . . .

He rode the tram towards the city then got off at the corner
of Smith Street. He pulled his collar up against the cold, releasing
the umbrella, then he quickened his pace along Johnston Street.
He slowed as he reached the start of the awnings, shaking the
umbrella then tucking it under his arm. He looked around this
little patch of the inner north, everything as it had always been
for all those years. He was embarrassed, but there was nothing
unusual about that these days, and as he skulked around the
corner he pretended he wasn't looking at the familiar building
across the street. He did the same thing after he'd doubled back
half a block, and then, once more, just to be sure. Eventually he
stepped into Marios Café and perched on a stool looking out
through the window onto the street. He was people-watching,
and laid his notebook open before him as evidence of this.
People-watching for his job, which was an entirely reasonable

thing to be doing. And he would have a coffee while he did this, and a Danish too, which was also markedly acceptable and not at all nostalgic because who in this entire café could ever have reason to call him a nostalgic man? Not a one, to be sure, he thought to himself, resting his chin in the cup of his palm and staring wistfully out at the gallery.

After some time, he pulled his mobile from his pocket and opened the internet browser. The previous search was still open – the one from the early hours of the morning – and he hurried to close it. He misjudged the screen in his haste, refreshing the search, but there was still nothing on the entirety of the internet about that poor poor man. Suddenly his throat tasted like bile and his heart was thumping about his ears and he could smell the rusty air that followed him across the ocean and into his nightmares and it was screaming – the air – screaming out to him, *Stop, please, I only want to help!* and all this happened in a sliver of a second. Rik pushed his fingertips into his eye sockets and pressed firmly. When this didn't work, he reached into his pocket for the foreign painkillers then sat very still, willing the headache away.

Eventually he was startled by the heavy thud of a delivery-man depositing a bound stack of newspapers on the bench beside him. The deliveryman slit the plastic binding with a Stanley knife. It was his newspaper. He folded a majority of the Danish into his mouth then gingerly seized the top copy. As he flicked towards *North Facing Window* he stumbled across a large beaming photo of Lotti, the caption proudly proclaiming her the recipient of the publisher's best new talent award. She looked suitably happy, her bright young eyes sparkling out at him. Rik stared at her a moment, all the hope and promise bursting from her face like piercing beams of light. Like the world was a satisfied oyster and not a cracked shell bogged with useless sediment and muck. Rik took up his pen and carefully measured out the beams of a rainbow, arcing from one eye to the next. He considered it a moment. It looked more like a monobrow. He added a little pot of gold then gave Lotti a fabulous bristling moustache. And some fawn horns too, just for good measure. And, because the horns seemed to demand it, the tight curl of a serpentine tail snaking up behind the shoulder of her smart fitted blazer. He was just deciding what to write in the Lichtenstein-esque speech bubble that now blossomed from her mouth, when a shadow fell across him. Rik looked up to see a camera pointed straight at him from the street outside. His hands splayed guiltily across Lotti's desecrated face. Then he realised the camera was focused on a figure to his right, a well-dressed silver-haired man delivering a piece to camera. Rik watched his broad back as his hands puppeted out occasionally. Eventually they finished and the man turned from the camera. As he did, Rik realised it was Harry, a former colleague who was now with one of the commercial stations. He'd made a generous toast at Rik's farewell do only months before. Rik tried to hide, a misguided action as they were less than a metre apart and separated only by a very large, frustratingly clean sheet of glass. He was mid-slither southward of his stool when Harry noticed him, his face breaking into puzzled surprise. You-wait-there, he gestured, heading towards the door, and Rik raised himself reluctantly from his awkward crouch. Harry greeted him with a warm handshake, then stuck his hands on his hips.

'Didn't expect to see you back so soon.' His face fell for a moment. 'It's not something terrible, is it? Not back for a funeral or something? How's –'

Rik shook his head kindly. 'No, no, nothing like that. Just back.'

He left it at that. Clearly Harry hadn't taken to googling him. This both hurt and relieved Rik. Harry watched Rik intently, his eyes now properly taking him in. Rik leant one hand on the paper, meaning to hide it, but it had the effect of merely sliding it closer to Harry. Harry's eyes tracked to the newspaper then to Rik, then, briefly, back to the newspaper.

'Working on a story?' Rik asked conversationally, nodding his head towards the cameraman outside who was now filming the busy street from various angles.

'Yep,' Harry replied with mock brightness. 'Residential parking permit brouhaha. Bit of a wank, really, but I've got a tit-for-tat where they let me do one of my pieces if I do one of theirs.'

Harry had started his career as an unpaid Indigenous cadet with free rein to report on anything he wanted, unsurprisingly discovering a distinct seesaw correlation between his preferred reportage and income earned.

'This one'll get me a minute or so on disproportionate representation in the child protection system.' He shrugged. 'But you've got to earn that crust somehow, right?'

'Me too,' Rik said, holding up his notebook as proof. The page was blank save for some splatters of Danish residue. They both politely ignored Lotti's graffitied face.

'So you've got work?' Harry asked, nodding his head encouragingly.

'Bits and pieces. Mostly just doing some freelancing. More time to write the Great Australian Novel.'

Rik watched this lie float out into the air between them. Never in his life had he ever had any intention or interest in writing a novel. Nevertheless, Harry seemed to accept this.

'Living the dream then, hey? I'd be there too but the wife wouldn't approve of it. Children, mortgage, blah blah blah. But it's good to see you making the most of it. The staff cuts, I mean. It's a massacre at the moment, even since you've been gone. Bodies piling up everywhere. Good luck finding an arts correspondent anymore. Good thing commercial telly's safe as houses, right? Look, I've got to keep moving but let me know if you want any extra work. We're always looking for freelancers these days and I've got a list up to here of pieces you could follow up. I mean, just as likely to be a piece on a baby elephant taking its first steps as the Calabrian Mafia fruit war, but give me a call if you want anything. Same number as before. Get that handsome bearded mug back on the telly.'

They shook hands once more and Harry gave him an awkward little salute as he headed back outside. Rik watched him, craning his neck with the certainty that he would, at some point somewhere down the street, report what he'd seen to the cameraman. Then it would only be a matter of time before he did a google search and that would certainly be the end of that. His eyes drifted over Lotti's heavy ink monobrow, knowing he would never contact Harry. He told simple stories. It was not entirely something he wanted, but this was what he did now. The door swung open and Harry was beside him again, his breath heavy from his brief jog back along the street.

'Speak of the devil,' he said, bending forward slightly to catch his breath, waving his mobile in one hand. 'Something's just come up. I'm triple-booked but it's the perfect piece for you. Social justice, sticking it to the man, etc. If you're in, I'll pass your details on to the producer and they can pick you up on the way.'

Rik didn't respond.

'Come on, mate. Do you good to get your teeth into something juicy again.' Harry motioned with his eyebrows at the paper.

Rik hesitated, then nodded reluctantly.

'Killer. Give me your number.'

Rik scribbled it in his notebook then tore the page out. Harry politely avoided the Danish smears.

'I'll get them to bring you a suit too. What are you, a thirty-four, thirty-five now?'

'Thirty-two.'

'Nice one. Did I tell you how trim you're looking? So trim. Not like the rest of us old blokes. Syria did you good, buddy. Anyway, thanks a million for this. Holler if you need anything.'

Rik smiled weakly.

'Give my best to Seymour too, mate.' Harry grinned as he strode towards the door. 'It's good to have you back. Welcome home, Patrick.'

11

Aida

Once more, it was the squeals of equal parts joy and disbelief that pulled Aida from her dreams. This time she had roamed the desert, thirsty and lost, searching for her father, before she was roused by Niki's cries of triumph from somewhere nearby. Aida heard her race through the house informing both Cyruses before finally bursting through Aida's door bearing her precious treasures. Aida provided appropriately impressed sound effects as Niki presented her findings: A pebble, a tangle of string, and an empty snail shell.

'*Afarin*,' Aida crowed. 'Well done!'

It had started with the tooth *pari* visit – a sudden willingness to involve Aida in the happenings of her little life – and Aida now found herself counted among the lucky few chosen to share in Niki's everyday discoveries. She let herself be led out into the kitchen where Elham stood scraping Niki's breakfast off the wall. It was raining again, steady and loud with wind that whipped at the windows, and as the day wore on, Niki soon grew bored. She yowled and whined like the Cyruses until Aida could take no more.

'Come, Niki. Let me tell you about Iran.'

As Niki begrudgingly pulled herself onto a kitchen chair beside Aida, Elham fussed about the kitchen. The kettle rumbled in the background as Elham placed three plates on the table, then proceeded to divide up fruit onto them. From the pantry she pulled a packet of dates, then placed a couple on each plate. She fished around in the fruit bowl and balanced a cucumber atop the small pile assembled on the plates. The kettle singing, she transferred the hot water into a teapot, setting out three small glass teacups as it steeped, then filled them with liquid. Finally, she took from the cupboard a packet of sugar cubes found in a Persian grocers, and placed this in the middle of the table.

'There. An Irani snack for an Irani story.'

Aida placed a sugar cube in her mouth and sipped her tea through it. Niki did the same, minus the tea. As Elham settled beside them, Aida cleared her throat.

'Let me tell you about the bazaar in Iran, Niki,' she began. 'This is where we go for all our shopping. The original Woolworths. Before you even leave the house you must check the air for pollution. Breathe in, Niki. Check it is clear enough or we'll all end up with red eyes and coughs. Too many cars, that's our problem. Maniacs on the roads filling the air with haze. So now that we know it's fine, we're going to catch the train. It's very busy in Tehran – eight million people in one city! – so squeeze in, Niki, or you'll be left behind.'

Niki was watching her with mild interest, a second sugar cube now wedged between her teeth.

'Off we get! Quick now, elbow your way out. Now hold tight to Maman's hand. The bazaar is full of people, pressed together, this way and that. Now, where should we start? You see, how the bazaar works is every section is different. Here we have fruit and vegetables. Over there is the fresh meat. Back this way you can get your nuts and pickled vegetables deep in their briny vats. And spices, too, piled high and colourful like a painter's palette. Now, if you head around to the other side, that's where you'll find the clothes: T-shirts and tailors and all kinds of scarves for women. Then the materials: your rich silks and deep earthy cottons, and yarn too, for weaving carpets. Speaking of carpets, I know someone who can give you a very good price, Niki-joon. Cousin of a cousin, good guy by the name of Ali. Ali Baba to his friends – just joking! – but you tell him Aida sent you. Specialises in mid-range pieces but he's got some special sixty-knot beauties out the back if you're prepared to sell your house for one. Tabrizi, Kerman, Naeen, some spectacular pieces from my mother's hometown in Esfahan province. Or basic pieces starting with a twenty-raj knot count if you aren't in the mood for anything fancy. Anything catch your eye?'

Niki placed her current sugar cube carefully on the table, then thoughtfully surveyed the invisible rugs Aida was gesturing to. Elham opened her mouth to laugh but then her voice caught and she shoved her fists into her eyes instead. She excused herself and darted out of the room. Aida thought to follow her, but her mobile rang. Niki, oblivious, continued scrutinising carpets, a third and fourth sugar cube pocketed in either cheek.

When Elham returned, red-eyed and quiet, Aida had cleared the table and was pulling on her coat.

'Sarah rang,' she explained. 'One of the news stations has contacted them for a story. Something about our visas, I think. Very last-minute but they just need us for some background shots. Maybe a couple of quotes. Lots of Sarah's clients are going. I didn't know if you and Niki want to come?'

Elham hesitated.

'You don't have to do anything you don't want to do. But it could be our chance to be heard.'

Elham thought for a moment then gave a half-nod.

'*Aallee*. Perfect,' Aida said. 'She'll pick us up soon. The trains aren't running because of this weather. Trees down on the line or something.'

Aida turned to Niki.

'You ready for your close-up, Miss Niki?'

Niki disappeared for a moment, returning with a hot pink legionnaire's cap and an extravagant pair of purple cat's-eye shades.

'*Kheili khoobeh*. Now you're ready.'

*

In the car, Sarah prepped them for the shoot.

'It's a bit of a "mood of the times" piece. The Minister's comments about refugees taking people's jobs while simultaneously being illiterate and on welfare, international criticism of the detention centres, the anti-immigration rallies that have been happening. They want something positive, about the contributions refugees make. They might ask you some questions but mostly they want footage of everyone being harmless and non-threatening to play behind their audio.'

Aida smirked as she stared out the car window at the bucketing rain.

'Harmless and non-threatening. Easy. I've been harmless and non-threatening my whole life.'

The crew had set up in the meeting room of Sarah's work, already in the process of filming two young men pretending to fill out forms. The reporter was positioned in front of them, attempting a piece to camera that he kept fumbling, forcing him to repeat the whole thing from the top. He looked nervous and pale, his suit ill-fitting, as he massaged his temples between shots when he thought no one was watching. Aida didn't recognise him from any of the stations. His features reminded her of the central Asian refugees she had seen in Jakarta, and she wondered if this was why he was doing the story. She looked about the equipment and was, momentarily, jealous. She spotted a few familiar faces from the many hours spent sitting in the waiting room and nodded in greeting. A tall woman in a deep blue abaya raised one eyebrow as the reporter stumbled his phrasing and laughed silently as he beat his fist against his thigh in frustration then started again. The young men sighed, preparing to retrace the markings on their forms once more.

They filmed Sarah's clients engaged in various tasks: chatting to each other, deep in mock appointments with Sarah, the children playing with assorted toys until Niki seized a ball from another child, causing both to explode in angry maligned tears. The producer had failed to organise interpreters so the reporter struggled his way through a number of confused off-topic interviews. His nervousness spread and soon Elham became anxious, pulling away from Aida.

'What if we get in trouble? What if the Minister sees it and decides not to give us a visa? What if we look ungrateful?'

The reporter watched them, sensing the apprehension in Elham's body language.

'Is she okay? Are you both okay?'

Aida shrugged. 'She's nervous.'

The reporter cleared his throat softly. 'Tell her that human stories are the only thing people listen to. It's the only way to remind people that you're people too.'

Aida translated and Elham nodded wearily.

'If you say so.'

The camera started filming and the reporter pushed his face into a sudden grave expression.

'Illegal. Illiterate. Dole bludgers. Job stealers. How does it feel to hear the Minister saying these things about you?'

Aida clasped her hands on the table before her, face composed, all those years of training kicking in.

'We understand the concern many in Australia feel. Jobs are hard to come by in Iran too. Your country has given us safety and we would like the opportunity to give back, to contribute to your economy, to work hard, pay tax and make a life.'

'Does it anger you to hear the Minister say these things?'

'As I said, all we want is the opportunity to contribute and work hard for this country.'

Aida's chest fluttered. It felt good to be back in the journalist seat, careful and purposeful with her words. Keeping on message, not letting emotions distract from the main purpose, avoiding tricky questions or set-ups.

'Can you tell me a bit about your journey here? What happened back home to make you leave?'

Aida froze, Elham waiting beside her for the translation.

'I'd rather not right now if that's okay with you.'

The reporter flinched.

'Are you sure?' he stuttered.

She nodded and he moved on, consulting the notepad in his laptop.

'How does it feel to have spent so long, first in detention, and now waiting to hear about your application? Is it unfair, this . . . this purgatory the government has kept you in?'

Aida took a measured breath.

'None of us has had an easy journey but our focus now is on how we can become part of this community. How we can contribute to this wonderful country and be part of the strong multiculturalism that has made Australia one of the best nations in the world.'

The reporter turned to Elham.

'Do you feel that the government has made a political issue out of your lives?'

'What do I know about politics? I just want a good life for my daughter. For her to be safe and free.'

Aida translated and the reporter paused, glancing at his notepad. As he did so, one of the young men who had earlier been filling in forms stepped in front of the camera.

'The Minister can get fucked. Fucking with us all! You let me have one job and I do it. My visa and one job! Back home I sweep the fucking streets. You want me to I do that here too. Better than dying on this fucking bridging visa for the rest of my life. You taking my mind, Minister. And my brothers on Manus. And my sisters on Nauru. My mind, my heart, every day taking taking. Sons of whores! *Haroom zadeh*!'

'Stop it!' Aida hissed in Persian. 'Shut your mouth. This is exactly what they want. You make us look like ungrateful animals.'

'Fuck you too,' the young man replied in Persian, gesturing rudely at her. 'With your fucking *Ingilisi*. What struggle did you know back home?'

Aida turned back to the reporter.

'Apologies for this man. You must stop the camera. He isn't well. This is what it does to people. All this waiting and uncertainty. It is breaking people. We are broken people. Please, stop the camera.'

There was a clatter of plastic then the slap of flesh on flesh from the makeshift play area and Niki emerged, sunglasses askew, clutching her cheek and howling with indignation. The reporter looked about nervously, his hands pressed to his temples.

'No more filming,' Aida said firmly.

*

The trains were running again when they finished for the day. Sarah dropped them at the station, already late for her next appointment. They sat quietly on the train, Niki asleep in Elham's arms, and watched the stations pass through the window. There was a burst of fresh air as the door between the carriages flew open and a group of men filed in, whooping and laughing loudly. Australian flags hung from their shoulders,

146

their faces covered by balaclavas and hoods. Aida held her breath, her fingers tightening protectively around Elham's wrist. The men made their way deliberately through the carriage. At the end of the carriage sat a young woman in hijab. *Slip it off*, Aida heard herself silently willing the young woman. The men passed the woman slowly, one by one, disappearing into the next carriage. The last man, the bottom half of his face obscured by a flag-print bandana, paused before the young woman. He leant forward slowly until he was inches from her. Her face remained blank, her eyes staring straight ahead.

'Go home,' he said, slow and purposeful, then pulled back.

The young woman didn't blink. She stayed like this, staring defiantly ahead, for the rest of the journey.

12

Patrick

MINISTER STANDS BY REMARKS
Reporter: Patrick Lee
18 May 2016
Transcript

(Footage of Melbourne pedestrians)

PATRICK LEE, REPORTER: Amid growing concerns over the conditions and wellbeing of asylum seekers both offshore and in Australia, the Immigration Minister has sparked criticism over his decision to label refugees innumerates and illiterates who would both take Australian jobs and languish on the dole. The comments have been met with outrage from both the Opposition and refugee advocates.

(Footage of woman sitting at a desk typing)

SARAH MONROE, SETTLEMENT CASEWORKER: What frustrates us about hearing these comments is firstly the fact they don't even make sense, but also that they shift the focus from our humanitarian responsibility to provide asylum for those facing persecution, to this idea of people seeking asylum and refugees as a burden on the economy or a threat. History shows time and again that once they've had a chance to establish themselves in the community, refugees have gone on to contribute greatly to Australia socially, economically and civically.

PATRICK LEE, REPORTER: For caseworkers like Sarah Monroe, comments like these are divisive and troubling, coming at a time when services are overwhelmed supporting thousands of asylum seekers, some of whom have been waiting years for the opportunity to apply for protection visas after the government introduced a freeze on visa processing back in December 2013. Only now does this legacy caseload have the opportunity to apply for what will at best be three to five year temporary visas to stay in the country, with limited pathways to citizenship.

SARAH MONROE, SETTLEMENT CASEWORKER: What we've got is thousands of people who have been stuck in limbo for years, who have spent a great deal of their recent life either held in detention centres or on bridging visas unable to work or study, who have fled persecution and fear, and who want more than anything to start the next chapter of their lives. To then claim that they are dole bludgers or job stealers; it's appalling to hear this coming from our elected representatives.

(Footage of two young men filling in forms)

PATRICK LEE, REPORTER: Ms Monroe works for one of the many organisations funded to provide casework support to asylum seekers and refugees. Here, in the outer suburbs of Melbourne, people are angry. Frustrated.

(Footage of man yelling)

'ALI', ASYLUM SEEKER: *The Minister can get fucked. Fucking with us all! You let me have one job and I do it. My visa and one job! Back home I sweep the fucking streets. You want me to I do that here too. Better than dying on this fucking bridging visa for the rest of my life. You taking my mind, Minister. And my brothers on Manus. And my sisters on Nauru. My mind, my heart, every day taking taking.*

(Footage of crowds protesting behind wire on Nauru, their faces blurred)

PATRICK LEE, REPORTER: *For many asylum seekers, unable to return home yet not welcome in what can only currently be described as their temporary new country, life has become hope-less. The hopelessness is palpable, many driven to desperation and mental despair by their time in limbo. And with more protests under way from far-right groups claiming to be anti-immigration and anti-asylum seeker, many here are feeling increasing despair.*

(Footage of two women seated beside a crying child. Close-up on child's face.)

AIDA, ASYLUM SEEKER: *We are broken people.*

LESLEY CRABTREE, PRESENTER: *That report from Patrick Lee. We're joined now by the Minister for Immigration –*

Part 3

13

Aida

When I was a child there were three things my father loved more than anything in the world. The first, though he never said the words, was my brothers and myself, his pride in us discernible from the smallest upward curve of the side of his mouth or the way he'd refer to us as 'his' children when we'd done something clever. Most of the time we were my mother's children, something she accepted with stage-like theatricality for all those within earshot: Look at the state of these children of mine! You'd never know they were mine by the look of their shoes! My own flesh and blood, yet the manners on them! This, too, evaporated quickly when I'd come home bearing a new award or near-perfect test score and they'd debate each other playfully as to who was best placed to take credit for my achievements. Was it my mother's nutritious cooking or the strong guiding hand of my father? They would celebrate, gloatingly, parading my accomplishments in the communal courtyard that joined our home to the neighbours', and Uncle Asadollah's first-floor apartment. It was an investment of my grandfather's, this property, Uncle Asadollah upstairs, my father downstairs, and tenants across the courtyard. In this same courtyard my older brothers took refuge against the more noxious eruptions their own underwhelming marks triggered, and it was where Uncle Asadollah commiserated drunkenly to the stars after each failed marriage and business venture. It was the backdrop of our lives, that courtyard.

The second thing my father loved more than anything in the world was my mother's tahdig, the layer of rice baked crisp at the bottom of the pot that we fought over each time we sat down to eat. Eschewing the practice of adding items like potato or turmeric or saffron, my mother's tahdig was simple but delicious, and my father claimed it could never be matched. This belief he advertised in all arenas save for in the presence of my grandmother, whose anxiety over the appreciation others felt towards her cooking rivalled none. I remember the first visit of Sohila, Uncle Asadollah's second wife, when she declared my grandmother's ghormeh sabzi merely 'very delicious', and my grandmother took to her mattress in unbridled grief, the level of which she usually reserved for the mourning of Imam Hussain every Muharram. Perhaps she, Sohila, would willingly replace her as chief cook of the family, my grandmother keened, prematurely bequeathing her treasured collection of heavy pots and pans. The rest of us, a practised audience in the stage show of my grandmother, watched with amusement, more certain that Sohila would be next for replacement if Uncle Asadollah's history was anything to go by. This was not Uncle Asadollah's fault, my father often reminded us, but a result of the over-mothering my grandmother had bestowed upon her final, long-prayed-for child, and it was a miracle Asadollah remembered even to feed himself given the circumstances. My grandparents, longing for a second child to complete their home, had travelled all the way to the shrine of Imam Reza in Mashhad so my grandmother could press her face to the zarih grill where fertility was supposedly granted, her elbows meanwhile fending off the throng of other desperate women clambering around her. His birth was a miracle, my grandmother was sure, and she raised him with the doting possessiveness of a queen regent. It was a miracle, my father would remind us again, that Asadollah had ever managed to leave the house.

The final thing my father loved most was the third shelf of his oldest bookcase. Here, separated from the tomes of his idols – Hafez, Molavi, Sa'adi, Ferdowsi, Khayyam – were the handful of first editions of his own publications. My father's interests spread far and wide: Persian literature, Persian history, and the intersection of Persian literature with Persian history. He watched with contemptuous disdain when we brought home newly discovered translations of modern foreign literature, his nose wrinkling at Austen or the Brontës as if they were flea-ridden, rheumy strays we had adopted off the street and dragged into his home. My mother, who finished her schooling at fifteen, was content for us to read anything so long as it kept us from the television which she insisted contained nothing but rot and nonsense. This was during a period when the satellite dish had been confiscated from our rooftop and we were yet to purchase another off the black market, so we were only able to access state-sanctioned channels. To my mother, most television produced within Iran was garbage. She would watch us disparagingly, one eyebrow raised, and mourn a childhood in which she'd spent her days roaming the streets and climbing trees with her friends. Our ears would prick up at these moments, springing on the sentiments like lions mid-hunt, and ask if this meant we were finally free to take to the streets with our friends.

'Of course not!' my mother would scold us. 'Who knows what kind of perverts are out there!?'

For my mother, the past was a time before strangers or danger or trouble.

I remember one Friday – it must have been a Friday because we were all at home – when my brothers and I lay watching cartoons, ignoring my mother's orders from the kitchen to help her with the chores. My brothers were grizzling – Alireza had probably tried to use Amin as a footrest or something similar – and I was telling them to keep quiet. My father, normally hidden away in his study while we were home, appeared from his refuge shaken and irate. He strode towards the kitchen, changed his mind, retraced his steps before changing his mind a final time. He stood frozen, halfway between my mother and his study, mute and quivering. My brothers and I, at the cusp of double digits, noted him with vague interest before turning back to the images flashing before us. Eventually, unable to contain his unnoticed emotions, my father let out a loud cry, throwing his arms out like an exasperated prophet.

'How dare they?' he raged to no one in particular, my mother's head popping up from behind the kitchen counter like a startled owl.

'How dare who?' she asked, but my father only shook his head, anger seething through the space between his teeth and tongue with a soft comedic whistle.

'How dare they?' he shouted again, this time catching our attention.

Alireza, used to our father's moments of academic frustration and venting, simply leant forward to turn up the volume, but I rolled away from the television, watching my father with interest.

'Censored,' my father spat, the word hurtling from his mouth as if he'd mistakenly bitten into rotten fruit. 'The manuscript. The publishers think it's too controversial, that there will be backlash from the government.'

His hands shook as if conducting a light-speed orchestra.

'Cowards!'

My mother made as if to come and comfort him but then thought better of it.

'Is it important? Is there something you can change?'

My father's orchestra went into overdrive. 'You can't change history! It is our duty – our responsibility – that it be told!'

He looked at my mother with a practised impatience that she quietly ignored.

'So what are your options?'

'Leave things out – important things – or find another publisher.' He glared bitterly at the tiles at this prospect.

'Will someone else publish it?' my mother asked him.

My father raised his shoulders in helplessness. 'Some might, but . . .'

He trailed off, his self-disgust evident.

'But what?' my mother prompted.

'But there might be repercussions. For me. For the publishers. For us.'

They both fell silent, their thoughts most likely drifting to the faces of friends and acquaintances who had been arrested – or worse – on account of their dissenting views. Later to be known as the Chain of Murders, the first decade of my life saw more than eighty writers, intellectuals, poets and activists disappear or die under suspicious circumstances, their mutilated, beaten bodies often found abandoned by the roadside far from their homes. Some my parents knew – had dined with, laughing long into the night amid glasses of black market wine only days before they were murdered.

'But you write history – not even modern history,' my mother protested, forgetting for a moment that neither reason nor logic played any part in the ways of the present-day regime.

My father shrugged again, his shoulders collapsing in defeat. 'Everyone is scared of inadvertent dissension. They're being overly cautious. No one wants to end up dead in a gutter of a heart attack.'

This was the official reason given for so many of the deaths. My father sighed heavily, his work rewriting itself before his eyes as he trudged back to his study. My mother watched him, her anger powerless against a force much larger than herself. She turned back to the potatoes, the knife grating her feelings into their skins. I watched them both a moment, my head tracing from one frustrated tableau to the other, before I too turned back to my television shows.

Not long after this, twenty-one writers were lured onto a bus under the guise that it would shepherd them to a poetry conference in Armenia. Mid-journey, it was said, the driver attempted to steer the bus off a mountain and they were saved only by a boulder that stopped them plunging a thousand feet down. Because of events like this many Iranian writers buried themselves under the cloak of self-censorship, clipping their voices or turning their creativity inwards. Forcing themselves – and their stories – to become invisible. Writing, just as I write now, about the trivialities of the domestic, or from the safety of mythology. Careful and cautious and quiet. Perhaps this is why we Iranians like poetry so much – who is to say what all that symbolism really means? Is the emptying cup the steady flight of Iran's best minds out of the country amid the pressures of censorship and restrictions, or is it just a simple cup, releasing its sweet wine to the thirsty open-mouthed world?

It had happened suddenly and unexpectedly, a phone call from out of the blue with the offer of a job at one of the many indistinguishable places she'd left her résumé. The days passed faster now, shaped around the steep learning curve Aida found herself struggling to scale in her new job, and soon the mid-year solstice was upon them. Each evening she would walk towards the train station from the café exhausted, marvelling at how winter stole the daylight so swiftly. The cold surprised her, confronting and heavy, and she would hurry along the streets despite her aching feet. She'd once thought this country existed in perpetual summer, but how wrong she'd been. A few weekends back, Sarah's organisation had taken them on a day trip to the state's historic goldfields. A place known for being the coldest in the state, they'd spent the day re-enacting the misery of panning for gold by plunging their hands into the freezing river as subarctic wind blasts whipped about them.

'Isn't this fun?' Sarah had called from somewhere within her parka.

The cold had stayed in her bones since. As a child, Aida had a habit of measuring the day's coldness not by the numbers on a thermometer or inches of slushy snow burying Tehran's footpaths, but by the density of the visible breaths that escaped her mouth with each exhalation. On their way to school she and Amin would see who could heave the longest breath, Alireza storming ahead, embarrassed by his younger siblings who spluttered and sprayed like asthmatic dragons.

'Today's a five!' they'd call out to him, timing the moment perfectly to coincide with the passing of Laleh, his neighbourhood crush.

Amin liked to joke that Alireza's ensuing anger was such that the smoke pouring out of his ears would be a ten, at the very least.

Today the sullen streets of Melbourne's north would be a six, perhaps a seven, the early moon rising in the grey mid-year sky. Aida shoved her hands deeper into the pockets of her coat, her breath tumbling out as she quickened her pace. A seven, for sure. The house was a four, the café an artificially sweltering zero, and the little cocoon made when she propped the cranky electric heater next to her bed was a two or three. It was costly, that little electric demon, but the alternative was to freeze.

When Aida had first started at the café a few weeks back the walk from the station to the front door hadn't seemed so long, but as the temperature dropped each walk stretched further than the one before. Sometimes she would pause, drawing her notebook from her bag to scribble down thoughts, but other times she daydreamed about universes where she possessed useful abilities. Waitressing skills, for instance, or the ability to memorise long orders. Peter, the café's owner, was adamant that his staff all master the art of paperless order-taking, something he had experienced once in a restaurant in Mykonos and thought classy enough to employ in his own suburban sit down/takeaway *gyros* café. Aida had attempted different strategies for this, such as making up songs or creating mnemonics, but most of the time when Peter wasn't around she just resorted to asking the customers repeatedly in between trips to the cash register. Her colleague Nina carried a contraband scrap of paper in her pocket along with a stolen minigolf pencil, and Kat, who was Peter's second cousin's daughter, just openly ignored him, much to the chagrin of Peter's wife Evangelia.

Evangelia seemed chagrined by a great many things. While Peter was the face of the business, Evangelia appeared to be the brains, as well as the mouth, the muscles and, Aida suspected, whatever it is that controls the body's ability to hand over money. The other staff seemed to fear her, for she never seemed satisfied with their efforts. She would appear at random, surveying the café as if it were a ship in distress, and it was not uncommon for her to seize a broomstick from someone's hands or the tongs from their grip and deliver a pointed demonstration of how things should be done. Subsequently, the staff spent much of their time hiding in the storeroom when Evangelia was about. Peter, too, who seemed possessed of some form of marital ESP that allowed him to escape to the back office moments before his wife swept through the front door. There was shouting, often, as if the high stakes of operating a middling quality rotisserie meat food service was on par with a Michelin star restaurant, and after she'd leave Peter would storm behind the counter to construct himself a towering *souvla*. He would eat it quickly and quietly standing over the hand basin, then turn to his hovering staff. 'Marriage, eh?' he would say with the conviction of a Shakespearian actor, the balled-up wrapper held before him like poor Yorick's skull, then retreat once more to the back office.

Aida knew the handful of notes Peter paid them each night from the register was less than legal, but after so long searching, any job would do. Nina was a university student and Kat a single mum, so the three of them existed in an unspoken coven of mildly committed social security fraud for the benefit of a few extra dollars in their bank accounts each week. For Nina it made up the rest of the rent and for Kat it allowed her children to go on school excursions, so for the sake of this stability they put up with Evangelia's nitpicking and Peter's short-changing.

The café's major trade revolved mostly around elderly southern Europeans and tradies on their lunchbreaks. The days were long, spent bustling about tables, directing the tongs between the steel food bins and chasing a broom after the mess arising from the charcoal ash and dropped lettuce. Aida's feet ached each night and her face felt layered in various meat greases, but it did allow her the chance to practise her colloquialisms. Since starting, Aida now felt confident employing a friendly 'mate' when required or flinging a casual 'no worries' in with the tomato, onion and garlic sauce. However, she'd yet to find a way to offer a jovial 'g'day' without it sounding forced and unnatural, so she stuck with the less off-putting 'hi'. She'd even attempted a couple of '*yassous*' for the Greek patrons, but she'd quickly stopped this as it routinely invited a long, demanding response in indecipherable Greek. It was the nose – one look at it and they assumed she was Greek too. She had learnt from watching Peter that '*nai*' was Greek for yes, so for these customers she simply responded to each shouted instruction with an obliging '*nai, nai, nai*' and corresponding nod of her head. Greeks, she was discovering, seemed to naturally communicate at a volume normally described as 'yelling'. It reminded her of her own relatives, of her aunts Simin, Sohila and Farzaneh, who had each entered her life at various points via a high-volume stream of grievances drifting down from Uncle Asadollah's upstairs apartment. They'd been so similar, each of his wives, with a similar chorus of complaints – the *doogh* had been left out of the fridge, the *farangi* toilet was clogged again and why did his clothes smell so constantly of finches? His refrain was the same following each divorce too.

'Never again, Aida-joon. This marriage business, it is like a brick. It will either help you smash through windows into glorious new worlds or pull you down to the bottom of the ocean.'

He would shake his head mournfully, letting his little finches out so they could fly about the place and rest on his shoulders.

'If you have love for yourself and the Almighty, that should be enough.' And he would offer her whatever sweets were left in the tin on the high shelf as he whistled softly to his feathered loves.

Despite Evangelia's dramatic visits, things could have been worse at the café. Nina and Kat made the day amusing, joking with each other between bursts of customers about the unappealing slabs the uncooked *gyros* meat arrived in or their own questionable hygiene standards. When she wasn't present, Kat pretended to be Evangelia, using the special voice she reserved for her children when they were being especially ratty. Nina would respond with her best caricature of Peter, a Gollum-esque miser who hoarded every last cent and refused to part with even the last stale circle of flatbread.

'Anything can be used again,' she'd explain in a deep voice, pretending to scrape together the ash and dust off the floor to funnel into a cone of pita.

'Petro!' Kat shrieked, hands on hips. 'You gonna feed the customers dust with no smile? Basic customer service, for god's sake, *malaka*.'

She'd turn to Aida, one angry foot tapping disappointedly on the floor.

'This man,' she'd say. 'This man I married . . .'

'The dust! You're scattering the precious dust!'

They'd fall about in fits of laughter, until the bell rang and they'd separate guiltily in case it was Evangelia. If it was, Nina and Kat would disappear into the back, leaving Aida to conjure her best foreigner smile.

'Is this meat ready?' Evangelia might quiz her, peering at the spit. 'Because we're not about poisoning the customer, here.'

Who was? Aida would wonder.

Occasionally she would field calls from Sarah, updates that weren't updates at all. No one had heard anything yet. Be patient. End of story. Apologies. Sarah had been able to provide a referral to someone who might be able to help with Niki's behaviour, but the closest appointment was months away, so like the rest of them Niki was waiting. Waiting, waiting, waiting. Neither of them had mentioned the news story, how it had made Elham cry, sinking into a silence she rarely emerged from, nor had Aida told Sarah about the shift a few days prior when she'd stood by the counter laughing with Nina, both women releasing the weight from their aching soles for a moment. She noticed a customer sitting at a nearby table watching them, her face twisted in anger. The woman had stood up, her chair scattering behind her, then strode over to them.

'You sit here laughing for what, you queue jumper? My family wait in line in a Turkish camp because you Iranians come here in boats wanting more money.'

She spat at Aida then hissed something in Arabic. Once the woman had left, Aida calmly wiped the spit from her cheek with a napkin. Nina stared, shocked. Aida hadn't said anything, folding the napkin into a square and placing it into the bin. Aida still kept an eye out for this woman.

Pulling her coat tight around her neck, she winced. The knot was back, aggravated by the cold weather. She stepped off the curb, checking the street for traffic, then crossed between the cars. She rejoined the footpath by a padlocked clothing store, the large glass windows shiny from polishing. She glanced at the sparkling gowns in the window, all plunging necklines and fishtail skirts.

Aida caught her reflection, her wide eyes set in darkness by the unlit store's shadows. She looked so tired and, she hesitated at the thought, so unlike herself. For a moment, she caught her mother from one angle, high cheekbones and arched brow, and from the other her father's sorrowful nose. Her mother had messaged early that morning, a restrained few lines about how the doctor had recommended her father spend a few nights in hospital as a precaution. She'd said no more, her superstition and fear filling the message's gaps. It hadn't surprised Aida, this news she had been suspecting, and when she'd sought more detail from her brothers, their silence only confirmed her suspicions.

Now that it was real and no longer in her head, it stayed with her all day, buzzing about her consciousness like the determined mosquitoes back on the island; hiding when she sought it and pouncing as she relaxed. She would not bury her father. Shackled to this country that did not want her, visa conditions meant she could not go back to Iran if she ever wanted Australia's protection. Not that she would anyway, not with the list of names it was rumoured they kept watch for at the airport. She would not bury him – could not. Her mind fled to the halls of her childhood, scrambling at the files and folders of her family. Her father's beaming face at her graduation. His great nose swollen greater after Alireza kicked a football square into it.

Quickly she heaved this door shut, blocking the memories that clawed to be free. In their place came those of later, of the period between the Green Movement and her arrest. An interview she'd conducted one deceptively pleasant day with a man who had lost his daughter amid the violence of the protests. His hands shook, never still for a moment, as if the unbearable nature of it all rattled inescapably within them. He'd sobbed, unrestrained and broken, and she'd hidden her head at the shame of witnessing a grown man's tears. It never left, the strength of those sobs or the tremor of hands, not for him or any of the others she'd interviewed. And in it she now saw her own tears, the ones she would cry when she finally received the news. Her grief would be the grief of any child the world over, but the difference was in her proximity to this. Three things the same, three things different . . . One, two, three, my grief, my grief, my grief . . .

Aida forced her mind to halt, scolding herself. Enough. No more of this. Where would this get her? Useless and broken, or else locked in a place for the insane, and none of that would help. She forced herself to look out at the world around her, the way the hastening darkness shrank the world thinner, or the way children invariably walk in great awkward zigzags instead of straight lines.

She turned into the suburban outdoor mall that led to the train station. A crowd stood in her path, soft music floating into the night. She joined the crowd's outlier, peering over the heads. A young man in a beanie and scarf was settled under an awning. His piano accordion came alive with home songs from faraway lands that belonged to neither of them. His fingers worked the notes as he sang along to the melody. He merged the old gypsy waltz into a new song. Aida recognised it, searching for the name. Adele, wasn't it? He played with his eyes softly closed, tapping a beat with one foot on a small wooden box. All around curious eyes bore into him, young and old, judging and appraising and dismissing him. *Open your eyes*, Aida thought. *See how the world closes in on you. See how it traps you and controls you, squeezing you in as you shrink and fade. How it pushes you smaller and smaller until there's almost nothing left of who you remember being.*

When she arrived home the letterbox was empty.

14

Patrick

North Facing Window: Çem Aksu
June 2016
By Rik Lee

If you'd told him ten years ago, Çem Aksu would never have believed that he would one day be elected to local council. 'It shows you anyone can achieve anything if they work hard enough,' Çem says from his desk inside Hume City Council, twin Turkish and Australian flags entwined in a statue behind him.

Or, Patrick thought, if they planted enough dummy candidates to swing the vote their way. He stared at his laptop for a moment, hands poised as if preparing for a piano concerto, then let them fall limply to the benchtop. It had been a short interview and he had been distracted the whole time. Distracted by the dip and swirl of the man's hands as he spoke, by the way the corners of his pilose moustache coiled under his top lip like a Gauguin self-portrait, by the scores of shiny faux-gold statuettes lining the shelves behind him. By the framed map on the wall, the great hunk of land bridging east and west. His eyes kept travelling back to the lower right border as the councillor spoke. The councillor had gestured to a pile of newspaper clippings, leafing through them to demonstrate his adroitness when it came to cutting ribbons, delivering stirring orations and posing in front of things with his arms crossed sternly and his face set with consternation. He'd nodded along, neglected notepad in hand, the map shrieking from the wall as the faintest pinpoint of the farthest reaches called him back for retribution. Huddled in the storm clouds, dragging itself through the mucky streets, singing like a beacon through the earth's orbit. And he had excused himself suddenly, because those little faux-gold statuettes were watching him, seeing through each of the flimsy layers he'd cloaked himself in, horrified by what they saw beneath, and because he couldn't hear anything anyway over the caterwauling of the map.

Hence, there was little to write of now that he set himself to the task, huddled on a stool in the window of Marios. He shoved some more Danish into his mouth. His head was sore, the pain spreading out in radial prongs from a point at the base of his skull. They'd been more frequent, these headaches that were really migraines, cascading over one another in the weeks since the television debacle.

She'd been so angry when she'd called him, Sarah the case worker. Livid. She'd shouted into the phone so vehemently he'd had to hold it from his ear for fear of aural damage. He'd apologised, of course he had, profusely and earnestly, but it hadn't made much difference. The damage was, as she'd reminded him several times, already well and truly done. And she'd used his name – Patrick – the one he hadn't needed for all this time, and each word had landed the harder because of this, tearing little pieces from his armour until he felt the version of himself beneath exposed once more. The worst part was that he'd tried to ensure this wouldn't happen. Had made careful notes of how it should be cut, but the producer he'd been working with had waved her hand dismissively when he held out the pages for her. 'Shoot me an email later,' she'd called as they let him out at his apartment. He'd been mortified when it had aired that night, and if he was any kind of journalist he would have marched down there and demanded someone important see him then give them a proper telling-off, or at the very least sent an anonymous tip to *Media Watch*. But what he'd done instead, because this was the kind of journalist he apparently was now, was write a politely worded email tentatively questioning why they'd chosen to portray his interviewees in such a dishonest way, and then wait meekly for a reply that never came. What did come was the briefest of phone calls enquiring if he wanted more work, in response to which he'd panicked and lied, telling them he was about to head overseas for a family holiday, and they'd told him to get back in touch when he returned.

That had been a fortnight ago, and instead of a glorious fictitious few weeks basking in the Balinese sun and drinking cocktails with little umbrellas, he'd spent them huddling under a real umbrella as the rain bucketed down upon the city. The staff at Marios had been very good about this, largely ignoring him despite his tendency to spend hours sitting in the window surrounded by a fleet of tepid, half-drunk coffees, a trail of Danish crumbs trekking across his whiskers as he watched the puddles pulse and quiver like something Brack would paint. This had been after the twenty-four hours he'd spent pinned to his pillow in the aftermath of the brain-strangling migraine that took hold following Sarah's phone call.

There was something his father had once told him, whistled from somewhere behind the tottering pile of Cantonese-language video tapes he'd procured from a distant relative in some obscure south-eastern suburb. 'You can't fail unless you give it a go!' his father had chuckled, resolved to finally master his ancestors' native tongue. Patrick's grandparents, proud natural-ised citizens, had spoken Cantonese only in private, for fear of poisoning their offsprings' acquisition of English. So his father's pursuit had seemed optimistic, when really it was misguided, because his father had disappeared into his study only to erupt again several hours later and topple the cassette tapes into the bin with a demonic defeated hiss. And this memory had come to Patrick as he'd laid there, Icarian in his bed, the knowledge that failure came only for those who tried.

There had been a lot of YouTube during this time, and he was now on first name terms with several delivery boys from the local Indian restaurant, so at least there was that. He had taken to enquiring about their days, listening earnestly as they provided vivid detailed accounts, delighted to be asked about something that wasn't to do with whether the pappadums were free or not. Alongside all that, it had all seemed to act as some sort of psychological plunger, demolishing whatever blockage had kept all the other stuff buried deep inside him. It came now in hiccups and gulps, little shattered rememberings of things he didn't want to remember. The underwhelming flash of metal. The noise like a shovel hitting wet cement. The blood, and how there seemed so much of it. The flight with not even the remotest ounce of fight in it. And as he'd lain there in the dark, bits of Patrick came flooding back, the bits he thought he'd left behind. How they'd groaned to a halt four separate times on the journey south-west, so that by the time the bus deposited him in the little coastal Anatolian town, it rode on four new old tyres. How winter had stripped the bougainvillea of its tyrian purple flowers, so that they reached and clawed their skeletal fingers across the shuttered-up shop windows. How the landlady had stared at him, baffled, as he'd proffered the lira towards her in the courtyard of the empty guesthouse. How the landlady's husband had studied him curiously, as he sipped his coffee in a sliver of feeble sun. 'Are you here because of the wreck?' he had asked, in confident accented English. And Patrick had not known for days that there lay beneath the waves an old DC-3 war plane sunk to the delight of divers, but it had made so much sense to him anyway.

Patrick turned back to his laptop and attempted another sentence. *Born and raised on the streets of Broadmeadows* – and then he was distracted again, his fingers slowing as his mind started racing once more, bouncing between catastrophes. Those poor women. Imagine how it must have felt watching themselves on the news. Maybe they hadn't seen it. You could only hope as much. And that young man . . . The ethics of it all grabbed hold of Patrick's brain, wringing it with both hands, and he was filled with the sudden throbbing promise of another imminent migraine.

He straightened, his balance wavering slightly on the stool, and his eyes suddenly locked on a familiar figure crossing the street. Patrick's stomach dropped, his legs forgetting themselves. Rocking back onto the stool, he watched as Seymour completed his jaywalk and passed by Marios. He continued on a few metres before stopping suddenly, spinning on his heels and doubling back. Seymour stood at the window before Patrick, pressing his face into the glass. He hovered there a moment, watching silently like a ghost as his breath fogged the glass in rapid tumbles, then his face contorted and he burst into tears.

Eventually Seymour was inside the café, standing a cautious distance from Patrick. As he collected himself, Patrick felt the gripping tension behind his eye sockets deepen, shuddering down his cranium and into his shoulder blade.

'I'm so sorry but will you excuse me one moment?' Patrick said.

Seymour's face revealed nothing.

'I promise I'm not running away.'

Seymour scoffed at this. Patrick slid off the stool and shuffled awkwardly to the restrooms. He slammed the door behind him, scrabbling in his pocket for the little foreign painkillers. He washed them down with a scoop of tap water, plunging his face into the stream as his fingers worked his temples. Despite the weeks of what effectively amounted to staking out Seymour's place of employment, Patrick did not at all feel ready for this. Perhaps he *should* run away? Slip out the back door, jump over the garbage skips like the hero of an action movie, and tear off towards the horizon. But he knew he couldn't do this because not even he was capable of something like that. Besides, he could barely walk now. His vision was clouding, and faint white auras were creeping into the world as the migrainous fog descended. He sunk onto the toilet lid.

'Are you okay in there?' Seymour's voice was hard and concerned, a balancing act he was struggling to master.

Patrick raised his head. The world was swimming, blurring, feeding into itself like when music videos discovered the echo effect in the nineties.

'Patrick?'

Patrick squeezed his eyes shut, cradling his head once more. The door opened slightly and Seymour peered in.

'What's going on? You look terrible.'

'Migraine,' Patrick replied through clenched teeth.

Seymour surveyed him, then clicked his tongue.

'Jesus. Here, let me help.'

He helped Patrick to his feet, then ushered him out of the restroom and through the café. Patrick leant into his shoulder, Seymour's familiar scent flooding him. He felt Seymour tense at the connection of flesh, pulling away to collect Patrick's notebook from the benchtop. Seymour guided him out through the front door and the world did a woozy Charleston.

'What's your address?' Seymour asked, thumbing the screen of his mobile.

He guided Patrick towards the car when it arrived. As he stumbled over the curb, Patrick forced an eye open. The rideshare driver was watching him curiously from the car. Patrick shifted his head slightly and his eyes met Seymour's.

'You're back,' Seymour said, his voice without tone.

'I'm back,' Patrick echoed.

'Did you ever actually go?'

Patrick's brow furrowed.

'Of course I did,' he whispered from somewhere inside the migraine. 'Just . . . not very well.'

'I see.'

His eyes dropped and he noticed a wad of cards tucked into Seymour's waistband. Seymour followed his gaze, frowning at the cards as if suddenly remembering them. One arm still holding up Patrick, he pulled the wad free and fanned them gently.

'Bookmarks. For Carole's new book. I'm meant to leave them in all the hip places where people go.'

Seymour slid them into his coat pocket. As he did, the pain reared up in Patrick's skull and he groaned loudly. He could feel Seymour scrutinising him and he stepped away from him, leaning against the car.

'You look like someone who has done terrible things and had terrible things done to them,' Seymour said.

The distance that stretched between them suddenly made itself known, and Patrick felt like crying because of everything that had happened and everything that he'd done.

'I wish they hadn't,' he said in a very small voice.

Seymour's jaw loosened, the briefest of movements. Worlds shifted in his impassive face as he watched Patrick.

'Are you back? Properly back?'

Patrick nodded slightly at Seymour.

'You coming or what?' Inside the car, the driver drummed the steering wheel impatiently with the fingers of his right hand.

Patrick opened the car door and slipped awkwardly into

the passenger seat. The driver gave a frustrated exhalation and flicked on the indicator.

'Wait,' Seymour called. 'Here.'

He seized one of the bookmarks then grabbed a biro from his lapel pocket.

'Call me if you have any problems getting home. I have a new number.'

He thrust the bookmark at Patrick then stepped away as the car pulled onto the street.

Back at his apartment, Patrick managed to navigate the way up the stairs to his front door, pulling it shut behind him. He groped his way down the hallway, eyes firmly shut, and shuffled into the little kitchen. He downed a glass of water then felt his way back towards the bedroom, stubbing his toe on the edge of the monolithic sideboard. He finally collapsed into his bed, pulling the cover over him to clothe himself in darkness. Reaching down to tug off his trousers, his fingers brushed the outline of the bookmark in his pocket. He smiled briefly, then the smile turned into a frown, and for a moment everything was too loud to breathe and he squeezed his eyes shut despite the fact that they already were. *Stop, please, I only want to help!* Patrick bit down on his tongue, his fists clenched tight, trembling as his head shook with everything that was inside.

15

Nell

– at which time the barrister for the applicant made clear that his client would proceed with the application for a full intervention order as concerns remained about the threat posed by our client (OC) to the applicant and their two children, with particular regard to alleged past abusive behaviour. At this point OC proceeded to swear at the other party across the room and Magistrate Davidson demanded she restrain herself. OC took her seat once more but not before conveying to the magistrate

'Fuck fuck fucking fuck.'

Nell had never seen DB properly angry but properly angry was what he had been, slamming his hand about the office walls and the desk until he'd hurt himself. Nell had looked around, embarrassed, but no one in the office seemed particularly bothered by this display. He hammered again, this time with his foot, the end of his tapered black derby pecking at the nearest desk leg like an outraged woodpecker. Eventually he had calmed himself, hurling his tall body into his office chair and slamming his elbows onto the desk in front of him. Nell sat tentatively opposite, her client notes half complete, waiting for him to speak. When he did, he looked like a combination of the bad cop in a good cop/bad cop pairing and a child who had just discovered the truth about Santa.

'She lied to us. She fucking lied to us.'

Nell made sure her voice was measured.

'We don't know that for sure.'

'Lied, withheld information, hid things – it's all the same.'

'I did tell you that –'

She'd stopped abruptly. Mr Williams was making his way across the office. Dressed smartly in a pressed off-white suit, he looked more like he was embarking on a picnic at his southern country manor than putting in a day's work at a top-tier law firm. His eyes sparkled expectantly as he stopped by their desk, leaning against it for support.

'Mr Arnolds. Helena. Successful day at the shop?'

Nell waited for DB's response. He offered a confirmatory thumbs-up, his face beset with a vaudevillian grin.

'Getting there. The ex is contesting the cross-application so we've got directions in a few weeks. Order is still in place but should all be sorted soon enough.'

Mr Williams nodded cautiously. He stroked his substantial girth as if it were a house pet.

'Who did you draw?'

'Davidson. I know.' DB gave an elaborate not-in-my-hands gesture.

'Unfortunate. Never met a magistrate so ill equipped to handle a lemonade stand, let alone a civil proceeding. Not much chop when it comes to family violence either from my understanding. Used to see him on the squash courts a bit. Terrible aim. Like playing against one of those inflatable things they have outside of car dealerships. All arms and no direction.'

Nell recalled the magistrate's face as he'd listened to DB speak, barely attempting to cover his yawns. He'd sighed heavily at the end, as if the list of things he would rather be doing was both extensive and significantly more interesting.

'Anyway, can't be helped,' Mr Williams continued. 'You've got your game plan worked out? You know how important it is for the firm that we see a win here.'

It wasn't a question. DB extended his thumbs again.

'Absolutely. Putting the ducks in a row as we speak.'

'That's what I like to hear.' Mr Williams smiled, though it was a quarter less of a smile than the initial one.

There had been a moment outside the courtroom when Nell had found herself alone. He had approached her, Madeline's husband, offering a tentative handshake.

'We've not met properly. I'm Eric Murray. I just wanted you to know I'm sorry about all this bother. About Madeline. She's . . . she's not well. She needs help. Psychological help. I've tried, god knows, but it's just been so difficult.'

He'd apologised again, his face racked with concern, then his lawyer had called him away. Nell had been too stunned to tell anyone but it had stayed with her, sitting uncomfortably in the pit of her already hesitant gut. In a place where things called for restraint.

Mr Williams offered a final encouraging thumbs-up. 'You've both got my absolute confidence.'

DB's eyes had followed Mr Williams as he made his way out of the office.

'Fuck,' he whispered, clutching his cheeks like a Renaissance painting, and then he went back to being angry.

*

When she came in for her next appointment, Madeline was angry too. She strode into the consulting room, hurling her handbag at the seat, showing no sign of her previous reserved self.

'You told me I would be able to see my children that day,' she growled. 'It's been two weeks and nothing has changed.'

DB folded his hands one on top of the other, his demeanour now calm and professional, the swagger all but gone.

'That was based on the assumption that what you'd told us was the truth. That you weren't omitting information, for instance, or lying.'

Madeline pushed her bag from the chair and sank heavily into it. The bag landed with a dull thud against the carpet, spilling its contents. She ignored this. How different she looked today, Nell thought, her eyes rimmed red and weary despite her careful makeup. Madeline crossed her arms and stared at DB sullenly.

'Did you not think it would be pertinent to mention the time the police were called to your children's primary school because you were drunk and/or high? And that this in turn resulted in a notification to Child Protection who paid your home a welfare visit? And that your husband spoke of your drinking but assured them it was under control? Did you not think your husband would include this in his application?'

Madeline shook her head with disgust.

'That's not how it happened.'

'Isn't it?' DB challenged her, fishing for the application from the file in front of him.

'Yes, but not like that.'

'Like how then?'

Madeline fell silent. She uncrossed her arms, pulling them to her lap and tightening them in her peculiar vice-like grip. She closed her eyes, her breath audible as she inhaled slowly, exhaled slowly, forcing herself to calmness. DB watched, unblinking. Nell, awkwardly aware of herself, reached out to fill their water glasses.

'So what happens now?' Madeline asked, her register lower.

'As both you and your ex are contesting the respective inter-vention orders raised against you, the magistrate has listed the case for directions in a few weeks. It's really just a procedural thing, five, ten minutes tops.'

'Like the last one, then,' Madeline scoffed. 'Getting my justice five minutes at a time.'

DB continued.

'Basically, it's pretty much a repeat of the first hearing and we get another chance to negotiate conditions. But if we can't get an agreement they'll give us a date for the contested hearing. That's the big one. For that we need to put together further and better particulars; things like witness lists, evidence, and of course your affidavit.'

'Like what I've already done?'

'More than that. It needs to contain all the relevant information, not just for this incident, but for the history of your relationship. How you met, when the violence first started, if it progressed, as well as specific information about the altercation and anything that happened up and until the point of the hearing. We need details for this. We need you to be honest.'

Madeline looked at her hands, her mouth drawn.

'So you need my story. Fine.'

'For the contested hearing, yes. Presuming neither of you change your mind before directions, which I think we can safely assume isn't going to happen.'

DB hesitated. His voice, when he spoke next, was delicate.

'Not only is he contesting the cross-application, but he is claiming a history of abuse perpetrated by you against him. Additionally, his lawyers are threatening to include costs as well, which means that in the event you are not successful, you would have to cover his legal fees. This means that he will be doing the same thing in preparation for the contested hearing: pulling together his affidavit, compiling witnesses. He'll be putting into writing all the same things: history of the relationship, past abuse and the like. Anything that provides evidence to his claims.'

'I see,' Madeline replied, her eyes downcast. 'And my children?'

DB's voice was gentler still.

'The interim order is still in place at this point, and until you either start mediation or get a parenting order, there's nothing much we can do.'

'So we start mediation?'

'You can start that process, but that's not something we can do here. You have to go to the Family Relationship Centre for that, and if he doesn't attend, you have to go through the Family Court to get the parenting order in place, and unfortunately all that takes time.'

'What kind of time?'

DB's face softened. 'Time. Months, perhaps. Unfortunately there are a lot of other people in a similar position to you.'

Nell noticed Madeline's hands trembling in their tangle. Madeline steadied them.

'I understand. So you need me to write you an affidavit?'

DB nodded.

'Yes. Well, not the actual affidavit, but the story. We can review it together in the next week or so then we will pull it into the proper format. Give ourselves time to make sure it's ready. And as you're going through, think of any witnesses who might be able to corroborate what you say. Any evidence. Things that will help the magistrate see that your story is the valid one. Unless of course you think you'll change your mind before the directions hearing?'

He ended the statement on a raised hopeful note. Madeline glared at him and DB rose to his feet hastily.

'I have a template somewhere with prompts for what to include. I'll just be a moment.'

He hurried out of the consulting room, leaving Nell and Madeline alone. Madeline looked over to her as if noticing her for the first time. Her brow creased.

'So what do you do?'

Nell considered this. Madeline's question was not unkind but the asking had made Nell realise that she didn't really know the answer.

'Support, mostly. Research, preparing documents, arranging our meetings. Once you've written your affidavit I'll be the one typing it up.'

Madeline surveyed her.

'Good for you,' she replied. 'Did you get all the way through that law degree just to be someone's secretary?'

It stung, and Nell could barely contain her reaction. She coughed, pulling herself taller.

'Ben is the senior lawyer. He has more experience. My role is to assist him and find him information or offer my opinion if he asks.'

Madeline looked amused though nothing amusing had been said. She leant forward, her body filling the space between them.

'And what opinion have you got on all this? Now that Ben isn't here?'

Nell felt her warm breath, sharp and close. She shifted back slightly. 'I would remind you that we can't take any instructions from you if you've been drinking. You need to be of sound mind. I'm saying that to help you, because we do want to help you, really we do.'

Madeline stared at her for a long moment, one hand hovering in front of her mouth.

'Fuck you,' she replied, placing her hands firmly in her lap.

*

That night Nell arrived home to find Seymour sprawled on the couch, though the mess consuming the kitchen counter suggested he had at some point been engaged in some form of productivity. The television was on but he seemed more preoccupied with his mobile, hitting the home button repeatedly so that the screen lit up.

'Terrarium,' he said, not looking up. 'Stupid idea. 'S'in the bin now.'

Nell surveyed the wreckage of foliage, dirt and pebbles. 'Couldn't be bothered cleaning up?'

Seymour pulled his eyes from his mobile, wounded. 'Bad day?'

Nell ignored him, sweeping her arm across the counter to shepherd the mess into the sink. It was meant to be dramatic and decisive, but instead sent pebbles and soil dancing into the air and skittering about the floor.

'What's up your arse?' Seymour turned down the volume of the television.

'I don't want to talk about it,' Nell said. She pulled a carafe of cold water from the fridge and poured herself a glass. She downed it aggressively, water sloshing out the sides of her mouth. She could sense Seymour watching her and brought her sleeve to her chin to mop up the spillage. Then she stood planted on the tiles, her arms rooted by her side, glaring tetchily at nothing in particular. Seymour waited, muting the television.

'I don't know what you're doing. If you want to talk about something, please just talk. I don't have the emotional insight to work out what is happening or why you are standing in the kitchen like an angry garden gnome.'

Nell took a breath. They were not, as a family, genetically predisposed to talk of their weaknesses. It was not something that came naturally to them, as if Darwinian theory had bled them of any ability to seek emotional solace or support.

'Am I affable?'

Seymour looked at her as if she'd asked him to perform some spontaneous, off-the-cuff calculus.

'You're not un-affable,' he said kindly.

181

'Do people like me?'

He shifted uncomfortably.

'They don't not like you.'

He pulled himself upright, swivelling his feet onto the carpet.

'Is there someone who . . . you want . . . to like you?'

His discomfort was obvious in the way it always became when the siblings were forced to discuss their romantic lives with one another.

'No.' Nell rolled her eyes. 'It's a client at work. I don't think she likes me.'

Seymour looked confused. 'Is she meant to?'

Nell shrugged offhandedly.

'Maybe she's put off by the desperate need to help everyone that you emit?'

Nell frowned. 'What do you mean?'

Seymour considered his words. 'Well, it's just sometimes you seem so keen to help people that it becomes more about your needs then theirs. And it's not about you, is it? Like the way you're always telling me to go out because you think it will help me forget about Patrick.'

His voice sounded funny at the end, as if he'd caught himself saying something illicit.

'It would help us all,' Nell muttered, and Seymour raised his eyebrows to demonstrate his point.

She stood there a moment longer, unable to articulate the tension running up and down her nervous system, pulsing through her veins in a way that unsettled and unbalanced her. She turned on her heels and marched out of the room.

'I am too fucking affable,' she mumbled.

That night she slept poorly, the flailing dervish sleep of the discontented people pleaser.

*

They met with Madeline again the following week. She arrived clutching a single piece of paper secured inside a plastic pocket. She nodded a greeting to DB then withdrew the page carefully and handed it to him.

I met Eric during my first year at university. We became engaged just after graduation and married twelve months after he finished his Articles. We underwent a short separation a year later after an incident in which we fought and he broke something precious to me. He apologised and soon after I became pregnant with our first child. Josh was born in 2006 and Leo in 2008. I became pregnant again in 2012 but lost the baby after an incident during which I was injured while locked out of the house. In retrospect, the abuse has been there throughout our entire relationship. It has caused me stress and anxiety and my drinking has been a result of this. The most recent incident, during which Eric called the police, occurred following a fight where Eric accused me of being an alcoholic. We fought and then the police turned up and Eric lied to them as usual. I just want this all to be over and for my kids and myself to be safe.

Nell read the page over DB's shoulder then awaited his reaction. He read through it a couple of times, turning the page over in case there was more, then placed it on the table. Nell knew what DB would say; that it was too brief, there were no details and, most importantly, that as a document it failed to incriminate anyone, really, except perhaps Madeline herself. She knew what DB would say but she waited now to see how DB would say it. He stared at Madeline's paper for a while then steepled his fingers. He searched the air as if he might find more information there, then, failing, settled his eyes on Madeline. The swagger was gone, so too the anger, and instead in their place was something close to deflation.

'Is there any more?'

Madeline crossed her arms. She reminded Nell of a child dragged before the school principal and asked to explain herself.

'Okay then,' DB said, clicking his tongue against his teeth. 'Look, to be blunt, there's just not enough here. I mean, for one thing, for the most part it reads like a normal relationship. You mention incidents, but what are they? You say there was violence, but where is it? There's just not enough meat in this to be useful for you.'

Madeline pursed her lips, her brows raised in an unimpressed scowl.

'It's not sexy enough?'

'It's not anything enough,' DB sighed. 'You need to be . . . sympathetic. Imagine I'm the magistrate. I want to see the damage this has done to you. I want to see the impact on you. I mean, you're the victim, right? As humans we're full of all this pride and our immediate reaction is to hide our scars, but the court needs to see them. You need to show them your wounds.'

Madeline shifted in the chair, recrossing her legs and pulling her hands into their usual tight little nest.

'I don't remember all those things. Who would want to?'

'You need to be reliable,' DB pressed. 'The drinking . . . it doesn't suggest that. What about witnesses? Who did you come up with?'

Madeline threw her arms into the air in wordless frustration.

'No one?'

'I didn't tell anyone,' she cried out, thumping her hands back down to her thighs. 'Who would I ask?'

Nell leant forward and pushed the tissue box towards Madeline, who batted it away like a softball player. The three of them watched it rocket off the table and crumple against the white wall.

'He has witnesses,' DB explained. 'The police, the school principal. People in positions of authority and credibility who can vouch for his story.'

'Of course he does.' Madeline laughed bitterly. 'He'll have it all sorted. That's what he does. Dots the i's, crosses the t's. He's got a big house and impressive career to show for it.'

She paused for a moment then reached for her bag.

'I have something.'

She fished about within it, pulling out her mobile phone. She fiddled with it for a moment, then held it up for them. An audio recording began, first crackly and incomprehensible before becoming clearer. A man was shouting, his voice distant and tinny as if coming through an intercom.

– What the fuck are you doing here?

'That's Eric,' Madeline interrupted, her own voice coming in over the top.

– I just want to see the boys.

– You know you can't. I've a bloody intervention order, you moron. And here you are lurking about the front of the house like a fucking stalker.

– I just want to see them. This is unfair. You know it is. This is all bullshit. I just want to see them. If this is about the house or the money, you can have it all. I just want to see my babies.

There was a pause and then the man began to laugh, cold and robotic through the intercom.

– You're pathetic, Madeline. Is that all the fight you've got in you? You're making this very easy for me. That's not the woman I married. You used to be such a good fighter. And now look at you. You're useless. A drunken wreck. You're an embarrassment. Lucky for you I'm always up for a fight.

There was a sob, so primal and raw it hurtled down Nell's throat and shattered the hesitancy of her doubting gut.

185

She avoided Madeline's gaze, but here in this room her eyes were fiery, her face determined.

– *Please Eric. Please just stop all of this. Stop your lies.*

– *But you're getting your day in court, darling. Isn't that what you wanted? It's only fair, after all. Isn't that what you said? Or have you forgotten all about that law degree you've got gathering dust? It'll be fun, won't it? Just like university all over again. Let's see who gets the better of the other this time.*

There was some more crackling then footsteps then the recording ended with the sound of someone fumbling to press pause. Madeline's whimpers were the last thing they heard. She looked up now, triumphant, the mobile raised before them like a trophy.

'Where did you get that?' DB asked softly.

'On the weekend. Played right into it, didn't he? He thought he was so clever installing that security system at the front gate.'

She stowed the mobile safely in her handbag. 'Don't worry, I've made copies.'

Nell's stomach dropped. She glanced at DB.

'That means you breached your intervention order,' DB said gently. 'We can't use it. It's inadmissible. Plus, you can't record someone without their consent. We can't use evidence that has been obtained in an illegal manner.'

Triumph fled from Madeline's face. 'But it shows that this is all a game for him. That he's making it all up.'

'You've breached your order. That's a criminal offence. He could report you for it and that's the last thing you need right now. You're lucky client privilege exists or we'd have to tell the police.'

Madeline's mouth tightened. 'So I can't use it?'

Nell felt the muscles tightening in her chest.

'We could,' she spoke up. 'There is a precedent. It's up to the magistrate, ultimately, but sometimes they grant an exemption and allow the evidence. It's happened before. But equally, Davidson might not. Ben's right. You may end up charged for the breach. It's a risk you have to make a call on.'

Nell watched as the momentary fight in Madeline seemed to shrivel away. She withered back into her chair, eyes dull, refusing to look at either of them. DB looked torn, unable to decide what to do next, his right hand tapping his biro repeatedly onto the notepad before him. He sprang to his feet abruptly.

'Nell, can we have a word outside?'

Nell rose, turning to Madeline.

'Can I get you anything? Tea? Coffee?'

'Merlot, if you've got it,' Madeline replied. 'That was a joke. I only drink white.'

She smiled to herself, a sad faraway smile. They huddled together outside the consulting room, voices low.

'We need more,' DB hissed. 'That's the worst attempt at an affidavit I've ever seen. It's more like the Wikipedia synopsis of a very sad movie than an actual legal document. We'll be eaten alive if that's what we submit. She's not doing herself any favours. And what if he reports the breach? Jesus . . .'

He fell back into the wall as if no longer able to support his six-foot frame.

'Maybe she doesn't remember?' Nell offered hesitantly.

DB ran his hands through his hair. 'Look, while I appreciate that, it's not going to help her in the end. I've seen his. Came through this morning. It's better. Way better. She comes off as a drunk and a risk to her children. And what she's giving us in that room isn't much of an improvement. She's not a good witness. She can't remember a bloody thing. And even if we didn't put her on the witness stand, there's nothing in that affidavit. She has no story.'

He stepped back, his hands on either side of his face like a panicking child.

187

'We could lose this. Shit shit shit. Williams will not be impressed if we lose this. It's meant to be our resounding pro bono victory. Redefining our whole goddamn social corporate responsibility ethos. They want to feature it in the bloody internal newsletter. And the annual report. I mean, it's four-fifty an hour we're not earning for this place. We need to make it count!'

He pulled his hands from his cheeks and started flexing them in front of him as if to tear a hole in the fabric of the space-time continuum through which to travel back to before. *What happened to Ned Kelly?* Nell thought.

'It's . . . stop that. It's okay. We've still got time. Why don't I speak to her? See if I can convince her to give us more detail?'

She had seen this, back when she was volunteering, the delicacy needed for a system that required its victims to speak the unspeakable. There was one woman, a victim of repeated and degrading sexual assault at the hands of her partner, who had wept openly for the full two hours it took to record her experience. Nell copied it all down because the woman herself refused to have it captured by her own hands in case it stayed there for good. She had done this, attended each session armed with her memories and a box of tissues, then once it was recorded she never returned, her court day coming and going without her.

DB agreed to Nell's suggestion and fled to make himself an espresso from the pod machine in the kitchen.

'Are you done whispering about me?' Madeline asked as Nell took a seat opposite her.

'Did you ever end up practicing law?' Nell asked.

This, of all of it, had shaken her the most. That amid all this horror there was something they shared. The question threw Madeline, who gave a half-shrug.

'No. I meant to, but I took a summer job working in the office of a local politician and then that turned into an actual job, and by the time I thought to go back and do my Articles or whatever it's called now there didn't seem much point. Eric seemed so far ahead of me by then it felt like I would be forever catching up, and then the kids came along and I ended up not going back to work at all.'

She raised her hands in mock triumph.

'So I'm an ideal role model for smart young female lawyers like yourself, obviously.'

'Do you remember much of it?' Nell asked, and Madeline made a face.

'Bits and pieces, I guess. But I'd assume it's changed some-what in the last fifteen years. You'd hope so, anyway. The Family Violence Protection Act, for one thing. That's new. Didn't think it would be used against me, though. I should have remembered all that rules of evidence stuff. Turning up like I was Sherlock fucking Holmes with my little recording. What an idiot.'

She slapped her palm to her forehead in pantomimic outrage.

'Well,' Nell continued. 'One of the things that is still the same with civil proceedings is that at the end of the day they're looking at the balance of probabilities that one of you did something wrong. It's a lower bar than criminal law. In criminal you have to show beyond reasonable doubt that someone did something, but in civil they're testing the evidence to see if the balance of probabilities is that something did or didn't happen. Because it's a cross-application, the magistrate will look at both your stories and evaluate each of them – did this happen and is there a risk of it happening again? So at the end of the day, it's about who tells the story best; whose version is the most convincing and reliable. Details, evidence – this is what helps to do that.'

Madeline's eyes were suddenly filled with tears. They tipped over her lids, pooling in the hollows under her eyes.

'Fucking details. You know the thing about details is that when all is said and done, it's the details you remember.

I couldn't tell you how many fights we had, how many times he punished me for all the various things I was apparently doing wrong. Hundreds? Thousands? Who knows? But you can bet I remember details. Particular phrases he used. Certain words that he knew were like bamboo under the fingernails. "Failure", that was one. "Disappointment". When the boys struggled at school it was because I was a terrible role model for them, sitting around on my fat arse all day doing nothing. Things like that. "I could wrap this car around a tree trunk and orphan our boys." That one word for word, and I can name the exact point on the exact road where he said it. Mimic the exact fluctuations of his voice and tell you what song was on the radio too. Tina Turner. Ironic, right?'

Madeline raised her eyebrows at this part.

'But the thing is, do I want all those details in court? Do I want to share them with a magistrate? With you? With that morose pup of a lawyer lurking about outside? It's bad enough knowing I was stupid enough to put up with it for so long, but to have everyone else know that too?'

Nell swallowed. 'I understand where you're coming from. Of course I do. But we want you to win.'

Madeline stared at her, her eyes hard and hollow, until Nell looked away.

'Do you really think any of us "win" from this situation?'

Nell changed tactics. 'Tell me about your boys.'

Madeline smirked. 'Good strategy. Get the woman talking about her kids then use that as leverage.' She pulled out her phone again, her face set with bitter mirth. 'Here.'

She flicked through some photos showing two young boys trapped in fits of hysterics. The older one had the same long face as his mother, while the younger one shared her smile. She ended with a photo of the three of them, lying together on a trampoline, their limbs tangled together.

'The older one is such a serious little man. Very into mecha-tronics and coding and things like that. And the younger one is the sweetest little bugger. That smile could charm Stalin, and he gets everything he wants, too. So now that we've gone down this path, I guess you're going to tell me that I have to do this for them?'

Nell met Madeline's hard stare.

'No. You have to do this for yourself. Write what you can and send it to me, and I promise you we will tell the best story on the day.'

16

Aida

Once, long ago, my father sat my brothers and I down to tell us about the labours of Rostam, hero of Iran. These seven struggles, his haft khan, shaped him from the boy he had been – the son of great Zal – into the man he would become – a ruler in his own right. My father

Aida paused, the silence distracting her from her writing. In this house of Niki and the Cyruses, silence was a rare, unnatural thing. Her arm darting from under the cover into the cold still air, Aida fumbled for her phone. It was silent too, the messages from her mother slowed now, as if reality was suddenly too hard to share. Aida glanced at the screen. By this time Elham should be up, clattering in the kitchen as the cats whined for milk, calling for Niki to sit down/eat her breakfast/no time for television/don't touch the cats. Niki should be protesting in response, scattering her breakfast across the floor, wailing by the mute television, hurling her clothes about like a tetchy tornado. Aida listened to the stillness of the house, her heart racing in her chest. Was that a soft feline cry she could hear? Or maybe it was her own panic, rising up from her stomach and thundering about her mind?

She rose from bed, hastily pulling a thick jumper over her pyjamas, and walked towards the bedroom door. She opened it anxiously, the quiet corridor greeting her. She glanced towards the kitchen, bathed in peace, then towards the lounge, similarly still. Perhaps they'd left early, so quietly and carefully she hadn't even stirred? That must be it, though their boots were still by the front door. Aida walked towards their bedroom, her breath catching in her throat. She gave a tentative knock. She knocked again, this time pushing the door open and peering in nervously. Elham lay on her mattress, Niki beside her. The little girl was stroking her mother's face, her pink fingers tenderly following the curve of her still brow.

'Elham?'

Elham didn't respond, her dark eyes staring into nothing. Beneath the sheets, her chest rose and fell in solemn rhythm. Aida had seen this before, eyes that saw only the past.

'Niki-joon, come here. Let's get you up and ready for kinder.'

The little girl refused to move, her eyes fixed on her mother.

'Come, Niki. You're going to need some food and I think we might just have to turn the television on this morning.'

At this, Niki's concentration wavered. She looked uncertainly at Aida then back at her mother.

'Let's leave her to rest,' Aida suggested, and Niki took a small step towards Aida, her eyes undecided.

Her round cheeks were red from the cold. Aida held out a hand.

'Maybe we can even eat our breakfast in front of the television?'

This won Niki over. She minced across the room towards the lounge, her step quickening as if expecting Aida to change her mind. As the television roared to life in the lounge, Aida knelt before Elham. Her sallow face offered no recognition.

'You just rest, okay?' Aida said softly, placing a palm against one of Elham's cold cheeks.

The recent federal election results meant more of the same,

so nothing seemed likely to change, and Elham had taken this heavily. Aida knew where she was, adrift somewhere amid the waves, the villages, the razor-wired cages, or the comforts and terrors of home.

'You come back when you're ready,' she whispered, pressing her lips to Elham's brow.

As Niki sat engrossed in the television, her breakfast falling blindly about her mouth, Aida hastily scrolled through her phone. Kat was unable to start any earlier but Nina said she'd cover for Aida until she arrived. She eventually managed to get Niki ready, the two negotiating a compromise in which a warm blue jumper was matched with the crumpled pyjama pants she refused to take off.

By the time they arrived at kinder the other children were well into their play. As Aida entered the code, the woman from weeks before came hurrying towards them. Niki ran off to join her friends and Aida tried to recall the woman's name. Beverly? Helen? The woman paused when she arrived, smiling expectantly. When Aida didn't fill the silence the woman reluctantly did.

'We're a little late today, aren't we?' she offered.

Aida swallowed all the snide remarks in her head and gave the woman her best 'no-English' smile.

'Heather,' the woman reminded her. 'Elham?'

'Aida,' Aida corrected her, enjoying the flicker of annoyance that crossed Heather's face.

'No, I meant . . .' she began, trailing off at Aida's reinforced smile. 'I wanted to check on how things are –'

'I must work now,' Aida interrupted her, turning towards the door. 'Please can Niki stay later today? I will pay.'

Heather hesitated then nodded. Aida knew she would have words for her, but that could wait for later.

She arrived at work to find the little café hectic with the late-morning rush. Peter had joined Nina behind the counter.

Aida cursed to herself. Her hopes of her tardiness remaining unnoticed quickly dissolved. Peter said nothing, simply thrust an apron at her, and she joined the meaty production line. The hours passed quickly, spurred by in inordinate demand for stuffed pitas that Aida could only put down to a mix of the cold weather and the launch of a new meat industry-driven public 'education campaign' championing a lamb-based reduction in iron deficiency. The staff called it Big Shawarma, a joke she'd had to explain to the others at first. Aida spent much of the day shrouded in silence, awaiting the inevitable disciplining that never seemed to come. The day's only lull came mid-afternoon, the sky already darkening beneath the low grey clouds. Peter had retreated to the back room. Aida pulled out her phone and called Elham. Eventually it rang out and Aida shoved it back into her pocket.

'Is everything okay?' Nina asked.

Aida looked at her, unsure where to begin. Nearby, Kat cleared her throat loudly, and the three women went back to their work as Evangelia bustled in. Giving their work only a cursory glance she strode through to the back room and they heard the sounds of raised voices before the door slammed shut. Working a broom across the tiled floor, Aida wondered what they were talking about. Her, perhaps, and she wondered how much longer she might have a job for. Nor did she know how long she could continue to pretend to know how to care for Niki. She wanted to ask her mother, to quiz her on how one went about parenting a child, but she knew it wasn't the time for this. Her father lying in the hospital, she couldn't add to her mother's worries, because worry she would, about Aida and about Elham and about the way their lives were tumbling wildly out of their control.

The bell above the door jingled and she looked up as a woman entered pushing a pram, two other small children flanking the sides chattering to each other. The woman paused, pushing her dark hair off her face, and for a moment Aida was transported. For the briefest second the air around her was hot and dense with the salt and tang of Cidaun, the air shuddering with the shrieks of the young Sri Lankan woman clutching wildly at nothing as the hall slowly filled with the lifeless bodies retrieved from the Indonesian sea. Her children – there had been two of them – first one then the other pulled from waters near the horizon as survivors told the story again and again of the ship that had seen them floundering but failed to stop. The bell jingled again, and Aida steadied herself. No, this was not that woman, standing here with her children close. Look how her nose curved differently, her cheekbones sat lower. This woman was here and so was Aida.

The rest of the afternoon passed and the café finally closed its doors. As the three women waited for Peter to tally the day's takings and hand them their pay, they exchanged looks.

'Here.'

Peter motioned to them, notes clenched in his hand. They approached, one by one. First Kat, then Nina, then finally Aida. When it was her turn she held out her hand but he didn't move. Their eyes met and she held his gaze for a moment before looking away. Finally, he placed a single note in her hand, less than half of what they usually made. She stared at it, her hand still outstretched.

'Is there a problem?' Peter asked.

Aida said nothing, her cheeks burning. On the train, Aida leant against the window. It was scratched with graffiti, inde-cipherable and coarse. At the next station two young men in ruffled school uniforms darted through the doors just as they closed, yelping with victory as they settled opposite her. The mobile phone in the taller boy's hand bleated and the other snatched it from him with a grin.

'What's the happs?' the young man with the phone hollered, pulling his collar from his neck.

He listened for a while, nodding enthusiastically.

'That's the tee-ruth, bra. Not my problem, TBH . . . Yeah, this is totally him.'

His friend grabbed at the phone.

'Give it to me, you fuckin' ESL-sounding weirdo.'

As they scrabbled in play-fight, cursing each other graphically, Aida watched the lightness of their youth. There, for a moment, were her brothers, lashing at each other with their long limbs, somewhere in the cusp between play and intent as their mother shouted at them to stop. There, too, was Aida and her best friend Shirin, squeezing into the overcrowded metro on their way to the movies or to wander the malls. Before any of the trouble that came later, lost in a youth that seemed so far away now. *Enough, Aida!* She pulled her mind from the past. Look at Elham, no doubt that was where she was stuck. The past was no place for anyone. For the rest of the train trip she made herself think of nothing, clearing her mind of the inexorable barrage that lived at the cusp of her thinking.

She found Niki, weary and cranky, at the doors of the kinder. Picking up her bag, she hurried her out the gate as Heather made her way towards them.

'Aida!' she called, but Aida pretended not to hear.

They walked in silence, and Aida worried about what they would find at home. Beside her Niki's grumbling became more audible. She stopped suddenly, refusing to continue.

'Tired,' she cried, sinking to the ground, her lip spilling forward into a pout.

'Please, Niki,' Aida said. 'Not far now.'

She felt warning throbs echo about her temples. It was too long a day for this.

'Tired,' Niki insisted, sinking lower.

Powerless, Aida sunk down beside her, the cold concrete radiating up into her skin.

'What can I give you, Niki?' she asked wearily.

Niki shrugged, pouting. Aida racked her brain. Her pockets were empty. She had nothing to give.

'How about a story?' she said desperately. 'One story and then we keep going?'

Niki nodded, a huge yawn enveloping her face.

'Okay,' Aida began. 'What story?'

Niki thought. 'Tiddilick.'

Aida stared at her. She had no idea what this was. She assumed it was something she'd picked up at kinder, just like the tooth fairy business.

'Well, I don't know that story. How about a Persian story? Do you know any of those?'

Niki shook her head.

'You don't know any? Niki! These are the stories of your people. What kind of Irani girl doesn't know her own stories? Good thing I'm here then.'

Niki looked like she didn't particularly share this sentiment. Aida thought for a moment.

'Okay, you know the story of Rostam?'

Niki shook her head again.

'Well, Rostam is one of the champions of Iran. He was a strong man, tall as a cypress tree and muscles like a mountain. When Iran's King Kavus is captured by the sorcerer King of Mazandaran, Rostam is sent to save him. On his way he has to overcome seven labours, his *haft khan*, each one harder than the next. He fights lions, witches and demons, all with his cunning horse Rakhsh. He even fights a dragon, Niki.'

Below her, Niki's eyes were wide with interest.

'This is my favourite part, the dragon. Rostam is sleeping near the dragon's lair, Rakhsh keeping watch. As Rostam sleeps,

Rakhsh sees the dragon, his claws sharp and his breath fiery. He wakes Rostam with a cry, but when Rostam looks around he cannot see anything so he falls back to sleep. Each time Rakhsh spots the dragon creeping towards Rostam he whinnies to wake him, and each time, the dragon hides in the darkness so Rostam cannot see him. Rostam becomes angry with Rakhsh because all he wants is to sleep. The third time the dragon roars and Rakhsh runs away in fear, but then he remembers his love for Rostam and returns to wake him. And this time the lights shine down upon the dragon and Rostam sees it and kills it. This is just one of his trials, Niki. Before he can rest, Rostam must lead the Persians into battle to defeat the sorcerer king once and for all and free King Kavus so that he can return to the throne of Iran. It is difficult, Niki-joon, but do you think he gives up? Never. Even when he is tired and weary. Even when it all seems too hard and he has nothing left. Even when he faces the sorcerer king himself.'

She paused, looking down at Niki.

'It's a pretty long walk home, isn't it? What do you think Rostam would do?'

Niki considered this.

'Do you think he would give up, like us?'

Niki shook her head. 'Walk.'

'You think so?'

She nodded with certainty.

'You think we should try?'

Niki mulled this over. Aida couldn't believe it was going to work. Perhaps this parenting wasn't so hard at all.

'Carry me.'

Almost. She leant over and lifted the little girl onto her hip, her body smelling of sweat and tears. As they entered through their little rusty gate Aida swooped down and checked the letterbox. Empty. Inside the house a light was on in the kitchen

199

and the smell of spices and tomatoes filled the hall promisingly. She released Niki, who ran down the hallway with excitement and burst into the kitchen, throwing herself around Elham's legs.

'Niki-joon!' Elham cried, smothering her in kisses. 'How late it is! You must be so hungry.'

Aida joined them in the kitchen. Elham was juggling Niki on one hip while she stirred a pot.

'And what have you been up to?' she asked Niki.

'Telling stories,' Aida replied, observing Elham. She showed no sign of her earlier torpor. 'Niki knows all about Rostam now, don't you?'

Niki nodded, her face buried in her mother's neck.

'Rostam!' Elham beamed. 'He learns how to be strong and good so he can take over from his father. It's a good story, Niki-joon. We all have our labours, big and small. But we need them if we are to grow up strong. You know, Niki, that story is from the *Shahnameh*. We learnt all about them in school. Everyone does in Iran.'

Elham tested the thickness of the stew. 'It means the book of kings,' she continued, 'because all the stories are about the great kings and heroes of Iran's past.'

'What do you think our book would be called?' Aida asked, stretching the knot in her neck.

'Ours would be the book of ordinary people,' Elham replied. 'And the exceptional Niki, of course.' She nuzzled into her daughter, who let out a delighted shriek. 'Now, who is ready to eat?'

Later, once Niki had fallen asleep on the couch, Aida turned to Elham.

'Do you want to talk about today?'

Elham's eyes remained on the television. Aida tried again.

'Do you . . . Do you think you need to . . .'

Elham cleared her throat.

'Stop it. I don't want you looking at me like that. With sympathy or pity. It's enough every day to remember you have no place without everyone looking at you with those sad unhelpful eyes all the time.' Elham sighed heavily, placing her hands flat on her thighs, the palms calm and steady.

'What about you, Aida? You want to talk about everything that has happened? Let it all out so that we can relive it again and again and again and still end up in the same place as before? You think I don't notice? That I don't have questions? Why don't you keep in contact with anyone from detention? Friends, lovers? You write all the time – always writing, never sharing – but where are your people? Go on, tell me your story.' She waited, small and fiery, but Aida said nothing.

'I didn't think so.'

Elham turned back to the television. Aida did too.

*

Days passed and Elham did not speak of much to Aida. Not of her sadness or her incapacitation, nor the lost day that had come and gone as if it had never been. Aida retreated into her own life, working long hours at the café and burying herself within her writing in the safety of her closed bedroom. She overheard Niki once, explaining to one of the Cyruses the cunning and intelligence of Rostam, though the story ended abruptly when Niki seized upon the idea that perhaps Cyrus could be her Rakhsh and attempted to mount the startled feline, who lashed out in panicked displeasure, leaving three little nicks in Niki's leg. But apart from this, Aida kept to herself despite the moments when the pitter-patter of those busy little feet hesitated outside her door and a small part of her wished they'd come in.

Elham, it seemed, had returned to her usual self, or at least a version of herself that refused to make eye contact, spoke mostly through Niki and gazed intently at the television, offering little

201

conversation. She fretted over little things: spoons that were missing, clothes that would not dry, and new chips in crockery that had been chipped to begin with. Niki's appointment with the specialist came and went and Aida never knew the outcome, for Elham awoke one day with a renewed determination to see everything in a positive light. She refused the idea that they might not get offered protection visas, laughed off the notion that Iran would do a deal to take them back involuntarily, and spoke of their financial struggles as if they were nothing but a game to while away the time until a more lavish lifestyle was at their disposal.

Aida now started work earlier and finished later at the café, though Peter still placed the same dismal amount of money into her palm regardless. It was something to do, she reasoned, even if it wasn't particularly enjoyable. Her nights seemed longer as she caught sleep in furious bursts of restlessness that pinged her from one vivid dream to the next. She fought them, writing long into the night until exhaustion caused her to fall into slumber, her notebook resting against her nose as she shuddered through sleep. It was on one such night that she awoke with a start, her phone singing beside her. She groped for it, lighting up the screen. 12.45 am. She didn't recognise the number, though she recognised the Iranian country code.

'Hello?'

'Aida-joon!'

The voice was crisp and full, as if coming from within the room. She sat up in bed.

'Maman?'

'Yes, *azizam*, it's me.'

'What are you doing calling? Is everything okay?'

Her mother's voice was reproachful.

'You've never answered when I've called you before and you're so unreliable with messages so I borrowed Farzaneh's phone.'

Despite being the most recent of Uncle Asadollah's ex-wives, Farzaneh and her mother had forged such a strong bond that this time round her mother had decided to keep Farzaneh instead of Asadollah. Her mother waited expectantly.

'You always call when I'm asleep,' Aida muttered, which wasn't entirely true.

Her mother, still baffled by the time difference, accepted this explanation.

'Anyway, now that I have you on the phone we can talk. Tell me what is happening. Your messages are so brief. One word, two words... Have you heard anything yet?'

Aida leant back into the pillow.

'Nothing. You know I'll tell you whenever I hear something.'

Her mother said nothing. Aida could hear the tension as she put flesh to her next statement.

'You know if you were to come home . . . maybe it wouldn't be so bad? Maybe they will have forgotten everything? Bita from down the road, her nephew returned and he's okay so far. He's not in the city anymore but no one has troubled him yet.'

Aida pressed her palm to her forehead, the cold of her flesh spreading across her brow. This was why she did not answer her phone. Because how do you argue with 'maybe'? Maybe I will be safe. Maybe I will be arrested. Maybe it all will be forgotten. Maybe I will be locked up or tortured or worse. Maybe I can start this all again . . .

'How is Alireza?' Aida asked, ignoring her mother's plea. 'And Amin?'

'As well as can be,' her mother sighed. 'Alireza's firm has given him some time off and Amin comes at night-time, so someone is with Baba all the time.'

She could sense in the silence her mother forming new words for the same thoughts. As if blinded to all that had happened before by the intense maternal yearning to shed this distance from their lives. Did she not realise how hard this was? This pleading for something Aida would do within seconds were things different? This thing that every pressure, every thought, every moment of every day was pushing her towards, when the ultimate fact was that she could not return. Even if she wanted to. And how very much she wanted to.

'Maybe they will have forgotten?' her mother tried again. 'Time has passed now. Ahmadinejad is gone.'

They both knew how wishful this thinking was. How unfair it was. How cruel. Inside Aida, the weariness of these last few years boiled over.

'Does Baba know you're talking like this?' Aida asked sharply.

She felt instantly guilty in the silence that followed. Her mother's breath as it travelled through the phone was laden with worry.

'He barely knows himself now.' Her voice was small and distant. 'He wakes sometimes but it pains him so much to be as he is that eventually they ease him back to sleep to stop his crying. He cries. Every day. Because he's not ready yet. Because . . .'

Because of me, Aida finished her mother's sentence in her head. Her mother sniffed, the wet *thwack* reverberating through the phone as she collected herself.

'Don't listen to me, Aida-joon. Of course you can't come home. Not now. It's not safe. Sometimes my head just disappears from reality. It's just so much without you here. Amin and Alireza, they're not much for comforting, and Asadollah is useless. He spends more time blubbering in the courtyard with his damn birds about how it should be him than sitting by the hospital bed. That man. Thank god we got Farzaneh, right?'

Her mother sniffed again, clearing her throat.

'And how is Elham? And little Niki?'

Aida thought of the last few weeks, how they'd twisted beyond her control.

'Fine,' she replied. 'They're fine.'

'You know every day I thank God that you have them,' her mother continued. 'No matter what happens, at least you have Elham and Niki. *Enshallah*, Aida-joon, *enshallah*.'

The phone call ended and sleep refused to return.

17

Evangelia

My mother arrived in Australia in the late 1950s, a quiet, courteous sixteen-year-old. She hadn't wanted to leave Cyprus but her family had no choice because the fight for independence from the British meant it was no longer safe and the family's business had been destroyed. My father first saw her at a dance at the Greek club and he suggested her to his family as a potential bride. My mother's aunt, a well-known matchmaker in the Melbourne circles, was sent to make enquiries. My maternal grandparents knew my father came from a good family, and that they were all hard-working, so eventually they agreed to their introduction. It was good fortune because my parents got on famously, and remained this way for the rest of their lives. My father always said that everything he had made of his life was because of my mother.

As young children, my mother worked hard to keep my sister and I well dressed and happy. She sewed us beautiful clothing using the neighbour's sewing machine that she would borrow. We'd take a trip to Myer, point out what we liked, and she'd work long into the night so we'd have something similar to wear to church at Easter or Christmas. My first day of school I wore my beautiful new frock with a matching ribbon in my hair and I remember the teacher telling me how smart I looked even though we were meant to be in uniform. I was selected to sit up the front at assembly and be one of the handful of students who got to sing the national anthem while they raised the flag. Imagine how proud I felt – and how jealous my older sister must have been because she had never been chosen for this honour before.

Evangelia glanced up from the page, interrupting herself.

'I can tell you what's wrong with it.'

Carole and the others were watching Evangelia expectantly.

'It's all about other people. Every time I try to write about her it slips into being about other people. I know it's meant to be about her, but the problem was she didn't do anything for herself. So it keeps wriggling out of my control and becoming about others.'

She gripped the paper, causing it to crinkle beneath her fingers, and shrugged her shoulders. It had been two months since she'd started the writing classes and she felt further from where she wanted to be than when she'd begun. The story was a fish, slippery and impatient, manoeuvring out of her reach every time she attempted to seize it. To make it what it should be. And each time she sat frustrated before the computer, she chastised herself for making such a mess of her mother's memory. It was a stupid idea anyway, this story that wasn't a story, and she'd used the recent school holidays as an excuse not to work on it.

'Sorry. It's not very good. I don't think I'm cut out for this.'

She fled to the safety of her seat, avoiding the others' gaze. They, in comparison, were thriving, apart from Damien, who had disappeared after the first lesson, never to be seen again. She'd heard something about him being in south-east Asia now as he had discovered Kerouac. The rest of the class, who hadn't needed to find themselves, were instead working away diligently on their biographies. Sita and Gwen had stumbled across a box of old council ephemera on one of their research trips to the town hall archives and were breathing new life into their pioneering councillor every day. And Terry had found a woman to write about, one who had been a prisoner of war in Changi and singlehandedly masterminded a way of smuggling medicines into the camp that aided in the rudimentary surgeries performed by the interned doctors. She was, according to Terry, a woman worth the ink.

Carole had, in her own aloof way, been supportive of them all, providing little hints and suggestions as they workshopped their pieces together. She'd been kind to Evangelia too, attempting to navigate the story towards clearer waters, but each week as she sat at home behind the computer, Evangelia managed to steer herself back towards uncertainty. She'd tried to make it rhyme, had written bits of it in poorly phrased Greek, had attempted a first-person structure until the weight of looking out through her mother's eyes had become too much and she'd retreated back to the safety of her own perspective. Nothing made it look how she wanted, and every time she felt herself close, she was dragged away by Peter or the children, or a frustrating phone call from Lydia about something inane to do with the school. Carole's suggestions had been thoughtful – perhaps there were diaries her mother had kept, recordings or scrapbooks, some source that would help Evangelia to gain entry into her psyche? But her mother had had no time for these things and had left behind no archives to assist Evangelia. She remembered the time she'd attempted to record her mother, who had waved away the voice recorder as if it were a knife held to her throat.

'I've told you everything already,' she'd said, glaring at the recorder. 'The people who need to know, know. I don't want my words living forever in that *kakos* little thing for anyone to find in the future.'

Then she'd clicked her tongue at the device and refused to have it back in her house.

So Evangelia had sat there night after night, pulling from

the closets of her memory all that she could recall. And when she laid it out before her, all she saw was a woman who utterly missed her mother, and there wasn't much of a story in that.

Carole was watching her, brow furrowed, considering her words.

'Thank you for sharing with us, Evangelia, and that was, once more, some good self-reflection on your work. Does anyone else have any other comments or suggestions they'd like to offer Evangelia?'

Evangelia knew they wouldn't. They'd already provided it in previous weeks, yet she couldn't seem to do anything with it. Besides, neither Terry, Gwen nor Sita were writing from personal experience, and this made them confused and uncertain of how to advise her. The best Terry seemed able to do was to ascertain time and again that she was absolutely sure there were no skeletons in her mother's closet vis-à-vis secret professions or untold adventures? For instance, Ruth, his subject, had later gone on to train as a covert operative under the newly founded ASIO program and was she – Evangelia – completely certain her mother hadn't done something similar? Housewife by day, enchanting deep cover operative by night? Evangelia, who now sat as far from Terry as physically possible, pictured her mother shuffling about the house of an evening with slippered feet and her hair in rollers, scouring the saucepans with steel wool and plucking the hairs from her chin in the reflection of her little hand mirror. Pickling the olives her father grew in the backyard and whooping at the neighbour's cat for shitting in the cucumbers. No, she told Terry with certainty, her mother was undoubtedly not a spy.

In lieu of anyone offering any practical suggestions, Carole once more reiterated that there were a thousand ways to tell a story and that Evangelia would one day find her own. Evangelia nodded and pretended to take notes and began to feel a familiar glumness that would last for the rest of the evening. Then she would go home and seek out Peter, because he was bound to do something minor that would warrant her having a good loud shout.

*

A few days later Evangelia sat in the car with the motor running outside the *gyros* store. She jammed the base of her palm down on the horn a couple of times then turned up the heating. What was keeping Peter? It was freezing outside and she didn't want to leave the warmth of the car. She'd convinced him to close up early but already the sky was darkening. Evangelia had always hated this time of year, her mood blackening and her patience shortening in direct relation to the proximity of the winter solstice. Lydia was the same, so growing up in their house had been a cavern of petty fights and collisions every winter as the two young women had slammed doors and thrown cutlery and hurled themselves dramatically over couch arms to weep at the slightest inclination. Her mother had always said this was because their bodies were set for the northern hemisphere and were expecting sun and sweet sea breezes instead of all this rain and gloom. Her father blamed the lax parenting of this new country and muttered about a time when children were not treated like royalty and were expected to pull their weight. They'd had no time to sulk in the village because they were always expected to help in the fields and with the animals, he'd grumbled. Whatever it was, she felt it now, as if being forced to fit her life into the shortened sunlit hours of the day made it heavy and unbearable.

She jammed the horn again, muttering to herself. He was always like this when they had somewhere important to be, no matter how much warning she gave him. She'd texted him reminders throughout the day and even set a false deadline in the hope this would compensate for his inevitable lateness, but still, here she was, freezing to death in the car in the dark, breathing in her own recirculated breath. She wound the window down a fraction, recoiling from the icy air that seeped in.

'Petro! Peeeeee-ter!'

She honked the horn a few more times, ignoring the glances from the street.

'Peeeeeeeeeeeeeeeeee-ter! Oh, for chrissake.'

Evangelia pulled her coat around her and hurried out of the car. She threw open the front door, ignoring the little bell, and strode into the store. The staff were hurriedly busying themselves, Kat wiping the counter as Nina pretended she hadn't just resumed sweeping the floor. The new girl was doing something awkward and pointless around the condiments which suggested the three of them had previously been gossiping. Evangelia eyed them. Peter seemed to have a way of hiring staff who managed half of what she herself could do in the same amount of time.

'Petro! How many watches do I need to buy you before you use one?'

She burst into the back office where Peter sat hunched over the small table. Always hunched over the small table. This was what he did. For the life of her she couldn't work out why he always seemed to be doing this, as the entire process of closing up the till each night took her fifteen minutes maximum and she could do the whole thing standing. He looked up, his thick eyebrows set in a scowl.

'Don't give me that look. You know we're late. Do you want to be late? Because I don't want to be late. Last time we were late, do you think Lydia could think of anything else to talk about for the next month? No. It was all about how we were late for the school concert and missed our own bloody children perform. After all those weeks of listening to Xanthe torture her

211

flute, we missed the stupid performance. And do you think I'm going to miss the start of this silent bloody auction so that Lydia can talk her mouth off about it for the rest of the term? No, I am not. I am not doing that, Peter.'

Her husband looked at her wearily.

'Why are you yelling?'

'I'm not yelling,' she yelled. 'I'm simply reminding you that you were meant to be ready half an hour ago and I have been sitting in the car for the last thirty minutes waiting for you, breathing in my own carbon dioxide, but do you care?'

He held his hands up before him in surrender.

'You think this is easy?'

He gestured to the little mounds of coins before him as if they were the controls of a spaceship.

'I think it is incredibly easy,' Evangelia retorted, stepping forward. 'I think it's far easier than childbirth, and I've gone through that twice with your giant *Kríti* babies. Go pay the staff and let me finish this.'

As he lumbered off, she sat at the desk and started counting the coins. Far easier than childbirth? Where had that come from? She knew where it came from – straight from the script of things her mother used to say. She was turning into her mother. It was inevitable. History repeating in a different set of clothes. She finished the work quickly then shut off the lights in the back room. Out the front, Peter was paying the staff from a wad of notes he kept in his pocket, releasing each one slowly as though he were selecting which of his children to offer up for sacrifice.

'I'll be in the car,' she announced.

As she waited for Peter, she watched the three women leave the store one by one. Kat and Nina got in their cars, waving each other goodbye as they drove off. The new one – Ada, wasn't it? – tugged the collar of her coat higher as she set off down the pavement. This surprised Evangelia, who had assumed someone picked her up each night. It was dark outside, yet Ada didn't seem worried. She wore the same resigned expression that Evangelia's mother so often had.

Evangelia was hit suddenly by the memory of her mother rising early in the morning and heading out to the factory. This had been the year her father's back had properly given up and he'd been unable to work for six difficult months. He'd joined the Greek Army during World War II, supporting the Allies as the Greek islands became the coveted strategic point between Europe and the Middle East. He was a teenager, a baby really, but so many of them were, those burly Greek boys with their beards hiding their youthfulness. His back had been injured in an explosion up in the mountains somewhere and it caused him trouble the rest of his life, helped little by the long shifts he put in at the brickworks in order to put food on the table.

This time when his back played up he had ventured down to Heidelberg to the veterans' hospital for treatment, only to be told to wait. Others came and went, and still he waited for hours. He'd watched them give the other ex-servicemen cups of tea and sandwiches while they waited, but there was nothing for him. He waited all day until the hospital drew to the very edge of closing time before they called him. First one there, last one seen. The doctor was quick, brisk, told him new Australians often exaggerated their pain. That it was all in their heads. Overtly emotional and whatnot. An unbalanced equilibrium of sorts. And he had been sent off just as he'd come. The other ex-servicemen were offered taxis, given vouchers, but her father had had to take the train back into the city and then another back out to Northcote. He had returned home late in the evening, his story unfolding as he sat exhausted at the table, avoiding her mother's eyes. He was a proud man but by the end of the story his eyes were flooded with tears, the first Evangelia had ever seen from him.

The next morning, her mother had set off early and marched through the cold dark morning to the factory and demanded she be allowed to work in her husband's place. They had not wanted to let her but somehow she had changed the foreman's mind, and for six months, she had risen before the sun every day, gone about her morning tasks, then set off through the changing seasons to cart sand and clay, and heft new bricks, amid men twice her size. She had woken often, tiny four-year-old Evangelia, and peered through the fogged-up window from the cocoon of her blanket to watch her mother depart, as Lydia snored obliviously beside her. And it had been that face – that face so similar to the one Ada wore now – that had bid her farewell each morning.

Evangelia sat back in the car seat, her chest heavy. She had not thought of this memory for decades – had not even realised it existed – until this moment. Here was a story, but like the others it was so full of questions and gaps that the only purpose it served was to remind Evangelia that the one person who could fill these was no longer here. And suddenly all the grief of these last few months came tumbling afresh to the surface and she bit hard on her tongue to staunch the tears. Peter appeared suddenly, his heavy figure filling the passenger side window, and he settled himself in the seat beside her.

'You okay, babe?' he asked, tugging at the seatbelt.

'Of course I am.'

She started the car and they drove off in silence.

*

They missed the start of the silent auction and arrived to find Lydia laughing loudly amid a gaggle of other mums. It was a hearty laugh, visceral and deep, and it was far too soon for Evangelia.

'We're barely out of black,' she whispered to Peter under her breath.

Lydia, it seemed, was done with dark shades now, arriving at the six-month *mnimósino* the month before in a bright red blouse and beads and forgetting to ask the priest to bless the grave. Spotting them from across the school hall, Lydia's face lit up with faux concern and she shooed away the other women. Evangelia slid into the seat beside her and reached for the open bottle of wine at the centre of their table. It was set amid a sea of platters displaying various delicacies because Lydia believed in quality comestibles. At the front of the hall a small stage was pitched from where the principal stood reading out the winners of the silent auction, an assortment of teachers parading around the items like tired underpaid game show assistants. Darren was peering at the list of auction items, working out how long he would have to wait until his items were announced. Not that it mattered. He would most likely win them as Lydia had a tendency to hide the bidding sheets after they'd filled them in, and no one on the school committee had cottoned on to this yet. Besides, even if he didn't win tonight, whenever they wanted something they just went out and bought it.

'Don't worry,' Lydia said soothingly. 'I bid on a stone Buddha for you.'

Evangelia stared at her sister. Why on earth would she think that was something they wanted?

'How much did you put?' she asked cautiously.

'Oh, not much. Four hundred or so,' Lydia said dismissively, dipping a wholegrain cracker into a tub of babaganoush.

Evangelia saw Peter's eyes widen and she attempted to give him a reassuring look.

'I hid the paper so no one else could find it.' Lydia winked at them, and Evangelia watched Peter's mouth tighten into an almost imperceptible point. She pushed a plate of antipasto in front of him then turned to her sister, annoyed.

'Yes!' Darren leapt to his feet and started pumping the air with his fists.

Lydia looked momentarily embarrassed, which made Evangelia feel a little better.

'Win something, did you?' she asked Darren.

He gave her a stoked grin.

'*Game of Thrones* box set. Signed by one of the show runners.'

He looked around for someone to high-five but found no one.

'Good for you,' Evangelia said encouragingly, knowing this would annoy Lydia.

Lydia did not like anything that reminded her of the significant age difference between her and her husband. It had been a point of pride initially, when it was she who was in her thirties and he a decade younger, but now that Darren was in this position it simply made her feel old and, Evangelia suspected, vulnerable. Peter was scanning the list of items, munching on a stick of salami.

'Look at some of these dinner packages,' he said, impressed.

'We bid on a bunch of those,' Lydia replied enthusiastically, sweeping her dark curls back over her shoulders in a way that made her silver jewellery rattle.

'Did you put our name on any?' he asked hopefully, and Lydia feigned surprise.

'I didn't realise you'd want that kind of thing,' she said.

Evangelia inhaled sharply, the nails of one hand digging into the flesh of the other. Lydia was surveying the room with eyes sparkling and Evangelia wanted to seize her, shake her, shout in her face until she remembered that their mother was no longer here and that they were meant to be bereft. She took another deep breath. Someone was wheeling the stone Buddha onto the stage. It was colossal, the folds of its huge belly peeping out from its robes in a way that reminded Evangelia of Peter circa now. She had hoped it would at least be one of those nice elegant Thai Buddhas, but it was the laughing kind, inexpertly carved so that it peered out at them with a sardonic jeer. She did not want it anywhere near her home.

'You've won!' Lydia exclaimed brightly, clapping her hands together in a pantomime of delight.

Peter glared at her, stuffing another salami stick into his mouth.

'Smile,' Lydia joked, and for a brief second Peter's grimace was an exact replica of the Buddha's.

Evangelia leant over to Peter.

'It's okay,' she whispered. 'We'll just go without picking it up. Eventually they'll leave us alone and just re-auction it next year.'

Lydia had other ideas.

'Let's go up and get it now. They're having a short break. The kids are performing a musical item.'

Up onstage, Andreas and Marina were preparing to perform, Andreas pulling his bouzouki from its case and Marina adjusting the microphone. They were dressed in some eclectic version of traditional dress, as prescribed by Lydia, so they looked like impoverished peasants preparing to busk for bread scraps. Lydia liked to pick and choose from costumes of the various regions of the Hellenic nations, because the point was to be cultural, she insisted, not accurate.

'They wrote this song themselves,' she said proudly as Andreas started to play, slow and dramatic.

She grabbed Evangelia by the hand and pulled her towards the Buddha.

'Isn't it lovely?' she gushed.

'Why don't you take it?' Evangelia suggested. 'Clearly you love it.'

'Oh, I couldn't,' Lydia insisted. 'You deserve it. Plus, it wouldn't really go with our aesthetic.'

So Evangelia handed over the money, feeling Peter's eyes like lasers on the back of her neck.

Lydia soon lost interest in the silent auction. She turned her back to the stage, reaching across to tap Evangelia's arm.

'We really do need to make sure we get the *mnimósino* right next time,' she said, her voice suggesting that it had been Evangelia's fault the Italian had not known to pray for their mother's eternal soul. 'The headstone should be ready too.'

Evangelia's face fell. For years their father had lain alone in the double plot, the bare headstone beside him waiting for the time when their mother joined him. Lydia was supposed to have organised this months ago. Had promised to do it at the three months after Evangelia had been upset to find the plain white wooden cross still acting as placeholder for the real thing, then again following the six months. And now their mother had lain in the ground for nearly seven months with no proper headstone.

'Why isn't it done by now?'

Lydia raised an eyebrow. 'I wanted to get it right.'

She picked a strawberry from a plate and nibbled it delicately, avoiding the leaves.

'Besides, I can't decide which picture to use. It wasn't an issue with Dad because he died so young he hadn't really aged that much. But Mum looked so different in her later years. Anyway, these are the ones I've whittled it down to.'

She held up her phone and starting swiping through images. They were all recent photos, their mother's dour, aged face staring back at them. Evangelia's own face contorted in annoyance.

'God, when you make that face you look just like her,' Lydia said.

'These are terrible photos. She looks terrible. No!'

Lydia's eyebrows shot up.

'Why are you yelling? This is what she looked like.'

Evangelia's hands pulled into tight fists and she struck them down upon the table.

'That's what she looked like when she was old and tired and worn down from living a hard bloody life. When she was sick. That's not how she would want to be remembered. And it will look weird. There's Dad, all handsome and vibrant, and then you want a picture of Mum looking close to death?'

She pushed the phone away from her, surprising Lydia with the force. Peter too, who was watching with interest from the other side of a meat platter. It was not often his wife stood up to her sister and he looked to be enjoying it. Even Darren, who had been lovingly cradling his box set, was looking at them with a mixture of curiosity and worry, as if he might be called on at any moment to say or do something, and he was rarely prepared for either.

'Why are you making such a big deal out of this?' Lydia asked.

Behind her, the Australian History teacher was promenading a framed signed Collingwood guernsey across the stage. Evangelia clenched her jaw. She didn't know how to articulate it. Lydia sighed patiently.

'Fine. What photo do you want? What magical photo that doesn't seem to exist? From what time period? From what country? Mum in the kitchen cooking our dinner when we were kids? Mum at the church fundraiser ragged from baking all morning? Mum sitting by Dad's bedside each time his back played up, when neither of them slept at all? Which interchangeable point in time would you like to memorialise?'

Evangelia squeezed her eyes shut.

'Oh, no answer! I see. Not so easy, is it? Not so easy being the one who does all the work keeping this family on track. You don't realise what it's like. You're not the oldest. You don't have the crushing weight of being the matriarch now.'

219

Evangelia squeezed her eyes tighter. Images of their mother were crashing through her mind. The factory. The cherries. Hiding from the Waltons man. Speckled by candlelight at midnight mass. Cracking red eggs. Squirrelled away in the tomato plants. Lifting her grandchildren high above her head. Spitting on her daughters' wedding dresses to drive away the evil eye.

'Hello? Evangelia? I said you don't know what it's like being in charge now.'

Evangelia's eyes flashed open and she seized the platter of meats in front of her. And before anyone could say anything, she hefted it across the table at her sister, showering her with salami, prosciutto and something that was, knowing Lydia, very expensive jamón. The hall broke into ecstatic applause as Evangelia grabbed her bag and someone bounded to the stage to collect their framed guernsey. Lydia was, for the first time in Evangelia's memory, stunned.

In the car on the way home, Peter reached across and rested his hand on her thigh. She glanced over at him, her eyes catching the Buddha strapped into the back seat behind them.

'Do you want to talk about it?'

'Of course I don't,' she snapped.

She watched the suburbs pass by.

'Your mother would have hated to see good meat go to waste like that,' Peter said gently.

Evangelia bit down on her tongue.

'But she would have hated that statue more.'

And they smiled, the three of them, pained, weary smiles that didn't for a minute have any answers at all.

18

DB

Jonesy!

Loved the safari pics. Never been that close to an elephant myself. Internet says they're dangerous but nothing stops the Jonesenator, amiright?! Pity about the lost passport, but as you said, it was almost full anyway.

Life continues this side of the Equator. Case is proving more challenging than we originally thought but you know me – glutton for challenges! Obviously can't give you details but the other party is a bit of a name in the legal profession. You've heard of him. That's all I'll say. Former university Law Society President. So that's what we're up against but you know I'm not a quittin' man. And Nell is not a quittin' anything, so there's that.

Rudy's fifth birthday this weekend. You're missing out on one stellar party, my friend. Upgraded the barbecue in preparation because it's going to be epic. Balloon guy for the kids, fully stocked tiki bar for the adults. Matching father-and-son chino polo combos plus Ray Bans. You know we do!

DB squinted at the screen. Should it be *you know we did*? He tried to recall the hip-hop he listened to in the car whenever Sylvie and Rudy weren't around, testing out both phrases in his head. *You KNOW we do.* Like that. That's how he wanted

Jonesy to read it. Because if he didn't it just sounded like DB had made a typo . . . Except, wasn't it *you know* how *we do*? That sounded better. *You know HOW we do!*

'Wozzle womble worry?'

DB glanced across the desk. Nell was looking at him expectantly. He stared at her for a moment.

'Yes,' he replied eventually, and this seemed to satisfy whatever question she'd asked.

She turned back to her computer and continued typing. DB watched her, immersed in whatever it was she was working on. Most likely the pro bono case because this was what she seemed to spend most of her time doing, staying late in order to manage the rest of her work and continuing to fuel his suspicion that she had little life to speak of outside of her day job. This suited DB since it had become apparent that they may not win this case after all. And if they didn't win this case it would not impress Old Man Williams and impressing Old Man Williams was something DB was passionately devoted to right now. He'd even invited him to Rudy's party that weekend. It was a strategic move – he'd seemed so enamoured of Rudy when they'd met at the golf course – and might prove handy if – and this was only an if – if they were to somehow, potentially, perhaps not win the case. Which they would. But just in case. He had only been invited to the second of Rudy's parties – the one with the petting zoo and tiki bar – and DB had been working hard to ensure this party would be the more memorable. Sure, there was Nino's party with its homemade cake and decorations first purchased in the 1980s, but that was more about them than Rudy, and he knew how impressed everyone would be by the extravaganza he was preparing. Even Sylvie, who seemed inexplicably weary of the whole thing. But it was all set in place now: Rudy was to have two parties, one after the other, in a sort of procession of celebrations like a Hindu wedding. Nino would hold his in the morning and DB theirs in the afternoon, and Rudy would helicopter into each like a celebrity. The guests could decide which party they chose to attend, potentially either and hopefully both, unless it was Naughty Niki who was at this point invited to neither as she had recently clawed superficial trenches into Rudy's cheeks when they were meant to be practising their sharing. DB wavered for a moment. Rudy had finally made the connection between very old people and the proximity of death, and was not un-vocal in sharing this information. And Mr Williams was an . . . aged man. But of course he would charm Mr Williams once more, because he was a charming young fellow, just like his father. And right now his father had a job to do and that job was to confirm the petting zoo man. Across from him, Nell stretched then returned to her goblin-like hunch over the keyboard. DB picked up his phone and dialled.

*

The day of the party arrived and Sylvie set off early with Rudy to help her parents prepare. DB had insisted on this arrangement, that Sylvie not lift a finger, and she had happily obliged. He waved them off from the driveway, then stole into the house, his dressing-gown whipping behind him in the breeze. The DJ had cancelled at the last minute – something Sylvie suggested may have to do with the two dozen or so instructional emails DB had sent him up to that point – so he'd been up most of the night putting together the ultimate party playlist. He wanted it to make a bold statement to the attendees about what kind of dad he was – why yes, that was The Specials playing at his son's party. The Pixies? They're coming up next! He'd cleared the backyard of the plastic paraphernalia abandoned by Rudy in past play, and dragged the outdoor setting from where it had been pushed to one side. He arranged the chairs around the perimeter of the yard, then decided this made it look too much like a 1960s prom, so instead he set the whole thing up to one side. He'd checked the barbecue had gas, there was ice in the garage freezer ready to be broken up and tossed into the drink stations, and he'd purchased enough fancy sausages to stock an Oktoberfest tent. He scattered items on the kitchen bench – venison sausages, salt, bread, a bottle of red – as if to say, 'Oh, hey, I was just being gourmet . . .' as guests wandered into the house. A whole section of the yard had been reserved for the petting zoo and DB imagined the sheer joy on his son's face when he arrived home from his no doubt pedestrian first party to find a veritable menagerie of creatures roaming his backyard. He planned to take a picture of Rudy patting a sheep or riding a goat, and get it printed nice and big so that Guiseppa could place it in the centre of her fridge door.

He spent the rest of the morning picking up platters from the deli, selecting craft beers, and negotiating the towering honeycomb double chocolate mud cake into the passenger seat. Once everything was in place, he showered, pulled on his carefully pressed outfit and styled his hair in the mirror. Rudy was already dressed in his matching outfit, which included proper big boy underwear because he was five now, and five-year-olds – Sylvie had assured Rudy – wore proper big boy underwear. It was almost time to pick up Rudy and Sylvie so DB headed out the front door, stopping to perform a last-minute scan of the house. As he closed the door a ute pulled up with the petting zoo's logo on the cab door. DB watched, frowning, as a young man climbed out smoothing the sides of his pompadoured hair.

'Here we are!' the young man, whose name badge read *Ravi*, announced.

DB peered into the ute's tray. There was a handful of cages housing an assortment of guinea pigs, rabbits and what looked like a terrifyingly obese rat.

'Is someone following you?'

Ravi looked confused.

'The animals,' DB clarified. 'Is someone following you with the rest of the animals?'

Ravi turned to his ute, gesturing as though its contents were the jackpot of a game show.

'This is it. The "Great and Small" selection. That was what you ordered, wasn't it?'

DB took another look at the cages. It was definitely an obese rat.

'Where are the great animals? The lambs and goats and things?'

Ravi's bright eyes sparkled.

'This is them – they're small but they're great! For instance, did you know that a guinea pig's coat is made up of five different types of hair? And that while they have four toes on their front paws, they only have three . . .'

Ravi trailed off, noticing the look on DB's face.

'I don't know what you were expecting, man. I mean, you picked the cheapest option so . . . Do you want me to go? You still have to pay.'

Ravi looked somewhat crestfallen and DB got the distinct feeling this had happened before.

'No, no, come in. They'll be expecting animals and these will do, I guess.'

He cast a disparaging eye over the obese rat, which seemed to be struggling to pull itself off the cage floor. Ravi followed him into the house.

'So where are the kids?'

'They're not due for another hour. I thought you'd need time to set up the animals. You know, release the lambs, tether the goats and whatnot. I was going to leave you to it while I pick up my wife and son from his grandparents' place.'

'Oh.' Ravi looked around the empty house. 'I mean, I need to bring in the cages but that takes, like, five minutes tops.'

So he left Ravi sitting in front of the television while he drove through the outer suburbs to Nino and Guiseppa's house. He had planned to pull into the driveway, leave the car running and dash in long enough to arrive to a hero's welcome, pluck Rudy and Sylvie from one party and lead everyone to the next. Only when he got there he had to drive up and down the Zambettis' cul-de-sac several times before he managed to squeeze into a narrow park. The whole thing was dense with cars, half-mounted across lawns, double-parked along Nino's driveway, boxing each other in with a snug familiarity. He spotted Tony's motorbike, parked almost across the threshold, like a shiny death-trap welcome party. From the house, the sound of laughter and accordion music danced through the air. DB squeezed between two cars, scraping his knee on a bumper, and grumbled up the driveway.

Inside, it was chaos. Children tore about the place, laughing with the joy of television commercial children. They clutched in their hands sugar-dusted biscuits and semicircles of *cassateddi*, Guiseppa's specialties. Parents stood in happy clusters, nursing plastic cups of wine and warming bottles of Carlton Draught. DB could smell the faint scent of grappa coming from somewhere in the house. He recognised only a handful of faces. A few parents nodded at him but most ignored him. He stepped into the backyard to find a swarm of children, delighted and screaming, crawling all over Nino as he played his accordion. Tony was nearby, lifting children like free weights as some of the mums looked on in admiration. He spotted Rudy, alone and shadow-faced by the grapevine at the end of the yard, and while it was a heartbreaking sight, a tiny part of DB felt better. At least someone was having a bad time. Rudy's face lit up when he saw DB and he bumbled across the yard with his awkward angular run.

'No one will play with me,' he whispered into his father's

ear, his warm breath scented with potato chips.

Sylvie, who was standing in the middle of a group of mums halfway through a story, raised her eyebrows at him as if to say, *Look how great this party is.* DB, Rudy in arms, raised his own and gestured to their child as if to say, *He seems to think it's shit.* And then Guiseppa appeared with a tray full of bubble blowers and the whole yard erupted in effervescent joy.

They drove home in silence, DB and Rudy. Sylvie had decided to stay, ostensibly to help her parents pack up, as had pretty much everyone else.

'We'll see you all in a little bit,' DB had called out as they left, though no one seemed to hear him above the fun.

Rudy had been sullen for a while then perked up suddenly.

'My zoo is waiting for me!'

DB thought of the lethargic rat and shuddered.

'You bet it is, buddy.'

When they got home the party was in full swing. That is to say, the balloon man had arrived and was now sitting on the couch alongside Ravi discussing the results of the previous evening's football.

'Help yourself to beer,' DB told them, because they already had.

There was the flush of a toilet and DB's father appeared in the lounge room. He crossed the room and handed a wrapped box to Rudy.

'It's a set of educational books,' he announced, before Rudy had had the chance to unwrap it.

'Your mother had a prior engagement,' he informed DB as he shook his hand in greeting. 'She's sorry she missed the party at Nino's because she's particularly fond of ethnic cooking.'

DB stole an embarrassed glance at Ravi. This was exactly how his mother would have phrased it, unflinching, as if it were still the eighties.

'My in-laws are Italian,' DB explained apologetically to Ravi, who looked up from the chip bowl, confused.

'This is some party,' the balloon man commented wryly, plunging a corn chip into the ramekin of guacamole, and DB pretended not to hear him.

In the meantime, Rudy had spotted the cages now sitting in the backyard and raced out towards them. Ravi pulled himself up from the couch, brushed the chips from his khakis, and followed him outside. DB was left in the lounge, staring between the balloon man and his father, who were now seated on the couch side by side watching a sports highlights program and eating the selection of expensive dips.

'I'll just pop some music on then,' DB announced and headed towards the sound system.

He un-paused the playlist and the opening chords to a Belle and Sebastian song began. There was the sound of the front door closing and Mr Williams appeared in the living area, proffering a bundle of helium balloons and an expensive box of whisky. The balloons said things like *Birthday Boy*, and *5 today!*, and *Congratulations!!!*, and bobbed around Mr Williams' head like bodyguards. DB realised that apart from the golf wear, he had never seen Mr Williams dressed in casual clothes, and that he had never imagined that these casual clothes would be so similar to a cowboy's. He even had a little buckle – well, a large buckle – that appeared to have a rearing horse on it.

'Young Mr Arnolds!' Mr Williams boomed, his face momentarily confused by the somewhat empty house. DB rushed over to relieve him of the balloons and whisky.

'That's good single malt there. Top shelf.'

'Laphroaig?' DB's father asked, turning from the television, and Mr Williams clicked his fingers in the affirmative.

The two men observed each other appraisingly, locking

hands in a bone-crunching grip. Neither of them mentioned the car park incident.

'One of my finest lawyers, there.' Mr Williams nodded.

'Takes after his old man,' DB's father replied.

DB looked between the two seasoned lawyers jostling for paternal recognition and his heart swelled outwardly until it butted into his ripening ego.

'I think it's time we barbecue,' he announced.

After some discussion they agreed that, seeing as it was DB's house, he should be the one who did the barbecuing while the rest of them stood around offering him advice. DB lined the hotplate with sausages in the event that there was a sudden mass arrival of guests from Nino's party. You never knew, what with the traffic, he explained to the others, and they nodded, kindly, in agreement. DB's father cleared his throat loudly.

'Ben's told us about the pro bono pilot,' he said, directing his conversation to Mr Williams.

The balloon man had made them all little balloon hats to wear and his father's was a nifty red and black pirate ship.

'Brilliant idea.' Mr Williams nodded, his rainbow top hat quivering as he did so.

DB's hat was meant to look like an elephant trunk with a pair of eyes set either side of it. He suspected from the way that everyone tittered whenever he spoke that it actually looked more like a penis graced by a tightly coiled scrotum.

'A lot riding on it, I imagine,' DB's father continued, sipping his beer. 'Reputation and whatnot. Rather embarrassing to catch a loss.'

'Quite a lot,' Mr Williams affirmed. 'But we're in safe hands, aren't we, Mr Arnolds?'

'I hear it's DB now,' his father replied, a merry glint in his eye. 'Or haven't you got the memo?'

DB jabbed at the barbecue with the tongs, slashing a gourmet sausage in half. Sometimes he disliked his father, who had never got his own memo that having a child occasionally meant allowing focus to be pulled from oneself. Sylvie had pointed this out to him, long ago when she was still attempting to get on with his parents, and he saw it now on frequent occasions. He suddenly remembered his own son and looked guiltily around the yard. Rudy and Ravi were huddled over one of the cages, peering grim-faced into it. Jesus . . . DB craned his neck to see them better.

'Watch the sausages, Benjamin,' his father scolded him, and then he'd been distracted by an argument between his father, Mr Williams and the balloon guy about the appropriate level of carcinogen required to perfect each sausage.

This had become quite heated, and everyone had insisted that everyone else was wrong, and the balloon man had taken offence at DB's father calling him a cheap purveyor of parlour tricks and left in a huff telling them it was weird to have a kids' party with no kids, and everyone had looked uncomfortable until Mr Williams started talking about the pro bono case again, and DB's father began pointing out all the ways they were going about it the wrong way, and suddenly DB could feel his chest getting tighter and the elephant trunk-penis felt like it was squeezing his brain to the point of explosion and the heat from the barbecue was radiating into his eyeballs and . . . there was Rudy like an escapee, holding the fat rat with a strange little look on his face, and DB realised the rat was quite dead and he'd wanted to shout out that the party was over there and then, even though it had never really been a party to begin with, so they could all just bugger off home.

'We need to bury Malcolm,' Rudy instructed the group, his voice solemn and respectful, for he had at some point christened the rat after their Prime Minister in what was an act of complete affection with no trace of irony.

'I really can't let you do that,' Ravi said, meeting DB's eyes. 'I need to account for all my animals.'

DB was ready to concur but then Rudy had looked at him with such hope in his eyes that he knew he needed this to happen.

'Please,' he whispered to Ravi. 'Please. It's his birthday.'

Ravi looked reluctant.

'I'll pay you more. For the dead rat and for the trouble.'

Eventually Ravi acquiesced, and the party had continued, just the five of them, only it had naturally turned into a funeral for Malcolm. They'd pulled their balloon hats from their heads as Ravi gently placed the rat in the little hole DB had hastily dug for it, then they'd looked on respectfully as Ravi scraped the dirt back over the top. Then they gathered in the house to eat venison sausages and commence the wake, Rudy adorned in a black cape he'd acquired somewhere, as well as a fresh pair of pants because he'd forgotten himself in the commotion and wet his old ones. Now, he moved between them all like a commiserating widow.

'There, there,' he told them each, patting their hands comfortingly.

'He watches a lot of documentaries,' DB explained as his father and Mr Williams looked on.

They lapsed into silence. In it, DB considered what kind of career move this was. Bold, he suspected, but in an adverse way. Mr Williams pulled himself to his feet, clearing his throat.

'We can't let Malcolm go without marking this solemn occasion with a good drop.'

He brought over the whisky and poured them all a glass.

'Perhaps a few words are appropriate,' he continued, taking up his glass.

He beckoned to Ravi, who shook his head. Mr Williams acknowledged this.

'Then I shall meet the task.'

He stood, gathering his thoughts, a finger to his lips as if quieting himself.

'I stand here today a man humbled in the face of death.'

DB glanced over at Rudy, who was utterly transfixed by the speech.

'I did not know Malcolm well but the few hours we had together demonstrated to me that he was a rodent of fine standing and good character.'

DB's father rolled his eyes but thankfully remained silent for his grandson's sake, perhaps because his mouth was full of whisky. Mr Williams paused, peering into his glass, rolling it gently in a circular motion. He shifted his weight from one foot to the other then continued.

'Some of you may know that I run a very large, very successful law firm.'

He paused, mostly for the benefit of DB's father, DB suspected.

'You may not know that my grandfather started this firm. His old man worked in one of the infamous Collingwood boot factories – you know, from *Power Without Glory* – and he made enough money to send my grandfather to university to study law, if you know what I mean.'

DB did and he was glad his son did not.

'So you can guess the kinds of upright citizens my grandfather started out defending. Arsonists, thugs, blokes who'd catch their wives up to no good with the milkman and sink their bodies in the Yarra. And those cases were the ones on which he built his career and the earliest days of this firm. It was my father who encouraged him to move away from criminal law towards commercial stuff, but my grandfather always had a soft spot for miscreants, defending them pro bono until he died.'

Mr Williams smiled fondly at the memory. To his right, Ravi glanced surreptitiously at his watch.

'Were they guilty?' Rudy asked, eyes wide.

Mr Williams gave him a conspiratorial wink.

'Not according to the jurors.'

He chuckled. So did DB's father, despite himself. DB acknowledged that this moment, though transfixing, was not his finest parenting hour.

'Anyway, what I mean to say is that my family has long stood by our principles of sacrifice in the service of others. Of offering our expertise to those in need, with no expectation of financial reward. And our belief that justice is for everyone, no matter who you are.'

DB glanced at his son again. Rudy had no idea what Mr Williams was saying but he seemed glad he was saying it.

'And in the same way my grandfather started our family's tradition of volunteering our services to those in need – something we are proud to continue to this day – today we have laid to rest a fine rodent who did the same, providing to the children of our community joy and happiness wherever he did roam.'

DB avoided his father's gaze, certain he would barely be containing his mirth. He wondered how much Mr Williams had drunk. Beside him he heard a sniffle.

'It's true,' Ravi agreed. 'No one really cared about him because he was gross and stuff, but he didn't let that deter him. He was always there, rain, hail or shine, no matter how much people preferred the guinea pigs or the rabbits. Even the mice. People preferred the mice to him.'

'I loved him,' Rudy spoke up, and DB saw the tears in his eyes. 'I loved Malcolm.'

'As did we all,' Mr Williams agreed. 'As did we all. On that note, I would like you all to raise your glass to Malcolm. A rat above all other rats.'

'To Malcolm,' Ravi repeated, raising his glass.

233

Then they all went outside and released the helium balloons into the air one by one. DB watched as the last one floated away. *Congratulations!!!* Malcolm. May death be kinder to you than life.

Later, once they'd had some cake and everyone had gone home, Rudy climbed into his father's arms. He had, throughout the whole afternoon, seemed completely unperturbed that no other guests arrived. Sylvie had messaged to say she would spend the night at her parents' as the party had kicked on into the evening and there was much cleaning still to be done.

'Did you and Mummy fight again?' Rudy asked, pawing sleepily at his eyes.

DB swallowed uncomfortably. 'Of course not. Mummy is coming back tomorrow.'

Rudy watched him a moment, then looked away, distracted. 'Everything dies,' he said stoically.

For a moment DB felt gutted at the strange and lonely party he had thrown his son, but then he saw that Rudy was smiling as he drifted into sleep. And he realised in a sad and peculiar way that this was probably exactly the party Rudy had always wanted, and that perhaps this was worth something in the end.

19

Patrick

North Facing Window: Michael 'D'accordion' Smith
July 2016
By Rik Lee

If you have two ears and have walked the outdoor malls of the north, chances are you're familiar with Michael 'D'accordion' Smith. 'I grew up near the SA border but have spent the last five years busking around the world. London, Berlin, a stint in Rome that didn't end too well. Mostly Europe, though, because they're more open to busking. The Balkans in particular were incredible – I learnt a lot there, both musically and spiritually.'

Now settled in Greensborough, D'accordion plies his trade right across the region. 'Anywhere my bike will take me – that's my rule. It's a pretty incredible way to make a living and counter-intuitively, easier than if I were to park myself in the middle of the CBD. There's more community in the suburbs. I guess that's it. People aren't as stressed.'

One of the biggest misconceptions D'accordion finds is that people assume he's a penniless artist. 'I do well enough. Plus, my girlfriend, she's a painter but she's also nearly finished studying early years education. It's not like we sleep under a bridge or anything.' D'accordion and his girlfriend are saving money to build a tiny house. 'Nothing special. Just a tiny place to call home.'

His favourite thing about the north is how many people seem to have spare change on them. 'It's the continental Europeans – people who carry all their cash on them – who are a busker's best friend because SOMETHING SOMETHING SOMETHING

Patrick hunched forward, squinting at his own indecipherable handwriting. The word looked like 'swamp fiend' but that couldn't be right. Something? Smarmy? Who was to say . . . He consulted his notes, trying to remember what he had been planning to write next but this train of thought was shuttered up in the depot now. He stood, stretching, then filled the electric kettle. He waited as it stirred to life, leaning his frame against the kitchen bench. *It won't boil if you watch it,* he thought to himself, casting his eyes across the rest of the small living area. It wasn't much to see, the sideboard crowding the space, proud and mighty like a fallen monarch. It masked the emptiness though, which had reminded him so much of the bare Anatolian guesthouse room, its wall-to-wall solitude disrupted only by the little bed he had dragged to the centre. How it allowed him to see all around, a tiny turret in the middle of the cramped bare room, where the quiet noises of the landlady's daily chores scraped in through the window and swept under the threshold and time passed as he tried to make sense of the senseless. How this hadn't worked, so he had eventually pulled himself from the room and wandered, disoriented, down the quiet streets peopled only by the wild-coated cats and dogs who knew nothing of the off-season, and it was in this manner that he had stumbled upon the barber, surprising them both when Patrick sunk into the worn red leather chair. He'd looked between the stylised images affixed to the wall, then pointed to one of a clean-shaven young man, his head clippered into a military-style buzz cut. The barber nodded, turning down the volume of the little television mounted on his wall, then set about pulling from his drawers the tools of his trade.

First, he laid out before him the electric razor and its assortment of heads, blowing into the blades to clean them. Then he gestured to the heads one by one, miming to Patrick their lengths as they tapered from his own longer locks to the soldiery shave of the poster. He waited, his rough dark hands stroking the ends of his Atatürk moustache as Patrick scrutinised the heads, giving an obliging nod when he selected the shortest. Then he set to work, removing Patrick's hair in great curving sweeps, the hair falling about the old towel around his shoulders. When this was finished, he removed the head and ran the naked blades along Patrick's hairline, delicately tracing the same arterial freeways of his increasingly frequent headaches. He worked slowly, carving new borders across Patrick's nape, along his temples, folding the tops of his ears to run the clippers down and back to where he'd started. When this was complete, he reached for a pair of long metal scissors, winding a cotton ball around the end, then dipped it into a clear solution. He set the cotton ball on fire then swiftly dabbed it against the outer rims of Patrick's ears one after the other, the hairs sizzling, then dropped the ball into the sink where it fizzled out. The barber disappeared for a moment, returning with two small metal cups. He poured hot water from one into the other, working it into a foamy lather with a wooden handled brush, then painted Patrick's throat and cheeks in soft arcs.

Patrick watched as the barber opened a drawer and pulled out a small straight razor, and suddenly his heartbeat quickened. The barber knocked the razor against his palm and the blade came away, then he replaced it with a fresh blade housed in a little paper sheath. He laid out a square of card on the bench to catch the foam as he shaved, then turned back to Patrick.

Patrick watched his reflection in the mirror, the razor moving towards him, and it started again, racing up and down the fresh lines of his haircut, pounding, scratching, throbbing with urgent pain. He couldn't breathe. His breath refused to draw. Then the razor was at his throat, the barber pulling it down his flesh in one long drag, and it was all too much. As the barber pulled away, Patrick slid from the chair and backed out of the little shop. Pulling a handful of lira from his pocket, he stammered an apology as he let it tumble to the chair, then he was gone, off, out into the street to blindly stagger back towards the empty guesthouse. *Stop, please, I only want to help.* And people had stared at him, the smattering of locals going about their daily business, startled by this wide-eyed man with a face full of foam and his hands clutching at his shorn temples, and it was then that he had met the Australians and the terrible situation was made that tiny bit worse. And now, sitting here in his boxy Melbourne apartment, now he could feel it again, the same tensing of muscles around his nape, as the limberness fled his body. Taut, coiled, ready to react, ready to spiral and stumble and nauseate him once more.

There was a knock at the door, first timid then flattening into a confident rat-a-tat. Patrick pressed his palms over his face, the cool of his fingers a brief relief, then rose from the table. He opened the door cautiously. Seymour was standing there, his hands plunged into his pockets. He read Patrick's surprise.

'The rideshare,' he explained. 'It used your address.'

Patrick opened the door and Seymour stepped inside. He led him down the dark hallway and into the cramped living area. As they pressed past the sideboard, Patrick saw Seymour trail his fingers lightly along its wood. In the kitchen the electric kettle was rumbling. It let out a loud click as it switched itself off, making them both start.

'This place is terrible,' Seymour observed, leaning against the counter, arms crossed in front of his body.

'The rental ad said cosy,' Patrick murmured.

This made Seymour snort.

'Our place is cosy. This place is like a crypt.'

They both waited until the word had run its course, ricocheting about the room and dusting them both with sadness. Seymour turned and reached up to the cupboards, pulling out two mugs. Patrick watched him navigate the little kitchen, finding easily the items required to assemble their tea.

'Top drawer for spoons, farthest right cupboard for mugs, farthest left for tea, just like at home,' Seymour explained, placing the full mug in front of Patrick. 'There's no milk, though.'

'I don't drink it anymore,' Patrick said, and Seymour flinched.

They sat opposite each other, sipping their tea. After a while, Seymour collected their mugs and rinsed them at the sink. He sat back at the little kitchen table-cum-desk and placed one hand on top of the other.

'Are you coming home?'

Patrick couldn't tell if this was an invitation or a clarification. He moved his hands awkwardly in some unspoken sign of the unresolved. Seymour exhaled sharply.

'What is going on? We take a break, fine. You need to go do your thing, fine. But you were always coming back. You were always meant to come back. Wasn't that the agreement?'

Patrick stared at his hands. 'I am back.'

Seymour looked critically around the room. 'Are you? Is this you being back? Living in a poky little apartment with hardly any furniture except Grandmother Lee's great bloody sideboard like you're some kind of Romanov? I don't recognise any of this stuff. I don't recognise you. You're thin and your clothes are strange. You look like a sad thin man with strange clothes and a patchy beard. What happened to you?'

Patrick shrugged, avoiding Seymour's look. Seymour let out a yowl, throwing his hands into the air with frustration.

'What is going on with you? What is going on with us? Why won't you say anything? I know things went weird over there. I have the internet –'

'Can we please talk about something else?' Patrick interrupted, not looking up.

Seymour sized him up. 'Fine. Let's talk about something else. The weather perhaps? It's shit, isn't it? Politics too. We've already talked about real estate so perhaps we've run out of topics.'

Patrick brushed this aside. 'How's the gallery?'

Seymour stared at him, then allowed himself to soften.

'Same old. Sales are up and down, and I live in fear of my young staff usurping me. They have so much energy. They'll be up all night working on their own stuff then turn up at the crack of dawn because they're too wired to sleep and be at it for hours while I'm on my third coffee after a big night in, bingeing on Netflix.'

'They will inherit the future,' Patrick said.

'They can pry it from my cold dead hands,' Seymour scoffed. 'The Vince Pemblebrook show is happening. Took months of negotiating with the little turd. You know he turned up with a list of demands as long as a Kerouac scroll and sat there waiting while I read through it. All the staff are contributing pieces, so you can imagine how focused they are at the moment.'

'Are you contributing anything?'

'God no. You know how I am with production. No, I'm too busy making sure we cater to Vince's whims and fancies. Currently I'm trying to source vegan mock *gyros*, and there's a

long and painful story of how we got to this point that I shan't
bore you with, but suffice it to say, it all better be worth it.'

'I'm sure it will be successful,' Patrick offered.

'Are you, because I'm not,' Seymour replied. 'And if it's not
successful I look like an idiot, and who wants to show their
work in an idiot's gallery?'

Patrick fought the instinct to reach out to him.

'Uni students and vanity artists?' he offered.

'We can only hope,' Seymour sighed. 'Because without the
gallery, I'm not really anything, am I?'

They sat in silence a moment waiting for Patrick to fill it.
When he didn't, Seymour rose from the table.

'I should leave you to your work.'

He hovered awkwardly, halfway towards the front door.

'I could stay?'

They were both surprised by this. Seymour looked around
the empty shell of a room. In his eyes Patrick saw a glint of
something that could have been pity or love, and he deserved
neither of those things right now.

'You could,' he replied softly, avoiding Seymour's gaze. 'But
I don't think you should.'

After Seymour left, Patrick tried to return to his work but
it was futile. All he could picture was Seymour's face and the
almost imperceptible flashes of hurt that had punctuated his
visit. And without warning Seymour's eye became that poor
man's, and his face twisted in a moment of indescribable agony
and it was the same look of agony that had set Patrick running,
spiralling back to this country because all it seemed he was
good for was hurting others. Where he had stood, jet-lagged
and shrunken, the sun shining on the polluted river with its
corpses and chemicals sunken below, and wept for being home.
He stood up, the chair skittering into the wall behind him,
and grabbed at his coat. Outside, the cold hit his cheeks first,

spreading across his exposed skin, and he shoved his hands deep into his pockets. He walked without purpose, stalking down the high street and along its branches in great pointless rectangles. Eventually he tired, crossing the street in search of somewhere to eat. He passed a young man, eyes and nose peering out from the depth of his scarf and beanie, a clipboard in his hands.

'Help a child in Syria?'

Patrick blinked. 'What?'

'Sponsor a Syrian child?'

Patrick squinted at the young man. He was dressed casually, the clipboard unexceptional.

'Did you know that there are thousands of Syrian children living without clean water or electricity? Unable to go to school? Unable to access basic medical treatment?' The young man motioned earnestly at his clipboard.

'Where are you from?' Patrick asked him.

'UNICEF,' the young man replied cheerily.

'Where's your ID?'

'Left it at home.' He shrugged, embarrassed.

'Why aren't you wearing a UNICEF T-shirt?'

'In this weather?' the young man replied lightly. 'It's a few layers under my coat.'

'Show me,' Patrick demanded.

The young man looked nervous, stepping back slightly.

'So far it is estimated that recent airstrikes in Aleppo have –'

'Show me your T-shirt.'

Patrick stepped towards the young man, seizing his lapels.

'Man, you're crazy! Fuck off.'

'Show me your T-shirt!'

The young man pushed at Patrick's hands. The clipboard fell to the ground, papers fluttering about. A few people had stopped to stare.

'Show me your T-shirt! This is a fucking scam. People are dying there and you're fucking scamming people.'

The young man scowled, slapping at Patrick's hands.

'Fucking let me go.'

'You lying little bastard. You should be arrested for this. I arrest you. This is a citizen's arrest.'

A crowd had gathered around them, fumbling for their phones. The young man grabbed Patrick's wrists, wrenching them sideways. Patrick held on, his fingers tightening.

'Let me go!'

'Never!'

The young man jerked to one side, his coat ripping as Patrick tumbled after him. Patrick righted himself as the young man seemed to pause to gather his strength, then he lunged forward, slapping Patrick across the cheek.

'Leave me alone.'

Patrick threw himself forward, wrapping the young man in an awkward hold, his arms pinned to his side.

'Someone call the police!' Patrick hollered as the young man struggled furiously.

Someone had indeed already called the police, who arrived to find the two men locked in an awkward, unwelcome embrace.

'They're fighting,' someone explained, and the officers looked unconvinced.

'This is a citizen's arrest,' Patrick crowed, before the young man got an arm free and smacked him in the mouth.

Later – and it was a considerable amount of time later – Patrick sat in the passenger seat of Harry's Mazda outside Preston police station. His top lip had started to swell and his cheek was crimson in the cold.

'They're not going to charge you with anything,' Harry explained, starting the car and turning the heat vents towards Patrick. 'Or the kid. I had a chat with them about everything.'

Patrick didn't respond. He felt exhausted. Harry cleared his throat.

'I know what happened,' he said gently. 'Over there. I ran into some guys from the network who were over there too, and they told me. I . . . Here's a number. Critical incident counselling. They might help, mate.'

Patrick took the piece of paper and shoved it into his pocket. No one knew what happened. Not all of it.

'Sorry I called you. They wouldn't let me go without someone coming to pick me up. I . . . there wasn't anyone else.'

Harry considered this for a moment, stretching his hands wide across the steering wheel. He turned back to Patrick.

'You probably don't know this but I studied physics for a semester. First year of uni. Bloody hated it. Too many letters masquerading as numbers. But there's this one thing that has always stayed with me. Physics 101, this classic Galileo experiment to prove wind friction or something like that. You take a feather and a bowling ball and drop them from the same height at the same time. Normally, because of the air resistance, the feather falls at a slower rate, while because the bowling ball is so much heavier, it's going to hit the ground faster, right?'

He waited a fraction of a second for Patrick to nod then continued.

'But if you put them in a vacuum and take away the air resistance, both objects fall at the same rate. Now to me – and I could be wrong because what would I know with one failed physics subject to my name and all – but I've always thought that's pretty neat. If you take away resistance, we all fall the same.'

They sat in silence for a moment before Patrick raised his eyes.

'Am I the bowling ball?'

Harry gave him a smile. 'Most of us are, mate.'

Hot air streamed from the vents and Patrick found himself leaning back into a fug of weariness. His eyelids drooped a moment and he wondered if he were to let them close how long Harry would let him stay here. The car came to a stop. Harry reached over and placed a hand on his arm.

'Is there anything I can do to help? I only want to help.'

The weight of his fingers brought Patrick back to the present and he reached for the door handle. *Stop, please, I only want to help.*

'I'm fine, Harry. Thank you for today.'

20

Evangelia

Turks and Greeks at Loggerheads
August 1974

Tasty coffee, delicious sweets – there's a lot to thank those new Australians for! But it's not all fun and games at the newly opened Consulate General for the Republic of Turkey, with Greeks descending en masse to protest what they refer to as the illegal invasion of Cyprus by Turkish soldiers. The long disputed Mediterranean island is now the scene of chaos and confusion as the United Nations seeks to broker a ceasefire between Turkish forces in the north and the recently installed pro-Enosis government in the south. Bolstered by signs in Greek that this reporter was unable to decipher, protesters donned head-to-toe black as they hurled abuse and rotten fruit at the locked consular doors.

Northcote resident Andreas Georgiou told reporters that the protest was to voice the concerns of Melbourne's wider Greek community at the treatment of their fellow Hellenes, as reports emerge of Cypriots from both sides being expelled across the buffer zone that has split the country in two since the early 1960s.

'The whole community is here,' Mr Georgiou said. 'My whole family, even the babies. We are here in solidarity with our people.'

A counter protest is rumoured, with suggestions Turkish-Cypriots will stage a similar action against the alleged mistreatment of their own compatriots. With many of the protesters taking time away from their day jobs working the fruit and vegetable stalls at the markets, if there's one thing this reporter is certain of, they won't be wanting for projectiles.

Representatives from the consulate office said that services would continue as usual, but to please telephone first.

Evangelia pulled the faded newspaper article closer, squinting at the grainy image accompanying it. She could make out her father, his face grave, and she supposed the infant in his arms was her. A small child grappling with a little Greek flag was most likely Lydia, her pudgy cheeks beaming for the camera in complete discord with the severity of the rest of the group. She recognised a number of people, faces discernible from the muddy waters of her memory, people she'd called aunty and uncle despite them having no real familial ties. Where was she? She scanned the faces again, then pushed herself back in the rickety library chair, her eyes tracking upwards to the great dome of the state library. Her mother was not there.

It had been Carole's idea to approach the library and seek out any place her mother might be mentioned in the clutter and collections of the state. They'd returned to her with a long list of suggestions: well-known broadsheets, Greek language newspapers, things – so many *things* – that had been donated by people who, unlike her, had discovered boxes of memories left behind by departed parents. And this, from a university student newspaper, cloistered by articles about controversial lecturers and the unwinding of the Vietnam War. She had spent days sifting through them all, bent over the desk as around her present-day university students jabbed at their mobiles and napped over their textbooks. She had pored through them with an eagle's eye, but still she could not find her. Her mother was not here. Her mother was not anywhere. Maybe she was out of shot, a slight outlier the camera had failed to capture. Maybe she was somewhere nearby, with the other women, preparing food as Evangelia always seemed to remember. Not quite a part of anything but off to one side, slicing up halva or waiting patiently over a *briki*. She'd made coffee while the world grew wings, Evangelia thought, but there wasn't a story in that.

Lydia might know, her memory blessed with the advantage of her slight seniority, but the sisters had not spoken since the meat platter incident and Evangelia refused to be the one to broker peace. They'd set up their buffer zone, somewhere north of Bell Street, and both were abiding by the terms of the dispute. There was no phone contact, no commenting on the Facebook posts of mutual acquaintances if the other had got there first. If they were to cross paths at school pick-ups, they looked away, either to their mobiles or at some distant curiosity, until they were no longer within speaking distance. The children were to follow this protocol too, proxies in a conflict they did not quite understand, though Evangelia sometimes arrived at the school gates to find them huddled together conspiratorially. She would call their mobiles, watching as they shrank guiltily from their cousins in a way that made her feel both vindicated and sad, and she would blame Lydia for this too.

It was strange, this not talking to each other, and for the first time since she could remember Evangelia felt something like freedom. For hadn't she always been there, Lydia of the raised eyebrows and judgemental lips? Stabbing a finger at all the ways Evangelia was getting things wrong. The way she'd worn her hair as a child, the fear that kept her from shaving her legs well into high school. All the things her mother had loved in her, but that made her too embarrassing for her elder sister. Lydia who had somehow succeeded in having her last name changed on the school roll so that she was Lydia George, exotic and gregarious, and nothing like stubby little Evangelia Georgiou, whose name confounded everyone and whose moustache sparkled in the schoolyard sun and who couldn't shake the woggy accent everyone teased her for. Who kept the lunches their mother made for them instead of throwing them in the garbage bin like Lydia did each morning. Who said somethink instead of something and practised her *kalamatianós* by herself in the backyard while Lydia was off pretending she wasn't related to them. Who had spent weekends helping pickle olives and turn the buckets of backyard tomatoes into *saltsa* while Lydia was off at university learning from textbooks how exciting it suddenly was to be multicultural, then returning home to tell them how they were doing it all wrong. That they were meant to be having parades and linking arms with all the other cultures of the city instead of shuttering themselves away in their diasporic little community and failing to learn the language properly. Who had never quite been exactly the person Lydia expected her to be because this person changed, constantly, and she could never work it all out even from the youngest of ages. Who had woken night after night as a child to the sight of a dragon, ferocious and startling, slithering through the bedroom towards her, only to disappear into the shadows when her shrieks sent their mother scurrying into the room again and again. And there had been Lydia, laughing in the bed beside her, taunting her sister about her nightmares. The *matáki* her mother strung up above the bed didn't seem to work and each night the dragon returned, silent and serpentine, its eyes on Evangelia alone. *That* Evangelia – that Evangelia felt free and she felt angry and she couldn't for the life of her work out where the hell her mother was supposed to be.

Evangelia collected her things and walked to the photocopier to make copies of the article. At least she would have something to report back to Carole and the rest of the class, proof of the gaping nothingness of her mother's life: a vacant newspaper clipping and a fraction of a factory story. She laid the page face down in the machine, closed the lid, then watched it spit out the reproductions. The pages shot out of the machine, and each time, her mother was still not there.

21

DB

Dear Jonesy,

I have of late found myself perusing the online biographies of life's great men: Weary Dunlop, Whitlam, Mawson and the Ice Men. And what fascinates me is the obvious connecting strand – and one I see in myself, and you – of a benevolent sense of command and restraint. Of control and serenity. A mastery of

There was a hammering on the toilet door.

'Other people in this house need to use the bathroom too.'

DB saved the draft email on his mobile and hastily pulled up his pyjama trousers. He opened the door to find Sylvie dancing about like a child, her knees clenched together.

'Are there not other toilets in this house you could use? I distinctly remember this being a selling point when we picked this place.'

Sylvie ignored him, pushing past. 'This is *our* toilet.'

The door slammed shut and DB stepped into the adjacent bathroom. He stood for a moment washing his hands, working the soap around the joints of his fingers and under his wedding band. As he did, he leant forward, peering into the bloodshot eyes reflected back in the mirror. He'd hit a rough patch of insomnia of late, his mind poring over the details of the pro bono case as the court date drew nearer. And of the terrifying potential fallout from losing. There was much riding on it – Old Man Williams had made this clear at Malcolm's wake and in the smattering of exchanges they'd had in the elevator since. And the thought of letting him down – of letting them all down – well, it didn't bear thinking about. But he wouldn't, of course. He was onto it. They were onto it, he and Nell. Madeline was working on a second affidavit. A better version. So it would all be fine. And he believed her, didn't he? And thus things would all be fine.

He raked his fingers down his cheeks, catching the sharp overnight stubble. It was all fine, all going to plan, on course for a win and that plum new office. Chin up, game face on, off we go! DB twisted the tap then leant forward to splash his face with water a few times. As he emerged, he noticed Sylvie's contraceptive pill packet sitting amid the clutter of toiletry items strewn across the vanity. He was peering at it as she came in, nudging him aside to wash her hands. When she was done, she reached for the packet, popping a pale yellow pill and swallowing it.

'That was Saturday.'

'What?'

'Saturday,' he replied, pointing at the writing above the pill casing. 'Today is Thursday.'

'Oh, that?' she said dismissively. 'They don't match up.'

She reached past him for her toothbrush. DB continued to stare at the packet, his brow furrowed.

'But how are you meant to know?'

Sylvie brushed this off.

'I forget sometimes and then make up for it when I remember. The days don't align anymore because I guess I've forgotten it a couple of times.'

DB considered this.

'But it's four days off.'

Sylvie spat toothpaste into the sink, then shrugged. DB did not know a great deal about contraception but he knew enough to know that it was meant to be taken every day. That if you didn't, the baby might be made. And if the baby was made, the baby was often born, and the baby being born was not part of their current schedule, and certainly not part of their current budget. It wasn't part of the plan. Suddenly, his heart seemed to be racing. If they abandoned the plan, they wouldn't be able to keep up with the mortgage, not on his current wage. And if they couldn't keep up with the mortgage they would have to go further into debt. And Rudy wouldn't ever be able to go to private school because they'd have to dip into the money DB had been saving for this, and this meant he would most likely do drugs, or sell drugs or, as was increasingly the case, cook drugs, and then sell them and do them, and then they'd never sell the house because no one wanted to buy a former crack house. He watched his wife calmly flossing around her top left incisor.

'How often does this happen?'

'Does what happen?' she slurred through the floss.

'The forgetting. Are you . . .'

Suddenly everything seemed to click into place. The mood swings, the fighting, the perpetual displeasure at everything he did. He stepped back, surveying his wife with shock.

'You're pregnant! This is why you've been so grumpy.'

Sylvie's hands dropped from her mouth and she spat into the sink.

'That's why you think I'm grumpy?'

DB thought backwards.

'When was your last period?'

Sylvie glared at him. 'I don't know. I skip them sometimes. A month or two?'

DB sank down onto the edge of the bathtub, head in hands.

'Stop being so dramatic,' Sylvie sighed. 'It hasn't happened before and I've been forgetting for years.'

'Years?' The whole carefully planned timeline of their life was now flashing sporadically. It could have happened at any time?

'Would it be such a bad thing, anyway?' Sylvie asked. 'We certainly don't want Rudy to be an only child.'

Sylvie thought only children were emotionally fragile. DB was an only child.

'It would be terrible timing,' DB wailed. 'We're not ready for this. Our finances aren't ready. Rudy isn't ready –'

'– what has Rudy –'

'– and you've been drinking and eating all that salami your father keeps hawking on us and –'

'– do you hear yourself right now –'

'– and I haven't done the maths. I'm not ready. My spread-sheets aren't –'

Sylvie's hands flew up and she stormed out of the bathroom, shutting him in. DB slid gently backwards until he rested in the bathtub, curling his legs to fit. He stayed there, his head alive with figures, as he tried to adjust their life to this potential – prob-able? – new course. Sylvie would take maternity leave – that was fine – but there'd be a shortfall if she went the full year, but by that time he'd have the promotion so presumably he still had another, what, eight months until the birth plus thirty-two weeks mat leave, which was surely enough, provided they took no holidays and did no more renos, which meant they'd have to wait on the plan to upgrade the second car, which wasn't ideal, but perhaps they could look at some kind of refinancing of the current car . . . Eventually, DB awoke from what had been an unexpected exhausted slumber. The cool of the porcelain had crept into his skin and his neck ached from the strange angle it was on. He eased himself awkwardly out of the bath, washed his face under the tap, then made his way out of the bathroom. The house was empty. He glanced at the clock on the microwave. Ten am. Bugger. He'd have to drive. He dressed hurriedly, then made his way to the garage. Sylvie had taken the good car, so he folded himself into the little sports car. They'd joked when they bought it that it would never fit a baby seat and this suddenly didn't seem so funny anymore. Shit shit shit. As he sped towards the city, DB tried to calm himself by running numbers through his head again. He hurried into the office, avoiding eye contact.

'Breakfast meeting,' he announced loudly, though no one was listening. 'That's where I've been.'

He slid into his office chair and roused his computer to life.

'I didn't realise you had a meeting,' Nell said, peering over her computer screen.

'I did,' he assured her, then pretended to take a phone call.

A few hours later, he felt himself caught up enough on work that it was okay to take a little break. He opened a new internet tab and typed in, *Can you get pregnant if you skip the pill?* Then he searched, *How many pills do you need to skip to get pregnant?* Then, *What happens if you are pregnant and are on birth control pills?* This last one, at least, relieved him. At least it wouldn't be a mutant baby. Just a regular run-of-the-mill money-guzzling baby. He scanned a few more paragraphs, anxiously angling a wedge of Turkish Delight into his mouth.

'Are you working on the Miller file at the moment?' Nell asked.

'Yes,' DB replied, and minimised the tab.

He made himself focus on work, which wasn't hard as there was enough of it to get through. The day dragged on and eventually the clock hit 6.00 pm.

'Madeline's just emailed through her new affidavit,' Nell announced, her eyes on the computer screen. 'Do you want to see it or do you want me to go through it first?'

DB's mobile vibrated beside him and he glanced down. It was a text from Sylvie. *Rudy and I are staying at my parents' tonight.* DB stared at the message, imagining his maybe-pregnant wife curled up in her childhood bed with their son breathing softly beside her. Nell cleared her throat. She was watching him, waiting for an answer. The pro bono case. It needed their attention now or else. Or else. If they got this right it might mean the promotion, which meant more money for the maybe-baby that was maybe on its way. He watched Nell watching him, one hand hovering near his mobile and the other at his mouse.

'What do you want to do?' she pressed, raising her eyebrows expectantly.

Columns shifted in his head, worlds, lives, pathways too.

'You start on it and I'll get the pizza,' he decided, pushing his mobile into his pocket.

22

Nell

Notes for affidavit – Madeline Murray

How do you even start this? Where do you begin? There are distinct points, obviously, like the first glimpse across a crowded Carlton pub or the slide of a diamond ring down a foolishly eager finger. But those are a bit too obvious, aren't they? A bit too same same, like a made-for-TV movie. Because that's what it is, really, when you look at the basic structure of my life. The big house – actual picket fence and all – the charismatic couple. I'd be played by some middle-aged actress who the audience recognises but can't quite place, whose Hollywood offers dried up alongside the spread of her crow's feet. Eric would be the male equivalent, only he'd probably get nominated for an Emmy and skyrocket back into the A-list. So typical it doesn't seem real or interesting at all.

Perhaps, for me, it all started at the breakdown of my parents' marriage when I was eight, my father relocating to continental Europe for a sabbatical that never ended. I blamed my mother, of course, for making him leave, never considering for a moment that he may, in fact, have chosen to leave and that it was, as I found out many, many years later, his decision entirely.

He was a genius, my father, or at least that was how people liked to portray him, a man of high standing whose infamous stubbornness and pig-headed perseverance saw a number of notable breakthroughs in whatever scientific research he spent much of his time immersed in. Physics of some sort is all I know because my mother never bothered to ask too many questions and he apparently wasn't that forthcoming with information. She knew he was important and won awards, and I suspect that was as much as he needed her to know.

I wonder sometimes if this was where it started, because his leaving so early meant I didn't truly have the opportunity to age in his presence and see for myself the impact of his moods at home which would, I imagine, have vastly changed my perception of him. Instead, I was left with an entirely unreasonable portrait of what to me was a normal functional relationship, and the blueprint for what I would come to accept in my own life. Brilliant mind = patient wife. This is not to say he was an abusive man exactly, but more that his stubbornness and temper fluctuations seemed to me a basic and acceptable hallmark of every relationship. My mother only spoke of these things decades later, at the time employing the fortitude and resilience often found in generations of women raised on the land. I suspect this influenced me too, this lineage of long-suffering women, there in our veins and pulse, helixed into our DNA and stored on the stiff starched shelf of our stout upper lips. Taught by my mother to just get on with things because that was how they were. He was a genius, she long maintained, and brilliance needed to be accommodated.

Eric was my first proper boyfriend. I didn't have much to measure him against except that to me, and those around me, he seemed perfect. Handsome and clever, the two of us raced each other for top marks each semester like some kind of legal studies power couple. The other girls in my share house were smitten with him too. He would show up at all hours unannounced, with flowers or longnecks or expensive items from the Lygon Street delis that none of us could afford. Checking in to see that I was okay, that I didn't want for anything, that I had everything I could need – the way we'd always imagined our boyfriends would be, but never seemed to happen in real life. Like a prince, as embarrassing as that sentiment is when put down on paper.

It's an insular little world that cloisters around the residences and share houses of Parkville, everyone in and about each other's business like the gossip columns of 1920s Hollywood. We would happily have been the golden couple if this was a title on offer, as if it were entirely natural and expected that the two students 'most likely to' were among other things most likely to end up with each other. And we were proud of this – both of us – because those things matter so much when you're young, don't they?

We had tremendous fun in those days, inventing games to aid our study, buying buckets full of sour warheads to keep us going and rewarding ourselves for our all-night study with a second full night down at the Tote listening to Magic Dirt or Spiderbait. We'd styled ourselves on the Clintons initially, his'n'hers lawyers set to take the world by storm, only to later use them as a cautionary tale for all that we wouldn't become. This was the time of his impeachment and I'd judged her so readily for her choices in a way I would never do now. 'I'd die before hurting you,' Eric told me at the time as we watched a media-lashed Hillary stand by her man, and I'd taken this as proof of his love. I sometimes wonder how early I knew things were wrong, somewhere deep beneath the excuses and accommodations I occasionally made for him.

When our final results came out I hid mine from him, letting him believe that he'd bested me for the fourth year in a row, sensing this was important. How prophetic that turned out to be, as it eventually became part of his arsenal of insults to hurl at me throughout our marriage. Second best, he would taunt, unaware he was mistaken.

Engagement seemed the natural next step, something our friends around us seemed to be doing, and seemingly inevitable when you'd reached the point our relationship was at. How proudly he displayed me around his office, his clever beautiful wife – second best, but nonetheless! – with her impressive job in politics and the promising future this conveyed. His colleagues' jealousy comforted him, as if I was a secondary validation for his achievements in life. They would joke at barbecues about stealing me away with jewels and travel and towering houses – as if that was all it would take – and he'd play along with the suggestion that the heavy gem on my finger was a security investment to keep me by his side. I would play too, despite my reservations, careful not to come across too flirty or coy because where once he had laughed at this, soon it aroused suspicion and irritation, particularly after we'd married. He couldn't bear to live without me, he told me, so I wasn't to joke about it. Besides, he was recently promoted and it was important he look the part, and what kind of man couldn't keep control of his own wife?

Marriage changed everything. It was as if that ring bound me to him in a way that allowed no room for independence or difference. Where once his suspicions had been endearing, they now became unreasonable, and he monitored every exchange I had with a male in his presence with the thoroughness and precision of a scientist. You were flirting with the butcher, he'd say, disgusted and wounded, as if a half-kilo of lamb chops was a euphemism for something unseemly. You do it to make me jealous, he'd say, convinced I'd made lingering eye contact with strangers I never even noticed.

Nonetheless, we bought the big house and the fancy furnishings to go with it, and things progressively got worse from there. He never actually hit me. He was clever like that. You don't actually need to, though, do you, if you go about it the right way. What he would do was punish me if I did something wrong. First with things like silence or a sudden feigned lack of hunger in the middle of an exclusive restaurant, then eventually with unexpected work emergencies that left me solo at family occasions, hurriedly untangling plans for couples' weekends away with friends or unpacking clothes from suitcases as planes took off without us. Then, after some unpredictable amount of time – two hours, one day, an excruciating weekend – things were suddenly back to normal and we'd giggle about his silliness. It was always little things – insignificant things – that led to these huge reactions. This is what caused the separation. I had a porcelain statue – an ugly little thing – but it had been my grandmother's and her grandmother's before that. A quaint hokey little eggcup shaped like a duck. It lived on the mantle by a framed photograph of my grandmother and was one of the few possessions of hers I had. I'd worked late one evening, arriving home to find him sulking about his spoiled plans to surprise me with a candlelit dinner. We fought, as we often did at that time, and when I got home the next day the eggcup was gone. It took me a while to realise, sitting on the sofa watching the television, but eventually my brain settled on why things looked ever so slightly off. I turned the house upside down, scouring each of its giant vacuous rooms after work each night, until one day I found it in the back of a drawer in one of the guest rooms. It was crushed into a fine dust, identifiable only by a few bright red shards. He never mentioned it but I could tell when I returned to the living room that night that he knew I knew. His smirk. You wouldn't understand, but it was his smirk that always gave him away.

Why did we get back together? What a wonderful question that is. I went to stay with my mother and no one – not she or my friends – could really understand what the fuss was about. Surely eggcups, even ancestral ones, aren't worth a whole marriage? they'd say. Eric too had started a campaign of redemption, showing up at my mother's door, emailing my friends, trying – they all told me – to work out what he had done wrong. He loved me unbearably, they relayed, and just wanted to make me happy. Perhaps, they suggested – his words in their mouth – it was the stress of my job.

It wasn't right to work such long hours and my wellbeing was more important than any employer. Eventually, I too decided I was over-reacting. It was, after all, a hokey old eggcup and not worth losing my marriage over. So I went back. And soon enough I was pregnant. And it wasn't hard, then, to be convinced that I needed to leave the job that had caused so much strain on my marriage and wellbeing.

The boys were a gift to both of us. To me they were these wondrous, helpless little creatures who needed to be loved and encouraged and cuddled. To Eric, they were the perfect conduit through which to berate and control me. You see, I was never very good with them. Latching issues, teething troubles, reflux, sleep-lessness and nappy rash; these were all evidence that I wasn't doing it properly. I didn't go back to work – children needed a mother at home, Eric believed – and besides, I'd lost my confidence by then. If I couldn't handle getting two kids under three to sleep each night I certainly couldn't manage a politician's office anymore.

Eric was a great father, except when he wasn't. Then he would mutter and moan, as if the boys' inability to keep their food down was a personal insult to him. It was always on his good work shirts, he once told me, as if they did it on purpose. He worried, too, about their intellects and milestones. They didn't do things fast enough for his liking and he was sure I didn't provide enough mental stimulation during the day. He would email me articles from work with instructions on the types of games to play with children to ensure the highest level of cognitive development. No play for play's sake, but targeted activities 'proven' to produce the most intelligent of children. Once, when he thought I was in the other room, I watched him playing with Josh, who in the middle of his terrible twos had decided everything around him was an idiot. 'You're the idiot', Eric snapped back at him, then became red-faced and angry when I reprimanded him. I was imagining things, he told me, projecting my insecurities onto him. He was worried about my mental health again – was I coping all right?

He worried about my wellbeing a lot. He knew how wearing finances were so he took care of all this himself. It was unnecessary stress – why would I argue with that? At the time I thought him generous and caring. Who wants to worry themselves with that kind of thing? But I realise now that I know absolutely nothing about our finances. They are, in a practical sense, his finances. The house, the cars, the savings – we could be on the verge of financial collapse or be completely mortgage free for all I know. And this makes me feel so incredibly stupid, how little I know of these things. Spending was similar too. Rather than bore me with all the various accounts, I simply had access to a debit card linked to a little household account from which to buy all our daily expenses. It was topped up automatically from his wages – I needn't worry about that, he said – and I didn't. I didn't need to. If ever big purchases were to be made I would do all the research then he would go out and buy them on his credit card, which was linked to his work or something; there was a complicated reason why it wasn't in both our names. And this was never a problem, until now.

The thing is, none of it seemed a problem at the time. Not on its own. Not as a collection of discrete distinct behaviours. But now when I piece it all together like some kind of terrifying tapestry I see how these things wove together to bend my actions – muffle my choices – to shape the things I did or said so that I wouldn't upset him. The way I retreated bit by bit until I had nothing left to control. The way I withdrew, shut off, became dependent. The way I let myself believe his concern came from a place of compassion and care, and that I was the one at fault. Because this is what they told me, those supposed sounding boards around me – my friends, my family, all assuring me that I was overreacting, imagining things, making mountains out of molehills and other damning idioms.

I don't know when I started drinking, or rather, when it became an issue. Or if it ever really was an issue in anyone's eyes but Eric's. I was fine during the day but what started as a gin and tonic as I prepared dinner eventually turned into a couple of glasses of wine over the course of the night. Never when it was just me and the children, and only after they'd been tucked into bed. It was never more than a glass or two to help me sleep, and when this stopped working, perhaps a glass during the day so I could manage a nap before picking up the children. Never anything dangerous, but of course why would Eric represent it as anything other than that? Easier to convince everyone I'm crazy, isn't it?

I fell pregnant again in 2012. Maybe it surprises you that I still had sex with him, but he was my husband. Often it was more out of a sense of duty – he would sulk and mope and make things miserable if I didn't – but sometimes it was something we both wanted. The pregnancy wasn't planned and I worried because of the drinking. I was a few months along and hadn't realised because my period had been irregular since the boys, which meant a few months' worth of drinking in that vital first stage. I told Eric one night, convinced he would share my worry and we'd work out what we needed to do to make things all okay. He didn't say anything, simply rising from the outdoor setting where we had hidden ourselves from the boys, and walking back inside. I watched him, hugging myself against the cold, as he turned and stared at me through the sliding glass doors. Then he raised his hand and locked them. I froze. I was convinced he was joking. That he would unlock them, hold me and comfort me, but he turned his back and joined the boys as they played on the carpet by the fire. I watched them for a while, that while turning into minutes, and eventually I walked to the door and knocked. It was freezing outside and I was hardly dressed for it. Only the boys looked over; Eric continued to ignore me. He must have said something because they looked away quickly. I continued to knock and eventually he rose, made his way over and flicked off the outside lighting.

I stood there for what seemed like hours, wanting to bang at the glass but anxious of startling the boys. Instead, I paced about *the yard. We'd built ourselves a fortress, you see. High gates, secure locks that needed keys. Eric had even set up security cameras at the entries and exits which he could monitor live from his phone, ostensibly to keep people out, but he could also see if I was coming or going. As I paced the yard, I realised I couldn't get out. I curled up on one of the pool chairs, too cold to sleep. Soon enough the inside lights went out and I stayed there until I could bear it no more. I started pacing again, shaking the fence, my bare hands numb. I was worried about the cold, you see, and what it might do to the poor creature growing inside me. Eventually I climbed my way up the high side gate, pulling myself up to the cast iron spikes lining the top. But my limbs were too numb and I stumbled, losing my footing and crashing back down to the ground atop the wooden outdoor chair I had used as a ladder. My chin split and a rib broke against the heavy furniture, and this was when Eric finally unlocked the doors. At the hospital they told me I had lost the baby. I don't know if it was the fall or if in that moment the poor thing realised it was better off somewhere else, but Eric never spoke of it again. I told the hospital staff that I'd come home late, forgotten my keys and, not wanting to wake my family, had attempted to get in the back way. It seemed like the best thing to do at the time.*

I don't want to suggest that Eric became a monster after this. He was still the same man who enjoyed playing with the boys, would smother me with attention and gifts, and promised me the world when he felt like it. But the time between his silences became smaller and smaller, and all those things that had once been so romantic morphed into obsessive and frightening. 'I can't bear to live without you' became 'If you leave I will kill myself and it will all be your fault'. I had stopped drinking when I found out I was pregnant but now there didn't seem to be a reason not to. I could have a quick drink in the morning, sleep it off after lunch, then be back on my feet to pick the boys up when the school bell rang. I was very good at it, you see. What I couldn't manage was my anxiety. It had started properly after the miscarriage, refusing to diffuse over the years. It didn't help that a perfectly happy family activity could turn suddenly depending on Eric's mood, and something that one day may have brought laughter and togetherness, the next resulted in mockery and abuse. I couldn't read him anymore and this unpredictability was terrifying. When he was feeling loving, Eric would fret over me and encourage me to get psychiatric help for the anxiety. Then when he was upset he would use it against me, threatening to tell people about my drinking and mental health issues if I ever tried anything on him. Then he would become concerned again, telling me I was overreacting, that he'd never say things like that, that my anxiety was making me imagine things. This is what made it hard to leave, my own internal doubt that I was justified in making that kind of decision. Besides, my marriage wasn't like my parents', I told myself. Mine wouldn't fail and my children would always have both their parents around. Because he was good with them, mostly, just like he was good with me, mostly, and it took a long time to realise this reason for staying was really the reason to go. This all led to the school incident.

You know what triggered it? You'd think after all this time it would have been something huge, but in the end it was a simple joke. I was driving the boys home from school one afternoon and they were sharing jokes in the back seat. Silly knock-knock jokes that had them in fits of laughter and had descended into them just saying whatever came into their heads. Josh: Knock knock. Leo: Who's there? Josh: Daddy. Leo: Daddy who? Josh: Daddy's home so we better run and hide! That was it. That was what pushed me over the edge. It bothered me all night and the next morning when I woke it was still there. It festered inside me all day until I could take it no more. This was one of the things the alcohol did – it made me brave enough to believe I was strong. That I could leave.

So after two glasses that morning I was adamant I was leaving. I would go to school, take the boys and just run. But what I hadn't realised was that the new medication I was on for the anxiety didn't mix well with alcohol, and instead of brave and confident, by the time I got to the school I was a complete mess. Eric blamed the alcohol entirely, feigning concern like he had done for years, and promising I would get treatment as part of the plan agreed to with the Child Protection worker.

I didn't drink again for a long time. Until recently, actually, after everything that happened with the police. I hadn't touched a drop the night he called the police. He knew I hadn't. I made dinner that night, we ate together as a family, and once the boys went off to watch television I told Eric I was leaving him. No tricks or plans. Straight out told him it was over and I wanted out.

When I tried to leave the kitchen he refused to move, blocking the doorway with his body. I asked him politely. I asked him again and again. I was leaving and he needed to move out of the way. He wouldn't though. Planted his feet and crossed his arms. I was being unreasonable, he told me. I wasn't in my right mind. I was a risk to myself and he couldn't let me leave. He wouldn't let me leave. Even if I tried, I would never be able to leave. And I would regret it, when he was finally through with me, if he ever let that happen. He smirked then, the way he always did, and that was too much for me. I yelled at him to move. I told him again that I was leaving. When he wouldn't move, I started shoving him, but he didn't do anything, just stood there blocking my way, and the walls of the house were suddenly closing in on me as he took a single step towards me. So I started throwing things at him, first plastic things then plates, glasses, anything to make him move. Scrambling about the kitchen, trying to get out. That's where the bruises came from. Like I said before, he's never hit me. He's clever like that. Just stood there smirking, taking it all. Not fighting back. And it was bursting out of me – this fire I'd swallowed up for so long – until I winded myself, struggling against the counter to try to open the locked window, and as I stood there doubled over and panting he calmly pulled his mobile from his pocket and made a call. And in less than sixty seconds he managed something I had dreamed about doing for years, and it seemed so easy for him.

When the police arrived I was momentarily relieved. I was so sure I would tell them everything and finally we would be free. But as my adrenalin wore off and reality set in, I recalled the words he'd told me so many times before: If you leave me I will take everything from you, including the boys. And what had seemed a hollow threat for so many years now felt more real and certain than anything else did. So I lied to them, covered it all up, because if I didn't he would take everything from me. And despite all that, he's done so anyway, hasn't he?

'What are you still doing here? They work you hard, don't they?'

Nell looked up from the computer, blinking slowly. There was a clatter of metal on metal and Lou, the office cleaner, emerged from the doorway.

'Just reviewing something,' she replied, minimising the screen. 'I'm done now.'

She emailed it to DB so he'd see it when he returned with the pizza. He'd review her notes and then they'd set about pulling Madeline's story into shape.

'I'm surprised, you know,' Lou continued, hefting the vacuum pack onto his back and connecting the nozzle. 'On account of me being late and all. Caught up in traffic. They've closed off the streets up by Fed Square again. Swanston and Flinders. Some candlelight thing for those poor bastards who died in the detention centres.'

He tugged at the cord, wrestling it into the wall socket.

'Poor bastards,' he said again. 'Every time you turn on the news it's this, that and the other thing, isn't it? All the killing and the war and the violence. But what you gonna do? State of this world, eh?'

Lou adjusted the straps of the pack, shaking his head.

'What you gonna do?' he repeated to himself, the vacuum roaring to life as he flicked the switch.

Nell watched him, her head suddenly overwhelmed by the hiss and thunder and everything else that ran rampant around the world. She laid her head on her desk, her arms shielding her ears, and tried as hard as she could to block out all the noise.

Part 4

23

Aida

As a teenager, my parents' home in Yusefabad in Central Tehran was both the centre and the end of the world. My mother, who lived through both revolution and war, discovered in peacetime a newfound anxiety about the world outside her home over which she had little control. She predicted death and misfortune every time any of us left the building, the strength and fortitude of her war years gradually replaced by a fatalistic, year-round sense of foreboding that was nourished by the American detective series she had taken to watching late at night on the illegal satellite channels. This meant that it was not until my later teenage years that I was able to join my friends in exploring our bustling city, the cinemas, galleries and fast food restaurants in which we passed our time and tested the boundaries of our changing identities. How far back could we push our scarves and what gait best attracted the right kind of attention? Who were we at home and who were we among friends? Even then I would have to wait by the window until my friends arrived in convoy to spirit me away into the outside world, in case, as my mother seemed to fear, I would spontaneously forget how to cross the street on my own and end up flattened by an errant taxi or affixed to the front of a motorcycle like a shrieking masthead on a ship.

These were the same young women I would soon attend university with, me studying English and journalism while they stuck to engineering and the sciences. Headscarves at all angles, makeup sneakily applied after leaving our parents' sight, we would charter our teenage course through the chaos of cars towards Tehran's artistic hub. Young men in uniform patrolled nearby, their eyes more interested in us than the streets, completing their two years of compulsory military service and keen to be anywhere else. Stuck in our final years of schooling, we felt the same way, our eyes and shoulder muscles enjoying the break from study as we laughed and joked our way through the crowded city.

Of all Tehran's streets, Valiasr is my favourite. A predictable choice you might say, but watch as it snakes its way for nearly eighteen kilometres through the city like a tree-lined backbone. It starts in northern Tajrish, nestled at the foot of the Alborz, where the cool mountain air in summer makes for expensive real estate, home to Tehran's elite and the former summer estate of the Shah. It ends at the railway station in downtown southern Tehran, amid the bustling hole-in-the-wall stores and the shabby slums housing the unemployed and vulnerable: Afghan refugees, stateless Feyli Kurds, and the city's poor urban drift. To travel it in its entirety is to journey through the many faces of this smoggy metropolis. The maze of off-white apartment complexes stacked like boxes, as if the mountains are a machine churning them out and spitting them across the city. Buildings half-complete, construction halted by the unpredictable economy that monies and bankrupts people with equal abandon. High-rises cloaked in graffiti honouring the martyrs, exulting the Ayatollah and, until it is noticed, calling for freedoms the whole world should have. Drivers beat at their horns, motorcyclists risk their lives and traffic lights flash a constant amber just to keep you company. Driving too has its own unique rhythm, Peugeots and Paykans and the Saipa Pride – our home-grown 'moving coffin' – weave and wheeze and create more lanes than the painted lines suggest. Horns bleat a chorus of complaints – Watch it, idiot! Green light, you fool! Congratulations on your wedding, friend! Often in winter, my friends and I would simply find a starting point and set sail along Valiasr, enjoying the chill on our cheeks as we forgot about our studies and anxieties.

One day during a rare break from studying for our upcoming exams we thought to go see a movie at the Artists' Forum. It was myself, my best friend Shirin, our classmates Sonila and Maryam, and Shirin's cousin Leila whose religious parents only let her out of the house if Shirin was with her. When we arrived, the line for ticket sales stretched almost as long as Valiasr itself, so instead we purchased plastic cups of tea from an enterprising young man and sat watching the line as it heaved and crawled towards the ticket stall: director types in thick square frames and clean-heeled boots, artsy older women in flowing tunics and muslin scarves, young couples defiantly holding hands, and worried moustachioed men clutching brown-suitcased lives.

Soon we grew hungry and made our way down Valiasr to Ferdowsi, tracing our fingers along the rough brown brick of the British Embassy as we walked in the footsteps of our parents and their long-gone days of activism. Inside Café Naderi, we ordered soup and tea, shadowing generations of writers, artists and intellectuals who had talked of different revolutions from the safety of these red-tableclothed confines. We'd taken to coming to Naderi as often as we could, spurred on by our burgeoning realisation that soon we would be free of our parents, coupled with the youthful desire for meaning. We talked of art, thinking ourselves smarter and worldlier than we were, discussing the work of Farideh Lashai and the Picassos, Warhols and Lichtensteins we'd seen at the Contemporary Art Museum. Shirin told us she had understood entirely what Picasso was trying to say and we all nodded in agreement with her. At this, laughter erupted from the table behind us. I looked around, embarrassed that we'd been overheard. A group of people sat there, older than us but still young. The women's scarves were pushed far back on their heads, delicately hanging at

275

the curve of their crowns with casual indifference. The men were tall and thin with holes proudly marking their dark sweaters. They smiled at us, not unkindly, and my cheeks blazed red.

'Do you think they're intellectuals?' Shirin whispered far too loudly, causing them to erupt with laughter again.

I doubted it – none of them looked like my father or his sombre-faced friends.

'Only Afshar,' one of the women replied, pointing to the solemn-looking man opposite her. 'He thinks he's an intellectual because he smokes and wears black, but I know for a fact he listens to pop music. He only says it because he thinks it will help him get more girls.'

Laughter rippled around the table again. Afshar ignored them, attempting refined dignity from behind his coffee cup. I watched, absorbed, their confidence unsettling and exciting me, wanting to be noticed and ignored in equal measure.

'What brings you here?' the same woman asked, her bright red lips smiling encouragingly.

We were silent. No one wanted to admit that these trips were part of the many little acts of subversion we attempted to cram into our day-to-day lives between school, homework and obeying our parents. That they were practice for the people we hoped to one day become. People, I thought, like them.

'Nothing much,' Shirin replied casually. 'Just chatting about art.'

'Picasso, right?' Afshar grinned and we all looked down, embarrassed.

'Farideh Lashai, actually,' Shirin continued, her feigned confidence impressing me utterly. 'We were discussing the post-revolution tensions of creating a new Iranian identity and the use of Persian and/or Islamic iconography in modernist expression.'

This was met with impressed looks from both tables, and only I knew that this was word for word the topic of an assignment we had recently completed in class.

'What did you decide?' Afshar asked, his dense eyebrows raised in interest.

Here Shirin squirmed, for she had failed the subject.

'It's complex,' I cut in, draining my teacup. 'Too many layers to get into. What were you discussing?'

'The election results, mostly,' the young woman with red lips spoke up. 'How Ahmadinejad will prove nothing but trouble.'

The others looked at her hesitantly.

'They're kids,' she replied. 'They're not going to cause us any grief.'

She turned back to us.

'He was an incompetent Mayor and he'll be an incompetent President, you mark my words. There'll be nothing but hardline religious conservatism from him, you'll all see.'

'You can't blame them, though,' added another young man who we later found out was Afshar's brother Hamid. 'Not after Khatami. There's only so much reform the Guardian Council will let through and Khatami pushed it to the brink. You know how many reformist candidates got disqualified from this election? We'll be lucky to see any kind of reform for another decade.'

We sat nodding in mute agreement, our home lives having prepared us in no way for this level of discussion. For the most part my father increasingly kept his views to himself or a select group of trusted friends, and my mother simply thought that all politicians were rubbish. A waiter brought fresh tea and the discussion continued, Shirin and I pitching in where we could. They were university students, all of them, and Lida – the one with the red lipstick – kept an anonymous political blog in her spare time.

'It's called Follow the Leader.' She grinned. 'Do you think anyone will ever guess?'

She told us more about her blogging and of other friends who also sought out the stories of corruption and nepotism that dogged *our country. We'd never met anyone so political before, who wore their beliefs so openly and proudly.*

'Aren't you worried you'll get caught?' I asked, cursing myself for sounding so young and cautious.

Lida simply shrugged as if this thought scarcely registered in her mind.

'How can I expect anyone else to tell these stories if I won't do it myself? But if something happens to me, hopefully there will be others willing to take my place.'

She sounded in that moment so much like my father. I remember feeling heavy and weightless all at once as the scale and possibility of my adulthood finally became apparent. You know the kind of epiphanies you have on the cusp of growing up, where things seem so clear and certain before life complicates matters?

'More importantly, though,' Afshar spoke up, 'is who will tell the story of Hamid's spectacular moustache?'

The table erupted in laughter once more, all except Hamid. Hamid, they told us, was an actor. Not in the way that all Iranians claim to be actors or poets or singers, but in a genuine demonstrable way. He'd almost performed under Bahram Beyzaie, Afshar informed us, only he'd turned up on the wrong day and had been replaced. Hamid had all the while sat in embarrassed silence, his fraternal tolerance tested as his large hands hovered self-consciously over his top lip. It was, in fairness, a wondrous moustache, long and tapered like a Qajar-era Shah.

'He means it ironically,' Afshar added. 'Though he keeps getting stopped because Ershad think it's too international.'

Unlike his brother, Afshar's pursuits were more political, with pre-sunrise proclivities for spray-painting state-owned walls among his many interests. He was also in an underground metal band who produced two versions of all their songs – one that was acceptable to Ershad, the Ministry of Culture and Islamic Guidance, and a far more political version they distributed via the internet. All these

things I would discover later, crammed together in the brothers'
tiny apartment swapping contraband books with Lida and helping
them re-alcoholise non-alcoholic beer in plastic jerry cans hidden
beneath the bathroom cupboard. And later, just the two of us,
listening to Afshar's music side by side on the couch as Hamid
begrudgingly roamed the streets with his comical moustache until
the cold forced him to return. All this from the girl who won the
national essay-writing competition! But all that came later. Right
then I was just a young schoolgirl charting a future that was full of
so many sparkling, dangerous possibilities.

Later that day, not wanting to return home yet, we walked
through Laleh-zar, the old entertainment district that now housed
various stores selling light fittings, lamps and other illuminating
paraphernalia. A single long street, it had once been home to
more than twenty cinemas before the revolutionary government
shut them down. Still today the posters of the movies that had
been showing at the time are plastered to the outside walls, frozen
and hopeful and sombre. We had joked often that where once the
rich and famous had their names up in lights, now only the lights
remained. One of the many ironies of the revolution, it didn't seem
as funny that day. We chatted, our feet dipping into the gutter as
we wandered aimlessly through the streets. About the tediousness
of classes, our frustrations with our parents, whether Shirin should
ask for a nose job for her birthday. About Lida and Afshar, and the
things we'd discussed.

'Imagine once we're at university,' I gushed, Lida's number
safely saved in my mobile.

'I'm going to wear lipstick every day,' Shirin announced, her
face defiant far from the presence of her strict doctor father and
engineer mother. 'Different from Lida's, though, maybe more of a
coral colour.'

We discussed her options given her fair skin tone, a remnant of
the Armenian ancestry somewhere in the branches of her family tree.

'We'll call her when we graduate,' I decided, emboldened, my future unfolding before me with the clarity and precision of the young and determined.

You know how sometimes people write a letter to themselves at sixteen? To impart all the things they wish they could have known then – the wisdom, the knowledge, the cautions? It's so easy to write that letter, but I wonder if, given the opportunity, you would ever actually send it? Or is the journey itself what everything is all ultimately about? And what would I have said to someone so full of all those dreams?

The meat was stuck to the floor, dull and defiant. Aida arrived at work to find Kat and Nina huddled together by the counter, staring down at it in confusion. Hairs had collected about it so it looked like a sad dead toupee, and a little trail of ants were engaging in an orderly early morning picnic. Something viscous – garlic sauce, perhaps – had crusted around it, white and faint like chalk outlining a body on a busy New York street. No one recalled dropping it and no one volunteered to clean it up.

'You'd need a bloody paint scraper.' Kat shook her head.

'All I'm saying is it wasn't there last night when I closed up,' Nina insisted.

'Well, it was there when I arrived, and apart from Peter I was the first one here,' Kat replied.

The three of them looked towards the back room where Peter was squirrelled away sifting through the cash log and trying to make his columns balance.

'We could rock paper scissors?' Kat suggested.

'I'll buy whoever cleans it a *cerveza* in Cusco,' Nina countered.

This had been a running joke for weeks now, ever since Nina had announced that following the completion of her final exam she was heading to South America. She was finishing soon and had invited them all along – Kat with her two small children and Aida with her empty bank account – and they'd been playing along since.

'Imagine me on the Inca Trail,' Aida had laughed, not reminding either of them that without a permanent visa, she could not leave the country.

They stood observing the increasingly rank hunk of meat on the floor.

'There's not enough beer in the world –'

Aida cut herself short as Evangelia burst in, her entrance accompanied by the spasmodic explosion of the little bell above the door. She looked distracted and tired.

'What are you all standing around for?' She frowned. 'Did someone die?'

The three women looked at the mess on the floor. Nina stifled a giggle. The mess stopped Evangelia in her tracks. She observed it with first confusion, then disgust, then rage, her face cycling through her own mini version of the seven stages of grief. *Seven stages of beef*, Aida thought to herself, though it was more likely lamb. As she stood before them Evangelia sought the appropriate words for this situation. The first she settled on was a cuss word, the second a command.

'What the shit is that? Answer me, someone.'

Kat shuffled her feet nervously. 'It's, well . . . this morning . . . just there.'

Evangelia frowned at her non-sentence. She looked to Nina for clarification.

'It's, well . . . Peter?'

Evangelia's frown sunk deeper into her face.

'It's certainly not Peter.'

'Not even after a big night out?'

The words slipped from Aida's mouth before she could stop herself. Nina's eyes bulged and Kat swooped her head to hide the laughter scrambling out of her mouth. Evangelia stared at Aida, her mouth open. A snigger slipped out.

'You might be right about that. I've never seen someone so enamoured of testing their own wares. I feel like the consigliore to one of those drug lords on the telly – don't get high on your own supply, I keep telling him, but he doesn't listen, does he? Promises he keeps away from the spit, but scales don't lie, right?'

She barked out a series of short laughs. The women joined in nervously. Evangelia looked at them for a moment with something close to warmth. A tepid, brackish warmth.

'Meat throwing everywhere in this family right now,' she muttered cryptically. 'Still, though, someone needs to clean it up. It's an OHS issue plus it smells terrible.'

'I'll do it for double pay,' Aida offered jokingly.

She sensed Kat and Nina's eyes flick to Evangelia. Evangelia raised an eyebrow. For a moment, it looked as if Aida was about to receive the kind of tirade they were all so used to. Instead, Evangelia pursed her lips.

'Don't push it. Remember whose name is above the door here.'

In reality it was actually Jemal's, the long-departed owner of the Mediterranean grocery that had graced the lot prior to Peter's *gyros* store, but this wasn't what Evangelia meant. So Aida begrudgingly scraped the muck off the floor for the same sub-minimum wage she always got while Nina and Kat retold the preceding events over and over, Aida becoming cheekier with each retelling. In the back room they could hear the comforting duet of Evangelia and Peter's usual marital-business discord.

Eventually, they fell back into their everyday rhythms. The day was busy, as Thursdays often were. The gradual spring thaw meant customers had once more started using the outside tables, so Aida spent the day shuttling out to catch the refuse and rubbish from the tabletops before it scuttled off in the breeze. She had just reached for a sauce-stained wrapper when someone caught her arm.

'Aida?'

She whipped around, startled by the Tehrani accent.

'It's me, Massoumeh! From MITA! Ahh, you look terrible. Your hair! What happened to you? We never see you!'

Though it took her a moment to recognise her, Aida remembered Massoumeh. They'd been in the detention centre in Broadmeadows at the same time, just before they were released into the community. Massoumeh was a hairdresser, comfortable and constant in sharing her opinions. She was blonde now, all detailed makeup and flashy clothes, when inside she had been duller, flatter. At one point she'd become prone to erratic crying, convinced the guards were keeping her mail. She'd come with her husband, Aida recalled. The whole family, in fact.

'Massoumeh! How are you?'

Aida leant over, kissing her cheeks, left right left. Massoumeh shrugged, her strong perfume wafting over Aida.

'Good as one can be, what with the waiting. Immigration here is slower than Tehran! Who thought that was possible? I'd go crazy if it wasn't for the hairdressing. You know what it's like – finally out of detention and all you want is some highlights to make you feel like a person again. Even the ones who want to keep wearing the scarf, they're too scared to, so you can imagine how busy I am! I could do yours, you know. No charge.'

Aida batted away the offer.

'And how is your husband? The children?'

'Mansoor? He's well enough too. You know him, never bends an eyebrow. The children too. You remember he had an uncle here? He's working with him, in a café closer to the city. Nice little place. Lots of customers, all the young hip people. Iranian food but also international dishes. Hot chips. Everyone always wants hot chips. The best *kabob* in Australia but people come for the chips. We're famous for them.'

Massoumeh's face grew secretive and she leant forward, one arm on Aida's.

'Say! You remember Fariba? Big lady with the funny teeth? Her husband is back in detention. Broke the code of behaviour. Driving without a licence. Back in MITA and maybe back to the island. Refuses to return to Tehran voluntarily so he's stuck in detention until who knows when. She can visit him, though. At least there's that. Not like the other ones – you know, the Sri Lankans and the Afghans – sent back without a word. Happened to one of the boys working for Mansoor's uncle. Went in for an interview and never came back. Shocking, isn't it? Still, what can we do but wait?'

She paused for a moment, then her face broke into a wide grin.

'Why don't you come work for Mansoor's uncle? He needs more staff. What do they pay you here?'

Aida told her.

'Is that even legal? You'd starve on that. You must come work for Mansoor's uncle, no arguments. It's the least I can do. You were always so kind, helping us with our forms and things. You still writing? I'm sure you are. Our very own Ferdowsi of the cell block! That's settled then, you'll work with us. Here's my number. It's much nicer there, closer to the city, not out here with the rest of the bridging visas. Nothing wrong with them but you know how it gets. So much sadness and never any good news to share. Exhausting. You come in Monday, okay? Take the weekend for yourself. Maybe get those highlights. You'll love it there. Sometimes we play the '97 Iran–Australia World Cup qualifier on the television just to heat things up a bit.'

Aida hesitated, breathless from listening to Massoumeh. Here she was different, nothing like she'd been inside.

'Monday? Are you sure?'

'Positive.' Massoumeh beamed, leaning in to kiss her good-bye. 'If we can't look after each other, who do we expect will?'

Massoumeh turned to leave then paused.

'You know what, give me your address. I'm coming round. Tonight, okay? We can't have you working in the café looking like this. You're a strong Iranian woman, not someone who lives in the forest. Okay? *Areh. Khodafez*, Aida-joon.'

She left in a cloud of perfume and exuberant waves. Aida walked back inside, her hands full of litter and her mind full of possibilities. She would take the job. Of course she would. She would get a decent wage. She would be treated with respect. She would need to tell Evangelia. Oh. She paused, sucking in deep breaths. Of course she could tell Evangelia. She had stood in the front of the crowd facing down Basiji. She had smiled as the vice police searched their car for contraband, never finding the alcohol hidden beneath the spare wheel. She had won the national essay-writing competition, for god's sake. She paused before the back room, knocking first tentatively then a little more confidently. Evangelia and Peter looked up in surprise when she entered.

'Is something wrong? Is there a fire?' Peter asked, confused as to why his staff would breach his inner sanctum.

'I've come to tell you that today will be my last day. I will be finishing this afternoon and I'd like my pay, please.'

Peter's mouth fell open. Red rippled across his face, starting from his ears and finishing around his jowls.

'You, you . . . Such disrespect,' he began, but Aida cut him off.

'Please don't talk of disrespect to me. Have a look at your-self first.'

Peter's eyes widened. 'Don't you start with me. My parents came to this country with no money and an empty suitcase and –'

'And did they get this kind of treatment? Were they cheated out of their pay? Is it now your turn to do the same?'

Peter's mouth fell open and he glanced at his wife, nervously scanning her face.

'What is she talking about, Petro?' Evangelia asked coolly. 'Because it sounds like she's talking about the kind of bullshit our parents put up with, and she better not be talking about that kind of bullshit, because we are not going to be the kind of people who do that kind of bullshit. Am I understood, Petro?'

Peter looked at his feet then at the ceiling then at an assortment of other places that were not his wife's face. The two women's eyes met. Aida held Evangelia's stare.

'Give her the money,' Evangelia said quietly. 'All of it.'

As she accepted her money, Aida watched Evangelia's curious gaze. It was not the respect of equals, but it was near enough. Then she left, with promises to catch up with Kat and Nina and her final full pay still sticky in her hand. As she did, she heard for the final time the explosion of marital discordance from the little back room.

*

Aida entered the house happy and hopeful, slapping the money down on the kitchen table. Elham, who had been sitting drinking tea, looked up, startled.

'Guess who starts a new job on Monday?' Aida announced.

Elham's reaction was slow but when it came it lit up her face.

'Oh, Aida-joon! Such good news. We will have to celebrate.'

'I saw Massoumeh today, a woman from MITA. A hairdresser. She's coming around tonight to do our hair.'

Elham nodded vacantly. She rose from the table, looking around.

'I . . . Oh, yes, I have something for you. I found it this morning on my way back from walking Niki to kinder. Perhaps it was in anticipation of this news.'

286

She disappeared for a moment then reappeared, dragging a great hulking object across the linoleum.

'What is it?' Aida asked as Elham nearly toppled over under the weight.

'Look!'

Aida approached the object, circling round. It was a mirror, ornate and cumbersome, its golden etchings chipped in sections.

'I found it on the roadside,' Elham told her. 'Someone wanted to throw it out but I thought you might like it.'

Aida observed the mirror. It looked like something from a mafioso's boudoir or a budget theatre production set in pre-revolution Versailles.

'I love it,' she approved.

She caught her reflection in it, a tired gaunt face framed by dark un-highlighted hair.

'And we must celebrate your wonderful news,' Elham said. She propped the mirror against the wall. 'A celebratory meal. It will be ready in time for Massoumeh.'

She crouched before the fridge, her mind assessing its contents. '*Ghormeh sabzi*,' she announced. 'Without the *sabzi*.'

Elham pulled items from the fridge then opened the pantry cupboard.

'Come, Aida.'

Aida looked at her, surprised.

'It's a celebration, not a restaurant. It's time you learnt how to cook.'

Aida crossed the kitchen to the counter.

'Okay,' Elham began, pretending to roll up her sleeves. 'You cut up this onion and I'll start with the meat.'

They worked side by side, Elham issuing orders as Aida fussed about the kitchen. The smell of frying onion filled the room and was then muddied as the lamb, turmeric and kidney beans were added to the pot.

'You can't get the right greens here but spring onion will do,' Elham said, scraping them into the pot with a knife.

She helped Aida measure out the fenugreek and parsley, then set the stew to simmer.

'Normally you'd leave it for five hours but we'll cheat a bit tonight,' she said. 'A couple of hours then we'll add the dried lime just before it's done.'

She stood back, hands on satisfied hips. Aida breathed in, the familiar smells transporting her across the oceans and into the kitchens of her mother and grandmother. She imagined her mother's face on discovering that her daughter had cooked something. She pictured her now, leaning over the bowl suspiciously, tasting the smallest morsel from the tip of the spoon as if testing for poison. The surprised smile spreading across her face as she found herself alive and, better yet, impressed. Perhaps Aida would make it for her one day, once she had her visa and could start to save the airfare. Her father's face flashed into her mind but she pushed it away for the moment. *Not now, Baba.* Now was for celebrating.

From the moment Massoumeh arrived the house was plunged into wall-echoing motion as she set about preparing her makeshift salon. After smothering Aida in a hug, she introduced herself to Elham, pulling her into her chest. Elham's startled eyes met a lycra-clad bosom, her eyebrows high in confusion.

'We'll definitely need to do something about those eyebrows too,' Massoumeh announced.

She stepped back, observing both women as if they were salvaged works of art in need of intensive restoration.

'Some thinning out and at least a few inches off the bottom,' she muttered to herself, hand on chin. 'And we'll obviously be putting some colour in because whatever you were born with is not worth keeping.'

Elham glanced at Aida, her household confidence muted by their brazen guest.

'We haven't got money for these kind of things,' she began, but Massoumeh cut her off.

'Who said anything about money? Think of this as charity. I certainly am.'

She laughed heartily to herself. There was a clatter of toys hitting carpet nearby. Massoumeh glanced over. Niki was staring at this new woman, her wide eyes tracking over the high-swept blonde hair, arched eyebrows and colourful makeup and clothing.

'Tooth fairy?' Niki whispered softly, her hands flying protectively to her mouth.

Massoumeh's eyes lit up.

'Who is this? *Salam, azizam*! How are you?'

She swooped upon Niki, grasping her cheeks in her hands.

'Aren't you precious, *khoshgel khanoom*! Beautiful lady!'

Niki's eyes bulged with fear as if Massoumeh's firm pinch might somehow wrench the teeth from her mouth.

'No, no,' she whimpered, pulling away.

Massoumeh, not noticing, released Niki and straightened up. She cast an eye over the room.

'Okay, what we need is a chair, some water and that fabulous mirror over there. Look at it! Perfect for a salon.'

They decided Aida should go first. She sat in the chair, a towel draped over her shoulders. As Massoumeh started coating Aida's hair with dye she began an exchange that was more monologue than conversation. Elham and Niki huddled to one side, watching Massoumeh with awe.

'The thing they say about this country is that anyone can make it here. Or is that America? I don't remember, and who knows with that clown who is running for President. But it's true here anyway. Look at me. Back in Iran I was nothing. No opportunity. No rights to anything. Every last rial gone to getting us

289

on those boats. I'm dust. But here, you look at Mansoor's uncle and everything he has achieved. These chips – you wouldn't believe me when I tell you how many people come for them! And there's so much less hassle. No sanctions, no one bothering you for money to leave you alone. Of course it is better here. Not always, I know. Not for us asylum seekers. But you wait until we get our visas and then what's holding us back? Take Mansoor's uncle. He came here as a student and once he got his refugee visa he brought over all the family. His children – all of them at school, all of them going to university. One daughter is even modelling. You've seen the flyers for his store? That's his daughter! No joke. Not a model at all, but his very own daughter Mojdeh. I did her hair.'

She paused for breath, laying aside the brush.

'You're next while this one sits,' she indicated to Elham.

Elham raised her hands in gentle objection. 'It's really okay. You don't need to –'

Massoumeh waved away her objections. 'None of that. You'll feel amazing. Have you ever been blonde before? You'll love it. All those men!'

Elham nodded reluctantly as she sat down, her hands gripping the bottom of the chair until they were a startled white.

'The thing is, now everyone is in a state about these letters. You know, the ones they're saying people are getting telling them if they don't submit their applications in time they'll be cut off from welfare? They say there are thirty thousand of us all lining up for lawyers. All processed at the same time. Lucky for us Mansoor's uncle can afford a private lawyer. So of course everyone is panicking. What if they get rejected? It means what? You either accept you must go back to Iran or they put you away in detention forever? Mansoor's friend – Milad – he says there's no way he can go back. They'll kill him properly this time. He was whipped before. He's a Kurd, though. So he's like a double refugee, isn't he? Iran and Australia – no one will take him. At least he's got the scars, though. That should help his application. They want to see persecution but how do you show them what it's like to always be discriminated against and picked on and barred from half the world because you're Arab or Feyli or Afghan or Baha'i? You can't show someone those scars. At least we got here before they shut the doors for good. Those poor people still stuck on Manus and the islands. With the heat and the rain and the tents so close together you can hear every fart and cry. The rashes, the headaches, the infections. I can't tell you how happy I am to see the back of that place. And the desperation. Here too, but it's different, isn't it? One of Mansoor's friends – friend of a friend, really – he was so terrified they wouldn't believe him he changed his story. Told them he had become a Christian and they'd persecuted him back in Iran, even though he had a perfectly acceptable reason to flee in the first place. The things people do!'

She sighed, stepping back to check she hadn't missed any hair. Elham watched her in the mirror, her soft brow furrowed.

'What happened to him?' she asked softly.

'Still waiting,' Massoumeh replied. 'Spends all his free time struggling through the Bible in case they quiz him on it, foolish man. But this is a depressing conversation! We have this conversation every day. And we'll have it every day until we get our letters telling us what is what. And even then, the visas are temporary anyway. Another few years and then you have to apply again. We'll be having this conversation for the rest of our lives at this rate. What a depressing thought. Let's talk about other things. Guess who I heard is applying for divorce?'

Soon, both Aida and Elham rose from their chairs crowned with their new haircuts and carefully shaped brows. Elham scuttled shyly to the stove to finish the meal while Aida helped Massoumeh sweep up the mess. When the meal was ready they ate in the lounge room, a tablecloth spread across the floor as their makeshift *sofreh*. Niki plunged into the food, rice and sauce splattering her clothing in a sign of five-star approval. Elham seemed not to notice, so Aida reached for the paper towels. The gaudy mirror had been dragged in from the kitchen and propped against the wall, an elegant companion for the television set. As she leant forward, Aida caught her reflection once more. The face was still gaunt, but softened of its hardness by the new curve of her hair and her strengthened brows. How that face had aged and changed in these last few years. But there was fire in those eyes, wasn't there? She'd stood up for herself. She had a new job. She was still here. What would come next? Perhaps she would study, once her visa came. Start writing properly again, get back into journalism. For, of course she would get her visa. How could she not? They had her story, they knew she was genuine. The thought came to her that she had forgotten to check the letterbox that day. Elham rose to put Niki to bed and Massoumeh stretched, her back cracking. Aida showed her to the door and the two women embraced.

'Monday, okay?' Massoumeh told her, wagging a finger like a teacher. 'Start earning proper money so you can pay taxes to prop up the detention centres, the Minister's wages and all those mental health services we all need now.'

'*Bale*,' Aida replied with a wry smile.

'There you go. Just like a real Australian,' Massoumeh said, kissing Aida's cheeks.

She saw her off down the street, waving from the weary fence. The letterbox was empty as usual. Yet despite this, it was the happiest Aida had felt in a long time. She looked up at the sky, stars peeping through the pockets of night-time cloud. Three things different: my hope, my hope, my hope.

When she woke up the next morning Elham was gone.

24

Nell

There were dreams she had sometimes – dreams that could not be real for she had been far too young to remember the events – yet dreams that masqueraded as memory of the time just before their father left. The second time he'd left, that was, because he'd left them twice – once when Seymour was seven and finally when Nell was still soft-crowned and sweet with the milky smell of infancy. There he was, draped in dusky shadows, watching from the doorway as his wife and son slept curled easily around each other's bodies. There she was, plump and cocooned in the bassinet, her eyes bright, and gurgling with all the hope for what their family could be. It was from these dreams that the others spilled, all the violent, wakeful thrashing of them, that left her tangled in the bedsheets and soaked and shivering in the early hours of morning. Glimmers of violent men, locked glass doors and slithers of porcelain waiting in drawers. Had her father been like this? She had never thought about it, his absence being a fact of life no one felt the need to address. They had just accepted that he wasn't there and no one ever seemed to miss him, his only legacy being the shared birth name Seymour no longer responded to. She'd always assumed he'd been a normal person who disappeared for normal-person reasons – fear of commitment, a secret family, unpaid Russian mafia debts – but abuse was so common, so prevalent, it seemed, that why wouldn't this be a possibility too?

Seymour was lying on the couch balancing a bowl of cereal on his paunch. He was watching early morning cartoons, the same station they had watched as children, and she was comforted by the blur and shriek of the wide-eyed anime characters. Seymour spooned mushy Weet-Bix into his mouth, milk spilling over the sides onto his T-shirt. He seemed heavier these days, for what reason she had no idea, weighed down by a gravity and burden whose origins she couldn't place. He lifted his feet when Nell approached, placing them back down on her lap after she'd manoeuvred herself into the snug. His feet smelt as they'd always smelt throughout her life, stale and warm and inherently Seymour. They watched the screen in comfortable silence.

In her mind, Nell saw herself as a child, a constant shadow in Seymour's wake. He'd always been so determined – they both were – confidently chartering a life they fully expected to claim, fuelled in part by their mother's insistence that not only were they capable of anything but that there was absolutely no reason life wouldn't turn out exactly as they planned. Her mind drifted through the past before settling on a memory from years before. Their mother, steadfastly determined to instil in her children a love and fascination with art, had – at Seymour's request – thrown them a surprise joint birthday outing to the National Gallery of Victoria. Seymour was known for this, instructing in great detail how exactly he wanted his 'surprises' to unfold. Their mother had wanted to take them to the visiting masterpieces but Seymour, fifteen and headstrong, had insisted on leading them through the upstairs galleries, the ones that usually housed the 'innovative' artwork. For all her years in academia their mother had never quite managed to shrug off the clear division her own parents had recognised in that there was capital-A Art, and then there was the rest of it. In keeping with this spirit, she largely found the upstairs galleries off-putting and unapproachable. Loud, too, for try as she might she did not understand the role of audio in art. As Seymour explained to Nell many years later, their mother did not like art that made her uncomfortable. On this particular visit she had begrudgingly humoured her son, seeing as it was his birthday, though she had lagged behind like a grouchy child.

'I just don't know what makes this art,' she'd sighed, passing a number of pieces without pause.

As if to make her point, the next piece had been a large cropped photo of a neon-lit vulva with graffiti scribbled across it and a classical soundtrack playing on a loop. She had sighed again, profoundly. Their mother liked Carracci cherubs and pre-Raphaelite paintings because they had the respectable kind of nudity, the nudity of proper Art. Soon enough she had wedged her way far enough under Seymour's skin that he gave up and they made their way down the escalators to Federation Court. Their mother spotted someone she knew and while the two women chatted, Seymour had led patient, sore-footed Nell into the Great Hall.

'Here.'

He'd pulled Nell up onto a cushioned bench, and they lay back, staring up at the ceiling. The siblings traced the kaleidoscope patterns of the stained-glass roof, connecting the mosaic's emperor yellow with its Krishna blue and Derwent box green. They'd not said anything, shoulders pressed together, tracking the rise and fall of each other's breathing as they lost themselves in the colours and shapes. And this became one of Nell's most treasured memories, though she'd never wondered why, only now she could see it was because of the safety she'd felt – so loved and secure – and she realised now the precious rarity of this.

Her focus shifted back to the cartoons before her, her lap heavy with the weight of Seymour's feet. They watched until an advertisement for a fast food chain broke their concentration. Nell turned to Seymour.

'What was our father like?'

Seymour paused, the spoon halfway to his mouth.

'Jesus. Where did that come from?'

'Why did he leave? Was he . . .'

Seymour read her silence. He guided the spoon back to the bowl, depositing the cereal with a claggy splash.

'Is this because of your client? I don't think so. Not that I remember. But I was so young . . . I think he just wasn't very good at being a father and sort of opted out. He wasn't around that much anyway because he travelled for work.'

'What did he do?' Nell asked.

Seymour scrunched his face in memory.

'I want to say travelling salesman? Like Willy Loman? But that could just be something I associated him with when I was little.'

Seymour placed his cereal bowl on the floor then pulled himself upright beside her. He put an arm around her, awkward and familial. His T-shirt smelt of sleep and dried milk, and of meals he'd eaten the previous day.

'Not all men are like that, Nell.'

He held her for a moment, then let go, reaching down to retrieve his cereal. Nell felt her body cool in his absence. *But some are*, she thought. And that was the worrying thing.

*

Outside the sun was making a valiant appearance in the mild springtime sky. Nell was not a regular jogger but this morning the cells of her body were tight and agitated, calling out to release the pre-court pent-up energy within. The air when it hit her was crisp and sharp. She set off at a leisurely pace, her limbs responding slowly. She quickened her tempo until it reached something of a brisk trot, her arms swinging against and then with the motion. Soon she found herself pressing forward, lurching into a jog-like rhythm that ate greedily at the pavement. Deep within her chest the burn and yowl of her recent sedentary lifestyle started scratching about, but she ignored it. She turned onto the bike path, narrowly avoiding an oncoming cyclist, then focused on the staggered white line stretching out before her. The bike path sloped down then up, and she found herself suddenly removed from the mutter and mayhem of the inner city. She'd forgotten this park was here, a nature reserve along the river, preserved and precious, housing community gardens and wide-open spaces to help the city forget itself. She hadn't been here since before she'd started at Williams & Williams – well before that, now that she thought about it. They'd come here for picnics, Rani and their other law student friends, until they'd graduated and everyone had taken their separate paths.

Her heart pounding in her chest, Nell slowed to a walk. She had met with Rani the night before, Nell's pre-court nerves getting the better of her as she prepared for battle. Rani had been waiting for her in the bar, having secured a small table by the window. Dressed casually in jeans, she'd reclined lazily against the chesterfield, pretending to swirl a glass of something strong, making Nell smile for the first time that day.

'Can I get you a real drink to ponder with?' Nell said, and returned soon with two stiff whiskies that made both of them gag.

'That was a very expensive joke,' Rani commented, ordering them white wine instead.

'This is why we'll never make the old boys' club,' Nell sighed, pulling the amber liquid into a satisfying swirl before abandoning it for the sauvignon blanc.

'How's life?' Rani asked, and Nell rolled her eyes.

'I hear you,' Rani replied. 'How's the case?'

'Contested hearing tomorrow. No one budged at directions. I don't know what's going to happen. It's so complicated. Both their affidavits are strong. And her ex the lawyer isn't making it easy for anyone. DB is confident, but I'm not sure.'

Rani wrinkled her brow.

'I swear we didn't realise it was so complex. Sorry this was the one we handballed to you.'

Nell shrugged. 'We're in it now.'

Madeline was, now that Nell reflected on it, at odds completely with the person captured on that paper. She was, for want of a better word, positively chipper now, enlivened by the prospect of finally being heard. At their last meeting she'd been so excitable someone had knocked on the consulting room door to check everything was okay. The only downer had been when they'd reviewed Eric's affidavit together, her face oscillating between hurt disbelief and table-pounding outrage. It had included the intervention order breach, though thankfully he hadn't reported it to the police.

'I sound like a train wreck,' she'd muttered quietly, before buoyed by a renewed burst of energy. 'That lying bastard. He'll get what he deserves.'

'Did the magistrate schedule one day or two for the hearing?' Rani asked, wineglass near empty.

'One. There are so few witnesses. We've got none. I'll be happy when it's over, to be honest.' She studied her wineglass for a moment. 'Doesn't it ever get too much for you? All those stories of violence and abuse, day after day? I mean, this is just one case and already it's messing with my head. He's supposed to be this fantastic person when he's not at home but some of the things he's accused of doing . . . It's like now I look at everyone and think "What are you capable of?" In the office, in the supermarket, on the tram home. Who knows what happens once each of those people closes their front door?'

'You know what's shit?' Rani said. 'You spend so much time listening to stories of all the horrible things people do to the people they're meant to love, and it makes your own relationship look perfect in comparison. I go home every night and feel lucky that Rob isn't a perpetrator, and that's fucked up. But I've worked with people from every single walk of life, and none of us are immune to this. I mean, look at Madeline. She was us right up until she met that guy.'

'Almost us,' Nell replied. 'I mean, there's the drinking and everything. It doesn't help us that she's not the most reliable of witnesses. It would help if she acted more like a victim.'

Rani tilted her head, squinting at Nell.

'What does a victim look like, Nell?'

'You know what I mean,' Nell said. 'She doesn't present well to the magistrate. She's not sympathetic.'

Rani placed her wineglass on the table. Outside the window a tram rattled past, packed full of evening revellers. Football finals were on and excited passengers waved their scarves out the windows. Black and white, navy and white, a sea of wool waving in the dying light.

'You know, the problem with victims, Nell, is it's a status that takes away people's agency. Their complexity. The nuances that make us human. They exist in shades of grey, which isn't the easiest colour to capture. None of us are sympathetic in real life because that's what it is to be human. But none of that negates our right to live safely, to command respect, to access the full extent of the law. There's a reason Lady Justice has that blindfold.'

Nell raised an eyebrow. 'It's not that the wool has been pulled over her eyes?'

'Does it matter either way?' Rani replied. 'You're her lawyer. It's your job to tell her story properly.'

*

299

They arrived early at the magistrates' court. Despite this, the waiting room was so crowded they were forced to stand shoulder to shoulder, or more like shoulder to shoulder to chest as DB towered over the two women, the lapels of his well-cut suit at eye level to them. They'd positioned Madeline between them, trying to block Eric from her view as he stood on the other side of the room chuckling at something his lawyer had said. He'd been to their place for barbecues, Madeline had told them the first time she'd seen Eric's lawyer. He and his wife had brought gluten-free sausages as they were paleo now. Their children too, though she'd found them hiding in the boys' playroom stuffing their faces with fairy bread at one point in the afternoon.

Madeline had dressed carefully today. Nell could see she had paid particular attention to her hair, her makeup, and had chosen a demure yet sophisticated blouse and blazer with a set of pearls she said she'd borrowed from her mother. Her mother who had that morning, Madeline informed them, told her that it wasn't too late to put all this silliness behind them and try to work things out. Counselling, she'd suggested. For the sake of the children. Friends, too, apparently mutual, had been sending messages full of love and best wishes and the awkward assurance that they would still be there for her no matter what the truth turned out to be. She was nervous, shaking, her hands clenching tightly before her. Nell suspected that if the press of bodies was to evaporate she would crumple without their support. Nell's own stomach was a mess, hyperactive butterflies that had caused her to use the bathroom already on multiple occasions for what DB sometimes referred as pre-court cramps. DB's face was set impassively but she could tell he was nervous. He'd repeatedly stepped them through the process and in his silence picked relentlessly at a non-existent spot on his suit.

As they waited to be called, Nell looked about the room. For the most part it consisted of other groupings similar to their own, though a significant number of individuals sat disparate and downcast, dressed in formal clothes they did not wear often enough to feel comfortable in. Some of them would seek out the court's duty lawyers, who would shake their hands, hear their story, then, depending on their assessment – and time permitting – either accompany them inside if they were lucky, or provide some brief advice and send them in to battle unchaperoned. Others would go it completely alone, armed with only a flimsy folder of photocopied documents. She could pick the private solicitors – all tailored jackets and buffed shoes – from the community lawyers, who often appeared in crumpled suits and well-worn shoes. She imagined them collapsing back into their suburban offices, stripping themselves of their finery, comfortable once more in their sweaters and flat footwear. Occasionally someone would burst into brief, mortified tears, either in the process of entering or exiting the court, or else hidden behind tissues as they waited to be called. There was security, too, a clear reminder that for some of the applicant/respondent pairings, acts of extreme violence had occurred between them.

From across the room Eric's lawyer caught their attention. He motioned to DB, who approached grimly. They stood in a huddle, gesturing neatly. Madeline gave Nell a questioning look.

'They're making an offer,' she said gently.

DB was statue-faced when he returned.

'They've offered us a bargain,' he informed them. 'Prepared to settle on the steps. You plead consent without admission. You'd get a limited order but you'd be free to see the children. Obviously, you'd drop your cross-application.'

Madeline looked between them, panicked.

'What does that mean?'

'It means you accept the intervention order against you but it's adjusted to a limited order, which means you can go to the house, see the children, communicate with Eric, etc, you just can't commit family violence,' DB explained. 'If you accept, we go in, tell the magistrate, and the magistrate gives the final orders straight away.'

Madeline was watching him intently.

'So I wouldn't get the chance to tell my story?'

'No.'

Her brow scrunched at this.

'So it would be like admitting to all his lies?'

'Technically no. Consent without admission means you're not contesting the order against you, but you're not admitting guilt either.'

'I don't think anybody outside this room gives a shit about technically. It's basically the same thing. Promising not to commit family violence when I never bloody did in the first place.'

She stared at them both.

'And no one would ever know the truth,' she continued. 'He gets to carry on with his lies. While it's forever known that I had a fucking intervention order against me?'

'It's not on your public record,' DB clarified. 'I mean, the police, yes, but it's not like future employers could access it.'

'That's not the point. People would still know.'

DB moved his hands in a more-or-less-but-not-necessarily kind of way.

'On the other hand, think about your reputation,' he cautioned. 'Everything will come out in court. Everything you say but also everything he has to say. And it might affect you further down the track when you go to the Family Court. Their priority is the safety and wellbeing of your children.'

Madeline looked crestfallen.

'And you think mine isn't? So you think I should accept it. Nell?'

Nell shifted uncomfortably. She knew what DB was thinking. This was more of a sure thing than the chance they'd win inside. And it wasn't a win, but it wasn't a loss, either. It was grey, the murky haze that Rani spoke of, where things were neither clear nor certain, and while it wasn't what they'd prepared for, perhaps it was the compromise they needed.

'Well, you can never predict the outcome of the court,' she said carefully. 'It's your choice. There's a chance you won't come across well on the stand, and like DB said, you'd be airing all these things in public. You'd have to talk about the incidents. You'd be examined, cross-examined, re-examined. They'll hone in on the drinking. And then there's the breach. And, well, like DB said, Eric could use it against you in the Family Court when you go for parenting arrangements. Even if you don't take the witness stand, he can still use your affidavit.'

Nell pressed her thumbnail into the flesh of her index finger, clicking it softly.

'Sometimes it's more about the long game,' she added, hating herself.

Madeline stared at the two of them for a long, bitter moment.

'I didn't realise the law came with that caveat.'

She looked over to where Eric and his lawyer stood, sharing a smug look. DB stepped forward to block her view. He looked exhausted.

'Look, we can't tell you what to do. You have to make that decision for yourself. We either go ahead, you tell your story and we hope for a positive outcome, or you take the limited order, get to see your kids and in all likelihood in twelve months the order expires and you've nothing on you anymore. You could walk away with everything you want, or nothing at all. We can't make that call for you.'

Nell felt Madeline's body press against hers, heavy suddenly with the weight of things. She brought her hand to her throat, her face pale as she clawed absent-mindedly at her skin. She straightened, suddenly, clearing her throat.

'Can I have a few minutes to think about it?'

25

Patrick

North Facing Window: Seymour Swansea
September 2016
By ?

Seymour Swansea was born in the north and, if his present circum-stances are anything to go by, he will die here too. He is a man of the world, in as much as anyone with an internet connection, a streaming subscription and the vague memory of a gap year two decades ago can claim to be so. Each day he cycles from his terrace house in Brunswick down the Upfield bike path, past Princes Park, hugs the crest of the cemetery and follows the bike lane all the way to his Fitzroy gallery. Sometimes he returns the other way, north up St Georges Road past the Edinburgh Gardens and west through Brunswick East, completing a ten-kilometre circuit that roughly encapsulates the girth of his life now, for rarely does he travel beyond this parochial rectangle anymore. He did once, before life trampled him down and he chained himself to the expectations of others, back when he looked out at the world instead of in on his own. Back when he saw opportunity instead of imminent disaster, and hope instead of worry. Back when he was a man for the world, and there was nothing not to love in that.

Patrick read through what he had written. His head was beginning to ache again, had been threatening to since midday. He deleted it letter by letter until he got to the stranded question mark. He couldn't bring himself to write 'Rik' anymore. It had been a whim, something he'd thought both clever and cleansing at the time, and he'd fancied it an homage to Rik Mayall as well as a reinvention of self. Only it looked stupid and made him sound like a middling pop singer and had failed to shield him from the claws of the world anyhow. His head was thundering and he pushed the laptop away. He grabbed the packet of foreign painkillers, punching the remaining two tablets out of the capsules. He swallowed them then collected up the empty plastic. That was it now. They were all gone.

His laptop sat before him, its blank white rectangle staring earnestly back at him. Empty, and refusing to be filled. Patrick seized the thing and hurled it across the room. It did not go far because it was a very small room, and it left a pathetic dent in the plaster from its pitiful impact. His head was buzzing, wild with today, and with yesterday and the long hopscotch of days before, all trailing back into each of his idiot decisions. He brought his fists to his temples as if to beat it all away, the memories and the pain and whatever else was lurking about inside there. When this didn't work, he stumbled to his bedroom and crawled into bed. It smelt of his failures, stale and tart, so he stripped the sheets and lay on the naked mattress instead. The migraine dutifully descended, stripping him of his vision. He lay motionless, his head set at the least painful angle, then pulled the naked duvet over his head. Here it was dark and here he would stay, forever at the very least. But no one can stay anywhere for long, and soon he was transported by the stillness back, back, back into that empty little Anatolian guesthouse room . . . And he was failing, failing to capture anything in the empty notebook that sat before him, fortressed from the world in his cramped island bed, hemmed in by the four heavy walls, even though the sequence of events played through his head like a film reel set to repeat. And all he could hear was the scrape of fork clearing plate and the phlegmy freeing of a throat and the *sweep sweep sweep* of a straw-bristled broom somewhere out in the courtyard. And the bare light bulb was too fierce, but the light that flooded past the nudged-aside curtain was too, and there was a mosquito, somewhere, and a dog barking, somewhere, and at the back of it all a man pleading pointlessly because he only wanted to help. And Patrick had heaved himself from the bed because it was too loud in this little empty guesthouse room, and taken himself out into the world with his face an unkempt garden save for the one careful row mown from gullet to jaw. And it had been beautiful out there – the way the sea hugged the stone harbour with a turquoise indescribable, and the boats had bobbed in the breeze in their multicoloured breeches, and the rich red flag had coiled in the salty air, offering its crescent for all to see, and it had smelt sweet and earthy – of something baked in syrup and something else cut fresh from a garden – and he had sat at a plastic table by the harbour with a glass of tea before him and there hadn't been any milk because you weren't supposed to drink it that way. And after he had drunk this milkless tea and stared out at the world he saw the beauty of it all, but when he tried to write about all that had happened he failed once more because there were no words to capture the reality of these things. Every phrase seemed wrong – too laden with cliché, too emotive; either bathed in simplicity or riddled with needless ornament. Unable to shape itself around the immensity of what he had experienced, witnessed, caused. *Caused.* There was a word that would stick. And in the back of his eyes and the canals of his ears, the film reel played again and again.

Under the covers of his bed in his boxy Thornbury apartment, Patrick twisted and turned in the twilight between wake and sleep. In the place where things are remembered and suffocated but find new ways to creep back up. He woke often, whimpering, each time drifting back into nightmares.

He was roused eventually by an incessant knocking at the front door. He waited for it to stop but it didn't, so eventually Patrick crawled out from under the duvet and felt around in the darkness for the light switch. He flicked it and nothing happened. He flicked it again, numbed by the post-migraine fug. He groped his way out into the hall and tried another light, but the effect was the same. He felt for the door handle, pulling it open. Where he expected sharp light flooding down from the landing's fluorescents, he was met by more darkness.

'Am I dead?' he asked the shadows.

'It's a blackout,' Seymour's voice came softly through night. 'The whole of the north is out.'

Neither of them said anything else and for a moment it was as if neither were there. Eventually Seymour spoke.

'You don't get to keep running away.'

'But I'm so good at it,' Patrick sighed.

'No, actually, you're not. You're terrible at it. If there was an award for most ballsed-up run-offs, you would fill the podium.'

They found their way into the kitchen, Patrick cursing loudly as he cracked his elbow on the edge of the sideboard, and sat at the kitchen table-cum-desk.

'What did I just step on? It felt like a laptop.'

'It was.'

'Oh.'

'I would offer you a cup of tea but I'm scared you'll throw it in my face. Besides, the kettle is electric.'

'Wise decision. Not the electric kettle. The other bit.'

'So.'

'So.'

Patrick waited, hoping Seymour would start. But then he realised that if anyone should start it should be him, because he was the one who had left so much unsaid. He sifted through various beginnings and realised none of them were any good. So he settled on one that was okay and went from there.

'I wish I'd done things differently.'

He sensed Seymour considering this, turning it over for scratches and dents. 'Which parts?'

'All of it, I guess.'

He listened to the silence that followed, how Seymour had left it open for him, and realised that if he didn't fill this silence, someone else would. And so he told him, because if he was going to tell anyone he may as well tell Seymour. He told him how it had crept up on him stealthily, the nagging feeling that he was wasting his life. That there was more to do and if he didn't start doing it then he would regret this forever. And that he knew if he let Seymour be a reason not to, then he would regret this too, and this regret would turn into resentment and that was a place couples seldom returned from. It helped too, that the world was crumbling around him, job cuts and voluntary redundancies bleeding the country's arts departments of their lifeblood. Trivialised and unprioritised, as if the darkening world had no more room for journalism of the aesthetic when there was so much real-life horror in need of reportage. So it had seemed like some kind of sign when the Syria offer came through – made sense that this would be his chance – except that it only made sense if you were Patrick and lived inside the little breakdown he was orchestrating in his own head because where in the world would it be useful for a forty-year-old career arts correspondent to stick a helmet on his head and march off into a war zone in the manner of a Will Dyson etching? But it was all so noble and good, wasn't it, because he was going to Syria – SYRIA – where he would make a difference and do something important and have an impact on the greater existence of humanity because that was the whole point, wasn't it? That was why words were created – for history and posterity and justice.

Only, he'd barely got a chance, because he'd got as far as Turkey, where he planned to spend some time with the two and a half million Syrian refugees clinging to the hope that they wouldn't get pushed back across the border, and then everything had gone horribly wrong. It had been days – mere days – and he'd made the mistake of sending through some images from a tussle between the Turkish police and a small group of Syrian agitators that identified too clearly one of the chief instigators just as the bandana around his face slipped. And these images had appeared online, causing trouble for the unmasked man, who had simply been trying to seek justice for the sporadic acts of violence his people seemed to fall victim to. And a day or so later – not even long enough for his stomach to react to the food – this man had sought out Patrick and he had been angry, because who wouldn't be, and he had shouted his anger menacingly into Patrick's face. In his hand was what looked like a knife, only a knife long dulled by use and hardly more than a modest letter opener, and he'd waved it about, making his point. And Patrick hadn't felt scared, he'd felt guilty. Guilty about his slip-up and guilty about the bruising that bloomed easily across the poor man's face and torso. And a passer-by had wanted to help, stepping in to calm the raging man and take the knife from his hand, only it suddenly looked as if Patrick was being attacked by these two men, and the police officer who happened to round the corner at that exact moment didn't want a dead foreigner on his hands – particularly one dressed in an untarnished helmet and flak jacket – so he'd done what he thought was right and hoisted his gun in warning.

Who could tell the order in which things happened next? There had been yelling and hands waving, and the passer-by had shouted, *Stop, please, I only want to help*, and the poor man hadn't been trying to stab Patrick in the face, it just looked that way, and so the collection of bullets deposited in the passer-by by the skittish police officer had been completely without reason. And it had smelt, suddenly, like blood, and Patrick's whole world had collapsed in every way imaginable, and what he should have done at that point, after he'd stumbled away from the police station where the Syrian activist remained in a cell, was to contact head office – ask to be debriefed, seek support from the employee assistance program, allow them to send him home. Instead – and here in hindsight was where he'd gone wrong – Patrick had gone rogue. Disappeared off the radar, telling no one and nobody where he was. Got on a bus, then another bus, and took it as far as he could until it deposited him somewhere far from one border and at the edge of another. And he had hidden for as long as he could, until the need for food forced him out of the guesthouse and into the world, and this was where he had found the painkillers – mild opiates, he suspected, but who was counting –

'And you brought them through customs?'

– and he'd brought them through customs, and this little coastal town was where he had tried for a haircut to pull himself back into the world, only it had sent him running from the glint of the razor, stumbling through the streets into a group of rowdy young Australians dressed for some reason in the flag of their shared country, clutching merrily at their bottles of raki, and they'd pushed him – or he'd pushed them – and at the age of forty, having never participated in a fight in his life, he had decided to fight them, including the embarrassing moment when he'd been caught on a camera phone in a lofty and misguided 'don't you know who I am' type declaration which of course had ended up on the internet. And he had looked deranged – raving – his face full of shaving foam and his eyes wild with rage, and the only saving grace was that he may have gone viral if not for a Kardashian breaking the internet again that week, and the fact that barely anyone outside of a small group of people did indeed know who he was. One of these, unfortunately, was his employers – who by this point suspected him kidnapped – and they had thought it best to sever their relationship. So that was pretty much that for both his career and his dignity, and he'd eventually returned to Australia because the temporary visa he had never got round to extending was set to expire and he couldn't face deportation amid everything else going on.

'That's what happened to you? My god.'

Not quite. There was also the cock-up with the television report, a moment that was meant to simultaneously be some kind of repentance and a second attempt at seeking absolution. And god only knew how unbearable it would be if he found out that it had in some way contributed to any of those poor people having their visas rejected. So there was that debilitating guilt too. And that more or less brought things up to speed.

'Jesus. How have you been managing any of this?'

Patrick shrugged into the darkness.

'I just figured I'd pretend none of it happened.'

'And on a scale of one to ten how much is that strategy working?'

'I believe the answer is quite evident.'

Patrick said this last part with a doleful chuckle, then buried his face into his hands, collapsing forward on the table.

'I just wanted to do something that mattered,' he whispered. 'But I couldn't even do that. And I figured that the least I could do was write about it – about him – but I couldn't. I can't. And I couldn't face you after. I couldn't face anyone.'

Seymour said nothing for a moment, shifting audibly in his seat.

'That's the problem with art, isn't it? Sometimes it can't capture what we need it to. Sometimes life is too much, too harsh, too indescribable to convey. And I guess that's why we just keep trying. Failing, but trying anyway.'

He swallowed softy, and the muffled sound thudded across the darkness.

'The gallery isn't doing that well. I never told you that. You never asked. If this show doesn't do well I'm not sure what will happen. And that was the one thing I was meant to be good at. I know that this pales in comparison to what you've been through but perhaps there is a semblance of comfort in that.'

Then Seymour started crying too, and they both sat together crying in the darkness, which was a lot more comforting than crying alone. Eventually Patrick straightened his shoulders, rubbing the tears from his cheeks with the heels of his palms.

'I honestly thought myself stronger than this. I just wanted to do something worthwhile.'

Then there was silence, stillness, in which their collective failures and worries coalesced in the night and tentatively wove themselves back into a familiar shared fabric. In the darkness, Patrick felt Seymour reach for him, placing his hands across his own.

'What's not worthwhile about this?'

26

Evangelia

There were more flowers on her father's side of the grave so Evangelia took a handful and slid them into the vase on her mother's side. Now both vases looked depleted, the flowers leaning awkwardly in the space around them. The little cemetery shop would have closed by now. Oh well. She'd have to bring more with her next time. Evangelia opened the delicate glass doors at the base of the headstones and refilled the oil candles, lighting each one before returning them. Then she dusted the headstone with her hand, her fingers carving the shape of the letters on her father's side and brushing the smooth empty expanse of her mother's. She sank onto the marble, pulling her feet up under her, and leant against the headstone. It was cool and solid against her forehead, and she closed her eyes, picturing her parents. She tried to find a memory without Lydia in it, but there weren't many. They were still not talking, over two months since the cured meats incident, and a week since the awkward nine-month *mnimósino* when they had sat on either side of the church flanked by their husbands and children, pretending the other didn't exist. They had ended up one before the other in the long line for communion, ignoring each other up the carpeted aisle as they accepted the wine, and once more as they collided at the *andíthoro* table. They had each grabbed a handful of bread, offering a quick respectful cross as they continued to blank the other. Nick and Xanthe had wanted to play with their older cousins, to hang off them with a reverence that now outright aggrieved Evangelia, but she had insisted they were late for their family brunch. If it was a family brunch, why couldn't their cousins come? the children had whined. Evangelia had explained that family came in varying degrees and sometimes it was important to do things with only the closest members of your family. But they were the closest members, the children had pleaded. They loved their cousins more than anything in the world, including sometimes their parents, so why couldn't they come to brunch? Evangelia had looked to Peter for help and Peter, eager to be done with all this family business and get back to the café, told them, 'Because I said so,' and that seemed to placate them.

Evangelia opened her eyes. It was getting dark. The cemetery would be closing soon. She pushed herself upright, taking in the headstone. The half-hearted vases bothered her but there was nothing she could do. She traced her hands again over the empty face of her mother's tombstone. Her father's was full of kind gold-plated words: *loving father, cherished husband, adored papou*. And then her mother's – bare and undecided as if no one wanted to claim her. Evangelia tried to think of what her mother would want here, which version of herself she'd have chosen to peer out for all eternity, and what epitaph would capture her worth. But she still didn't have this answer, even though she'd given up trying to write her mother's story weeks ago.

It had been unbearable, watching the others' successes. Sita and Gwen had an almost complete first draft and a meeting with the Mayor to pitch its publication. They read from their manuscript each week, the trials and triumphs of their turn-of-the-century glass ceiling shatterer, each week growing stronger and more confident under Carole's steady hand.

And Terry . . . Bloody Terry had gone and got himself a publishing deal off the back of the first chapter of what he called his 'lady spy' biography, which in itself should have been reason enough for him not to, but there you go. And the following week, after his announcement, Evangelia had left home fully intending to attend class but had found herself driving past the TAFE car park and out through the suburbs, ending up outside the cemetery not far from closing time. And once she was there, it had made far more sense to sit with her mother's blank headstone than in the classroom with the embarrassment of her own blank canvas. She hadn't told Peter, and each week now she had been making this journey, sitting in the stillness of the cemetery and watching its solemn restfulness. There were so few visitors, even when she came earlier in the day. Maybe a handful of people, often alone and hurried, who hovered a few moments over their loved one, preened and dusted a little, then scampered off without a second thought back into their busy living-lives.

Evangelia glanced at the headstones again. The near-empty vases were really bothering her now. And then she was back in a time decades ago, clinging to her mother's hemline as they zigzagged between the graves. Her *papou*, long dead, was buried somewhere nearby and her mother could never quite remember the best way to find him. They would weave and wander, a mother duck and her baby, and it must have been the year Lydia first attended school because she wasn't part of this memory. Which meant it was the year of the back injury, when her mother had demanded her way into the factory, so it must have been one of the few days her mother was not hauling bricks in and out of the kiln. They had rounded a squat weathered obelisk and suddenly her mother's face broke into a smile.

'*Yassou*, Baba.'

They tidied the stone, dusting it with their hands and tracing the letters to edge out the dirt, then her mother struck her forehead with realisation.

'*Ta loulouthia!*'

The flowers were sitting on the kitchen table at home, exactly where Evangelia had forgotten them. Realising her mistake, she had curled her lips, a sob forming in her little chest.

'Nothing to cry over,' her mother had soothed her, taking her cheeks in her palms. '*Papou* would hate to see you cry.'

Then her good church-going mother had peered around the quiet cemetery, before leaning into a funny little stoop and darting from tombstone to tombstone, grabbing a single flower from each. Evangelia had laughed at this, her eyes still wet with tears, overcome with how funny her mother looked in her panicked half-run. Her mother arrived back, panting, a hasty bouquet now in her hand.

'Good young, good old.' She'd winked at her daughter, and they had set the flowers in the vase by her *papou*'s headstone.

Evangelia remembered this now. 'Good young, good old.' Her mother used to say this all the time, her measure of someone's worth. Evangelia smiled, her eyes filling with tears. *Stop that*, she thought. *Mama would hate to see you cry.* Dusk was creeping into the edges of the day now and the cemetery would soon close. She pulled herself to her feet, dusting off her trousers. She turned to leave, but before she did there was one more thing that needed doing. When she walked out through the cemetery's heavy iron gates, each vase at her parents' grave was crammed with vibrant, mismatched flowers.

Usually Evangelia would drive to class, but her car was being serviced so she took the train instead. It was a hassle, but she needed to maintain the illusion that she was sitting in her writing class instead of wandering the north in the dark. After a few stops, she got on a tram heading east and alighted after a short time. This was the other thing she had been doing.

The old brickwork was faded, but inside, the factory had been renovated to form a dozen apartments with a little café at the front. She hadn't realised this when she'd first ventured out this way, searching for the factory that had supported her family during those six difficult months after her mother had demanded assistance. A small part of her had hoped it would still be operational, churning out bricks, while the rest of her suspected it would be empty and derelict, most likely housing squatters or long-dead machinery and hazardous chemicals. She'd been surprised by its new character, and amazed to find the café housed in what had once been the foreman's quarters. Named, helpfully enough, The Foreman's Quarters, the café was open well into the evening with a little sign at the entrance explaining that this had been where the foreman sat at his great wooden desk, watching over the workers as they loaded the kilns. Evangelia had wandered inside, her eyes drinking in the masonry and steel frames. This would have been where her mother had stood and demanded she take on her husband's work. When this realisation hit, Evangelia had collapsed into tears, large and profound as they cascaded down her cheeks, and a worried waitress had rushed over and asked if she needed anything. She had needed her mother, but because this was not an option, she instead ordered a chardonnay and had sat quietly in the café until it was time to go home.

The next time she'd sought out a table by the brickwork, leaning her head against the rough surface and imagining her mother bracing herself against this wall. Refusing to leave. Refusing to be forgotten. There she would have stood, all five feet nothing of her, her words sharp and purposeful in her mother tongue as she talked the poor foreman into meeting her demands. And Evangelia was so sure, as her skin pressed into the bubbles and indents of the brickwork, that her mother's palm had breathed into this wall, into this very spot, and here they were connected after all these decades.

Today Evangelia sat in her seat, drinking the wine the wait-ress now knew to bring without her having to order, and wept for her mother. She knew how this looked – the strange woman who sat in the same seat crying to herself for forty-five minutes once a week – but she did not care in the slightest. Let them talk.

Soon enough it was time to go. The biography class would be finishing and she needed to make her way home, where her children would be racing around rabid with end-of-term excitement. She realised as she stood that tonight would have been the last class. Her stomach dropped. That meant an end to her weekly visits. What excuse could she give Peter now that wouldn't seem too obvious? It had been okay before, an omission rather than an outright lie, but anything beyond this would be purposeful deception and she had read enough gossip magazines to know how that usually went down. They were talking today, mostly because it was too difficult maintaining multiple family grudges, after a prickly evening following her discovery of his tendency to underpay their staff. Besides, they were now two staff short – she had made him pay Nina in full before she'd left on her adventure – and with today marking the beginning of the busy school holidays she had no excuse to not be at the shop.

Evangelia hurried out of the café, refusing to acknowledge that this would be her final visit. She caught a train that would take her up past the TAFE and out to the shop where Peter and the children were waiting to take her home. She watched the houses shudder past, her mind still, her body rocking and settling as the train drew breath at each new station. As it took off from Bell Station, there was a cry from the door and a woman fell forward, papers flying from her arms. As the woman pushed herself upright, Evangelia realised it was Carole.

'I'm okay,' Carole said loudly, pulling herself to her feet. 'Everyone go back to your phones.'

Evangelia hurried over and swooped down to help her with the papers. Carole looked surprised.

'Fancy seeing you here!'

Evangelia held out the pile of battered papers.

'Are you all right?'

Carole's cheeks flushed red.

'Yes, yes. My head was somewhere else completely and I've got on the wrong train. I'm meant to be heading towards the city. God knows what's out this way.'

'My home, for one thing,' Evangelia replied, and Carole flushed a deeper red.

The train curved to the right, sending Carole skittering towards the wall. Evangelia held out a hand to steady her.

'Are you sure you're okay?'

Carole looked close to tears.

'Not really. I . . . I haven't been sleeping that much lately and didn't have time to eat, and class completely takes it out of me.'

The train began to slow as it approached Preston Station.

'Here, I'll help you off,' Evangelia said.

'Don't be silly,' Carole said, but she took her arm. 'You must think me some silly old woman. I'm really not, despite what my children seem to think. I'm not actually that old. I'm just –'

'It's fine,' Evangelia interrupted. 'Really.'

'You can just leave me here,' Carole began. 'There'll be another train soon enough.'

'Stop that,' Evangelia said. 'We're getting you some food. Me too. I'm starving.' And as she said it, she realised it was true. It took a lot of energy to sit and be sad.

They settled at a table in a quiet restaurant and ordered large bowls of pho. The waiter brought them longnecks of beer and Carole drank at hers thirstily.

'Don't you have somewhere you need to be?' she asked.

Evangelia shrugged. 'It's fine. I texted my husband to say

we're out celebrating the end of the course. He doesn't expect me back for a while.'

Carole watched her.

'You stopped coming to class . . .'

Evangelia ducked her head. 'I . . . I wasn't any good. I couldn't tell her story the way I wanted to.'

Carole snorted through her mouthful of beer. 'You think any of us can? You think I've ever written anything that looks even remotely like I want it to? Inferior versions of the projected desire, that's what the literary world is based on.'

'I wanted to tell her story so much, but the problem was she didn't do anything amazing. She didn't do anything at all.'

Evangelia dropped her head again, her eyes wet with tears. The shame of the funeral came flooding back.

'After the funeral service, at the wake, my sister Lydia read a eulogy. Didn't tell anyone she was going to do it. Just stood up and began this eulogy that none of us knew about.'

Evangelia felt a sob rising up and tried to swallow it. This was ridiculous. She was sobbing like a child. Clearly this was her thing now, crying in public.

'It was so short. You have no idea. It was so short, and all about us. Well, mostly about Lydia and her children, but it wasn't about my mother at all. Not her as a person. It was all about who she was to us. And it made me so angry. I was so angry. But I didn't know what to say, you know. I didn't know how to wrestle the microphone from my sister's hands and tell my mother's story the way it was meant to be told. And I still don't.'

A new sob burst from her throat and she failed to catch it. Carole handed her a wad of napkins and she blew her nose loudly. The waiter arrived and attempted to place the huge bowls of steaming noodles discreetly in front of them. He backed off carefully, and his trepidation caused them both to burst into laughter. Evangelia pressed the napkins to her face again.

'Jesus. I'm crying in a restaurant. How pathetic. You must think I'm a complete mess.'

'Not at all,' Carole said.

'You must,' Evangelia insisted. 'I show up week after week with my terrible writing. How embarrassing. What a stupid idea to think I could tell her story.'

She couldn't meet Carole's eyes. Carole pushed the bowls out of the way and reached across the table. She took Evangelia's hands. Finding the soggy napkins, she put these to one side and then took them again.

'Can I tell you a secret?'

Evangelia shrugged.

'I was only doing that class to sell more books. Initially, anyway. My publisher told me it looks good on your résumé and it's a chance to build up word of mouth publicity, etc, etc. Only there really weren't that many of you, and I'm not entirely sure Terry would have spoken to anyone about anything but his own book. So that was a bit redundant. But the thing is, initially I took one look around the class and thought, what the hell am I doing here? This isn't going to help sell the book and that means fewer people are going to read my story and understand why we need to put our women back into history. Women like your mother. When you started talking about her, I thought, yes! Here's my opportunity! Only then you stopped coming. I thought I was doing this amazing thing helping coax it out of you, but then you just disappeared, and I was stuck with Sita and Gwen, who were fine without me, and with bloody Terry.'

Evangelia cringed. 'Sorry.'

'That's not the point of this story.' Carole clicked her tongue against her teeth. 'The point is, you have a story worth telling and you're going to find a way to tell it the way you want. To work with what you've got. And to not think you need something spectacular to make it matter. That's a bloody cop-out, and that's why women have been left out time and time again. Because they weren't doing important things? Bullshit they weren't. You tell me who decides what is important and what isn't.'

They ate their soup and Carole told Evangelia about how she'd learnt long ago to ignore the voices telling her it wasn't worth seeking out these ordinary people from history. That this was the old school – the dusty keepers of history who had set the rules long ago – and it was about time those rules were changed. Because those rules kept them all out – the people whose gender or colour or disability or sexuality kept them from the pages of history. She had just begun an energetic oration on the value of reconceptualising the unknown when the restaurant fell into darkness.

'Power out,' the waiter told them apologetically, his face lit up by the light from his mobile. 'The whole of the north, they reckon.'

'Traffic will be chaos out there,' Carole sighed. 'We'd better leave now because it's only going to get worse.'

They got into taxis pointed in opposite directions, and Evangelia waved through the back window as they departed. The traffic lights were out, and the driver approached each one at speed, demanding his right of way. Evangelia squeezed her eyes shut, the world dark save for the car headlights, and felt terrified and alive. There were rules but those rules needed to be changed.

When she arrived home, the kids were running feral about the darkened house. Peter had gathered together all her scented candles, and the house smelt of a pungent mix of citrus and spices.

'Thank god you're home, babe,' Peter said, kissing her cheek with the earnest affection he had adopted in their post-argument wake. 'They're lost without their technology.'

He explained that the children had been going from room to room, shrieking in disbelief each time they discovered a new piece of equipment that could not work without electricity, their

323

propensity to forget to recharge their various devices finally catching up with them. Evangelia watched her children, bathed in the privilege of never knowing need, and knew this was what her mother had wanted. These spoiled little goblins, exactly as she'd hoped for.

'The computer doesn't work either,' Nick called from the study, his voice bordering on hysterics.

'I told you before,' Peter said. 'Nothing that uses electricity will work.'

'But it all does,' Xanthe wailed. 'All of it.'

Peter's eyes rolled in the flicker of a vanilla bean candle, and Evangelia swallowed a smile.

'Oi, you lot, come here.'

She assembled her weary children around the kitchen table and surveyed them.

'We're going to try something new.'

They looked at her suspiciously.

'We're going to tell each other memories.'

The children exchanged looks.

'Boring,' they uttered in unison.

Peter looked like he agreed.

'No, it won't be. This is what they used to do back in the village before they had electricity. And all these memories are going to help me write a story about Yiayia's life.'

Xanthe sighed heavily. 'This sounds lame.'

'Sure, it sounds lame. But it's what we're going to do. Because the power is out and the night is long and I'm the mother here.'

The children nodded begrudgingly. Nick's head slumped to his hands in defeat.

'Good. Now I want you to tell me some of your memories of Yiayia.'

Nick thought for a moment. 'Her chin was hairy. Like, really hairy. And some of the hairs were so long I wanted to grab them with my hand and pull and pull and pull until it burst out like one of those magician's scarves.'

Evangelia stared at her son. 'That's not the kind of memory we're looking for. Think of things Yiayia would want people to know about her.'

'Her cooking,' said Xanthe. 'She was the best cook. Better than you. Even better than *thea* Lydia.'

'And her cuddles,' Nick joined in. 'Her cuddles were really strong like she thought you might die if she let you go.'

'She did,' Peter said. 'She thought you kids were going to die all the time. Every cough, every cold. She was convinced everything was coming to get you. It's a wonder we ever got you to kinder.'

'And her songs,' Xanthe said. 'You know that one song she used to sing . . .'

She started humming it, clapping her hands to the beat. The song pulled at Evangelia's chest, sending memories of her own childhood skittering about her mind.

'You mean this one?' she said, and she began to sing.

Παλαμάκια παίξετε
κι ο μπαμπάς του έρχεται
και του φέρνει κάτι τι
κουλουράκια στο χαρτί.

'Yes, that one!' Xanthe cried. 'What does it mean?'

Evangelia sighed.

'How many years of Greek school and you don't know what the lyrics mean? It's a song for little kids. Come on, guys, the words are really simple.'

They worked through the lyrics together, Evangelia and Peter doing a bulk of the work and coming to the final conclusion that Greek school, and indeed the language of their forebears, was lost to their children.

Clap your hands,
his dad is coming
to bring him something,
cookies in paper.

'That's what it means?' Xanthe looked disappointed. 'That's pretty dumb. It sounds much better than it means. Why would Yiayia sing us that? It's all about a man. And you never gave us cookies in paper, Dad. You never gave us cookies at all.'

'There's another verse, you know,' Peter said, ignoring this.

This surprised Evangelia. 'Really?'

Peter nodded. 'Hardly anyone sings it, but my mum used to sing it to me.'

He sung the verse to his family. As he did, Evangelia's eyes filled with tears. This time it was the mother coming home and she would take her small child onto her lap.

'Wait a moment.'

Evangelia reached down into her bag and pulled out the remnants of her leather-bound journal, the scribbles and photo-copies of her half-discoveries wedged between its pages. She wrote down these lyrics. When she was finished, she looked up at her family, their faces bathed in sickly sweet candlelight.

'What else do you remember?'

27

DB

Jonesy.

DB stared at the blank space. He stared at it some more until his eyes went fuzzy and he remembered he needed to blink. He brought his hands to his face, cupping them over his chin as if to wrench words into existence, but this didn't work. After some time, he moved his hands to the keyboard and rested them there, hovering, as if waiting for a non-existent light to turn green. *My hands are waiting for Godot*, he thought to himself, and realised at this moment how very tired he was.

'There's nothing left now.'

He started and looked over his screen at Nell. 'Pardon?'

'All the paperwork is complete. For Madeline's case. I just have the closing letter to do but other than that, that's everything. Does this mean it's all over?'

That was what it meant, wasn't it? He nodded. Nell kept watching him.

'I . . .' she started, then stopped herself.

She looked exhausted, her skin slack and pale, and crowded

with angry red stress blemishes. Her shoulders sagged like empty windsocks, her eyes flat, and he noticed her nails bitten ragged as she held a hand to her chin.

'Do you ever regret things?' she asked, her voice small. 'Cases?'

Of course he did. All the time.

'There's no use in regretting them,' DB replied. 'You just have to try to do things better next time.'

His father had told him this once, and it had never really helped. Nell looked bothered by this.

'That's our luxury, isn't it?'

'And our curse.' DB offered her what he hoped was a comforting smile. 'You did your best. Just remember that.'

Nell tilted her head to deflect the praise. She neither accepted nor returned the compliment. DB waited a moment more then stood and stretched.

'I'm off now. Got to get to Rudy's kinder before they lock him in for the night. You heading off?'

'Soon,' Nell replied. 'I just need to do the closing letter. Do you want to see it before you go?'

DB shook his head. 'I trust you to do it.'

Nell tilted her chin a moment, then nodded. 'Enjoy your weekend then.'

DB closed the empty email and put his computer to sleep. He drove north in the sports car, voracious hip-hop blasting from his car speakers. He bobbed along as he drove, turning it down whenever he pulled to a stop beside other cars. Once he hit the freeway he wrenched the volume as high as it could go, feeling the bass shudder through his muscles and ricochet about his brain. It took nearly two full rotations of the CD to get to Rudy's kinder. As he turned the corner, he muted the volume, then fumbled to switch to one of Rudy's CDs. He picked the least mind-numbing and primed it ready for Rudy's arrival.

It took DB a couple of minutes to find the entrance to the kinder and he ended up following a harried-looking woman in a suit through an unassuming side gate. It had been months since he'd been here, he realised. Not since the day they had brought Rudy in for enrolment. The woman had entered through a second gate which swung shut behind her. DB realised it needed a code. He had been given it, he vaguely remembered, but hadn't bothered to memorise it. He called to the woman ahead of him.

'Sorry, but I seem to have forgotten the code. Are you able to remind me?'

The woman gave him an understanding look but shook her head.

'You know we're not allowed to tell other people. I'll let one of the staff know you're there.'

'Thank you,' he called, but she had already turned away.

DB waited, embarrassed. As he stood there, a man in jeans and an oil-stained polo shirt hurried past him, jamming the code into the little box. He held the gate open, beckoning to DB, and DB followed him through quickly, fearing that alarms might start going off.

'Can I help you?'

Another woman was standing before DB, arms planted squarely on hips. DB wondered if he had met her all those months ago. She raised her eyebrows at him, equally warm and suspicious.

'Ben Arnolds,' he said. 'Rudy's dad.'

'Rudy's dad?'

The woman looked surprised, as if until this moment she had assumed Rudy had sprung fully formed from Sylvie's skull like a Greek god.

'This is a first, then.'

DB suppressed the urge to respond.

'I'm here for my child,' he muttered.

They drove eastwards accompanied by the chirpy trill of Rudy's CD. Rudy sang along, his tinny soprano cutting over the music. DB watched him in the rear-view mirror every so often, watched his little eyes close as he swooped to high notes that weren't actually there. Eventually they pulled into his parents' driveway, coming to a stop behind his mother's Prius. Rudy looked at his father questioningly.

'We're going to stay with Nana and Grandfather tonight,' DB explained. 'For fun.'

Rudy nodded as if this made perfect sense.

'You're staying with Nana and Grandfather, and Mummy is staying with Nonna and Nonno. And I'm staying with everyone.'

'Yes,' replied DB, and because he didn't want his son to think he was about to cry, he gave him a toothy Cheshire grin instead.

His parents' house sat comfortably in the middle of a spacious block, willows and other swooping deciduous things embracing the red-brick cottage. 'Cottage' was his mother's term for the house, which had a faux turret, formal and informal sitting rooms and enough studies for every occupant. They had renovated it 'old', meticulously keeping with the heritage value of the area and engaging an architect friend famed for her knack at upholding tradition while ensuring the latest of technological creature comforts. DB let them into the house, jamming his leg across the doorway to stop the inevitable.

'Stay, Woofer,' DB growled, but the little white demon ignored him, valiantly trying to vault his leg despite its lack of height.

'Bad Woofer,' Rudy chided the dog, and DB felt a striking affinity to his son.

His mother was bustling about the kitchen, throwing cutlery on the table and bread into the oven.

'Five minutes,' she informed them, giving Rudy a quick cheek-squeeze and reaching to refill her wineglass. 'Your father's on his way back from the drycleaners. We took some of your shirts too because god knows what state they're in. Anyone can see they've gone through the machine.'

DB ignored his mother, taking Rudy through to the bedroom the three of them would be sharing to dump his little bag.

'Who sleeps here?' Rudy asked, pointing to the crumpled, hair-lined bedsheets.

'You, me and Woofer unfortunately,' DB replied, watching his son compute this.

'Woofer will die one day,' Rudy replied. 'Just like Malcolm.'

DB ruffled his hair affectionately.

'Yes, he will.'

'I'm going to tell Nana,' Rudy added.

Often his nana gave him prizes like pencils when he told her something clever.

'By all means,' DB encouraged him, smiling as Rudy marched confidently out of the bedroom.

His mother had made some kind of exotic stew for dinner. This was what she had called it. An exotic stew from the Middle East that she had found on the internet. It had figs in it and tasted exactly like one would imagine a stew with figs cooked by someone with no experience in this would taste. Rudy poked at it with his fork, fascinated by the viscosity.

'What's this animal?' he asked, stabbing at a piece of fig.

'Fig,' his nana replied, leaving Rudy to imagine what a fig would look like roaming the untamed savannah.

Unlike Sylvie's family, DB's family tended to eat in relative silence, consuming at least three-quarters of their meal before it was deemed appropriate to talk. His father cleared first his plate then his throat, settling his fork and spoon down in the middle of the empty dish.

'How was court yesterday?'

Despite the long history of psychological disaster it had

caused, DB was in that moment thankful for his parents' inability to discuss matters either emotional or personal. Neither had mentioned Sylvie nor questioned his desire to not return to his own house.

'Settled on the steps,' he replied. 'Consent without admission, limited order. Our client dropped the cross-application but she gets to see the kids. Not exactly a win.'

'Strategically a good outcome, though,' his father replied. 'And not an absolute embarrassment for the firm. Well done.'

Strategically, yes, thought DB, but this didn't make him feel any better. He could see Madeline's face now, the way her whole body had shrunk at her own decision. His father topped up their wineglasses.

'Your mother and I have decided that fifty dollars a week is sufficient for board,' he continued.

'I'll transfer the money tonight,' DB nodded.

'No rush.' His father smiled generously. 'Tomorrow is fine.'

DB took a large mouthful of wine. This was the longest he had been back in his parents' home since he'd first moved out during university.

'Would you like Nana to read to you before bed?' his mother asked Rudy, indicating a pile of books she had purchased from the Oxfam shop.

'No, thank you,' Rudy replied, and they went back to eating in silence.

'Your mother also bought him some underwear,' DB's father added after a time, directing his conversation to DB. 'We all have to grow up at some point.'

'I'll take that on notice,' DB replied, avoiding his father's gaze.

Later, once he'd tucked Rudy into bed and checked to make sure Woofer wasn't smothering him as he slept, DB grabbed a towel and jogged down to the aquatic centre around the corner from his parents' house. His parents lived in the affluent part of the north-east and apparently this entitled the area's residents to exercise until late at night if they so desired. An entitlement they apparently didn't action, because the pool itself was empty but for a bored-looking staff member pushing a broom around the locker area.

DB slid into a lane and spent some time adjusting his goggles. He hadn't swum since the fight and his body was feeling it. His shoulders were tight, his neck strained, and there always seemed to be a constant, tender pang of pain behind his eye sockets. This may also have been a result of the lack of sleep, but who kept count of these things anyway? DB pushed himself into the first lap and tried to clear his mind. Only his mind wasn't prepared to be cleared. As he touched the far end with his hand, he gave up suppressing things and let his mind start swirling.

It had been a terrible fight, the worst they'd ever had. Things had never picked up again after the birth control incident and instead they'd niggled and picked and poked and stretched each other until it had exploded into a nuclear argument wrought from something tiny he couldn't even recall now. Some poorly constructed sentence that had electrified the field of shallow buried landmines, and they'd hopped from one explosion to the next in a fraught choreographed disaster. They were like the scavenger birds in Rudy's documentaries, picking away at each other until nothing remained but bleached calcium phosphate. And then things had gone ballistic and they'd both said all the things they'd stored away – all the things they'd never said for the sake of maintaining harmony – and now neither of them could unsay them, let alone look at one another. The next day Sylvie had texted him at work to say she was going to stay with her parents for a little bit and he'd managed two hours in the empty house before the silence had driven him crazy, and neither of them had been back since. And neither had really spoken to the other, apart from the minimum amount required to organise Rudy. Though, in fairness, she had texted him that morning, brief and succinct: *Not pregnant, arsehole.* So there was that.

The pool suddenly fell into darkness. As DB reached the end, he pulled himself upright and looked about blindly. Through the floor-to-ceiling windows he could see the darkness stretch out across the suburb and realised it must be a blackout. He paused, panting, then pushed himself off the wall and into a new lap. His heart was pounding in his chest but he continued pulling himself through the dark. Without light to contextualise the world around him, it felt like he was freefalling – gliding – drifting through a heavy darkness that pulled at him and buoyed him, and his head spun with the sensation of statelessness.

It was all meant to get better once the case had finished and everything was back to normal, but now that it was over, Madeline hung about him like a ghost. It had started when he'd first read through the affidavit, bringing to life that damaged, rotten marriage. He was nothing like Eric, he knew this, but it forced him to dredge through his memory for evidence of recent moments when he and Sylvie had been properly happy. When he hadn't had half his mind on work – or else been physically at work – because somewhere it had become less about living and more about making a living. After Sylvie left he'd walked into that empty house and he'd been crippled with the embarrassingly clichéd realisation that he'd bought a big house and filled it with nice things and for the life of him couldn't work out why this hadn't worked. And he realised that if someone had asked his own wife to do the same – to put upon paper her own version of their marriage – he was not at all certain of what it would say. He could not, despite his efforts, shape the words she would use, the adjectives she'd rely on, the metaphors she'd fish from the bottom of her reserves to conjure their marriage in these last few years. When he tried to, all her words were his, said in his tenor and formed from his lips. And his child's teacher had no idea who he was, and his parents had given his bedroom to the dog even though there were other spare rooms, and they'd settled on the bloody steps because this was the only way that poor woman would be able to see her children, and he'd gone and lost all the things he was lucky enough to have in his life because he figured they'd hold until he was ready to start living properly, which would never bloody happen because he was nearly forty and if his life hadn't already started there was something worrying and esoteric about that. And he was angry with Sylvie for not being clearer about what she wanted, and he was angry with himself for not listening properly, and he was angry with his parents because there were other bloody spare rooms the dog could have taken, and he was angry with Madeline for accepting the impossible deal, but mostly he was angry with himself because he had a hand in so much of it, with the exception of the dog. And he knew that there was nothing he was going to do about any of it because it was all too hard and he didn't admit defeat, and he wasn't entirely sure of what he was supposed to do anyway, so he swam and he swam through the darkness and the uncertainty, until eventually they had to poke him with a pool noodle to tell him it was time to go home.

DB made his way carefully into the darkened house, navigating from memory the passages and steps until he doubted himself and opened the torch app on his mobile. Shielding the light, he gently opened the bedroom door, and his heart dropped suddenly to his stomach. The sheets were tucked in as he had left them, Woofer curled up in one corner, and Rudy was nowhere to be seen. DB rushed into the room, pulling up the sheets as if he might find his son underneath their taut surface. He crouched down, the light of his mobile illuminating the emptiness beneath the bed, then he straightened, terrified. Perhaps Rudy had awoken to find DB gone and wandered off in search of him? Or he might be with his grandparents, though DB knew this was unlikely. DB crashed out of the room then stood in the hallway trying to decide which way to go. He turned towards the front door and had set off at a great loping speed when there was a flush from the darkness behind him. He turned, tripping himself up, then looked down the hallway to see Rudy wander casually out of the bathroom, his pyjamas pants askew and his eyes lit up like a dozy rabbit in the light of DB's mobile. DB pulled himself upright then half-crawled towards his son, who allowed himself to be swallowed up by DB's hug.

'I did it on my own,' Rudy informed DB, his voice muffled in fabric. 'The toilet. I was very brave.'

They lay in the bed side by side and Rudy pressed his body into the cave of his father's.

'I wish Mummy was here so I could tell her,' Rudy sighed, burrowing against DB's chest. 'She would care the most.'

As Rudy's breathing became measured with sleep, DB realised his son was right. Sylvie would care the most because that was what she did for them. She cared for them both in a way that no one else did – individually and as a family – and this capacity for genuine love had been one of the reasons he had fallen for her in the first place. Had been the reason he had worked and saved and accumulated around them this fortress of possessions because he knew no other way to match this unwavering love she had for them. As he stared into the darkness, caught between the shudder of Rudy's sleep and the whimper of Woofer's slumber, DB worried that this realisation had come far too late to matter.

28

Nell

Reference: 3284/16BA
Williams & Williams
Queen Street, Melbourne 3000

16 September 2016

Dear Ms Madeline Murray,

Re: Closing your case

Thank you for allowing Williams & Williams to represent you in this matter. Your case and our representation of you are now concluded. As explained at our last meeting on 15 September 2016, we are closing your file and will take no further action on your behalf. We are returning all original documents and papers you gave us in connection with this case. We will also retain a copy of your file for a period of seven (7) years, after which the file may be destroyed at our discretion, provided there is no action on it, in accordance with rule 14 of the Legal Profession Uniform Law Australian Solicitors' Conduct Rules 2015 under the Legal Profession Uniform Law 2015. You are advised to keep all your information concerning this matter in a safe place in case you need it in the future.

If we may be of assistance in the future to you or to your friends or family members who may need legal help, we hope you will contact us.

Yours faithfully,

Helena Swansea,

on behalf of Benjamin Arnolds, Williams & Williams

Nell reviewed the letter, the same letter sent to each of their clients when things were complete. Of course, it was missing something, something along the lines of an apology or a supplication, but these were all empty platitudes, as DB had told her so many times. A selection of words bundled together that offered no real balm or absolution. Scanning it a final time, Nell printed the letter then sealed it in an envelope and placed it in the mail tray to be sent the following week. She collected her things then left the quiet office.

The tram was near empty as it rattled its way out of the city, too late for the post-work rush and too early for any homeward-bound Friday night revellers. Now and then a passenger or two boarded, but never more than alighted, making it feel as if Nell had survived some kind of apocalyptic event and existed now alone in this empty, barren world. She and the elderly woman in a *salwar kameez* who had fallen asleep and the young man with facial piercings who was cradling a basket full of dirty laundry. The tram pulled to a stop yet again, its doors opening to expel the young man and his sodden laundry. A woman stepped inside and it took Nell a moment to recognise her as Madeline. Gone was the makeup and jewellery of yesterday. Her hair was pulled back into a messy ponytail and she was dressed casually in jeans and an old T-shirt. She looked around, noticing Nell, and offered a small wave. As she approached, Nell shifted her handbag, knocking it to the floor in the process. Its contents spilled everywhere, mints and hair ties and empty chocolate wrappers fluttering about. The bookmarks too, a feminist rain shower all over the sticky public transport floor. Nell had never given them out, completely forgetting they were in there. Stooping to help Nell shove things back into her bag, Madeline seized one. They settled back into the seats and Madeline reviewed the bookmark.

'"Where are all the women?"' she read aloud.

'My mother,' Nell offered by way of explanation.

'She made all these bookmarks?'

Nell nodded.

Madeline squinted at the bookmark in her hand. 'This one has a typo.'

'Where?' Nell pictured her mother's embarrassment when she found out she had sent forth into the world error-ridden statements. 'Oh, no. She's spelt it like that on purpose. Gets rid of the word "men", see?'

Madeline held the bookmark up again.

'Ah, I see. Clever woman. What does she write about?'

'She finds women who have been forgotten from history and writes them back in. All the places they've been left out. She's been teaching classes, too. Women's biography.'

Madeline nodded at this, her eyes on something out the window.

'Sounds like the kind of class I need.'

They sat in silence as the university passed before them, the medical building, the music conservatorium, vet and agricultural sciences. And behind them the rooms where they'd both dozed off during tutorials or torts or statutory interpretation. The tram stopped to let in a few more passengers.

'Did I make the right decision?' Madeline asked, her voice a whisper.

Nell didn't know how to respond.

'I read the newspapers,' Madeline continued. 'I know all these changes are meant to be happening to the legal system.

Maybe I should have held off longer. But the problem is, he reads the paper too.'

She sighed.

'You know, for a long time, years now, I dreamt about how it would feel to leave. Yearned for it so desperately. But it's not all it's cracked up to be. I live with my mother, I have no money and now I have this intervention order to my name.'

She kept looking at the university out the window, her head tilted away from Nell. From this angle Nell could make out the faint white zigzag of a scar along the underside of Madeline's chin. She'd never noticed it before, though she'd stared at her face countless times.

'Do you think I could go back there?' she said, indicating the buildings with her head. 'Seize myself by the shoulders and shake until I see some sense?'

Madeline raised her hands to her face and let out a small moan.

'There's so much still to come. Property, parenting orders, the rest of the boys' lives . . . The rest of my life. And he won't make any of it easy.'

She made a sound, a frustrated yelp, then ran her hands back through her hair.

'But at least I'm free. Or whatever version of freedom this is meant to be.'

She pulled the cord to indicate she was getting off then rose from the seat. She turned to Nell, her mouth forming a sentence as Nell interrupted.

'Please don't thank me.'

Madeline let out a gruff laugh.

'I wasn't going to. I was going to ask if I could keep this?'

She waggled the bookmark between her fingers. The tram groaned to a halt and then Madeline was gone. Nell stared at the empty seat, the vacant space where Madeline no longer sat, and understood now what her mother had been searching for all these years. What Rani had been trying to say. All those stories no one told. All those Madelines who were forgotten, again and again, but whose stories were longing for telling because they were complex and uncomfortable and this was why they mattered. She looked at a bookmark in her hand. Where *were* all the women?

When Nell arrived home the house was bathed in darkness. She flicked the light switches but nothing worked, so she groped her way down the hallway. Seymour's door was closed and she paused before it, pressing her ear to the wood, but inside was quiet. In her room, she shed her clothes then sat on the edge of her bed, staring out at the shadows. She looked, blindly, at where her hands should be, then held them to her face, pressing her fingers into the ridges and furrows, running them along the lines of her jaw. Would she recognise this face if it were placed before her, with only the memory of touch to assist her? She explored her face a moment, before realising the strangeness of this action, then let her hands drop to her lap. She expected herself to think of things – to feel things. Guilt, for instance, or perhaps sadness. But surprisingly she felt nothing, which was easier than she thought it would be, so she remained like that for some time until eventually she curled into sleep and dreamt of going back and starting things again.

29

Aida

Once more it had been the silence that had startled Aida as she pulled herself from dreams of her father stumbling blindly through the darkness. That same foreboding silence, a darkened mirror of all those weeks earlier. Perhaps, she had thought, it was another bad day. She'd padded down the hallway and knocked gently upon Elham's door. The first thing she noticed was Niki's little mattress, the sheets rumpled and discarded from where they'd recently been slept in. Niki was now at Elham's empty bed, coiled around the bottom like a forgotten kitten. She looked up sleepily as Aida entered the room, her dark eyes sticky with tears.

'Maman?'

It was a plea more than a question. Aida knelt beside her, holding out her arms.

'Why don't we check the house?'

Niki crawled into her arms, surprising Aida. She clung to the little girl, terrified. She was back on the island, watching in mute horror as the officers cut the young man down from his fan cord noose. As another still body was rushed away for its stomach to be pumped or skin sewn back together. *Please don't let us find her*, she prayed. Not like that. They wandered through the house, neither saying a word, before finishing in the empty living room.

'Why don't you wait here for a moment, watch some television?' Aida started, but Niki refused to let go.

So the two of them made their way back to Elham's room where Aida scanned her belongings. It was a room of little character: their bedding, Niki's toys and a half-filled wardrobe dominating the space. The few clothes Elham owned were still there; only her coat and handbag were missing. As they left the room Aida noticed Niki's lonely mud-speckled boots by the front door. Elham was gone.

They stood frozen in the hall, Aida's mind racing. Aida tried Elham's number, but each time the phone went straight to the message service, her mobile powered off. She was gone. Elham was gone. Aida racked her brain. She should tell someone. But who would she tell? It was Friday and Sarah wouldn't be back in the office until Monday. And maybe Elham wasn't gone, after all. Maybe she had left the house to run some urgent errand. She could be back at any moment. You couldn't report someone missing until twenty-four hours had passed, that was the thing, wasn't it? That was what they said in movies and movies were usually right, weren't they? Well, not all movies. Or most movies. But that bit was probably right. And she might not be missing, she might just be out at the store. Surely there were stores open at this time of the morning? There would be an explanation for all this, something other than the only one she could think of right now, which was that Elham was gone and that they – Aida and Niki – were still here. Niki. She looked at the little girl tangled in her arms. That is what she would do today: focus on Niki until Elham returned. And if she didn't – no, focus on Niki.

'Maman has gone to an appointment,' Aida began, pounding her forehead with an exaggerated slap. '*Khaleh* Aida completely forgot about it! Silly me. Maman had to go but she'll be back later, okay? Today we get to spend the day together! Isn't that wonderful?'

She ended on a patently false high note, convincing neither of them. What would her mother do right now? She rattled through the drawers of her memory. The slow, solid *thwack* of slipper on palm rose up in her mind. She shoved this aside. Something else . . . Food! She would feed them! There was nothing in Iran that couldn't be fixed with a good hefty meal . . .

'So we start with breakfast,' she announced, and they set off for the kitchen.

She leant forward, attempting to lower Niki from her arms. The little girl clung to her like a terrified koala, her fingernails digging into Aida's flesh.

'Ahh, Niki! I can't make breakfast with you in my arms. Hop down, I promise I'm not going anywhere.'

Niki allowed herself to be released onto the floor, grasping the hem of Aida's pyjama top and following close behind her as she prepared their breakfast. She made a proper Irani breakfast – eggs, cheese, jam, butter and bread – all to distract Niki, who peered anxiously towards the doorway every couple of minutes. As Niki ate, Aida checked her mobile. Nothing. She rang Elham's phone. No answer. She put it to one side. Once they'd finished eating, Aida looked at Niki for inspiration. They needed to leave this house, for one thing. Every corner and shadow shrieked of Elham, her scent embedded in the furniture and her absence thundering about the walls. She couldn't deal with this upsetting Niki; not with the gnashing of teeth or the intensifying wails.

It was a long walk to the playground, Niki refusing to relinquish her stranglehold on Aida's clothing. They shuffled along the pavement, crab-like and stumbling, as Aida chatted away like a deranged suburban David Attenborough.

'Oh, Niki, look at the butterfly over there. See how it is eating the flower? Or maybe it's drinking? Oh, wait, I remember, it's pollinating it, which is kind of like, never mind, let's look at something else. Look at the puppies over there! They're – oh, let's look somewhere else. Wow, it's definitely springtime out here . . .'

By the time they arrived at the playground Aida had provided rudimentary explanations of how worms could see, why some cats have no tail and a range of other flora and fauna–centric titbits, most of which she had largely made up and none of which Niki exhibited the slightest interest in. The sun had pushed through the clouds and shone down on the playground as if it were a holy temple at the end of an arduous mountain trek.

'Here we are!' Aida beamed, trying unsuccessfully to pry her shirt from Niki's fist.

It was a neat suburban playground, the play equipment fenced off behind brightly coloured bars and a safety gate. Aida held the gate open for Niki, who hesitated. Her eyes surveyed the high bars and she shook her head firmly. Aida followed her gaze.

'You'll be able to come back out, I promise.'

Niki shook her head again.

'What if I come with you?'

At this, Niki hesitated. She looked around, her eyes flitting from the tall fence to the swings and back to Aida. Uncertainty and conflict battled across her face. Aida bent down, lifting her onto her hip, then entered the playground. Niki flinched as the gate clanged shut behind them. And side by side, the two of them conquered the slide and became masters of the swings. After a time, Aida grew tired. Her neck ached from stooping to fit the play equipment and her arms were tired from Niki's weight. Before her, Niki hurtled down the slide, chortling with glee. She landed on her bottom at the base of the slide and looked up to Aida for validation.

'*Afarin*, Niki-joon! Well done!'

Aida stretched her neck, feeling the taut familiar pull.

'Let's do something else for a bit.'

Niki seemed reluctant but scurried after Aida as she made for the gate. They wandered through the playground until they found a bench warm from the sun. Aida sat down, pulling Niki up beside her. She checked her phone for messages then tried Elham's number. It went to her message service, again. Niki watched her expectantly.

'Maman back home now?' Niki asked, her deep brown eyes peering into Aida's.

In those eyes Aida saw faces from the past – her father, Shirin, Lida, and all the pain attached to this endless ocean of loss. Her mother's voice on the end of that faraway phone line. The familiarity of its sadness.

He asks for you. Begs for you to come see him one last time. I tell him you can't, that he must understand this . . .

She blinked, blurring her vision, then looked away. She cleared her throat.

'Not yet. But I think it's time I told you another Persian story. You remember how I told you about Rostam before?'

Niki nodded.

'Well, today I'm going to tell you about his father, Zal. Zal's father Sam was a champion of Iran. He was lord of many parts and very noble. When Zal was born his face was paradise but his hair was pure white.'

Niki frowned at this.

'Why?'

Aida thought. She didn't know.

'Not everything has an answer, Niki-joon. Now listen. Sam thought this was a bad omen, a sign of horrible things to come, so he took his baby son and left him near the place of the Simurgh. A Simurgh, Niki, is a giant bird, like a phoenix. Now, the Simurgh took pity on poor baby Zal and took him to her nest on Damavand, the tallest mountain in the Alborz.

She raised him like he was her own child, until he was tall and strong like a cypress tree.'

She paused.

'Are you listening, Niki? This story is more than a thousand years old.'

Niki reluctantly withdrew her finger from her right nostril.

'Now back at Sam's palace he had a dream about his long-lost son and woke up feeling guilt and shame for abandoning him. So Sam rode off into the mountains to find Zal. Simurgh saw Sam coming and told Zal that he would soon be returned to his father. Zal, who was now a young man, didn't want to leave the Simurgh and the place that had been his home for all these years. So the Simurgh gave him two great copper feathers from her wing so that he would always live under her protection. If at any time he needed something, he should just throw a feather into the fire and the Simurgh promised she would come and help him. So Zal returned to his father and is finally treated like the prince he is. When Sam goes off to fight great wars for Iran he leaves Zal in charge, and Zal becomes a great ruler.'

Niki was watching her, fascinated.

'Two feathers?' she repeated.

'Yes,' Aida confirmed.

She searched the grass around them. There were leaves and detritus, and what was possibly a condom wrapper.

'Ah, here!' Aida plucked two feathers from the ground, dusting them off on her jeans. They were a greyish black, possibly from a pigeon, but they'd do. She handed them to Niki.

'Now many, many years later, Zal's wife Rudabeh was having trouble giving birth to their baby. Zal burnt a feather and the Simurgh appeared before him in the flames. She told him to run the remaining feather over Rudabeh's belly and the birth would be fine. Zal did as he was told and his baby was born safely. That baby was Rostam, and you know all about what kind of hero he becomes.'

Niki was staring at the feathers in her hand, transfixed. She twirled them in her pudgy fingers, then ran them along her cheek. Aida hoped they weren't full of lice.

'Well, that's two Persian stories you know now, Niki,' Aida said.

Niki nodded promptly.

'Who told you?' she asked, stroking the feathers along the back of her little hand.

Aida's breath caught. 'My baba, Niki-joon. He told me and now I'm telling you.'

Her face flushed with a sudden heat and she blinked quickly.

'Let's head home. It's well past lunchtime.'

And they headed off out of the park, hand in hand, the two feathers trailing in Niki's free hand. They took the scenic route, passing by the small shopping strip on the main street. The café tables were full as people took advantage of the springtime thaw. They stopped to buy sandwiches from a small family kiosk, eating them on a bench in the sun. Nearby, pigeons were squabbling over chips. Two small girls charged at the throng, shrieking with excited disgust. One of the girls lashed out with a foot, bursting into stunned tears when it unexpectedly connected with a tardy bird. Niki tut-tutted, her precious feathers clasped firmly in her fist. Aida stretched back, turning her face to the sun. In the distance she heard the clanging of bells from the Orthodox church and wondered if this meant someone had married or died. Small groups of elderly men sat cloistered around tables, calling to each other in Kurdish and Arabic and what might have been Italian. What had once been so foreign now felt so familiar.

Niki tugged at her sleeve, bringing her back to the present. Aida took the crusts from her hands, breaking them into pieces, and tossed some to the pigeons, Niki joining in. When the feeding frenzy died down they set off for home.

The house was empty when they arrived, but Aida wasn't surprised. They spent the afternoon sprawled before the television, napping in turns and wandering through the channels. Occasionally Niki whined for Elham and Aida sought creative new ways to postpone her arrival. Night-time crept across the house, and soon Aida rose from the couch.

'I'm going to the kitchen to make dinner,' she told Niki, who nodded, the two feathers still clutched tightly in her hands.

Aida had just opened the fridge when the house was plunged into darkness. In the sudden silence, Niki whimpered from the living room. Using her mobile for light, Aida found her, then the two of them examined the house. Nothing worked. For a moment Aida's world spun – perhaps she had forgotten to pay the power bill? She could have sworn she had. What if there was a reconnection free? She could never afford that, not on her own. She opened the front door, peering out. The whole street sat in darkness.

'It's a blackout,' she told Niki. 'Nothing to worry about. See – all the houses are like us.'

Back inside she searched the house for candles, knowing there were none. Bundling Niki into a jumper, they made their way down the dark street, Aida hoping the little store was open. They arrived to find it lit up like a well-stocked séance. Candles had been placed all about the shelves, capturing the various products in an ethereal glow. Tinned soup cast shadows onto the egg cartons and bread loaves shone as the light caught the edge of their plastic wrappings. It was magical and comical, and for a moment Aida thought back to the stories her mother had told of the war years just before her birth. Of the barren shelves and queues for sugar, flour and rice. The young man sat behind the counter, unloading candles from a box. He grinned when he saw her and motioned at the carton.

'Let me guess . . .' he said, pretending to be deep in thought. 'You're lucky we found another box,' he said as Aida counted out candles. 'It was like an Apple store earlier – lines around the corner. Apparently the whole north has been affected. Some issue at the substation.'

He noticed Aida counting the coins in her pocket.

'These ones are half price,' he told her. 'On account of their age.'

They both stood in silence as the lie drifted out into the darkness, wafting curlicues amid the candle smoke.

'Thank you,' Aida replied.

The young man reached across the counter and handed Niki a chocolate bar.

'It's nothing,' he said, looking up as a new wave of customers entered the store.

'Let me guess . . .' he announced, pretending to be deep in thought.

Back at the house, Aida lit a couple of candles. Niki watched with excitement, blowing them out with all the faux birthday strength she could muster.

'No, Niki, they're not –' Aida began, but gave up. 'Fine, a couple more.'

Eventually Niki tired of this game and the candles remained alight. Aida placed them about the living room, then had an idea.

'Let's take them outside. See what the stars are doing.'

They spread out a blanket then sat upon it cross-legged. Aida looked up, the night sky stretching before her. She knew these were foreign stars, upside down and inside out, and that somewhere up there was the Southern Cross. But she knew so little of her own stars, Tehran's nights too heavy with light and smog pollution, that this sky seemed neither new nor familiar. Beside her, Niki snuggled into her side. She yawned mightily, her heavy-lidded eyes mesmerised by the flickering candle. Suddenly Niki scrambled upright again. She seized a feather from her pocket and held it towards the flame.

'Wish?' she asked Aida.

Aida hesitated, then nodded. She moved the candle onto a patch of cement then motioned to Niki. Together, they held the feather over the candle. It trembled as the flame caught hold of it, lifting it into the air as it spewed putrid smoke into their nostrils.

'Maman, come home now, please,' Niki instructed the dancing feather.

As the feather burnt into nothing, Niki pressed her eyes shut tight. Aida copied her silently. Niki wished for her mother and Aida wished for her father.

*

They slept that night together on Elham's single mattress, her scent and worry wreathed around the two exhausted sleepers. Neither dreamt, their slumber as dark as the world around them. Aida woke early, as new light tiptoed through the window. Soft footsteps sounded in the hall and soon the door creaked open. Elham lay down beside her, Niki undisturbed between them. The two women watched each other. Finally Elham spoke, her voice barely audible.

'I got my letter. Two days ago . . . I . . . I thought she would be better off without me. That they'd take pity on her and let her stay.'

Her face was hard with the reality of what she'd done.

'But you came back,' Aida whispered, and with that Elham's body lost its rigidity, defeated as she pulled her daughter towards her.

They stayed like that for some time, the three of them squeezed onto the narrow mattress. Aida, Niki and Elham, still dressed in her coat. Inside her pocket, the rejection letter wedged itself between them, this new little family. Together again, if only for this moment.

Part 5

30

Aida

At times of seemingly dubious import – existential homework crises, the tail end of dinner parties, various family celebrations and milestones – my father was well known for conjuring silence with a single raised hand and embarking on his prized philosophical treatise. It varied little at each retelling yet never once failed to rouse a tear from his own stoic brown eyes, nor from my mother's, who often mouthed the best bits along with him. It went something like this: After reminding us all of his remarkable academic prowess in the fields of both history and literature, my father would squint into the distance, tangled deep within his own thoughts, then suddenly seize the air before him as if plucking the very truth of life from amid the atoms and particles. It's not what history makes of you that matters, but what you make of your history. He would wait then, for applause, before continuing his previous conversation as if nothing had happened at all.

I have thought of this often over the past few years, in these long unrelenting periods where there is nothing to do but think or go mad, or one then the other. My father's voice whispering gnomically in my ear as I ponder my present situation: what to make of it all when your trajectory does not land as you'd planned? Sometimes I wonder if it is possible to find a single trigger point in my history that set things in motion, each action and decision contributing to *the domino avalanche that brought me to this point? Or do they all bleed and blend into one another, largely inconsequential on their own but accumulatively inescapable? If there is one moment, what would that be? Did it start with our decision to frequent Café Naderi, with Lida and Afshar and the others? Or in the tangled sheets of Afshar's bed, where we promised each other defiant young eternity before I snuck back to my parents' home? Or with my fascination for stories and truths that led me to study journalism? Was it earlier than this – my father's tears at the censorship of his work, my anger at having to wear a headscarf when my brothers did not? Or was it all inevitable, this rising tide of frustration and disillusionment the only natural response to all that was happening around us? The stripping of university funding, the job shortages, and the crushing down of artistic and basic freedoms? In the tide of anger gathering as yet another of the magazines Hamid now worked for was shut down, or Shirin's university cutting scholarships before she could claim hers? Or had it started decades earlier when Khomeini's revolution failed to turn out as it had promised?*

I asked Afshar about this once, cross-legged on the couch while Lida and Shirin smoked by the open window. Their breath tumbled out into the evening chill, escaping into the smog.

'Nothing happens for a reason,' Afshar sighed, his recent apostasy at an all-time high. 'Not for any god-given one, anyway. It's all brought about by people – you, me, people we know and people we'll never know. It's that butterfly in the Amazon thing. Some power-hungry suit gets miffed because he is left off a taskforce and refuses to cast the deciding vote, and we're the ones who get stiffed. An entire village votes a certain way because they believe the fear-mongering, or a prodigal son returns in a Mullah's robes and tells them it's for the best, and women get banned from the stadium. A kid happens to leave his Facebook profile open and his mother recognises his friend in an underground band and the audience gets beaten up at a gig. It's all chance and luck, really.'

By the window Lida rolled her eyes.

'Old age is making you bitter,' she teased him. 'You really think there's no point to any of this?'

'Not that there isn't a point,' Afshar replied, reaching across the table to seize a handful of sunflower seeds. 'But that there's just so much beyond our control that influences everything in our lives. How much power do I really have over anything if somewhere someone else can make a snap decision and my life comes crashing down as a result? When you look at it like that, does my vote really matter? If there's one less person in that crowd at the protest is anyone going to notice?'

'If there's one less moody punk song will anyone really care?' Lida teased him, but he shrugged in response.

'Does anyone really care?'

'But surely that's the point?' Shirin spoke up. 'Because if everyone thought like that, no one would bother to do anything.'

Afshar didn't reply, splitting the shells mechanically between his teeth.

'It's about what you make of it,' I said slowly. 'What you make of your history that matters.'

Shirin grinned, having heard my father's monologue on count-less occasions.

'Because I might just be one person, but I'm me, and that matters. My voice matters. My story matters. And every single other person out there – they're "me" too. And we all matter. All of us.'

Afshar paused, his hand hovering over the bowl.

'And that's why I like you so much.' He beamed, leaning forward to kiss my forehead.

Lida laughed as Shirin tittered red-faced on the window ledge. And it became just another day in the mad rush towards everything that would happen.

If there was one day that led to all this, perhaps it could be this one: On that day in 2009 it all started with Lida's phone call, four long years since we'd first met in Naderi. The election results had been announced early – before all the polling stations had closed – a bullshit second term for Ahmadinejad. People were taking to the streets, Lida told us. Shirin was on her way. Millions, it turned out, were on their way. Of course we would come, Afshar told her. There was never the thought not to. When we arrived at Azadi Tower the streets were already full, people from all walks of life determined to seize back justice from the rigged election. University students, artists and intellectuals, but also religious conservatives, the elderly – everyone draped in shawls and scarves and cotton strips the vibrant green of our candidate Mousavi and our country itself. We didn't want a revolution – we'd had several of those and they hadn't worked out so well. What we wanted was democracy and reform. You could see it in Afshar's graffiti, his messages clearer and angrier. His music too, no longer sanitised anywhere near enough for Ershad approval. Online and in the streets our world exploded. Enough. Enough of it all.

I wasn't long graduated from university and these would become some of my first proper assignments. Much of my work piggy-backed on the contacts of more established journalist friends, helping me to publish at home between media bans as well as internationally. We milled about the sea of millions. Mobile coverage was out but I recorded as much as I could on my phone, changing the memory cards each time they filled. For nine days we were on the streets, the dirt and dust Ahmadinejad so easily dismissed as if we were nothing but a handful of belligerent grumblers instead of the seething, teeming millions demanding justice.

After a week or so it was clear the results would not be changed, but we stayed because our anger needed to be heard. We were exhausted, forgetting to eat, forgetting to sleep. My friends marched in the front – Shirin, Lida and Afshar – signs lifted high above their heads. 'Where's my vote?' 'Sorry our backs hurt your knife.' I existed amid it all, a furious blurred line between journalist and citizen, all my worlds colliding. Drifting between my friends and strangers, recording all I could. When the Basiji started killing people – spraying bullets through the air or beating people senseless with rods and canes – at first we couldn't believe it. Iranians killing Iranians, something none of us thought could ever happen. We found one boy lying on the street with blood pouring from a wound. We used his scarf to halt the flow, the swift crimson staining deep into the proud green fabric. I knew my parents would refuse to let me leave again if I returned home so I stayed with Lida instead in the tiny apartment of two activist friends. She wrote her name on her legs, just in case something happened to her – so they knew how to contact her family.

Arrests increased, my journalist and blogger friends plucked from their homes and tortured into confessions for crimes they hadn't committed. The government posted photographs from the marches in the streets and on the internet. Do you know this person? they asked, inviting people to turn each other in. I remember seeing Afshar's face amid a crowd shot, something he laughed off nervously. So many people left then, the fear of arrest and torture too much. A friend of my father had spent time in prison after the revolution because he didn't support the new regime, and when they found him protesting in the Green Movement he was executed straight away. Shirin was beaten so badly she lost half the teeth from her mouth, her face so swollen I walked straight past her hospital bed. Parents searched the hospitals for weeks after, trying to find their disappeared children, waiting outside Evin Prison to check the prisoner lists. Some searched for a month – a whole month not knowing whether they should mourn their child. I was there amid it all, bearing witness as best I could.

I know you want me to talk about this more, that this is where the crux of my story lies. That ultimately the outcome of my visa will depend on my ability to tell this story, every detail, every horrible memory. Reliving it again and again, for the people from *immigration, for the lawyers, for journalists hungry as I was. So many times that it begins to sound just like the stories my father and grandfather used to tell, as if it wasn't me but some other mythical figure at the centre of this grand cautionary tale, and Lida, Shirin, Afshar and my parents all merely supporting characters. Here is what happened, the paragraph you use to win the audience over to the wretched plight of people like me:*

The government crackdown was fierce, a rattled cobra lashing out at everything in its path. Mousavi was placed under house arrest while activists, journalists and bloggers languished in jail. Lida was arrested, plucked one night from her bed while her mother begged the agents for mercy. We were unable to see her for many months and when we did she was a broken, withered shell, her body ravaged by the hunger strike she refused to abandon after receiving a twelve-year sentence for crimes against national security. Afshar was arrested too, cautioned overnight and released because his father had connections within the government. He returned sullen and silent, his casual self-assurance beaten right out of him.

A year and a half after the fraudulent election, protests broke out again. People raged, their Persian anger in solidarity with the Arab Spring erupting across the region. I was there, my phone recording everything I could, my pictures and words beamed out across the world under a by-line I'd made up for protection. This wasn't enough. My phone was confiscated when I was arrested, hauled into the van with so many others and unloaded at a police station dense with the sweaty beaten bodies of my countrywomen and men. The stench of imprisonment, torture and decay was all-consuming as they marched me into the holding cell.

It's not what history makes of you that matters, but what you make of your history.

The train arrived at the station and Aida put her notebook away. She could sense the security fences already, waiting patiently for her arrival. It was the proximity to the living that had surprised Aida the most. This had been when she was first released into the community after so long behind wire, first on the island and then in the detention centre in Broadmeadows. A Kmart, some fast-food restaurants, a petrol station, a business park, then there it sat, flanked on all sides by residential houses. Existing, behind its barbed wire and locked doors, amid the everyday. This small unbearable world surrounded on all sides by the normalcy of life. Now, as she walked the final distance from the train station to the detention centre, she trailed her hand along the fenced perimeter. How much power these simple structures had, splitting the world into hope and horror, divided by simple wire and steel. She had thought of this last night – and the night before that, and the night before that – every night since Elham and Niki had gone back into detention. In the warm still night she had lain on her side watching the moon out her window. She was never quite sure if it was coming or going, pregnant with possibility or wasting away into nothing.

Tremors of something – fear perhaps, or triumph – ran through her as she signed into reception, leaving behind her mobile phone and valuables as the guard checked through the bag of gifts she had brought with her. There were others, too, signing in. An elderly Sri Lankan couple laden with spicy-smelling tiffin trays; three young women with political slogans across their T-shirts; a family dressed in sombre colours, the small children bickering despite their parents' stern warnings. As she made her way to the security door, she paused to let past a woman who was coming the other way. The woman pulled her headscarf tightly around her, her face creased with distress. It looked so different inside now that Aida looked with the eyes of a visitor. Knowing she could leave at any moment made the walls seem higher, the couches and tables more cramped. Two guards sat at the desk by the door, one of them fiddling with a small radio.

Every bit of furniture seemed occupied by people – detainees and their visitors – as they spoke in restrained voices. The security door behind her opened and all eyes flickered momentarily in its direction. Aida's body ached with memory of that expectation – that hope – for someone, anyone, to visit. She spotted Elham across the room. Her skin was pale, dark roots spreading into the retreating blonde of Massoumeh's dye. Elham smiled broadly and they embraced.

'I was looking at the door and look what it's brought,' Elham said, a hand on Aida's cheek. 'You don't have work today?'

'It's a public holiday,' Aida reminded her. 'For the horse race. Massoumeh sends her love.'

'Is it going well?'

It was, but Aida felt ashamed to say this.

'It's fine. You know how work is.'

'And the house? Have you found someone else? And the cats?'

Aida tilted her head. Sensing the change in occupants and weighing up future food prospects, the cats were long gone.

'Have you heard anything? About your appeal?' she said instead.

Elham sighed, deep and weary.

'Nothing. The lawyer says wait. As if we haven't been doing that already. It goes to court, I think, and then after that, nothing. I can't go back to Iran so . . . Maybe they will send us back to the island? I don't know. No one tells me anything. The lawyers try to but they're so busy. They have so many people to help. And I forget, or, I don't know, I hear but I forget the English, and then I don't remember what they told me.'

'And Niki?'

'She's here somewhere,' Elham said, craning her neck. 'She keeps asking for her friends. The cats too.'

Aida spotted Niki, prowling about the new visitors.

'Niki,' Elham called. 'Come say hello to *khaleh*.'

The little girl ignored her and continued to teeter around a nearby table where the Sri Lankan couple was laying out the food from the tiffin containers for their waiting family members. Aida offered a wave but Niki's eyes were fixed on the food.

'Niki!' Elham repeated impatiently.

Noticing Niki, the woman reached over and handed her something from one of the tins. Niki clutched the fried triangle in her hand and dove under the table, devouring it greedily.

'The food here is terrible,' Elham sighed. 'Not as bad as the island, or your cooking, but not good. She misses proper food. Always asking for fresh fruit. She misses kinder too.'

'Has she made friends?' Aida asked.

'Some,' Elham shrugged. 'The ones who are like us, put back in detention. They're okay. But the ones who have just come from offshore for medical treatment . . .' She shook her head. 'I worry about her being around them. They . . . their behaviour is not like children's should be.'

'I brought some toys,' Aida said. 'Books and things like that. Underwear.'

Elham took the bag from her. Seeing this, Niki darted over, wrenched the bag from her mother's hands and began searching it.

'*Salam*, Niki-joon,' Aida said, and Niki looked at her shyly. 'Forgetting me already?'

Niki shook her head. She considered Aida for a moment then offered her a small, sticky hug. Aida pulled her onto her lap as Niki picked through the shopping bag, discarding the underwear in a pile on the table. Aida and Elham watched her. Static erupted from the wireless in the corner, the guards leaning in intently. A voice drifted out across the room.

. . . and it's all systems go as they head towards the finish in this, the penultimate race before the big one. It's Turpentine and Island Sun

fighting for the lead. Darwinian Theory's behind and the bookies'
favourite Brilliant Mistake II. Island Sun is giving her all but can't
quite edge out Turpentine. Brilliant Mistake is falling behind.
And it's Turpentine by an inch – Turpentine has won by a nose!
Island Sun in a close second, followed by Darwinian Theory, then
Uncle Max. Brilliant Mistake II, the crowd favourite, finishing in
fifth place, ending her racing career with this disappointing result.
A tragedy, surely, for such a fine racer . . .

The guards shut off the radio and one of them handed the other
a five-dollar note, patting his shoulder in congratulations. No
one else had taken much notice. Niki seized a book from the bag
then shimmied off Aida's lap. She sat under the table, turning
the pages. Elham rubbed her eyes.

'You know what the hardest part is? I would do anything
to see my family. For them to be able to meet Niki. I thirst for
them, desperately. But I can't go back. I can't. You try so hard
to forget everything, all the horrible things, but they make you
relive them again and again. How many times have I told it?
How many interviews? That horrible application form, page
after page asking you who, how, why, why, why? Demanding
you justify every little detail. Again and again, each time
someone pressing you, challenging you, making you prove your
memories are real. And you have to tell it a certain way. The
way your mother's heart broke when she kissed you goodbye,
the way you breathed in, knowing you might never smell your
country again; these aren't the details they want.'

Elham stopped, her hands drawn to her face. She pressed
her eyes then looked back at Aida.

'After a while – after hearing all those other stories – I
started to worry. I heard what others had been through and
I thought maybe mine wasn't so bad. Maybe it wasn't enough
for them to let me stay. You see all those other people – the

horrific things they have been through – and I got scared. What if my story wasn't enough? What if it wasn't enough for Niki?'

Elham paused then leant forward.

'I changed my story. Not the entire thing, but bits of it. Told them they'd got it wrong originally – that there were mistakes in the translation. And then it just got away from me. Too many details that didn't match up. Sarah tried to warn me but I insisted it was the translation that was wrong, not me. The lawyers tell me it failed the merit review and now we have to ask the court for a judicial review. I don't know. It's so confusing. They tried to explain why I did it. Something about exceptional circum-stances? But everyone says it is messy. And now what can I do?'

Elham wrapped her arms around herself, sitting back in the chair.

'When I think about it I get so angry. I've never been lucky – it's written on my forehead. All the omens were there: my scarf catching on my earring as I pulled it from my head when the plane took off. Nearly missing my connection at Doha, my luggage bursting open onto the tiles as I ran the length of Hamad Airport. Niki has always been cramped, even inside of me. I never thought this would be my life. I never got to study but you know what I would do? I would do a PhD in Anger.'

Aida watched her, that raw anger seething from her eyes. It was a weary anger, fed up with the cacophony of misfortune and struggle that wove itself into life. It was an anger she had seen so many times before, waiting to be processed at the police station in Tehran, standing futilely on an Indonesian shore as rickety boats were tossed about by the waves, slowly decaying while the world sought somewhere to store you. Elham hammered the table with her fists, then forced herself out of her rage.

'But those are stories for sorrow and you don't need any more of those. Tell me about you, Aida-joon. How are you? How is your father?'

At this, Aida could not reply. Her brothers were there, waiting now. All of them crowded around the inevitability that lay in that bed. Everyone was waiting now. There was the sound of scuttled breathing and Niki appeared from under the table. Aida felt Niki's eyes boring into her own, capturing each tear and curiously drinking them in. She pulled herself to her feet, her hand shoved deep into her pocket.

'Here, *khaleh*,' she whispered.

She placed her last feather into Aida's trembling hand.

*

When Aida eventually left the detention centre she found the sky heavy with dark clouds. She made it halfway to the train station before the clouds fractured and she was soaked within seconds. She continued her trudge, one hand buried in her pocket wrapped protectively around the feather, the other clutching her notebook to her chest. Cars raced along the road beside her, oblivious to the spray of muddied water shooting up from their tyres.

When she arrived home, the house screamed emptiness. The empty room she kept shut up, the empty bowls where the Cyruses no longer fed. The letterbox empty all week and the emptiness in her chest, awaiting the grief that would soon descend for the empty space in the hospital room where her father lay emptying of life. She grimaced as she caught her reflection in Elham's gaudy mirror. Her face was wan and sunken in a way that would make her mother fuss. There were wrinkles now, well before their time, creased into her forehead from worry. She watched herself, each movement a disconnected jarring thing as if she were watching through a window rather than a mirror. *I won the national essay-writing competition*, she thought, *and look at me now*. The weight was unbearable, clawing and cawing inside her, exhausting her.

She changed into dry clothes then curled herself into a little ball on the couch, eyes heavy and willing. It was a brief sleep – restless and violent – her limbs flailing wildly as she spun through the madness of slumber. Poisoned grapes and pomegranate juice – that's what had killed Imam Reza. But suddenly it wasn't Imam Reza anymore, but a bedside in a hospital cluttered with downcast people. Amin and Alireza, faces taut with the effort of not weeping, their mother beside them pulling her flesh in disbelieving handfuls. Asadollah cradling his girth as tears tumbled down his whiskered cheeks. And the keening wail of bereavement echoing about the tiles though no one's lips were moving. It was her, Aida realised, the source of all this noise. The walls, lined with tomes from her father's own collection, rattled a moment as if shaken by some distant geological disturbance, then they stepped forward, Amin and Alireza, to close their father's eyes and begin the process of washing him. She could smell it, vibrant in her sleep, the camphor mixed with tears, the pure white of the cotton shroud that would bind him. A mullah drifted into the room, his black turban sullen on his head, to hover by the crumbling walls. And she pictured her father all those years ago – *against my dead body* – he'd always said, eyes shiny with his own wit. But when the man opened his mouth it was not the *namaz-e meyet* he called out but something different. *It's not what history makes of you that matters, but what you make of your history*, he said, their mother mouthing along with him, and when he was finished, the books on the shelves exploded into fine white powder. She stuck out her tongue and tasted the flour, tart and sullen with the density of childhood.

Aida woke with a start from what had barely been sleep to begin with. Her heart was racing as she struggled to place herself. And in that moment she knew it was over, that her phone soon enough would bring to life a mourning sung across the oceans. And there was relief, too, in all that pain, as suddenly everything seemed clearer. Because there they all were – all those stories. The avalanche of everything that had weighed on her for these months and years, amassed and stored and none of them ever forgotten. Haunted by these stories, those collected and kept, their ghosts walking through her each day until they could wander no more. Hers and others, all jostling inside her. From the streets and the prisons, the protests and grieving homes. The mourning on the shorelines and the helpless waiting and waiting for letters or loved ones or boats that never arrived. For visas that were never granted. For hope that was never resuscitated. They all sat inside, clambering and crying to be told. There were too many stories to tell, but everyone wanted them told. Everyone, everywhere, wanted them to be told. Even she.

And in that moment, Aida knew she would write them. Not just her own, but others too. She would wrench them from within her and breathe them into the world. And not just write. She would take them, person by person, story by story, and set them free. And they would be all of the stories – the good and the bad. The wretched journeys from home to hopelessness told alongside those of beauty and laughter and life. All of the people – those real intricate people she had met – made faceless by reality. She thought of a woman she'd met on the island, tired and weak from the tropical heat, her grown-up daughter long settled in Sydney. She'd told Aida, laughing with pride, about the phone call she'd had with her youngest grandchild who had gone on a swing by himself for the first time that week. How it had taken her far away from that sorrowful island through the temporal jungle of life to her own childhood in a small Iraqi village when she'd raced her own sisters to the newly built playground and they'd competed to see who could swing higher and higher and higher until the clouds were their gardens. This story, and so many like it, including her own, ready to be poured out into the world so that they were real and heard and mattered. It might be a book or it might be a memory, but she would release them into the world.

Aida staggered to her bedroom, seizing the notebook from under her pillow, then moved towards the kitchen. She sat down, all the world before her, and she started to write the stories of all those precious ordinary people.

31

Nell

I would like to start by welcoming everyone here on this momentous day! (pause for applause) First, let me acknowledge the traditional owners of the land on which we meet, the (TBC) people, and pay my respects to any elders past and present. (respectful pause) I would also like to acknowledge the Attorney-General for his attendance, and the Minister for the Prevention of Family Violence, who sends her apologies, as well as extend my appreciation to our partners and commend them on their finery. It truly is the race that stops a nation if we've managed to get you lot here today and away from the office! (pause for applause and/or laughter)

As you all know, today is not just about the Cup, though you'd be forgiven for thinking it was given the amount of bubbles already flowing. And may I take a moment to congratulate the ladies on their magnificent hats! Bravo! But before you get back to those delicious canapés and, of course, the punting, I'd like to touch on a slightly different topic. (ensure solemn tone)

Family violence is a scourge upon this nation – a national shame – and far too prevalent in our society. While Williams & Williams is primarily a commercial law firm, what really lies at our heart is people. And it was in this spirit that we launched our pilot pro bono venture some months ago, a program which we can now share with you has officially been rebadged 'Williams

& Williams for Women' or 'W4W'. (potential applause – read the room)

As many of you are aware, the program ran its first test case over the past few months, unburdening one of our hardworking local community legal centres of what proved to be a complex and challenging family violence case. I am delighted to report what could be considered the success of this case, for what could be more successful than a mother reunited with her children? (applause/ tears? Photographer briefed to capture this moment) On that note, may I congratulate the two fine Williams & Williams lawyers who ran this case – our pro bono guinea pigs, if you will – Ben Arnolds and Helena Swansea. (BA and HS to acknowledge AW and audience) This case marks a new way forward for the firm and we are pleased to announce that the program will now be rolled out across our offices as an opt-in social corporate responsibility initiative for any employee wishing to take part (pause for applause. Check watch) Time is fast approaching for all you punters so I'll leave it at that, but let's conclude by raising a glass to the official launch of W4W. And best of luck for the day!

(End of official proceedings – photos to be taken with dignitaries etc)

'What do you think?'

Nell glanced up from the printout. DB was shifting from foot to foot, his Stetson in hand. In his pinstriped suit and jaunty hat he looked like a High Street pimp as he danced about nervously. They hadn't used any of what she'd sent them. None of it. Nell pressed her thumbs into the printout, creasing the margins, but didn't say anything. DB seemed to take this as a sign of agreement and reached for it.

'Better get back to the marquee – it's almost time.'

He took the speech from her hands. She offered no resistance.

Instead, she bent awkwardly in her spring frock to grab her clutch from where she'd wedged it between her ankles.

'Off we go, then,' DB sighed, and trudged towards the marquee like a man off to his own execution.

Williams & Williams hired the same marquee every year, engaging their events team to fashion it into a changing themed extravaganza. One year it had been Roaring Twenties and they all got about drinking cocktails in flappers' frocks and tails, and another year it had been 1950s Hollywood Glamour resplendent with champagne fountain and photo booth. They always chose periods of affluence and excess; there had yet to be a Depression-era theme in which they wore mismatching shoes and drank gin from shared jars.

This year the theme was, inexplicably, Safari Days, and the marquee had been fashioned to look like a giant colonial safari tent complete with cane furnishings and caged parrots the events team had somehow managed to source. The parrots looked utterly unimpressed with the event, refusing to repeat any of the phrases jabbered at them, and instead emitting only drawn judgemental whistles whenever someone passed by in an outfit they didn't like, causing the more sensitive attendees to avoid the cages altogether. The Partners were there, red-faced and merry as they congratulated each other in turn on their choice of costume, choice on the field, and choice of plus one. Mr Williams floated between them, outlandish in safari suit and hat that made him look like a cartoon big-game hunter come to life in inner-city Melbourne. Scuttling along after him in a borrowed hat was the Attorney-General, who had either forgotten or failed to acknowledge the theme and was in his usual all-purpose navy business suit. Staff were already tipsy in the slightly discomforting way that always happens when people with very serious jobs find themselves plied with alcohol and forced to socialise. HR in particular had gone all out – costumes and personalities – and were currently circulating the room with unconvincing English accents as they made jokes about the racetrack savannah and the thoroughbred game.

All in all, Nell felt utterly out of place. As she followed DB through the crowd, all elbows and apologies, she realised that while the event itself was embarrassing and excessive, it was the premise of the thing itself that sat so poorly with her. To start with, the coupling of the program launch with a day that encouraged inebriation and the discarding of large sums of money on the racing of animals seemed entirely inappropriate. Worse still, the speech was itself a fallacy. A disjuncture between words and deeds. For anyone to call what had happened a success was a complete misinterpretation of the word and demonstrated to Nell either a refusal or inability to truly understand the nature of things. It had gutted her, once the dust had settled – the whole thing leaving her racked with a sense of failure, of lacking, of impotence to do the one thing she thought herself trained to do. For this to be success in anyone's eyes was truly frightening.

She stepped out of the way as the HR team conga-lined their way through, letting DB slip away from her. She watched him take his position at the front of the marquee, to the side of the small stage from where Mr Williams would be making his speech. The tapping of cutlery on champagne glass began, and while the rest of the marquee assembled before the stage, Nell edged towards the back of the crowd. Mr Williams surveyed the room, proud and regal, then unfolded the paper DB had handed him and leant towards the microphone stand.

'I would like to start by welcoming everyone here on this momentous day!'

In the pause for applause, Nell slipped out of the marquee and into the piercing grey light. Rainclouds were gathering overhead and she thought that perhaps, if she ran fast enough, she might avoid them when they burst.

32

DB

DB stood at the front of the marquee feeling ridiculous in his hat and outfit. He hadn't wanted to return to the house so he had made do with items from his father's wardrobe, and it appeared that at some point his father had gone to a party as a hustler. DB felt stupid. And tired. He missed his wife. He missed tucking his son in every night and he missed doing so in a bed that wasn't infested with stale canine hair.

Madeline's ghost hung around him like a constant companion now, poking his ribs while he slept and running across his keyboard during the day, causing him to forget what he'd been writing and veer off into strange worrying sentences. Only it wasn't a ghost, was it, because she was still alive and wading her way through the Family Court system just so she could raise her children in safety. She peered at him from the corner as he sat on the couch beside his parents watching whatever shows they wanted to watch, sang through his mobile phone, asking why he didn't press a few buttons and apologise to his wife. She taunted him in the shower, as he urinated in the office toilets, as he swam his late-night laps. He had transposed the living, breathing Madeline into some kind of Ghost-of-Separations-Present type thing, and he realised the utter ludicrousness of this.

There was a tap on his shoulder and he turned to find Mr Williams beaming in his safari suit. DB handed him a copy of the speech and he took it with a nod.

'Solid work, DB,' Mr Williams smiled. 'You've made me a happy man.'

Mr Williams offered a cheerful salute then stepped up to the microphone. As he began the speech, DB noticed Nell slip from the marquee. He watched her for a moment, quickening her pace as she fled from the celebrations. He envied her, suddenly and intensely, running like a convict towards some kind of freedom.

'I would like to start by welcoming everyone here on this momentous day!'

DB's mobile vibrated against his thigh. He pulled it from his pocket. Tony? His heart started racing. Something was wrong with Sylvie or Rudy, he knew it. DB edged his way out of the marquee.

'Tony?'

'Ben. Mate. I'm just calling to see if you know where Sylvie is. I'm gonna call her this arvo and wanted to know when to call.'

DB let go of the breath he'd been holding. The bloody Zambetti communications tree.

'She'll be in class,' he replied, looking towards the marquee.

'You sure?' Tony asked. 'On account of it being a public holiday and all? I figured she'd be at Mum and Dad's. Rudy too. I figured they'd just be hanging about all day.'

DB frowned. What was he going on about?

'You know, I've been thinking,' Tony continued. 'I know how good my life looks. Eat, sleep, gym, repeat. I know, living, right? What can I say, life is pretty sweet.'

DB pulled the phone away from his ear for a moment and stared at it. Perhaps Tony had hit his head on some gym equipment? Perhaps he had concussion?

'But sometimes,' Tony went on, 'and this is just sometimes, mind you – sometimes I look at what you have and I'm jealous. Not like being married to my sister. We're not in the village anymore. But, I mean, you know.'

And DB knew. Tony was definitely concussed.

'But like I said, my life is pretty good. Just, you know. You know. Anyway, listen, we should lift sometime, mate. You, me and Rudy. You hear me?'

'I hear you, Tony.'

'So anyway, you think that if I were to call Sylvie at say 3.30 pm she and Rudy will be sitting around at Mum and Dad's? Just waiting? At Mum and Dad's. At 3.30 pm?'

'I'm certain of it,' DB replied.

He ended the call then looked towards the marquee. People were clapping, wildly, and someone had started the music back up. DB glanced down at his watch. He might just be able to make it.

It took two trains and a moderately difficult jog-walk-jog, but eventually he arrived at the cul-de-sac just as the rain did too. He was instantly drenched, the world suddenly grey, and he recognised the appropriateness of this. The house was quiet as he approached, save for the gentle sound of sobbing coming through the windows. At this, DB's heart broke. He pictured Sylvie now, curled up on top of the crochet-covered single bed in her room, heartbroken and bereft, pining for her wayward husband. He imagined her uttering one final heart-wrenching sob then pulling herself up stoically, washing the tears from her cheeks, and plastering on a bold face with which to show their child that she was holding up just fine.

Their child! Sweet, strange Rudy! He would be seated on the couch, perhaps on his nonno's lap, bravely watching his cartoons while he pretended with all his heart that the arms around him were his father's. His beautiful family, longing so desperately for him. Sending coded messages through Tony. How they would run to him when they saw him! He allowed himself a moment to imagine the warm, wild embrace, then set to business.

DB sidled around the house and stopped beneath Sylvie's bedroom window. His plan was to pull himself up atop one of the rubbish bins and rap gently on her second-storey window, rousing her mid-sob and very possibly climbing through Romeo-style as she opened both her window and her heart to him. He danced about the bin a moment, working out how to hoist himself up, then eventually managed to mount it using an awkward half-drag half-shimmy motion. He steadied himself on the brickwork then slowly inched further up until he was standing in a sort of crouch. The window was higher than he'd thought and he couldn't quite see in, so he reached his hands up and knocked gently on the pane. Beneath him the bin wobbled, slippery in the rain. He locked his knees, keeping his balance, then knocked again, a little more firmly. He was about to knock a third time when there was a crack beneath him and he suddenly found himself crashing through the broken bin lid, cracking his left knee on the sharp edge and landing on the rubbish inside. The smell hit him immediately and he knew Guiseppa had made seafood soup that week. Then the front door slammed and he looked up to see Sylvie coming round the corner, a broom raised above her head. She stared at him for a moment, her eyes wild, then lowered the broom.

'What the hell are you doing?'

She looked at him harder, pushing her wet hair from her eyes.

'And what the hell are you wearing?'

He had forgotten about the pimp suit. His knee was throbbing and the fishy scent was making his eyes water.

'I was coming over to apologise and beg for your forgiveness, only I seem to have fallen into your parents' rubbish bin.'

'I can see that. Why are you lurking around the bins in the rain? What's wrong with the front door?'

His knee really was hurting.

'I heard you crying. I thought I'd come to your window and surprise you. Like Romeo.'

'Like a pervert, more like it. What crying? We're all watching mum's Italian soap operas in the lounge room.'

'But I heard crying . . .' he wavered.

'Maria's husband died in a tragic nightclub fire despite having only just got his memory back and she's asking Giovanni to raise her son as his own. On the show.'

Oh. He should have felt embarrassed but he was in too much pain.

'Look, you don't think you could help me out of here, do you? I really think I've hurt myself.'

Sylvie leant the broom against the wall and came to his assistance. As he put weight on his left foot his knee exploded in pain and he stumbled forward, screaming.

'Jesus,' Sylvie exclaimed. 'The neighbours will think someone is getting murdered here.'

She bent her head to look him in the eyes and DB felt her strong grip on his arms.

'Are you okay?' she asked, and for the first time in a long time he remembered how tender they could be with one another.

'I'm okay now that you're here,' he replied gently, leaning into her body.

This made her laugh, a short spontaneous bark that she tried to smother, but it was enough for him to hear.

'I'm sorry,' he said, pressing his face into her shoulder. 'For everything.'

He decided now would be a good time to cry, and he did, from relief and pain and sadness. Sylvie pulled him closer and he felt her press her lips into the top of his head.

'I'm sorry too. We're both such stubborn idiots.'

He shifted his weight and a new burst of pain shot through his leg. Sylvie pulled away from him.

'This doesn't mean we don't have a lot to talk about, though.'

'I know. And we will, I promise. But can we please do it later because I think we may need go to the hospital.'

She helped drag him into the house. Rudy looked up from his position on Nino's lap.

'Hey, Dad,' he said nonchalantly, then turned back to the television.

'We're going to the hospital,' Sylvie announced, grabbing her handbag. 'Romeo here took a tumble in the rain. I'll call you when we know what's happening.'

Guiseppa and Nino surveyed him with a look of concern, which DB met with a brave grimace.

'Okay,' Guiseppa conceded eventually. 'We'll have dinner waiting when you get back.'

Then they all returned their attention to the television, and DB realised he was home.

They went to the closest hospital – the one DB always hated because it was under-resourced and understaffed and they always had to wait a long time – and they waited a long time because it was under-resourced and understaffed. While they waited, they talked, and this time when they talked they listened to each other too. They talked about things they hadn't talked about for a long time – things that were difficult or uncomfortable or that they knew they didn't agree on – and it was difficult and uncomfortable and while they still didn't agree, they tried to see each other's perspective. After a while, Sylvie wandered off to find them something to snack on. She paused before a vending machine, feeding money into the slot, and he watched her peer at the items on display. Her hand hesitated over the key pad then she selected a combination. The machine sprang to life, nudging free a bar of Turkish Delight. DB watched it tumble, freefalling momentarily through the air, and he was overcome with a sudden surge of love that left his body trembling. For her pragmatism, her dependability, for the fact that she was, despite everything, still here. And he realised suddenly all the ways her love had shifted things around to accommodate him and that it was high time he did the same. Of how the things he had once fallen in love with were not as important as the things he loved today, and that these were the things worth fighting for.

When Sylvie returned, he shuffled himself forward on the plastic waiting room chair.

'What are you doing?'

'Ow, shit. Ow. Can you just pretend that I've gone down on one knee?'

'The busted one?'

'Yes, that one.'

DB took the chocolate bar from her then held her hands in his. He looked into her eyes and knew that while this was not the decision he had wanted to make, it was absolutely the decision he needed to make.

'Sylvie Zambetti, will you move to the outer suburbs with me?'

Sylvie laughed her deep, coarse laugh, then took his face in her hands.

'I thought you'd never ask.'

33

Evangelia

In the end, Evangelia gathered up everything she had found into a folder and set off for the cemetery. There wasn't much – scraps of her own memories, of Nick and Xanthe's, and a clutter of largely meaningless photocopies from the library that spoke more of her mother's absence than of her presence. It had been exciting that night, unspooling from her children the stories they cherished of their grandmother, but it hadn't really amounted to anything that would move her mother's story forward, and nearly a year after her mother's death she still had very little. It would make a brief collection of anecdotes, something to save in some never-to-be-accessed part of the computer, to sit and be forgotten. Maybe one day the children would rediscover it, scroll through the pages fondly, then leave it to gather more temporal dust in the recesses of the hard drive. And perhaps that was all it needed to be, the notes on this ordinary unexceptional life.

Evangelia followed the familiar path to her parents' graves, the afternoon sun warming her cheeks. From a distance she saw a figure bent over the headstones, and as the figure straightened she realised it was Lydia. Evangelia paused, watching her. Lydia finished cleaning their father's side of the plot then crossed to their mother's. She scooped the withered, mismatched flowers from their vase, replacing them with fresh white roses so that they mirrored those standing tall on their father's side. She swept the base of the headstone with her hands then stood there for a long moment, her hands brushing her cheeks. Lydia made to leave and Evangelia started, ducking behind a too-short grave-stone. She stood sheepishly as Lydia noticed her and beckoned her over. The sisters stood before one another.

'I didn't realise you came here.'

'Of course I do,' Lydia replied, her face stern, hands dusting dirt from her trousers.

She surveyed the cheap flowers in Evangelia's hands.

'I don't have to leave them here,' Evangelia said sharply, glancing at the expensive roses already set out.

'They're fine,' Lydia said after a moment. 'Here, let me help.'

The sisters divided the flowers between the two vases, circling the roses with supermarket daisies. Evangelia flicked the water from her hands then bent to retrieve the folder. Lydia eyed it suspiciously.

'What have you got there?'

Evangelia had planned to read through the papers one last time, sitting beside their mother, before putting them away for good. Her cheeks flushed.

'Nothing. Just some papers. Memories and things from the kids.'

Her sister's face was unreadable.

'Can I see?'

Evangelia's hands moved instinctively behind her back.

'Eva, show me.'

'No.'

'Eva,' Lydia insisted.

Evangelia eyed her mother's grave. She could not make a scene here, not with God and all the departed watching.

'Fine. Here.'

She thrust the folder at Lydia then watched her sister leaf through the papers. Lydia paused when she reached the photocopies from the library, peering at herself in the image.

'Mum's not there,' Evangelia informed her. 'She's not anywhere. I mean, she's probably in the kitchen cooking but no one ever took photos of that.'

Lydia traced a finger over the image, haloing their father with her fingernail. Evangelia noticed for the first time how tired her sister looked, her face drawn with the same weary lines their mother had had, as her own was now.

'She didn't go. That's why she's not there.'

'What do you mean?' Evangelia frowned. 'It says the whole community turned up.'

'She didn't go. She protested the protest. People wouldn't speak to her for weeks. Dad was mortified. She said she couldn't abide by any of it – Greeks hurting Turks, Turks hurting Greeks. That wasn't the Cyprus she remembered.'

Evangelia stared at her sister.

'How do you know that? You were too young to remember anything like that.'

'She told me.' Lydia's eyes were suddenly full of tears. 'She'd tell me stories. Later on. Recently. I realised that I'm supposed to be the one that knows these things now. So I asked her and she told me.'

The tears spilled then, cascading down her cheeks in little rainstorms. Evangelia looked away. She'd never thought to ask Lydia, had never imagined her as the one who would carry this knowledge forward. And she realised that she had always supposed herself to be this person, despite being younger, because it had always seemed that way growing up. Had always seemed to be what everyone expected, even Lydia. And now tears were falling from her own eyes, great cascades of frustration and sadness because they were two grown women standing

383

beside their mother's grave learning something new about each other after all these years.

'I miss her,' she whispered, searching her bag for tissues.

'Me too,' Lydia said, handing her one from her own bag. 'It just hit me, suddenly when she got sick, that I'm supposed to be in charge now. And I don't know how to do anything. I never bothered to learn and now I'm meant to be the one. You know how often I have to google shit? Like sit there asking the internet how I'm supposed to do our traditions? It's embarrassing. She'd be horrified.'

Lydia drew a fresh tissue from the packet then blew her nose noisily.

'I can show you,' Evangelia said. 'I know things. You were off being *cultural*.'

She said the last part with an exaggerated flourish, which made Lydia laugh.

'I'd like that,' Lydia sniffed.

The two sisters appraised each other.

'We're the frontline now,' Lydia said. 'It's us until our kids.'

Evangelia thought of her children, their stilted ineffectual Greek and their noncommittal dancing.

'God help us all.'

She shoved the soggy tissue into her sleeve.

'I'm sorry about what happened. About the meat.'

Lydia raised her eyebrows. 'It was very expensive jamón . . .'

Evangelia hid a smile behind her hand. 'Do you have any more stories?'

Lydia made a face. 'Plenty. Names, phone numbers, details. That woman was like a sponge. What I know could fill a whole bloody book.'

Evangelia shifted feet, clearing her throat gently.

'Could you tell me more? I have memories but they're all incomplete. Like, I remember she had to go to work when we were little and Dad's back was playing up, but I don't remember anything else. And I remember her coming into our room each night when I thought I saw the dragon but I don't remember what happened.'

Lydia's face brightened.

'You don't remember what happened to the dragon? Eva, she slayed it. She had no choice. You were certain it kept coming back. She tried the *mati*, *ikoni*, everything she could think of, and when that didn't work, she burst in one night dressed like the tin man. Pot on her head, hiding behind this big old saucepan lid like a shield. She was armed with the mattock from the garden and she fought that dragon like she was *Saint George himself* or something. The poor dragon never had a chance. She buried it in the garden and we had a bumper crop of tomatoes that season. How do you not remember that?'

Evangelia frowned, watching the light fall across her sister's face. Somewhere inside things shifted ever so slightly and a glimmer of something forgotten began to shine through.

'You want stories, I've got stories,' Lydia said, and she held out her hand to her sister.

34

Patrick

The journey was longer this time, now that he didn't have a station van to drive him. As the suburbs passed before him, Patrick realised he'd rarely ventured this far into the outer north. Nor had *North Facing Window*, which was a salient point of note. He would have to make an effort to get out this way more if the column truly wanted to reflect the people it claimed to. He watched the factories through the window, hard at work manufacturing all kinds of things he didn't understand. Car parts, maybe, though who knew if they made those anymore. After a while he pulled out his mobile and called Harry.

'Patrick! What's up? Did you have a flutter?'

'Pardon?'

'Cup Day. Yesterday. I picked the nag.'

'Oh. No. I completely forgot about that. I've been busy. Look, I need your help.'

'Christ, you're not in the lock-up again, are you?'

'No, no, nothing like that. There's a show I need you to cover.'

'Art show? That's not really what I meant –'

'If not you then someone else at the station? Maybe you could give someone a nod in the right direction?'

Harry whistled softly.

'Please, Harry. Can you please just do this for me? It's a really important show. Think *The Field* at NGV. Think the Heide Circle. It's about Australia and our history and how we've got it all a bit wrong. Plus, I reckon there'll be some controversy.'

There was a pause.

'What kind of controversy?'

'The vegan *gyros* kind.'

'People do like controversy . . . Look, I can't make you any promises but I'll see what I can do.'

'That's all I need. Thank you. It's worth it, I promise.'

'Do I bother asking why?'

'Why do any of us do anything, Harry? Sometimes it's just time to stop being the bowling ball.'

Harry clicked his tongue at the other end of the phone.

'You've got me there. Send me the details.'

Because he didn't have an appointment, Patrick was forced to lurk about the waiting area until Sarah eventually emerged from one of the consulting rooms. Her eyes narrowed when she recognised him and she looked over her shoulder as if seeking back-up.

'What do you want?'

Patrick rose quickly, his hands outstretched as if to fasten her there.

'You wouldn't return my calls –'

'Why would I ever want to do that again?'

'It's just I need to ask you a favour.'

Sarah looked at him with utter incredulity.

'A favour? After what you did to my clients? Do you realise the sense of trust you jeopardised for me? Not to mention my professional standing. I encouraged them to participate and –'

'I understand and I'm so, so sorry. But please just hear me out. I need to speak to them. To your clients.'

Sarah shook her head in disbelief.

'You have no clue. We've lost contact with Maziar. Or "Ali"

as you dubbed him. We've no idea where he is now. And Elham – the woman with the child – they're back in detention. Their application was rejected. These are real people.'

Patrick felt himself pale. 'Is this my fault?'

He must have looked as horrified as he felt because Sarah's face slackened.

'Elham, no. There were issues with the information she provided but we're hoping she can make a special appeal and change the decision. But Maziar, maybe that's on you. I mean, it happens. People disengage for whatever reason. Sometimes they move, sometimes they don't need us anymore, sometimes they find someone who can provide more appropriate support. But I don't imagine your stupid stunt helped.'

Patrick sighed, momentarily relieved before realising his culpability changed nothing for either of these people.

'What about the other woman? Aida. The one with the excellent English?'

Sarah eyed him. 'What about her?'

'Please, can I have her number?'

'You're joking right? You know I can't provide a client's information. It's illegal, not to mention unethical.'

'Could you call her then?' he pressed, and he told her what he wanted.

Sarah regarded him sceptically.

'Please,' Patrick repeated. 'Just ask her. That's all I ask of you. It's either that or another *North* fucking *Window* about some guy who runs a suburban souvlaki shop, and no one wants to read about that.'

Sarah looked away for a moment. She drummed her fingers across the file in her hand.

'Fine. I'll ask. And if it's no, that's it. You leave us alone. Happy?'

Patrick smiled gratefully. 'More than you can imagine.'

And he was, sort of, in a way that he hadn't been for months. On his way back to the boxy apartment in Thornbury, Patrick reviewed the list he'd written a few days earlier. His counsellor had suggested he do this, create lists of things that kept him awake at night so that they'd keep until the morning, and this list had turned into a list of problems, and another of possibilities, and a final list of things that could be done in order to somehow in the tiniest way right the trail of wrongs he'd left behind him. He made a gentle mark next to Sarah's name and scanned the remaining items. The property manager had been contacted, the sideboard had been picked up, and now all that was left was to buy a plane ticket. This time – the whole time – Seymour would know exactly where he was. And while this wouldn't fix things, because in life often things might never be fixed, it did create a pathway through which he could seek bit by bit something very much like amends.

35

DB

Jonesy!

Sorry for the radio silence. Life has been busy and not much time for the old email etc. So much to catch you up on. Here's a brief snippet: I've been off work for a month recovering from a partial patellectomy – that's right, half my kneecap removed and I'm off my feet until it heals properly. Turns out I had more than enough annual leave once the sick leave wore off.

But it's not all been lying down for me. We're moving sticks to a new place out near Sylvie's parents. Should be in by Christmas if we can get all our junk into boxes in time. Walking distance to Rudy's kinder – once I'm walking again – and plenty of train time to catch up on my reading once I'm back at work. The mortgage has shed half its body weight and we'll probably have another baby now that we can afford it. To be completely honest, having a sibling might be good for Rudy. He's moved on from death now and is fascinated with birth, so that's an omen if anything was. I hear what you're thinking. We will probably become those boring people who live in the suburbs with all their children doing boring suburban things, but that's not the scariest thing in the world, now is it? On some days it even looks a bit exciting.

On a final note, because I've really got to run (ho ho), when are you planning on making a visit here? There's a spare room in the new place, at least until there's a baby, and email is just so impersonal, isn't it? Put us on your travel list and let's catch up face to face. It's been far too long, my friend, and I've so much I'd love to tell you.

More soon and don't be a stranger.
Ben.

36

Evangelia

Initially, Lydia had her reservations.

'That's not how it's done,' she told Evangelia down the phone line. 'What will people say?'

'I don't give a shit, Lydia,' Evangelia replied brightly. 'It's how we're doing it. Bring your children and that fucking bouzouki, and we're going to do it our way.'

It had begun the night of the cemetery visit, and there had been so much more to follow. She had started with Lydia, stories spilling from her over bottles of wine. From this, Evangelia found names, numbers, details of houses where acquaintances and relatives might still be found. Her mother's neighbours, the owners of the shops she used to visit, the friends long forgotten and far away. Evangelia sat by bedsides and in trickles of sun in nursing home courtyards, wading patiently through the confusion of today to where long-ago memories lay as sharp and clear as diamonds. She built it, brick by brick, the story of her mother. She wrote it gradually, with false starts and dead ends, sitting at the table by the brick wall where she knew for sure her mother had pressed her palm all those years ago. Her phone pinged with messages of clarification and discovery shuttled to and from her sister. And one evening she overheard two staff members talking about the café's previous owner, the son of a foreman who had worked his way up and eventually bought out the building, and she had followed this lead and found a middle-aged man who very much remembered the story his father used to tell of the woman who had waltzed into his factory and demanded he give her a job.

Then the real work began. She advertised in the Greek language papers and pinned up an invitation on the noticeboard at the church. Some of the women had looked on in concern, because it was not, after all, how things were done, but Evangelia didn't care.

'I do hope you'll be there,' she said, beaming at them, and soon the news was shooting out across the tendrils of the Greater Northern Metropolitan Grapevine.

Did you know for Xanthoula Georgiou's twelve-month mnimósino her daughters are throwing a party! Yes, a party. I don't know where – at some café, I think. Of course I'm going, aren't you? Whoever misses this is going to regret it forever! Holy panagia mou . . .

She accosted the Italian one morning after service and made him promise three times that he would be available to bless the gravesite after the mass.

'I promise, I promise,' he said, his hands shielding him from her stern glare. 'Rain, hail or shine?' she demanded, and he nodded weakly as he took the full envelope she thrust at him.

On the day of the service, she made her family stand before her, preening and de-fluffing and adjusting their clothing. All the appropriate shade of black, even if Peter's shirt strained a bit across his girth.

'My goddamn beautiful family,' she announced, and made them pose for photos.

She watched the liturgy like a hawk, her fist clenching in victory when the Italian recited her mother's name. Then she waited by the narthex until he was finished and shepherded him to the car.

'Let the *pappá* take the front seat, Petro,' she informed her husband, bobbing about until the Italian fastened his seatbelt, then closing the passenger door firmly.

She led the procession of mourners to her mother's gravesite, waiting patiently while the Italian swung the incense and sang his prayers. She sought out the words now etched across the surface of her mother's headstone: *Xanthoula Georgiou, good young, good old. She made her family who they are.* It wasn't how things were normally done, but it was damn well how they'd done it. Her mother surveyed the whole thing from the little memorial photo in the centre of the headstone. It was the perfect image, discovered by Lydia at the bottom of a neighbour's drawer, her mother at the cusp of ageing, her face still lined with the determination of youth as the wisdom of age began to blossom. And there was warmth too, her love for her people radiating out into the cemetery. *She would have liked this*, Evangelia thought, and that was what mattered.

After the blessing, she released the Italian of his duties, and the mourners piled into their cars. Then they pulled out one by one and formed a long snaking procession towards their final destination. The Foreman's Quarters had rearranged the tables so that they skirted the perimeter, leaving a large space in the middle. Evangelia waited anxiously, her body pressed against the brickwork, as guests slowly arrived. They kept coming. Lydia, Darren and the children, who she parked in the corner and instructed to start playing. The families of her mother's siblings, her father's siblings, cousins and second cousins. Kat was there with her children and she had dragged along Nina, already back from her trip overseas, which touched Evangelia far more than she expected. There was Carole, nodding to her with Gwen and Sita beside her. Terry, thankfully, was nowhere in sight. And there were others too, people she didn't recognise, draped in their dark mourning scarves and finest jewellery.

Perhaps they were friends of her mother's, but perhaps not. It didn't matter. What mattered was that people were here. They milled about, sipping their port as they entered and pausing before the large images of her mother displayed about the walls. As a mother, as a daughter, as a grandmother, as herself. All the faces she'd worn in her seven and a half decades on earth.

They picked at the meat platters, loading their plates with mini quiches and sausage rolls, dolmades and olives, and craning their necks to see what would emerge next from the kitchen. Evangelia's children promenaded around the room, accepting compliments from strangers and not understanding any of the Greek spoken to them, as their talented cousins played perfectly in the corner. Once everyone was settled, Evangelia pressed her palm into the brickwork, took a deep breath and pulled the sheets of paper from her handbag. This wasn't how it was normally done, but this was how she was doing it. She cleared her throat and began to read.

On a cold winter's morning in 1975, Xanthoula Georgiou set out her family's breakfast for when they rose, pulled on her best – and only – black coat, marched into the local brickworks and demanded they give her work. Her husband was injured fighting for freedom and he needed to recover, she told the startled foreman, so she would take on his work until he did so. The foreman looked at this tiny woman, all elbows and angles with little strength about her. He would later tell his son that he had laughed then, big and unyielding from the bottom of his stomach, and then told her he had no work for someone of her size. Xanthoula had planted her feet, her palms pressed flat against the brickwork as she stood her ground. 'Tha mou thóseis thouleiá.' You will give me work. The foreman laughed again, softer now, and uncertain. 'I understand your problem,' he said, because really he did, 'but we haven't any work fit for a woman. Perhaps my wife can give you some psomi to take home with you?' Xanthoula scoffed at this, staring him hard in the eye. Then she rolled up her sleeves, her bony elbows set for work, and marched into the factory proper.

The men, already hard at work lifting sandbags and packing in clay, froze. There were never women on the factory floor. Some recognised her, Andreas Georgiou's wife, and wondered if their friend and co-worker was dead. Why else would his wife be on the factory floor? Unless she had gone mad, which they knew sometimes happened to women. Too much time in the kitchen, not enough fresh air. The stress of womanhood was a well-known phenomenon, everyone knew that, something to do with the ovaries and time. It made them bitter and shrill and argumentative and nothing like they were meant to be. One worker would often tell the story of how he had crossed himself, muttering a little prayer for the mad woman, then almost fell to the floor when she proceeded to lift a huge sack of sand and cart it about the place. 'Like this?' she asked the foreman, pouring it into the mixer. 'Nai,' he muttered, beside himself.

The foreman was uncertain. If word got out there was a woman doing the same work as men – a mother, no less, for Andreas often talked about his small children – it would be very embarrassing for the foreman and he feared his boss would fire him. But the foreman, who had a wife and a mother and plenty of sisters as well, knew from the determined look in her eye that Andreas's wife would not leave until she got what she wanted. So he sought a compromise. 'I can't pay you his wage,' he said, wringing his hands at the look of it all. 'How would the other men feel to be paid the same as a woman? But you are half the size of Andreas, so I will give you half the money.' Xanthoula did not like this arrangement but she had haggled enough in the marketplace to know a deal when she saw one. 'It is done then,' she said, and she stuck out her hand to shake. The foreman shook her hand hurriedly, worried the other men would see this and think him weak. And for the next six months Xanthoula worked twice as hard as any man for half the money. Because of this, her husband Andreas could rest his back properly for the first time in fifteen years and every single night they had enough food on the table and enough money in their pockets to pay the bills.

Two decades later the church you just sat in was in turmoil. A new priest from Athens had arrived with the blessing of the Patriarch in Constantinople himself, and rumour got around that he had been an informant during the dictatorship, weeding out anti-junta republicans. This left half the congregation in despair – a traitor administering their communion and christening their babies? A man who may well have caused the torture of so many of their fellow countrymen, of their own family members, no less? No thank you, they would prefer someone else, and they nominated an up-and-coming young priest from Parramatta instead. But the other half of the congregation, they knew gossip when they heard it, and if this man was good enough for the Patriarch he was good enough for them. No one knew how to fix this problem. Families were fracturing and service had become a mess, with half the congregation sitting in protest in the church courtyard, where their chosen young priest performed the rituals in the early morning sun.

Then one day the problem was suddenly resolved – the Patriarch recalled his Athenian priest, who was now desperately needed in a church deep in the mountains near Albania, and who better to take over than the young priest from Parramatta? The congregation was overjoyed – finally a solution that left no one without face. What a clever Patriarch their church had, benevolent and infinite in his wisdom! Little did anyone know that this solution came to the Patriarch not through the word of God, but via airmail from a determined woman called Xanthoula Georgiou, who told him she would not stand by while her church fell into disrepair. But Xanthoula never told anyone this, because that wasn't how it was done.

Let's skip back now to the RMS Strathmore *as it cruises through the Indian Ocean in 1957. Up on the railings a young woman is perched, her body leaning towards the grey sea below. Tears fall down her sixteen-year-old cheeks as she draws her foot up another rung and closer to her fate. It is quiet because everyone is down below enjoying the celebrations, for they have finally crossed the Equator, and only a young Xanthoula Anastasiades is about, singing to herself as she breathes in the sea air. She spots the sobbing young woman and rushes over to her. Eventually, the young woman confides to Xanthoula that she has left behind a secret sweetheart, only no one in the village knew. Now, however, her belly is growing day by day, and when the uncle who sponsored her in Australia finds out, she will be ruined and who knows what will become of her. Xanthoula calms the young woman, pressing her hands against her wet cheeks, and convinces her to climb down from the railings. 'There is always a way,' she says, and while neither of them know what it will be, Xanthoula comforts the young woman because they are going to a new country and maybe it will be different from the old world.*

Eventually they disembark in Melbourne, and Xanthoula demands her family make room for the poor young woman. Her husband is dead, she tells anyone who will listen, and any Christian would make room for her in their heart and their home. So the young woman gains a dead husband as well as a new life, and eventually she marries and lives a wonderful life, and it is not until many years later that she tells Xanthoula's daughter her secret in the dying afternoon light of a nursing home in Melbourne's north.

These are but a small handful of the many stories about Xanthoula Georgiou that circle and swirl in the atmosphere. There are too many to be told, because she lived a giant life in the smallest possible way. History tells us to seek out the extraordinary people; to find exceptional people who altered the world in monumental ways. But in doing this alone we forget the ordinary ones who were extraordinary in their tiny circles and created miniscule ripples that made the world better in uncountable little ways. If you had asked my mother what she wanted from life, she would simply have told you that she wanted her children to live a better life than she had. My sister is the first in our family to go to university. I am the first of us to own a small business in Australia. Our children are happy and healthy and surrounded by opportunities. She found pride in all these things, all these things she said she wanted. But her real legacy is in all the tiny acts she performed without acknowledgement or reward, and without ever expecting this. So this is part of the story of Xanthoula Georgiou, and there are many other parts out there that none of us know. She was good young and good old, and she will live on in each of these stories forever.

37

Nell

Nell poured herself a glass of water and sipped it in quick mouthfuls. Her eyes hovered to the far corner of the window where a moment ago she had seen Madeline pass by. Nell had risen to rush out and call to her, to grab her attention, but then realised there was no reason for this. What would she say? There wasn't anything. Besides, Madeline had seemed busy, her two boys pulling at her sleeves and getting under her feet, the younger one skipping about and the older one watching in brotherly exasperation. She had left them to themselves, sliding back into her seat. Nell checked the door, then her phone, her tummy grumbling at the enticing fried potato fug. Soon, Rani rushed in, her arms spilling with folders. She let them cascade out across the table as she fell into the chair.

'Sorry I'm late. I'm starving. Let's order something.'

They looked about the crowded café, trying to catch the wait staff's attention.

'God, it's ridiculously busy these days,' Rani said. 'They had some write-up in one of those popular e-newsletters and now you can barely move in here. They're asylum seekers, did you know that? The family who run this place. Former clients of ours. Officially refugees now.'

A woman with bottle-blonde, sky-high hair arrived at their

table. Her eyes brightened when she saw Rani, then she swooped in to kiss her cheeks, left, right, left.

'Look at this place!' the woman crowed. 'You wouldn't believe how far people come to eat over-fried potato. But who am I to complain? And to think we all came on those boats. Anyway, no need to order, Rani-joon, I'll get Mansoor to make you something special. Proper Irani food, not this potato chip nonsense.'

Rani beamed. 'Thanks, Massoumeh.'

The woman left, elbowing her way through the crowd. Rani turned back to Nell.

'How's everything? How's your mum? How's Seymour?'

Seymour had been parading about like a rooster since the gallery was featured on television with the word 'seminal' mentioned at one or more points, and important people suddenly wanted to know who he was. And their mother had thrown herself into teaching another women's biography class in some sort of new-lease-on-life-Stella-getting-her-groove-back type of whirlwind. Both texted Nell constantly, emoji-laden spiels full of self-affirming phrases and adjectives dripping with zeal, and she was adjusting gradually to their happiness. It was a new state for the Swanseas, akin to watching a newborn giraffe learn to walk. And, without fanfare, the antique sideboard had reappeared in the house one day, back in its position as if it had never gone away.

'They're good.'

'And work? Have you heard from Madeline at all?'

Nell thought of the Madeline she had seen moments earlier, her children tugging at her sleeves. Her mother had turned up at Seymour's for lunch one day with a basket full of paperwork and Nell had noticed Madeline's name on the enrolment list for her mother's next course. A tiny flicker of self-forgiveness had fluttered about her chest, then she went back to slicing the sourdough as if nothing had happened.

'Mediation failed so they're heading to Family Court now. She's hopeful. I mean, what else can she be?'

'There's always hope,' Rani sighed, pawing at the folders before them.

She found the one she was looking for, then slid it to the top.

'Right, Swansea. Are you ready to finally enter the world of legitimate legal volunteerism? Because this backlog of asylum claims waits for no woman.'

She pushed the folder towards Nell.

'Elham Tasviri and her daughter Niki. Back in MITA after failing the merit review, so our only hope is a successful judicial review in the next few months. That and an appeal to the Minister to get another bridging visa granted so we can at least get them out of detention in the interim. There's a strong chance we can convince them, but I'm thinking we're going to have to apply some additional public pressure.'

Nell glanced down at the thick file before her.

'Her housemate works here, actually,' Rani continued. 'I should introduce you. I have a feeling you'll get on well and she could be very helpful to us for the public campaign.'

Nell nodded as Rani continued talking about hearts and minds, and special circumstances and compassion. She reached down, pressing her hands against the file's weight and urgency, then carefully, purposefully, laid it open.

38

The last chapter before the next chapter

A Well-Founded Fear of Persecution
December 2016
By Aida Abedi with Patrick Lee

Most of us never think about the power of waiting. We're told it is a virtue, a strength, an admirable quality we should all strive to master. We don't think about all the ways it can destroy you: swiftly, without warning, because you've left it a moment too long, become too complacent or hoped against hope that perhaps they wouldn't come for you. Or slowly and deliberately, chipping away at you molecule by molecule, at your bones, your mind, your soul, because a wait with no end is truly unbearable.

How do you pick the time for action? Must you wait until the moment inaction becomes a death wish, or do you call fate's bluff early? How do you time the unthinkable? Make the choices we make when there are no others possible? When 'I do not want to leave' becomes 'We must in order to exist'. And how do we bundle the unfathomable into one coherent sixty-page document for review by an unknown person sitting at a desk who wasn't there and didn't experience it and will never know the tears and sweat and adrenalin of clutching onto that choice?

In the life I lived long before this waiting game, I was a journalist. I sought out these kinds of stories and presented them with what I thought was an abstract eye. As if I could be removed from the words that flowed from my fingers. As if I wasn't a part of it all. And then, unexpectedly, I was, much more than I could ever have imagined, and suddenly my life veered drastically from where I always planned for it to go. Forced onto a pathway I never contemplated having to take.

Perhaps for me it was easy. When the gun is to your head, flight is a logical option. I had a loophole – pure luck – because the police cells were too full to hold me in the days before my court date and my passport was not yet cancelled. A tiny window of urgent oppor- tunity. For others it is like alchemy, weighing up the ingredients of probability and chance. Every day calculating their own risk matrix and trying to determine the mythical point when fleeing becomes acceptable. Because this is what we are judged by – a clinical external assessment of each of our fight or flight mechanisms.

Take my friend Elham. She could have waited for her husband to kill her. Could have weighed up his words with the potential for action and hoped for the best. But picture the columns shifting in her head – in Iran she had no right to divorce, could no longer work because her husband forbade it, and the child growing inside her would be his property in the eyes of the law. She could have waited for the beatings to get worse, for the prison around her to shrink its walls ever closer, and for her husband to draw the energy to tell the authorities that she was banned from leaving the country. Perhaps she could have waited.

Or my colleague Massoumeh. Her husband praises the ground she walks on, abhorring our country's unequal laws, and perhaps this is what brought him to the attention of the local paramilitary forces. Too vocal in his political discussions with other bazaaris, his stall soon became the target of repeated vandalism by Basiji. Massoumeh and he waited, though, sweeping up the shattered glass each time. Soon it was their apartment too, yet they continued

404

waiting, scrubbing the graffitied threats from their walls. Then it was their bodies, bruises blossoming like flowers by the light of the morning. And when it became their children, who cried at night from fear after being followed home from school by terrifying men, then they could no longer wait.

And so many others, who had the wrong politics, the wrong religion, loved the wrong person or just happened to be in the wrong place at the wrong time, so their life was sent shuddering rudderless when for others it was not. Each of them forced into the unfathomable decision to prolong or end the waiting. Though who among us realised that all we would be doing was exchanging one waiting game for another?

Before I left Indonesia I collected the stories of others waiting for their boats, pooling them together into a recipe of pain, sorrow and defiance. I collected these stories in case anything happened to them, so that there would always be a record of who we'd all once been, not who we were in that moment. Who we were before the waiting started and our lives progressed in this strange holding pattern like a forgotten bag on an airport carousel. I asked them to tell me the memories that made up their life, to choose the version of themselves they wanted to be remembered as. Not as statistics or tragedy, not as case studies or cautionary tales. About everything they were and everything they would be – the first and third acts – not the horror and harrow of the here and now. And each time I asked them to share with me the warmest memory they possessed so that this would become their legacy.

And soon I will be writing them, one by one, week by week. This project, Stories of Ordinary People, will appear each week on the pages and website of this newspaper, written by myself and my colleague Patrick Lee. You will have the chance to meet us all, transcending the bars and barriers constructed by governments to keep us from each other. And perhaps this may make the waiting less unfathomable.

But before we introduce you to the others, it is only fair I share my own story first – my warmest memory – which pulls me along through each hour of the long dark night. The history I want to reclaim:

For me, it is a moment, simple and pure. It is me, hurrying down the street, dodging the harried pedestrians and erratic motorcycles, anxious not to be the last to arrive. Slipping through the front door of my parents' home, pulling off my scarf and shaking out my hair as I shower my family with kisses and hugs. It is Nowruz, our new year, and I assure my mother, like I always do, that this year her Nowruz table has truly outdone itself: apples, hyacinth from the garden, coins, sumac and vinegar. My father's prized Hafez instead of a Qur'an, already open and waiting for us to read aloud to each other as the evening stretches on. The sabzeh I planted the previous week is green and perfect, its shoots alert and ready for the year ahead. My family is already gathered, my mother and her sisters busy in the kitchen, my brothers and cousins joking with each other while my father pretends not to laugh from his perch on the couch. Even my uncle Asadollah is here; though blighted by a cough he sits on the daybed shouting commands in his pyjamas like Mossadegh. The house aches with the smell of sweets and pastries, fish and rice with dill wafting from the kitchen, and my father sharpening his claws in anticipation of wresting the tahdig from us all.

We eat, our bellies full of the tastes of our past, the walls dense with our stories and laughter, and above it all, hope for the year to come. From behind his teacup my father's hand emerges, halting us mid-conversation, and he commences his philosophical treatise, my mother mouthing along like prosaic karaoke. It's not what history makes of you that matters, but what you make of your history.

We hold our breaths – watching the countdown on television – and at the exact moment of equinox the room is a sea of bodies, hugging and shouting and laughing. My mobile buzzes with messages of love and goodwill. And we are weeping, all of us, because we are together and we have lived another year, and before us lies a whole new year that we will struggle and laugh and love through together. And from deep in his memory my father finds a well-loved story and clears his throat for silence.

I know what you are thinking. What is the use of this story? What is there for you to do with it? It's nice, sure, but there's hardly a headline in it, hardly anything to shift the hearts and minds of the great story-hungry masses. And perhaps you're right about that. Perhaps it is the wrong story for me to leave you with because it doesn't serve the purpose you want it to. But it is the story I choose – the one that I want to be remembered by. And next week it will be someone else's. Week by week, story by story, until we seep into the everyday from our current home in the shadows. Ghese ma be sar resid, kalaghe be khoonash naresid: *Our story has finished but the crow has not yet arrived at his house. This is how all Persian stories finish, and I am finished writing my stories – for today.*

Acknowledgements

This book would not be possible without the kindnesses of a great many people. First and foremost Mojdeh, my hamdel and my darling friend.

Thank you to Mathilda, Cate and Haylee for taking turns helping steer this story away from the rocks of my own making, and to Jemal for helping me salvage the wreck of the first draft. To Bec and Brianne for your supportive and loving editing.

Thank you for answering my many, many questions: Petie, Des, Rani, Tanya, Sarah, Carmela, Dalal, Haseeb, Rodgers, Jana, Charley, Beth, Lil' Daniel, Dave, Lisa, the Reza's, Elham, the Abedis and the Tasviris.

To the Farsi-speaking women's and men's groups at WCC for teaching me so much, and to Omid and Nida for inspiring me with your passion and compassion.

To Renee, Nouna and Spiro for your Hellenic insight and spellchecking.

To Pip for being my first reader and to Grace for your kindnesses every time I rang to say that writing a second book is like parading naked in front of strangers whilst one's soul is crushed in a vice and one's dignity cast upon the unyielding spikes of judgement and despair.

To Philomena for your supportive and caring sensitivity read.

Immense gratitude to those who gave me the space to work on this at various points in its life, particularly Jo, Aunty Chrissie, and Laura, Dave and Kenzie.

Thank you to WCC and WHV for all your support – you are the best kinds of folk. To John, because you have to put up with me every single day and, like a fire that burns near flammables, I demand constant attention and care. To Brian, Matt, Lauren, Max and Imo for being my cheer squad. And to my Ma, for everything always.

A note on spelling and translations: decisions on spelling for the anglicised Greek and Persian are based on consultation with a number of native speakers and translators. While I have endeavoured to ensure the wording and phrasing is 'correct', the language also reflects how language evolves following migration and is changed through everyday use.